Award-winning author Marylyle Rogers weaves a special, enticing magic that brings her historical romances to vivid life. Here she sweeps us back to the opulence of Victorian England—the perfect setting for a grand, undeniable passion....

"You are so cold it would require a blast furnace to even thaw you!"

In direct contradiction to her charge, silver eyes darkened into the smoldering coals of a barely restrained blaze.

"Cold?" Many had named Gray the same, but that this one woman had done so stung him into rash action.

An inward bell rang, warning Liz to retreat. For the first time in her life she felt the strong arms of a man not her kin wrap completely around her. He relentlessly drew her nearer to the unsuspected vortex of fire at the core of his ice, a fire so hot it melted her resistance as his dark head bent to take her mouth in a succession of tormentingly brief kisses.

The man Liz had recognized as a danger to any woman's self-possession easily tempted her beyond an initial intent to resist. Yielding to his devastating kisses and lost to rational thinking, she softened against him. Then the ship's constant rolling worked to Liz's advantage. Where once it had thrown her into Gray's arms, it now atoned and set her free. Only after she stood a safe distance from the arrogant man and his wicked wiles did she feel the lashing whip of self-betrayal.

"You may have my father's money, but I'll be *damned* if you'll ever have me!"

Books by Marylyle Rogers

Chanting the Dawn
Dark Whispers
The Dragon's Fire
The Eagle's Song
Hidden Hearts
The Keepsake
Proud Hearts
Wary Hearts

Published by POCKET BOOKS

THE KEEPSAKE

MARYLYLE ROGERS

POCKET **STAR** BOOKS
New York London Toronto Sydney Tokyo Singapore

An *Original* Publication of POCKET BOOKS

A Pocket Star Book published by
POCKET BOOKS, a division of Simon & Schuster Inc.
1230 Avenue of the Americas, New York, NY 10020

ISBN: 0-671-74562-X

First Pocket Books printing April 1993

10 9 8 7 6 5 4 3 2 1

Printed in the U.S.A.

To Caroline Tolley
(without whom this book would not exist)
in appreciation for the patience and support
with which you calm this nervous author's fears.

Dear Readers,

Those of you who've read any of my previous nine books know that *The Keepsake* is a departure for me. I assure you that my home is in the English Middle Ages, but this tale represents a brief vacation into the late Victorian era. I think of this period of time as the "Regency revisited" because although it's Bertie, not Prinny, once again the arbiter of society is a Prince of Wales intent on his pleasures. But this time American heiresses were invading the marriage stakes for British peers.

This tale is a festive jaunt (despite the fact that someone is trying to kill our hero and there are white slavers about). I hope you'll come with me, join the whirl of garden parties, teas, and balls—even a mad dash or two into perilous places. I enjoyed this "vacation" with Gray and Liz, and I hope you will, too!

Marylyle Rogers

AUTHOR'S NOTE

During Queen Victoria's sixty-year reign, her oldest son and heir, Albert Edward, Prince of Wales was given no serious duties to occupy his mind. Left with little to do but have fun, he attacked this pastime with gusto. He beggared more than one of his friends by giving them the dubious honor of entertaining him at their expense—on the requisite lavish scale he deemed due a future monarch (Edward VII). And once married to a pretty Danish princess, Alexandra, he was free to entertain how and whom he chose, despite his royal mother's distaste for most of his companions.

The older and more conservative members of the British nobility looked upon the Prince with growing disapproval, but he recognized no boundaries and welcomed as companions the same *nouveaux riches* rejected by the staid members of New York's Knickerbocker Society. These were people with resources vast enough to entertain him in the style he demanded.

It was during this time period that a great many English aristocrats began to realize that although their personal fortunes were adequate to maintain the life-style they'd been born and raised to inhabit, their agrarian resources were inadequate to maintain their vast estates and enormous country homes. They, too, looked abroad to find new sources to fill the need. Enormously wealthy American papas and pushy mamas rejected by snooty New York society mavens found welcome . . . of a sort.

The 1872 wedding of Jennie Jerome to Lord Randolph Churchill (Winston's parents) was the first ripple of what became a high tide in fortuitous marriages. Soon American merchant wealth in the form of wealthy heiresses flowed across the Atlantic in exchange for marriages to British titles. A famous illustrator of that day, Charles Dana Gibson (of Gibson Girl fame), gave us the tale of two such American beauties traveling through Europe, culminating in Britain, in the delightfully drawn adventures of Mr. Pipp, their father.

During 1891–92 members of the House of Lords investigated the white slave trade and issued *The Report of the House of Lords Committee on the Law Relating to the Protection of Young Girls.*

Unlike the Middle Ages, in the 1800s marriages between cousins were neither forbidden by the church nor at all uncommon. However, I want to point out that the cousins in this book are *not* blood-related.

THE KEEPSAKE

PROLOGUE

Eastern Wyoming
in March of 1882

"Whoa, boy, whoa."

Liz gently patted her favorite mount as he came to a halt at the barn door. Ignoring the questionable support of a stable boy's offered hand, she slipped from the saddle. Grinning, she instead ruffled the pint-size lad's sun-streaked hair and tweaked his freckled nose.

"Ouch!" Sandy jerked away, ruefully rubbing the abused area. "Miss Lizzy—" Voice suffused with mock indignation, he repeated the message he'd been sent to deliver. "There's a telegram waiting for you at the house."

Liz's teasing smile disappeared and fine brows drew together, puckering a forehead turned golden by hours spent outdoors unprotected from sunlight whose potency increased when reflected by snow. The word *telegram* was synonymous with *trouble.* Tossing over her shoulder a wind-tangled mass of carroty hair flowing free to her waist, Liz promptly strode toward the house. Overwhelmed by anxiety, for once, she spared no doting glance to the flat vista of her beloved Double H Ranch's snow-laden lands.

Liz hurriedly ascended veranda steps and wordlessly took the telegram from the plainly worried foreman's hand.

There, in pitiless black and white, lay words she dreaded to see: *Your father lies near death. Come immediately.*

"Harvey, bring the wagon around. If we leave in the next quarter hour, I can make the 3:10 train." Wasting no time on further words, Liz rushed into the house and up the stairs.

The foreman knew as well as she that this being Friday, by missing the afternoon train she'd be doomed to wait three wretched days until the next arrived on Monday. The small burg of Clearwater wouldn't have train service at all were it not the railway owner's hometown, but not even Samuel H. Hughes's daughter could demand a change in the schedule.

No matter what it took, by Monday Liz meant to be a great deal nearer New York and her ailing father. Nearer also to the mansion her mother had chosen and carefully decorated with understated elegance only to be rejected by the snobbish leaders of the Knickerbocker Society. They'd condemned the Hughes family for being nothing more than another addition to the unwelcome and unrefined *nouveaux riches.* Liz had been twelve when her mother died and had never forgiven those rigid dictators of Society for rejecting her sweet if ambitious mother.

In her room Liz threw open the doors of a ceiling-high wardrobe cabinet backed against one wall. Disdaining the large, heavy portmanteau, she pulled out a soft satchel and flung it atop the bed.

"Might I help?"

Casting a quick glance over her shoulder, in the still open doorway Liz found the girl who served her as a maid—of sorts. Liz was uncomfortable with the custom of having a trained lady's maid constantly hovering near, getting in the way and choosing "proper" clothing for her to wear. But oddly placed buttons and other such intricacies on the fancy clothing she wore as rarely as possible sometimes made help necessary. To meet such demands, she'd chosen this sweet, gawky girl to help with the confidence that Millie would never presume to comment on either her mistress's choices or actions.

"Yes, Millie. You can put my hairbrush, combs, lotion, and . . ." She grimaced and nodded toward the few personal items scattered across the top of her bureau. "Put all of that into my reticule. My father's gravely ill and I'm off to New York."

"Will you need a maid to accompany you?"

Liz heard the excited hope beneath a doubtless honest concern for the ailing master of the Double H.

"Not this time, Millie. Before permitting me to haul his fifteen-year-old daughter off into the sinful dangers of the big city, your father would likely quit, and I daren't risk losing so fine a foreman. Most particularly not when the Double H's boss lies so near death that I must rush away to be with him." Liz's teasing grin faded into somber lines.

Into the satchel Liz hurriedly stuffed two changes of clothing. Two changes ought to suffice for the journey. And considering the abundance of prissy "city" dresses she'd left behind in her father's home, she shouldn't need more. That those outfits were years out of style and had been designed for a schoolgirl surely wouldn't matter. With her father gravely ill she was unlikely to leave the house between her arrival in New York and return to Wyoming.

To lessen tension while she found and packed a second pair of shoes, Liz purposely allowed thoughts of the wardrobe waiting in New York to revive memories of Miss Brown's School for Young Ladies and put a crooked smile on a generous mouth prone to saucy grins. She had finished—no, excelled in—her education there, albeit with an ulterior motive beyond an avid love of learning. By accomplishing that goal, she'd fulfilled her part of a bargain struck with her father. Once Liz had her diploma in hand, he'd been forced to follow through with his end and permit her to return to the Double H rather than join her debutante peers in the expected sport of husband-hunting.

Her pride in successfully arranging that coup was now blighted by the reality of the many miles between herself and the much-loved father who needed her. She inwardly bemoaned that vast distance but faced the problem head-on, lips firming while determination glittered in turquoise eyes. Having never removed her thick wool coat, she had only to accept the heavy reticule from Millie and grasp the satchel's handles to begin the journey to his side.

CHAPTER 1

"Papa!" Liz dropped to her knees beside her father's bed and clasped between her palms the hand she remembered as big and strong but now seemed frail. Heavy drapes were drawn across the windows, blocking late afternoon sun and leaving the bedroom so dark its fine furnishings were little more than ominous shadows.

"Ah, Miss Elizabeth, thank the good Lord you've arrived at last . . . and in time."

Piercing blue eyes shifted to the portly physician standing at the foot of the bed. Always a mild, self-effacing man, Dr. Farrell looked alarmingly anxious. *In time?* What, precisely, did that mean? Was Samuel H. Hughes's end so very near?

Heart punishing her with its urgent pounding, Liz again peered through the gloom at the indistinct figure buried in quilts. It was terrifying to think that this weak, bedridden man was the same ruddy-complexioned father, hardy as a horse, she'd known all her life. As worried as she'd been by the telegram, this sight increased her fears fourfold.

"I set out within an hour of receiving the telegram,

but before we reached Omaha, a snowstorm seriously delayed the train." Lingering frustration over winter's ill-timed fury still clouded eyes usually a startlingly bright turquoise.

"Elizabeth—" Samuel struggled to lift his head but his thready call faded into silence, and he dropped back as if exhausted by even so small an effort.

"Come away, Miss Elizabeth," Dr. Farrell urgently whispered. "Not knowing the hour of your arrival, I gave your father medication which will assure he gets a dose of desperately needed rest. Come—" With a rueful smile, the doctor motioned her toward the door. "The best we can do for him now is to allow him to sleep. And while he does I'll tell you how things stand."

After kissing the limp hand in her hold, Liz laid it neatly atop her father's chest and reluctantly rose to accompany the family physician from the sick room. Admittedly headstrong by nature, she was never one to sit idly when taking action, any action, offered even slim hope for a speedier conclusion. In meeting this serious illness, that trait collided with something she had no power to change. The inability to *do* anything added further layers of frustration to her escalating alarm.

"Oooph!" Liz gasped as Marnie, once her nursemaid but now her father's housekeeper, yanked the cords of her corset one last time. To recover her poise she took several shallow breaths while the ends were neatly tied at her back.

The beastly corset was a symbol of all Liz found detestable about city life—so tightly constraining it threatened to suffocate her. She grimaced with self-disgust. Little over one full day in New York and already she longed for the wide open spaces of the Double H and the freedom to rule her own life. But not now. Not now. How could she be so selfish as to think of her own wishes when her father was so sick? If he could put himself to what must surely be far greater pains to welcome a foreign guest, how dare she complain about this comparatively mild discomfort.

"For Father's sake." Turning toward the cupid-edged mirror her mother had chosen for a little girl, Liz made a face at the reflected image of formally upswept hair and the fussy laces edging a lawn chemise crushed by whalebone stays.

Dr. Farrell had firmly cautioned Liz to keep her father calm. Most particularly, he'd warned her to "at all costs prevent the explosion of Sam's infamous temper." Should her efforts prove in vain, the ailing man's fragile heart might well fail him.

"Only for Father." Liz twisted about to roughly jerk a gown from the polished cherry wardrobe with no concern for which among the many her hand had fallen upon.

"Did you bring nothing more suitable, Miss Lizzy?"

Liz looked from the white folds of a half-donned gown to Marnie and shook her head.

"Not with Papa sick. I gathered up only enough to get me here. Besides, I thought I'd be taking care of him, not entertaining guests." Her nose wrinkled in irritation. It was the honest truth but not all of it. The practical garb she inevitably wore weekdays on the ranch, even the simple gowns reserved for church and country social gatherings, would have been only marginally more acceptable.

Designed for a schoolgirl, the frilly gown was inappropriate for a twenty-year-old. But no matter, Liz thrust her arms into place. Never before had she bothered with what was or was not fashionable, and this was certainly not the time to start despite Marnie's poorly hidden dismay.

Upon reaching the ground-level parlor, Liz went immediately to where her father waited, sitting propped up by a mass of chintz-covered pillows.

"Papa." On her knees at his side Liz tentatively broached a subject she feared might dangerously waken his temper and put him at risk. "Are you certain it's wise to attempt a social engagement under these circumstances?"

"More certain than I've been of anything in many years." His enigmatic answer and the gleam in eyes as blue as her own roused further questions in Liz, but there was no opportunity to seek explanations as at that moment their butler, Davis, announced their evening guest's arrival.

"His Grace, the duke of Ashleigh."

Expecting an ancient, withered nobleman but knowing it her duty to greet him politely, Liz rose and took several steps toward the door only to stop abruptly.

The duke was stunningly handsome with raven black hair emphasized by wings of silver at each temple that matched the silver frost of his eyes. Her defenses leapt to life. Liz didn't trust exceptionally handsome men. The few she'd observed, from the safe distance of adolescence, during her father's business-related social gatherings had been too practiced, too certain of their own exaggerated importance. She'd watched while they proved themselves a danger to the hearts, even virtue, of foolishly susceptible females. This man was by far the most attractive she'd ever seen. And the most dangerous.

"Grayson, allow me to introduce my daughter Elizabeth." The seated man's voice was faint but steady.

"Samuel, are you ill?"

Liz watched as the visitor strode past her with amazing grace for one of his exceptional height. The man settled on his heels beside his host.

"You should have sent me a message," the dark guest gently chided. "Our dinner could have been postponed until a more convenient time."

"Pshaw." Samuel faintly waved a limp hand. "There may never be a more convenient time for me. And, too, I am aware of the limits placed upon your visit to our land and the need to conclude our business posthaste."

"Daughter—" Lifting his face, Samuel sent Liz a fond smile as he continued. "Meet Grayson Brandt, eighth duke of Ashleigh."

The quiet "Pshaw" from a man whose expletives generally ran along saltier lines had sparked Liz's ready humor. As their guest rose to his formidable height, barely restrained laughter danced in the depths of a blue gaze directly meeting one of silver.

Gray moved to take his hostess's hand while taking close inventory of the woman for whose New York arrival he'd been waiting. The suspicion of impish amusement lurking behind the carefully correct lines of her face so intrigued him that it pushed aside his initial shock over her startlingly vivid figure. Samuel had told him of her red hair, but he'd thought to meet a woman with locks either the golden rose of sunrise or the deep, rich red of a fine brandy. But, no, hers were as bright as newly harvested carrots. Even more surprising, her skin was tanned to a golden tone, a condition that would've put the women of his acquaintance into a strategic decline until all traces could be eradicated. Her eyes, however, were beautiful—large, widely spaced and a startling, brilliant turquoise . . . if a good deal too direct for maidenly decorum.

"I'm delighted to meet you, Miss Hughes." As Gray bent to brush a light kiss to her fingers, he wondered if by wearing the virginal white garb of a schoolroom miss she thought to mislead him about her age.

Liz blinked, gazing down at the back of the dark head, becoming disgustingly aware of his magnetism.

Releasing his hold but still standing near, Gray met her unflinching, honest gaze and dismissed the possibility that she'd meant to fool him about her age or about anything else.

Gray mentally shrugged aside the faint sense of having been deceived. Although in no way was Miss Elizabeth Hughes what he'd expected, he hadn't been misled. Instead, he had been frankly if rather offhandedly informed of her age, red hair, and spirited nature. Looking at her now, he feared that the term "spirited nature" might be as complete an understatement as the bland mention of red hair. Signed already were the all-important documents by which the American railroad magnate parted with a sizable sum of money to see his daughter become a duchess. The self-mockery curving his lips compressed in acknowledgment of a solemn fact. Even had the papers not been signed, Gray had given his word and never did a gentleman—much less a duke—renege on an oath.

Discomfort intensified by their guest's penetrating scrutiny, Liz's eyes narrowed with what she hoped he'd recognize as an unspoken warning not to waste his time attempting to charm her. She was wary of men—didn't want to be subjugated to a husband's control. She needed no man beyond a foreman to oversee the hard labor that kept the ranch running smoothly. And, of course, her father. The thought of Samuel Hughes brought Liz back to the present with a thump. Her attention abruptly shifted to the speculative gleam in the older man's gaze. Rats! Apparently she'd watched the wretched duke too long. So long that her father had mistaken warning for interest.

"Papa, perhaps I should leave the two of you to discuss whatever . . ."

"Dinner is served." Davis's sonorous announcement interrupted the offer. The butler next stepped back, leaving the door open for the parlor's company to enter the dining room.

"Permit me." Gray offered his arm to the woman plainly caught between worry for her ailing father and irritation with the situation . . . and likely him.

Liz had no option but to place her fingers lightly in the crook of his arm, yet as they moved forward, she lifted her chin while proud disdain radiated from every line.

As the younger two moved toward the dining room, Davis stepped behind his master. In their wake he pushed the wicker chair, which even Miss Elizabeth had failed to realize was equipped with wheels.

"Have you traveled to the Continent, Miss Hughes?" Gray politely asked once they'd been seated and the first course of trout in a light wine sauce had been served by a dark-suited, white-gloved footman.

"No." The briefest of glances accompanied Liz's single-word answer. She didn't add that there was little to interest her across the Atlantic. The fact that it would've been rude had nothing to do with her restraint. Rather, its source was a determination for her father to quickly recognize she was not, absolutely *not* interested in this more than eligible suitor.

It had become disgustingly clear that her father had arranged this dinner solely for her to meet the duke. Only by effort of will did Liz prevent her teeth from grinding. Illness, it seemed, had turned her father into as shameless a matchmaker as any debutante's mother. Liz wouldn't have it! She wouldn't do anything rash to rouse her father's temper, but neither would she do anything that the duke might conceivably interpret as encouragement!

The meal that followed would've been consumed in near silence had the matter been left in Liz's hands. This, despite the duke's courteous attempt to draw his hostess into conversation. His gallant efforts were rewarded with steadily averted eyes and such unrewarding monosyllables that in defense he turned to Mr. Hughes and embarked upon a mostly one-sided discussion of the relative merits of American and British rail systems.

All three participants were relieved when the waste of a fine cook's talents finally came to an end. Women always left men to their port at a dinner's conclusion, thus Liz thought she'd be able to escape the men's presence. She was wrong.

"Liz—" Samuel's weak voice was perversely lent strength by its tremble. "Ring the bell for Davis to see me into the study."

Anxious to take any step that would hasten her freedom, Liz instantly lifted the small silver bell ever awaiting a hostess's hand. Even as its jingle sounded, her father continued his instructions.

"You will join Grayson and me in the study."

"Why?" Liz sought to reject the unexpected and unwanted invitation although it was plainly not an invitation but an order.

"I have important news to share with you."

Liz looked from her father to their too devastatingly handsome guest with growing dread. What kind of news so confidential it could only be revealed in the study's privacy would be of any concern to the stranger whose gaze rested heavily upon her? In desperation she mentally searched for some innocuous purpose. Was it related to her father's railroad? Had the duke something to do with those in his own country? Was that why the subject had dominated dinner talk? A hollow feeling in the pit of her stomach mocked that possibility as an unpleasant joke.

Samuel Hughes, chair pushed by Davis, led the way. Trepidation growing, Liz stared at the strip of thick Turkish carpet stretching down the corridor they traversed to the small, book-filled chamber that had been her father's retreat for as long as she could remember.

Davis stepped around the bulky wheelchair and soundlessly opened a well-oiled door. A broad mahogany desk straddled one corner of the room while a plant stand holding a fern Liz's mother had selected stood in its depths. The fern had grown to incredible size, but though its green fronds threatened to fill the space behind her father's usual chair, he wouldn't allow anyone to move it from the position his beloved wife had chosen near a decade earlier. As Samuel was maneuvered into place behind his desk, Grayson held a wing chair for Liz before taking a seat on its twin.

"Elizabeth—" Leaning forward to rest his arms on the desk's satiny surface, Samuel paused to clear a voice apparently strained by the few words he'd spoken at dinner.

Liz straightened into an uncomfortably rigid posture. Save for introductions, her father *never* called her Elizabeth.

Recognizing the all too familiar stubbornness beginning to firm a gentle jawline, Samuel purposely disarmed his daughter with a wan smile of supplication.

"I am rapidly nearing the end of my days." Liz opened her lips to deny his gloomy prediction, but Samuel lifted a trembling hand to wave her demurrals into silence. "The approach of my inevitable end has made me more sensitive to unkept promises given your dear mother on her deathbed."

Without rational thought, Liz slowly leaned back, pressing into the chair's thick padding as if it were somehow possible to evade what she feared would follow.

"You know that I gave my oath to see you as well educated as any debutante."

"And you have, Papa, you have. Indeed, I surpassed my classmates at Miss Brown's School for Young Ladies. You know that I was their best pupil in everything from languages to riding."

Again a trembling hand waved away her protestations. "You were indeed. However, that was only the first of the two promises I gave."

Thick amber lashes dropped to rest on sun-bronzed cheeks. Never had they spoken of it but from Marnie she knew. She knew.

"I promised your mother that I would see our daughter well set up, and despite your belief and intention to claim that the good care you've given the Double H is a satisfactory fulfillment of that oath, it is not true. No, that promise I have failed to keep, for she sought and won my oath to see you safely and comfortably wed."

Liz's eyes snapped open and she began to so firmly shake her head that it endangered the firm mooring of fashionably upswept hair.

"Some days past," Samuel relentlessly continued, voice growing suspiciously strong. Liz was not calm enough to notice, but the duke's eyes narrowed. "His Grace and I signed formal documents concerning your future."

Turquoise flames flashed as Liz leapt to her feet. "I will *not* wed him! Neither you nor he nor any other can force me to say the words that would make it so!"

Grayson was well bred enough to have sat as quiet witness to the growing discord between father and daughter, but this last was an insult he could not, would not, ignore. There were a great many women of noble blood and far greater beauty in his own country who would joyously welcome the honor this American female rudely spurned.

"So be it." The duke stood and from his impressive height gazed icily down at the unwilling bride. "The contract is null."

Liz returned his freezing glare with one so fiery that by rights it should have burnt the man to cinders.

Then, before another word was spoken or action taken, the brittle tension of their confrontation was shattered by a sharp cry of pain followed by a loud crash. They whirled toward its source.

Clutching his chest in agony, Samuel Hughes lay awkwardly atop fragments of pottery, mangled fern fronds, and the smashed pieces of a wicker wheelchair and toppled plant stand.

CHAPTER 2

The ceremony was complete and for the first time since the Reverend J. L. Phillips had begun, Liz lifted her attention from where her stricken father lay on his bed, half smothered by piled blankets and a richly embroidered counterpane. The icy-faced duke now—horrors!—her husband looked to be no more pleased by this *fait accompli* than she.

Gazing down into his bride's brilliant eyes, Gray silently acknowledged how different she was from the woman he'd expected; how complete an antithesis she was to his first wife—Camellia, as pale and delicate as her namesake. The memory of white skin and fine golden hair cast a shadow of pain over his already cold expression.

Liz saw the darkening of his gaze and her fine auburn brows met, furrowing a sun-gilded brow. Though a tall woman, when standing so close to the coldly controlled duke, his shadow enveloped her as he gently pulled her to rest against his powerful chest. Despite the reverend's instructions, she was unprepared when he lowered his head for a kiss. Her senses tilted awry when his mouth met hers with tantalizing pressure. How was it that a man so cold could brush her with fire? Dangerous! Proof the too handsome duke was dangerous!

Gray was knocked off stride by the taste of this unconventional beauty's untutored but very real passion while Liz was unnerved by the experience. It was a reaction foreign to her and one she assured herself was extremely unpleasant. She determinedly doused the kindling flames by reminding herself of a chilling concern for her father's health and wretched awareness of just how sweeping a commitment she'd given and the complete mess it made of her plans for the future. In the precious few hours between her previous night's refusal of the match and this moment, the course she'd carefully plotted for her life had been abruptly, thoroughly rerouted.

Stoically firming lips still burning, Liz reminded herself that for love of her dying father she'd have conceded even more.

"Thank the Lord, that's over." Samuel threw heavy blankets aside, bounced up from the bed, and stripped off his nightshirt to reveal himself fully dressed beneath. "When that wretched snowstorm delayed Liz's train I feared all was lost, but we brought it off in time! Didn't we, Grayson?" His hearty voice was in no way muffled by the handkerchief being exuberantly rubbed over face and throat.

Shocked, Liz blinked at the vision of her "ailing" father suddenly vibrating with good health and actually wiping away his sickly pallor. Powder? White powder! She'd been gulled! Gulled by such artifice as was used for the stage, tricks a woman more concerned with the all-important need for a milky complexion would likely have recognized from the first.

Gray was equally shocked, but he might have found the unbelievable scene amusing were he not the butt of its jest.

Planting fists on hips, Liz turned fully toward the

one man in all the world she'd have sworn could be trusted. "You've played me for a simpleton!" Blue eyes glittered with fury. *"My own father* made me a fool! A fool and something I despise even more—a wife."

"Now Lizzy, lambkin—" Samuel tossed the soiled handkerchief aside and reached out to clasp his daughter's shoulders. "You know I would never do anything to hurt you. Never. I've only found for you a husband such as any of your former schoolmates would swoon to win."

Gray was appalled as the inference of Samuel's initial statement sank in. Although the other man's words would have it seem otherwise, he was an unwitting party to this ill-timed scene. Moreover, it was with growing distaste that he watched the heated interaction between father and daughter. These Americans had no sense of propriety, no inbred restraint that would prevent an exhibition of private disharmony from playing out before the reverend and, worse still, the two servants present to witness hastily exchanged vows.

From the corner of her eyes Liz saw the duke's frown and recognized its source. She wasn't sorry in the least. She'd be pleased as punch for the whole world to know this marriage was a mockery. Liz twisted free of her father's hold.

"Then you should've introduced my former schoolmates to him!" A fiery glare stilled hands again reaching for her. "You betrayed me! You used my concern, my tenderest emotions to trick me into this . . . this marriage. You've robbed me of *everything* I love, everything from the Double H to the father I thought loved me enough to respect my wish for an independent life in Wyoming."

Samuel's face went white without the aid of powder. "Lizzy, I do love you. I love you so dearly that I've done all that I've done—*for* you." The unsteadiness of his mournful voice held a supplication of its own. "And I've not stolen the ranch from you. Indeed, by the terms of the marriage settlement, the Double H Ranch has become truly yours and yours alone—my wedding gift to you."

"Mine? Of what earthly use can the Double H be to me now that, by the arrangements you've made, I will be banished from my own country . . . and my ranch."

Without the rigid social conventions which no gentleman would flout even need he not—for political reasons—be ever vigilant to protect his spotless reputation, Gray would have been more than willing to consign his new bride to her uncivilized Wyoming ranch. She obviously preferred its wilds to the status much sought after by others among his equals in aristocratic English circles, a status for which she was clearly ill suited. For the sake of good manners he had restrained himself from earlier interfering in his host and hostess's disagreement, but enough was enough and this was too much.

"Miss Jones—" Gray turned toward a young, goggle-eyed maid standing captivated by the titillating scene. "Would you be so kind as to see my wife dressed for our departure in two hours?"

Liz watched as Miss Sarah Jones straightened and reluctantly lowered curious eyes as she dropped a respectful curtsy. Almost Liz could see the wheels turn in this youthful but dedicated gossip's mind. She was certain to have divined that this unexpected trickery was the reason behind Marnie's suspicious illness and refusal to stand as witness to the vows given by the master's daughter. Liz's mouth curled in disgust. Sarah knew the dutiful Davis would never repeat the details of the heated exchange between father and daughter—but she would. Liz strode down the corridor, never doubting that as Sarah followed behind, her thoughts were filled with delighted anticipation of the attention this juicy tale would earn her from those belowstairs.

Once Sarah had cleared the doorway, Lizzy kicked it shut with a resounding slam. The vicious physical assault on an innocent door accomplished nothing . . . but it made her feel better!

"Your travel dress has been cleaned and mended where the braiding was ripped."

Liz glanced toward the bed from which Sarah was lifting the serge gown she'd worn on the train her first day out of Wyoming. Its hunter green hue was as practical as the simple no-frills cut, but the sense of approval it normally brought was dampened by the tremble in hands holding it up for inspection. The same burst of anger that had made her feel better had frightened Sarah.

"Please forgive my temper, Sarah." Liz shrugged apologetically. "I fear the prospect of imminent departure on an unexpected voyage has made me more nervous than I like to admit." Liz suddenly realized her statement likely revealed too much and immediately spoke again in a belated attempt to limit the scope of the girl's conjectures. "I've never been on a boat of any kind—much less a huge iron ship." Stifling unabated frustration along with an honest dread, Liz sent the curious upstairs maid an engaging smile. "To me the notion that anything made of something so heavy as iron actually floats defies logic."

Sarah nodded her agreement, not that there was the remotest possibility she would ever have the opportunity to test such a theory. Anxious to be done with duties and free to carry her gossip below, Sarah laid aside the green gown and made haste to see Miss Elizabeth out of her wedding garb and dressed for the first part of a long journey.

While Sarah folded the discarded dress into a trunk,

Liz again nibbled her lower lip. The vague image of a massive ocean liner loomed ominously in her mind. Within hours she and the dangerous, incredibly handsome duke would board the steam-driven beast waiting at the docks to carry them across the Atlantic.

"Elizabeth, are you ready?"

Liz glared at the connecting door between her room and *his*. Two hours out of harbor and already the dinner bell had rung.

Ready? No! She was not ready!

"In a mo—ooph . . ." Her response ended unceremoniously as she landed hard against a bureau fortunately fastened to a rolling floor. The night seas were rough and this appalling, constant tilting from one side to the other made the simple act of disrobing more of a challenge than riding the meanest stallion in the Double H's stable. And removing the practical travel garb was only half of the feat expected of her.

Clinging gratefully to the bureau, she tried again to speak. This time she succeeded in gritting out an answer to her tormentor's question while at the same time shrugging out of her green dress.

"I'll be ready in a moment."

Leastways her severely limited wardrobe, made for a years-younger-her, had neither the multitude of layers nor the endless rows of tiny buttons that adorned the garb of fashionable women. It was strange comfort, but Liz welcomed it. Ignoring the pool of green serge still encircling her feet, Liz firmly held the bureau's edge with one hand while with the other pulling on yet another too girlish gown.

"Might I offer assistance in fastening your dress?" Having considerable experience with such often-complicated devices, Gray had reason to suspect his help might be necessary and made the offer without an ulterior motive.

Liz didn't believe him capable of so altruistic an action, and it was a wonder the door did not explode in flames beneath the fiery gaze bent upon it.

"No, you may *not!"* How dare he? After discovering that they'd been booked into a suite with separate bedrooms, Liz had been convinced that she'd safely landed on the far side of the first marital hurdle. This discovery that the duke was sensitive enough not to rush her into frightening intimacies had for the first time softened her toward her groom. Now his "kind" offer to perform so personal a service trampled budding relief and again hardened her heart against him.

"I merely suggested my willingness." The thread of laughter running through his statement increased Liz's ire. "Knowing, as I do, that you've no lady's maid to perform the task for you."

Looking at the situation through the eyes of humor was Gray's only hope for dealing with it in the short term. And although Elizabeth was unlikely to believe it, he was as displeased by the position in which they found themselves as she was.

His bride was in no way the kind of woman Gray had thought he was marrying, and it would require time and careful planning to establish their future course. Nonetheless, he couldn't truthfully claim, even to himself, that he found Elizabeth physically unappealing—merely unsuited to be his duchess. Not solely because of her saucy tongue and defiant ways but also because he thought he'd chosen, had meant to choose, a wife who would be no danger to his emotional control. Gray had had enough of love and the pain of loss. He sought a stable life without the danger of either unreliable feelings, certain to be met with disappointing realities, or the golden illusion of happiness, inevitably revealed as worthless dross.

While on one side of the connecting door Gray pondered the future of their relationship, on the other

Liz stepped free from the ring of her fallen travel clothes to lean flat against the steadfast support of the wall next to it. She silently fumed and hastily thrust the few front buttons into their respective holes. Then, as the second and final dinner bell sounded, she pulled the door open—an ill-timed action. The ship crested a particularly large swell and pitched wildly over the far side. Liz found herself in her husband's arms, clasped tight against a powerful chest while he fought to hold them both upright.

To mask the response aroused by the feel of her more than adequate curves, Gray looked with distaste down the figure again inappropriately garbed in a too youthful gown.

Liz felt his disapproval as fully as if he'd spoken it aloud. Her face flamed anew and she heatedly defended her appearance.

"When I came East I hadn't any intention of embarking on a sea voyage let alone marriage to a hoity-toity Britisher."

Gray's face went to stone while ice glittered in his eyes.

Liz's smiled with bitter satisfaction. The duke's coldness pleased her. She would make it her goal to keep his response to her chilly and see that he never bent the heat of his undoubted charms upon defenses she was not certain were able to withstand such an assault. A wickedly determined curl deepened the grin on her peach lips. Giving free rein to the temper that so plainly put him off ought to go far in achieving that end.

"Besides—" Liz scornfully added, "I doubt you'd be any better pleased by the buckskins I usually wear on the ranch. The only other clothes I possess are two traveling suits and these dresses left in New York once my school days ended." It wasn't true; leastways not the whole truth. Liz did have a number of rustic dresses in her wardrobe at the Double H, but what she'd claimed would surely get her point across more effectively.

"I cannot be sorry that after tricking me into marrying you, as part of the bargain you struck for my father's wealth, you've been landed with the unacceptable encumbrance that you find me to be." She motioned toward herself. "And I won't change to make myself more acceptable to you."

"I was led to believe before we met last evening that you had accepted—nay, more, that you welcomed the arrangements your father laid for your future."

"Hah!" Liz gave a most unladylike snort. "I'd sooner trust a rattlesnake than believe anything you say. Besides, you *did* know how I felt before the ceremony this morning."

"Yes." Light from a gas lamp attached to the wall gleamed over smoothly combed black hair as Gray nodded slightly. "But I, too, was duped by your father's performance into an action I would never elsewise have committed. That I married you even though his claim of your willingness proved untrue demonstrates only that I am not cad enough to walk away from a dying man and leave the daughter he'd affianced to me alone in the world."

He gave her the grimmest smile Liz had ever seen, and she shivered, feeling as if he'd closed his coldness around her.

"I assure you that I am no more satisfied by the outcome of this bargain made and fulfilled under false pretenses than are you. Yet, no matter the circumstance or person responsible for the deed, we are married."

For near the first time in her life, Liz was taken aback. Her belief in his perfidy faltered as she acknowledged that he did seem remarkably irritated by his success in tricking her into this union.

"It's past time for us to make our way to dinner, but I will leave you here to go hungry until you swear by your mother's grave that you'll at least try to act civilly in public."

His dismissive glare left Liz in no doubt that he thought her manners so atrocious as to be beyond repair. This action and his cold words stabilized the momentary wobble in Liz's certainty of his villainous nature. Her temper blazed higher. If Grayson Brandt, the high and mighty duke, thought she'd meekly put up with his inference that she was some graceless barbarian incapable of good manners . . . Well, he was due a lesson in that art himself. She wasted no attention on the fact that this was a complete reversal of her earlier plan to freeze him with her uncivil temper.

"I agree we must leave now or we'll be late for dinner, and to prevent making a scene, we can delay no longer." The dulcet tones of her gentle rebuke were accompanied by such a sticky-sweet smile that he looked at her suspiciously but promptly offered his arm and led her from their suite.

"I've already taken steps to correct your sad lack of garb appropriate for the duchess of Ashleigh." Gray quietly spoke while they made their way down the corridor, pausing every few feet to allow Liz to steady her balance. Although it would have been irrational not to appreciate his solicitous action, it left Liz more aware of her clumsiness compared to the duke's gracefulness. And, for all his icy control, he did move with the sinuous grace of a big black panther.

"Upon reaching Liverpool we'll change ships and set out immediately for Paris," Gray continued, unfazed by his partner's uncertain balance. "I've cabled ahead to the Rue de la Paix. As I bring him a duchess in need of a complete wardrobe, M. Charles Worth will doubtless welcome us."

From his precise description of their destination and its purpose it was clear he suspected her too uncultured to know who the famous man was. That wasn't so. Even during her years spent in the relative seclusion of Miss Brown's School for Young Ladies, she'd heard her peers speak with awed reverence of the famous wardrobe designer Charles Worth. Her father had been right. Any one of them would've given anything to be in her shoes—wed to a nobleman, a duke no less, and on her way to be fitted for not merely a dress but an entire wardrobe by Worth. Nonetheless, Liz had rather be back on the Double H.

The first-class dining saloon, glittering with cut glass goblets and glowing silver, was nearly full, but as others were still arriving the lateness of their appearance went unremarked. They were led to a table for four, and as they approached, the only person already seated there politely rose.

"I say, Ashleigh." The blond, dark-eyed gentleman smiled in welcome. "I hadn't realized you were on this side of the Atlantic."

Liz felt the imperceptible tightening of the arm under her light touch, but the duke's bland smile revealed nothing of his honest response to the speaker. His reaction was curious, most curious. Hers, on the other hand, was an instinctively uncomfortable reaction to the man's smirk.

"Had I known, we could've met for dinner or a livelier evening like those we shared during our Oxford days." He grinned at Liz and added, "We had some jolly times. Remember when that bit of fluff got you into . . ."

The stranger's words trailed off at the sound of a feminine throat softly cleared. Liz's action was a gentle reminder both of her presence and of what men of refinement might and might not discuss in a lady's presence.

Gray's acquaintance cast Liz an apparently repentant smile and abandoned the subject for one more innocuous. "I'm glad to find I'll have friends with whom to visit during our return voyage."

Considering her escort's response to the man, Liz wondered if he hadn't been presumptuous in claiming Gray as a friend, let alone a complete stranger such as herself.

"Elizabeth, allow me to introduce you to Lawrence Burry, earl of Hayton." Silver eyes shifted from wife to self-proclaimed friend. "Hayton, meet my bride, Elizabeth."

Blond brows arched. "Married? Never thought you'd shackle yourself again."

Again? Liz was startled by this news of a previous wife but not so startled she failed to notice as the earl smoothly claimed her hand to brush a light kiss over its back. It was a perfectly acceptable exercise in good manners, but the quick wink that followed decidedly was not. Though distracted, Liz responded in the only possible fashion for a refined woman. She ignored it, taking the seat Gray held out for her without a moment's pause.

Course followed course, and the tables around them began emptying of people who looked distinctly green, but Liz and her two dinner companions continued unaffected. Nonetheless, after hours of holding her tongue to avoid speaking her mind in a way few women and certainly no new brides were permitted, and after exercising the rules of etiquette ground into her at Miss Brown's, Liz was relieved when the meal came to an end. As the duke stood to lead her back to their suite, their fellow diner spoke.

"I'm charmed to have met you, Elizabeth." Hayton rose and again took Liz's hand, this time kissing it in farewell. "Dare I hope you'll regard me as a friend?"

Aware of the instant chill this invitation called from

her husband, Liz knew a cool smile should be her answer. But after exercising dutiful restraint for so long, she couldn't suppress an impish wish to twist the panther's tail.

"If we are to be friends, Lawrence, then please call me Lizzy. All of my friends do."

"Your *American* friends." Gray hastily intervened, containing a strong desire to immediately chastise his unconventional bride. Here, in the urge to cause such a barbaric public scene, was proof of the danger she could be to his position in civilized society and to his long-practiced emotional control. Tucking her hand into the crook of his arm, with a patronizing smile he calmly pointed out the error in her thinking.

"Lizzy is hardly an appropriate sobriquet for the duchess of Ashleigh."

Liz realized that in the space of two impetuous sentences she had completely negated the purpose behind uncomfortable hours spent affecting a stilted etiquette. Oh, well, it was doubtful her frozen-faced husband had been impressed by her careful display anyway.

Hayton stepped aside to ease their departure, but as they passed, he winked conspiratorially at Liz. This second wink left her unpleasantly wondering if acceptance of his invitation to friendship hadn't been an act of supreme folly.

Liz was growing accustomed to the ship's roll, thus Gray was able to escort her down the corridor toward their suite with less difficulty than encountered on their journey to the dining room. It was a trip accomplished in silence while Liz longed for the suite's privacy, thinking that once inside they'd each seek their own bedrooms. She thought that was the way it would be. Thought? No, she hoped, even prayed it would be so. It was a hope doomed to disappointment as, despite her faint resistance, the panther she feared as a predator drew her into the sitting room they shared and carefully closed the door, shutting them inside . . . alone.

"I must speak plainly to you—of many things." Yet, rather than speaking, Gray began to pace like a stalking cat, and not until long moments later did he abruptly turn toward the bride whose apprehensions had grown with his every step.

"First—" he harshly began, again striding from door to far wall. "Hayton is *not* a fit friend for you to welcome."

Although she'd reached the same conclusion herself, Liz bristled, temper fired by the combination of rarely experienced fear and the restless excitement only he had ever aroused. Gray's attempt to control whose friendship she would or would not accept reversed her recent decision to distance herself from the earl. Never would she seek him out, but neither would she refuse the social advances he was certain to make.

"Furthermore," Gray came to a halt, looming over his bride. "It's past time for us to discuss the expectations we each have concerning our union."

Why, Liz wryly wondered, did she suspect that this discussion would be totally one-sided—that these expectations would be all what he expected of her and nothing of what she might wish. While Gray continued, peach lips firmed and turquoise eyes began to glow with the stubbornness Liz's father had teased her about for years.

"As we earlier agreed, neither of us sought this union—"

"Oh, but *you* did." Liz instantly refuted his claim. "You chose to sign an agreement with my father to wed me—sight unseen—for the sake of my inheritance."

"Unseen, yes, but . . ." Frustrated by her ability to

strike at the weakest point in his argument, silver lightning flashed from Gray's eyes while his voice took on the cutting edge of a bared blade. "To base my decision upon, I was given wholly inaccurate information, not to say bald lies, about your appearance and, more specifically, your character. Had I known the truth, never for any amount of wealth would I have chosen you." This woman was so completely the opposite of what he had sought for a bride that the sincerity of his words couldn't be questioned.

Feeling unaccountably crushed by her handsome husband's disdain, Liz glared back at the icy gaze slowly taking her measure from head to toe and blatantly finding her wanting.

"We could seek an annulment." Liz fired her retort at him with the speed and power of a gunshot, confident that this flash of inspiration was the answer to their quandary, an answer able to put both the panther and herself out of their misery.

"No, we could *not!"* Gray's chill rejection deflected Liz's attempt for a reprieve with disgusting ease. "Not after you've been publicly presented as my bride."

"Surely not to anyone who counts." Even as Liz made the desperate plea she was hit by a disconcerting realization: Were they parted she would miss the battle of wits with and, yes, the mere sight of this devastating man who could, and had, thoroughly upset her usually stable sense of balance.

"Oh, the earl of Hayton counts, more than I'd like to admit." Gray saw her odd expression, wide eyes staring at him as if some mythical character had taken his place, but went on to emphasize an undeniable point that left no grounds upon which she could base continued pleas.

"Moreover, there is no doubt but that Hayton is eager to spread both the news of our union and a detailed report of our encounter to anyone willing to listen. And, believe me, many will soak it all in with delight bordering on malice."

Liz heard the logic of his words, but it was the recent discovery of her own traitorous feelings that so overwhelmed her that with slumping shoulders she sank down onto one of the overstuffed chairs.

"We are," Gray added, "as you so tactfully put it, 'stuck' with each other. But there are rules I must live by, rules my duchess *must* observe—a necessity I fear you incapable of meeting. You seem unable to observe even the most basic precepts of good manners."

That hurt after she'd worked so hard to prove herself throughout the endless evening meal.

"Still more unpleasant—and, I assure you, for *both* of us—I must have an heir and you must give him to me."

This blunt announcement addressed the single issue at center of her deepest apprehension. But even worse than that bald statement, he'd added insult to injury by declaring his distaste for her despite his insistence that she submit. Liz leapt to her feet and struck back at what her two years of dealing with ranch hands had shown her was every man's most vulnerable point.

"You are so cold it would require a blast furnace to even thaw you, let alone ignite the blazing heat surely necessary to father a baby."

In direct contradiction to her charge, silver eyes darkened into the smoldering coals of a barely restrained blaze.

"Cold?" Gray's single word was not truly a question. A fact made plain by his sensuous smile, which seemed to steam with the danger of dry ice. Many had named him the same, but that this one woman had done so stung him into rash action.

An inward bell rang, warning Liz to retreat but she found herself welded in place by the flashing power of his silver gaze. For the first time in her life, she felt the strong arms of a man not her kin wrap completely about her. He relentlessly drew her nearer to the unsuspected whirlwind of fire at the core of his ice, a fire so hot it melted her resistance even as his dark heat bent to take her mouth in a succession of tormentingly brief kisses.

Gray again and more fully tasted the heady wine of sweet innocence and alarm on his rebellious bride's lips. His own instinctively gentled to lure her beyond fear and into pleasure.

The man Liz had recognized the moment they met as a danger to any woman's self-possession easily tempted her beyond an initial intent to resist. Yielding to his devastating kiss and lost to rational thinking, she melted against him. A strange, wild little cry escaped her tight throat while, shaking all over with the need to be nearer and nearer still, she pressed herself fully against his long, hard form.

Gray forgot the reason for his action, forgot his anger with her in the need to crush her soft body closer and savor her mouth's intoxicating peach nectar. As he deepened their kiss into something wild and overwhelming, it swept Liz ever farther into the depths of his fiery vortex and she clung to him with something akin to desperation until . . .

For a change the ship's constant rolling worked to Liz's advantage. Where once it had thrown her into Gray's arms, it now atoned and set her free. Only after she stood a safe distance from the arrogant man and his wicked wiles did she feel the lashing whip of self-betrayal. Liz boldly fought back with the single weapon in her arsenal, despite its proven vulnerability.

"You may have my father's money, but I'll be *damned* if you'll ever have me!"

To hide an urge to flee in fear of his undeniable ability to expose the weakness of her claim, Liz stormed into her bedroom and shot home the bolt that would insure he couldn't get near her—at least not tonight.

Gray shook his head to clear it of passion's irrational fog while frustration heightened a revived anger. He clenched his hands, fighting an inner battle to stifle first the desire and then the fury resurrected by her rejection of a passion she had assuredly shared.

Her further exhibition of an ungovernable temper and language that no lady would *ever* use had merely reinforced the rightness of a fact earlier acknowledged. Never would he dare present Elizabeth to the civilized company of the London Season or Parliament soirees. No, it would be best for her to remain at his country seat while his sister Euphemia, with years of experience in serving as his hostess, continued supervising his London home and social calendar.

Elizabeth would, of course, eventually have to learn that laws governing wives in his country were quite different from those in her wild land. Gray paused at the sideboard and from one of the ornate silver stands attached to its polished surface lifted a cut glass decanter to pour himself a stiff whiskey. In point of fact, Elizabeth belonged to him body and soul. All wives were their husband's chattel. And she'd "damn" well do whatever he demanded. He tossed the drink back in a single swallow and poured another before resuming his pacing.

Not that he'd force himself upon an unwilling bride. It wouldn't be necessary. He'd proven that already. Yet, disgusted by his loss of control moments before, he swore that never again would he allow her fiery temper to burst through the wall of his famous icy restraint. Instead, he'd use his experience to woo his bride and temper her flames into more useful directions, into the passion that would get him an heir.

Before his father's death he'd lived the irresponsible life of an idle nobleman, ignored the older man's wise counsel, resisted his attempts to restrict wild ways. But death had hopelessly shattered the pretty glass ball of Gray's youth with its round of parties and heedless pleasures. Harsh reality had then stepped in to require that he shoulder the sobering responsibilities of his heritage—from marriage to a seat in the House of Lords. Nonetheless, he had gained more than enough experience with the frailer sex during his irresponsible youth and in discreet alliances since its end to be confident of his ability to seduce a reluctant bride.

Glancing irritably about the half-lit chamber, he sharply turned and strode from the suite. In the smoking lounge he'd find company more amenable to a gentleman of good breeding.

"I say, Ashleigh, aren't you going it a bit heavy?" Hayton took a seat beside Gray and bent to peer into unfocused silver eyes beneath locks of dark hair fallen over his forehead. The earl hid his amusement with the unfamiliar sight. Never, even when young bucks on a lark from university, had he seen Gray drink to excess.

"Hayton, you'd know ol' boy." Gray's words were as blurry as his view of the other man. "Got experience. Never had to force a woman. Never will."

Having restrained himself to a mere two pints of ale, Hayton's eyes were clear as they narrowed on the rare vision of a thoroughly sotted Ashleigh, an Ashleigh as a lonely bridegroom. The earl nearly crowed with delight that some whim of fate had brought him here at this moment. Was it destiny?

"Right, you've no need to force a woman. They stumble over each other trying to win your attention and the chance to melt your famous ice, leaving themselves vulnerable for you to take your choice and prove the folly of their thinking."

"Won't have to force own wife. Melt Lizzy, too." Black hair gleamed as Gray tilted his head back to swallow another potent drink in one long draught.

With soothing agreements and occasional words to direct near incoherent words, Hayton extracted from Gray the tale of a reluctant bride.

CHAPTER 3

Liz gazed through the window of an impressive ducal carriage, blind to glistening moisture left on passing hedgerows by recent rainfall. Sunlight peeking between clouds laid shifting patterns over rolling green fields while the restless clenching of her slender fingers threatened to shamefully crease an exquisite traveling suit. The outfit was gray but, like *his* eyes, its color almost glowed. Subtle yet anything but drab, it provided a perfect foil for her intricately twined red hair and brilliant blue gaze.

Liz wished for the first time that matters were not so strained between herself and her husband that casual conversation was a challenge. It seemed neither of them was willing to humble their pride enough to breach the tense silence. Never had Liz been prone to the nervous fits common amongst "high-strung" society women, but imminent arrival at an unfamiliar home so unsettled her that she would've welcomed even the most banal of conversations to distract her from courage-stealing apprehensions.

Strangers awaited their coming, strangers who were unlikely to be any more pleased with their new duchess than their master was, particularly not after the bridal couple's uneasy relationship became evident. Liz was nervous. In her experience, curious servants were able to sense the slightest, most well-concealed discords.

Gray shifted uncomfortably on nicely padded red leather upholstery, repositioning long legs cramped in even so luxurious a vehicle as this one. He was aware of his wife's deepening dread. Under other circumstances he'd have tried to ease a companion's distress. His compassion, however, had been sorely strained by the act she'd put on following their disagreement over what he expected of a wife and her rejection of their single shipboard embrace. Throughout the rest of the voyage she feigned *mal de mer,* never leaving her bedroom. That unwelcome action had, however, brought one positive result. It had blocked any further advance Hayton might have thought to make toward her. A vague memory of Hayton's leering face and the next morning's fierce headache were all Gray remembered of his evening spent in the ship's smoking lounge.

Once they transferred from the transatlantic liner to the smaller ship for the voyage to Paris, they'd wordlessly adopted a stilted formality that had continued whenever circumstances forced them into proximity during that short round-trip and their stay in France.

Gray vehemently resented her apparent insistence that he play the repentant fool. He had done nothing that required forgiveness. She, on the other hand, had proven herself willing to use the same ploy of simulated illness that she'd disdained in her father's determination to see them wed. Despite her assumptions to the contrary, he had not tricked her into marriage. And there was nothing unreasonable about expecting her to fulfill the obligations accompanying the vow she'd given.

Moreover, he had gone to great lengths to see his

bride appropriately garbed even though the cost of her extravagant Worth wardrobe could have been better spent reroofing Ashleigh Hall. A fair man, Gray had to admit that the result justified the exorbitant cost. The Paris gowns made a stunning asset of her unusual coloring. From the first he had found her attractive, although utterly unsuitable as a duchess, but after hours well spent in the couturier's talented hands . . .

Feeling the weight of dangerous silver eyes on her restless fingers, Liz was abruptly aware of the damage she'd unthinkingly inflicted on innocent cloth too beautiful to deserve such abuse. This careless treatment of a very expensive suit doubtless gave her husband still another reason to find fault in her. She began anxiously smoothing heavy silk fabric beneath flattened palms in an unconscious effort to shift his dangerous attention from herself.

"Ashleigh Hall lies there." Love for his home shaded Gray's announcement as with a wave of his hand he directed the path of his nervous bride's attention.

Liz welcomed the diversion. Recognizing the emotion in his voice, she wanted to see what lent such warmth to normally chilled tones and leaned forward seeking an unhindered view. They had been steadily progressing down a long drive lined with stately poplars, but now the carriage began a sweeping turn to circle a huge fountain flanked by formal gardens already ablaze with tulips and irises.

The carriage slowed to a halt while blue eyes took in the impressive building. Rose-colored stone soared several stories high and stretched an equally formidable distance on either side of massive double doors.

"Our servants are waiting to meet their new chatelaine. Those who toil outside line the brick-laid path from drive to steps, and those who serve within the house stand on the steps in order of ascending importance." Sunlight gleamed on the silver wings in Gray's dark hair as he nodded first toward those awkwardly gathered at the edges of the drive and then toward the thirty or forty figures primly lined up from bottom to top of a grand stairway.

"Ascending importance." It wasn't a question but rather a wry restatement of what to Liz was a foreign concept. Oh, she was familiar with the theory of a servant class hierarchy. At Miss Brown's School she'd been taught the rules of managing servants on great estates but had no practical experience in dealing with the custom. By choice there were few servants in either her father's New York house or on the ranch in Wyoming, and all were treated with equal respect.

"Yes," Gray stated flatly, exasperated by what he heard as an unexpected complication, one for which there was no time to educate her to meet. "In England the multilayer system governing servants has existed for centuries. Those who labor inside are more highly regarded than those who toil outdoors. The demarcation between front of the house servants—butler, housekeeper, maids, and footmen—and those in the back—cook, bootboys, and so on—is as well defined and strictly observed as the line between master and servant." Silver eyes met turquoise steadily as Gray firmly stated an incontrovertible fact. "They would not appreciate an outsider meddling in their affairs. And further, they are easily offended by any perceived slight to their privileges. If you wish to get on with those responsible for your comfort, I counsel you to remember what I've said and tread lightly."

Gray wondered if it was possible for Elizabeth to exercise the subtle combination of delicacy and strength required. Her strength he couldn't seriously doubt, but had she even the smallest measure of delicacy?

Liz's temper simmered. The wall of unnatural

courtesy erected between them during their week in France crumbled beneath this insult to her upbringing.

"I am accustomed to dealing with servants." The words crackled with restrained indignation.

Gray nodded. "But I fear dealing with the servants in your country is a rather different matter than overseeing those in mine."

Liz had no doubt that it was true but resented the implication that she was unequal to the task. Though refusing to verbally answer, she met his icy gaze with an unwavering fire in her own.

"The butler and my valet are addressed by their last names." With this information Gray continued the lesson for a woman instantly steaming at this inference that she might be unaware of the traditions of address common to both countries. Gray hadn't meant it as an insult but as simple advice to possibly save her later difficulties. That it had upset her reinforced a decision made days earlier. Anyone so easily slighted would be a disaster if loosed amongst Society where pointed barbs abounded.

"The cook, housekeeper, and lady's maid have Mrs. added to their surnames no matter their marital state, while all lesser servants are summoned by first names." For her own good, Gray continued with details whose knowledge would make her life smoother. "To use the wrong form of address would be an insult to them and would be a sign of your foreign and—some will doubtless believe—inferior, background."

The carriage gently rocked to a halt and Liz scooted forward on the seat, anxious to be as far from him as possible.

"Lastly—" Gray held her back with a gentle but inflexible grip on her arm. "And I cannot emphasize this enough, *never* are private matters aired in their presence."

Liz recognized this as still another disparaging reference to the heated dispute with her father just after the marriage ceremony. Surely even these refined English people would find her reaction justified by a father's betrayal.

The carriage door was opened by a liveried footman, and to waylay dangerously escalating tension, Liz concentrated on irrelevant details. The man was handsome, though in no way as devastatingly so as his duke. All footmen were good-looking. They were hired for their attractive appearances just as all parlormaids were hired for their beauty.

Irritated by his wife's lengthy examination of a male servant, Gray stepped down, pleasantly aware that it broke her line of vision. While turning to offer his hand to aid her descent, he grimly wondered if in this she presented another problem for him to face? Did the fact that she was American and presumably thought all men equal mean that she would find no wrong in a relationship with this footman? Fighting a sudden urge to immediately discharge the man, and angry with himself for allowing this rare flash of jealousy to even enter his consciousness, he clamped an icy control over his expression but could do nothing to mitigate the silver storm raging in his eyes.

Apprehensions over the waiting people faded to nothing when Liz looked up and met Gray's fury. What had she done? And more, what could she do but accept his extended hand's help in stepping down. Although thoroughly rattled, she intended to employ the proper method of a lady departing a carriage. However, when she made to delicately lift the skirt's hem, her hand was shaking so badly that it rose too high and inadvertently revealed a glimpse of well-turned ankle.

For whose benefit, Gray wondered, was that tantalizing display? He nearly gritted his teeth, certain she hadn't meant it for him.

On firm ground, but feeling overshadowed by Gray's overwhelming height and horribly aware of his anger, she slowly moved with him up the long line of servants while he formally introduced her to each. She was able to manage a smile but left it to him to accept the congratulations accompanying either a bow or curtsy.

It would be impossible to instantly memorize everyone's name, but Liz tried to push aside the uncomfortable weight of her husband's baffling anger by making a concerted effort with those of the upper servants. Bremmer was the butler; Mrs. Haines the housekeeper; Dulcie and Esther the parlormaids. Of the housemaids and footmen there were too many to recognize so quickly, and no one would expect her to remember the names of the tweenies, bootboys, or any of a multitude of anonymous others who served belowstairs. Liz's attention was, however, caught by Mrs. Simms, a pinch-faced woman identified as a lady's maid. Liz was surprised . . . and dismayed. It seemed arrangements had already been made for this woman to attend her. A depressing prospect.

Not once had her bridegroom mentioned the existence of a family. Therefore, Liz had assumed he had none. It was a shock then when, after passing beyond a door held wide by the butler, they were met by a formidable woman who not only wore arrogance like an all-enveloping cloak but bore a definite resemblance to the duke. Hair and eyes of cold slate gray, she wordlessly inspected the creature daring to enter the house as if "it" were a mongrel dog trespassing on the mansion's manicured lawns.

"Sister, meet my bride, Elizabeth." Gray motioned his wife forward.

Liz's heart dropped. She already had before her a plate full of troubles and this further, far more threatening difficulty she did not need! Nonetheless, she forced a looming sense of defeat aside and boldly faced the other woman's disapproval with no betrayal of her flagging spirits.

"Elizabeth meet my sister Lady Euphemia." Despite a lingering anger, Gray felt sorry for the bride received with so little cheer and decided to do what he could to improve the situation. He would take his sister away with him as soon as possible.

"Welcome to Ashleigh Hall . . . Duchess." The chill in the elder woman's greeting completely negated its ostensible message. This while both the pause before the last word was said and the acid it held left no doubt but that the recipient had been found unworthy of the title.

"Thank you," Liz responded with not a jot more warmth. Plainly, though the woman had expected the arrival of a bride, she was unprepared for one whose appearance lacked subtlety. More importantly, one unwilling to demurely look down and play the correct role of humble intruder.

Gray saw a storm brewing and intervened before it could break.

"Euphemia, we must be off to the City as soon as possible. I have hopes of catching Sir David this evening to discuss with him, as M.P. for our district, the introduction of a bill into the Commons."

The prospect of a quick departure succeeded in diverting his sister's attention. As she gave Gray an abrupt nod, the sunlight falling through a long window lent a dull sheen to iron gray hair fashionably knotted atop an again haughtily tilted head.

"You are nearly too late to see anything done." Euphemia's rebuke of a younger brother was restrained but unmistakable. "Parliament opens in two days and with it the Season."

"Unforeseen and unavoidable delays held me back." Gray wouldn't bother trying to explain either snowbound trains or why a side trip to Paris had been necessary. "I'm relying on your skilled touch to help me achieve my goal . . . as your wise counsel and deft handling have done so often before."

Euphemia's stern expression melted into pleasure under the charm her brother effortlessly wielded.

While siblings spoke, Liz watched the arrogant pair ignoring her. She'd no desire to be the center of attention, but it was insufferably rude to treat a new arrival as if she did not exist. British aristocrats were reputed to be the epitome of good manners. Hah! But then, perhaps these two merely deemed her unworthy of their efforts. It had assuredly become clear that to them she represented nothing more than an inconvenient appendage to a crass yet needed merchant wealth. This attitude was to be expected of the sister. And, yes, of Gray as well. Yet it wounded Liz to realize that the man she reluctantly found ever more fascinating looked through her as easily as he doubtless looked through the teeming rabble she'd read filled London's slums.

"Bremmer—" Lady Euphemia called to a shadowy figure hovering in the background. "See that the footmen unload Her Grace's trunks immediately. Then repack the carriage with those waiting in my suite."

On hearing this order Liz suddenly understood the full meaning of the siblings' conversation. Her husband intended to set off for London with his sister, leaving her confined to the Ashleigh Estate like some naughty child to the nursery. Never mind that had her preferences been sought with even minimal politeness, she'd have happily remained in the country. His high-handed manner roused the rebellious side of her nature. And, despite her distaste for both the social scene's foibles and infinitely more serious political intrigues, no matter what might be required, Liz was determined that she *would* foil his intention for her to remain here in seclusion!

At last the duke's attention turned to his bride—too

late to calm Elizabeth, even had a still irritated Gray wished to do so. Meeting her ever-direct gaze, that irritation increased with the knowledge that he would only make himself appear foolish by chastising her for merely looking at another man. Not only would he *appear* foolish, Gray chided himself, he *was* foolish to allow so simple a thing to bother him. The truth of this did nothing to sweeten his temper.

"Elizabeth, please come with me into the study. There are issues to be discussed before I depart."

Issues to be discussed? There most certainly were! Fuming, Liz followed the inexplicably angry man into a book-lined room whose pleasant scent of leather and old books she was too upset to notice. He settled behind a massive desk while she sank into the huge black leather chair where he had indicated she should sit.

"As you heard—" Gray tamed his ire, forcing it under tight restraints while with a practiced and charming smile he began, deep voice softening to a dark velvet few women had been able to resist. "I have duties that require my immediate attention in the City."

Too aware of her own weakness where this man was concerned, Liz distrusted his devastating smile and gentle words. She wasn't about to forget how easily he had with a few kisses overcome her resistance aboard ship and meant to never again be caught so ill prepared to reject his wiles.

"Rather than rushing you into London's whirl of unfamiliar faces and customs, I'll leave you here in Ashleigh Hall with the hope that it will provide a period of adjustment to your new responsibilities and life-style."

Period of adjustment? She'd lay any odds he meant it to be a period without end. Liz's answering smile was grim and the glitter in blue eyes ominously defiant.

Elizabeth's rebellious expression reinforced Gray's confidence in his decision. She possessed neither the social experience nor quiet tact so necessary for a political hostess—traits ingrained in Euphemia.

"This doesn't mean you will be alone. My stepniece, Drusilla, will also remain in residence."

"A child?" Liz asked acidly, wondering if this was supposed to be a comfort to her when it merely validated her initial impression of being consigned to the schoolroom like an erring student.

Although inwardly cursing himself for being fool enough not to have anticipated this contrary woman's reaction to his plan, Gray calmly rebutted her suspicion. "Dru recently celebrated her eighteenth birthday."

Thick bronze lashes dropped over turquoise eyes. The news that her companion-to-be was eighteen roused Liz's curiosity. It was the practice for a girl to "come out" at seventeen. Therefore, Gray's stepniece had likely been a debutante the previous year. That this Dru was to remain at the family's country estate while the new Season opened made it clear she, too, was being disciplined for unacceptable behavior. For the first time since stepping on British soil Liz found something to anticipate. She couldn't wait to meet her companion in confinement and possible confederate in insurrection against their bonds.

The faint smile of peach lips and nod of blazing red hair increased Gray's uneasiness. Still, what mischief could this foreigner in an unfamiliar country possibly get up to that might endanger his carefully protected reputation and family name? This proved not to be a comforting thought. Gray didn't want to seriously consider such possibilities.

"There is no reason for you to be offended by these arrangements." While speaking quickly to divert his concerns, Gray experienced a twinge of guilt. He immediately suppressed the unpleasant sensation with the honest belief that once she'd calmly contemplated the matter, she'd be happy to remain at Ashleigh Hall. After all, within minutes of their marriage she had announced her preference for life in the wilds of Wyoming. So, surely she would choose his country estate over city life and the company of an unwanted husband. "Truly, I thought that given the option, you would prefer this home with its relative privacy compared to London's demanding schedule of social obligations."

Remembering her determination to maintain an inflexible shield against his wiles, Liz refused to let the seeming sincerity of Gray's words dent her wordless defense.

"You'll have access to my sizable stables, as I've already directed my head groom to provide whatever you ask." Gray was irritated to discover that even in his own ears the words had the hollow ring of an inadequate bribe. "The quickest way from the house to the stable is through there." He nodded toward the french doors she'd mistakenly thought were merely full-length windows on the wall opposite where they'd entered the room.

Elizabeth was not mollified. The offer of horses to ride meant little when, as his duchess, surely they were hers to command anyway. Under the certainty that his entire speech had been offered to dupe her into being an amenable country wife, she allowed her simmering ire to overflow into ill-considered words.

"At least you'll not be around to insist upon fulfilling what you termed the 'unpleasant' duty of getting the heir you say I must provide." Liz stiffly stood up, lips curling in exaggerated disgust. "Your name is appropriate for a politician like you—neither black nor white, neither cold nor hot . . . merely tepid."

"Tepid? Haven't we had a conversation very like this before? Although last time you claimed I was cold." Finding himself caught between anger and laughter, Gray smiled—a slow, sensual, and potent smile that stilled his opponent's breath. He rose and began moving around the desk with the intimidating grace of a panther. "Have you forgotten how that challenge ended?"

Gray vividly remembered how they'd physically dueled and how she had lost, yielding her softness in his arms, giving him the heady peach wine of her mouth. But most of all, he remembered the hungry passion in her wild little cry. Despite an honest need to soon depart, he wanted to hear it again.

Liz recognized the mistake she'd made, one that he clearly heard as an offer to become the panther's prey. The fearful suspicion that she had unconsciously wanted to do that very thing held her immobile and unable to retreat while Gray approached, molten silver gaze luring her with promises of delights unknown.

"Perhaps you merely wished to entice me into another demonstration of the error in such thinking? Hmmm?" Gray's voice was a deep purr as he stopped just in front of the fiery woman gone silent. With unexpected gentleness he brushed his fingers over her cheek and down her elegant throat.

Apprehension and shocked awareness so heightened Liz's senses that his curiously light touch sent a tremble of pleasure through her. Then, still standing a whisper away, Gray bent and rubbed short tantalizing kisses to the corners of her mouth, across her cheeks, eyelids, and in the sensitive hollows beneath her ears.

Lacking Gray's experience in passion, Liz's knees threatened to give out as wild sensations throbbed within. She swayed into his waiting arms and, once inside their circle, the feel of his broad, muscular body overwhelmed her with dangerous sensations and drove the last tendrils of rational thought beyond her reach.

Gray took her mouth in a warm assault that quickly

parted her lips, allowing him to search within while she sank headlong into a hungry blaze, instinctively arching deeper into his embrace. Dazed by sparks of hot pleasure, she wrapped her arms about the steady center of this firestorm, mindlessly savoring the strength of his broad back before lifting her hands to twine fingers into cool black strands.

With one arm Gray locked her against his powerful body while the other hand began a tempting tour from her waist to under an arm clinging to wide shoulders and then forward to cup the tempting weight of one breast. The action won a soft, intoxicating whimper, and a smile of male triumph curved the lips he moved to trail liquid flame down her throat to the primly covered dip at her throat's base. Suddenly his mouth dropped to nip at the peak of aching flesh cradled in the palm of his hand.

Liz's heartfelt moan accompanied the uncontrollable quiver shocked from her depths. Fingers involuntarily winding tighter into black hair, she pulled the source of an unfamiliar but incredible burning pleasure closer.

Restraining an urgent need to do away with the cloth impeding the kind of intimate caress his trembling bride naively demanded, Gray buried his face against her lush curves. He desperately wanted what he couldn't have, not here and not now. Gray lifted his head, struggling for control, but foolishly gazed down at the enticing vision of fiery hair encircling a passion-rosed face, eyes deepened to a dark blue drowsy with new desires, and peach lips, moist and softly swollen, yearning up toward his. That delicious sight put any hope for restraint in serious jeopardy.

He had set out to prove to his wife how easily he could seduce her into willing surrender. An intention gone badly awry as the untutored, reckless passion with which she responded strained his practiced control, leaving him all too aware of an unaccustomed vulnerability. Once again the woman threatened to shatter his carefully guarded emotional bonds and Gray didn't like it at all!

Gray abruptly pushed Elizabeth back to hold her at arm's length while with a sardonic smile and silver glittering from half-shielded eyes he mocked her easy surrender. "You'll give yourself to me and provide the heir I must have with little enough effort on my part . . . a few kisses and you're mine."

Feeling as if she'd been dropped into a vat of icy water, Liz gasped but very quickly extricated herself with a burst of temper. She whirled and dashed from his study and the house.

Gray slowly followed to watch from the french door his passionate wife had left ajar. The cynical smile twisting his lips deepened with self-disdain. She clearly believed he'd won another round in their ongoing battle, but he knew it wasn't completely true. She had shaken him as nothing and no one had done in many years.

He leaned against the door frame and waited. Her traveling suit was not the best choice for a midday ride, but he understood the compulsion driving her. During his youth, more times than he could count, he had resorted to long, energetic rides to calm bouts of temper. He thought her plan to do the same was a fine idea . . . until the stable doors were thrown wide and his own temperamental stallion bolted from its shadows with a fiery-haired woman riding not only bareback but *astride!*

He instinctively rushed outside intending to chase after the black beast and its equally temperamental rider. Within two strides he stopped, restraining the urge to capture and chastise her, to make her understand just how terribly inappropriate such behavior was for any female—and far, far worse for a duchess. Midnight was the fleetest mount in his stable, and by rushing after his bride he'd more likely make himself look a fool. And that was something he would not do. Instead he would simply depart with the memory of this impulsive action to further prove what a complete disaster she would be within the tight confines of London society. In the City, despite discreet liaisons and the political infighting roiling beneath its correct surface, the first rule was the inflexible demand for impeccable manners and unblemished appearances. Clearly, Elizabeth could never fit that pattern.

CHAPTER

Liz's temper merged into exhilaration as her powerful mount covered great stretches of green earth at amazing speeds. Wind tore the pins from red hair which, once freed, became a bright flag streaming out behind until the black steed slowed, carrying her into cool woodland shadows.

"Who are you?" A male voice suddenly demanded from directly in front. "And how did you come by my cousin's most prized stallion?"

Drawing the beast in question to a complete halt, Liz curiously studied the young man of about her own age standing boldly in the narrow path ahead. Sunstreaks lightened brown hair to a tawny hue while a frown banished the habitual warmth indicated by the pleasant lines of his handsome face. Liz was surprised. She'd been told of a stepniece, but no cousins had been mentioned.

"I am the duchess of Ashleigh." Amused by his loyal challenge of her apparent misdeed, Liz grinned and promptly shot back, "Who are you?"

This announcement plainly startled the pathway's human barrier. The disbelief filling a dark gaze taking the measure of this unladylike specter made his skeptical opinion of her claim clear.

"No, Timothy. Likely it's true." With the soft words, a sweetly rounded feminine face encircled by dusky curls peered shyly around the young man's shoulder. "Stepmama has been expecting Uncle Grayson's return for days."

Never one to hesitate in leaping to conclusions—usually correct—Liz felt certain that this petite girl must be her companion in confinement at Ashleigh Hall.

"If that's true, why didn't you tell me before?" The gently scoffing words made it plain that the young man suspected the timid girl's compassionate nature of inventing a tale to temper his actions.

The girl defended herself with enough heat that it lent sufficient courage to speak more clearly. "Stepmama couldn't, until this morning, bring herself to tell me that uncle would probably be accompanied by a 'half-savage American wife.'"

Suddenly conscious of the unintentional insult she'd just delivered to the newcomer, cheeks brushed by the ringlets escaped from a charmingly untidy chignon went an attractive shade of scarlet.

"Yes." Liz laughed freely as she swung down from the black stallion's back with no more effort than if he'd been a child's hobbyhorse. "I am the 'half-savage American wife.'" Her unfaltering smile went wry with awareness that, by their standards, she probably did embody that description.

"Pay no attention to Aunt Euphemia's outrageous prediction." Acknowledging his error, the young man was quick to repent his initial disbelief and attempt to undo its potential damage to a fresh relationship. "She is the original snob, prejudiced against any policy that hasn't been practiced since the Conqueror's time or anyone who wouldn't bleed as blue as she's certain she would."

"That's not fair." The bonds of Dru's usual reticence had been loosened by the newcomer's open laughter, and her dainty foot silently stomped earth padded by recently sprouted grass and fragments of leaves fallen the previous autumn. "Stepmama supports uncle's reforms for the poor."

The young man twisted about to give the dark-haired girl a fond smile, but it did little to lessen the sarcasm in his words. "Anything for her brother—so long as it smacks of the traditional role of a master deigning to provide for his inferiors."

"Don't listen to this wretch." The girl playfully slapped her companion's arm as she stepped around to stand beside him on the well-trod path. "Uncle Gray is sincere in his attempts to better the lives of all—not just those here in his district but in the London slums as well."

The sweetly chastised man looked repentant. "That's true. Gray *is* sincere." Holding an open hand alongside his mouth, he leaned forward to loudly whisper. "What I said about Aunt Euphemia is equally true."

Liz was surprised by this offhand revelation of Gray's admirable efforts on behalf of the "teeming rabble" to whom, not so long ago, she'd assumed he'd be blind.

Making a show of ignoring her companion, the girl moved forward to properly introduce herself.

"I am Drusilla Elway, Lady Euphemia's stepdaughter and the duke's stepniece." She delicately spread the fine lawn skirt of a lovely pink daygown to make a sweeping curtsy.

"I am pleased to make your acquaintance, Miss Elway." In a parody of one particularly offensive, arrogant social hostess she'd had the misfortune of meeting in New York, Liz gave the briefest of nods before pursing her lips and lifting her chin to a supercilious angle. The condescending expression was apparently familiar internationally, as it won a spurt of laughter from her audience.

"And this mug—" To lend the introduction a proper tone, Drusilla smoothed amusement from her face and cast the young man a stern look of disapproval, one which failed to either douse the gleams dancing in sky blue eyes or drain the affectionate pride from her voice. "—is Timothy Brandt, cousin to the duke of Ashleigh and secretary to the House of Lords."

The subject of these words turned to Liz with a grimace and fervent entreaty. "*Please* don't call me Mr. Brandt. Family members do that only when they're upset with me."

"A not uncommon event." It was Drusilla's turn to lean forward with a *sotto voce* comment.

"What then shall I call you?" Liz asked, absently patting the amazingly patient stallion's neck.

The young woman answered for her companion. "Timothy, of course, but I'm just Dru."

"Or Silly." Timothy grinned at the girl who looked back, gaze melting into his. "That's what I call her . . . it's more appropriate, although officially she is Lady Drusilla."

As the girl was part of a duke's family, her title was no surprise to Liz. Moreover, it couldn't and didn't distract her from the playfully innocent but unmistakably sincere signs of a flirtation ripening to a deeper relationship than the mere kinship of stepcousins. When the pair caught her knowing gaze upon them, they straightened guiltily. She soothed their distress by airily waving toward herself and continuing the subject of their conversation without a missed beat.

"I'm Elizabeth Hughes—or leastways I was." Her hand dropped aimlessly as she gave a self-conscious shrug, acknowledging an all-important omission. "Now I, too, am a Brandt, but I hope you'll call me Liz. Or Lizzy, as my closest friends do."

"Lizzy?" Timothy repeated the name, gazing up into the pattern of branches almost meeting overhead with the assumed air of a sage's contemplations. "Lizzy," he said again as if testing the way the name rolled off his tongue. "I like it."

Though amused by his antics, Liz felt compelled to make an admission. "In fairness I must warn you that your cousin, my bridegroom, decidedly does not."

"Ah, hah!" Timothy sounded delighted. "Then you may be certain it's what I'll use."

"Do you not get along with the duke?" Straightforward by nature, Liz asked the question without thought of subtler methods to learn the same information.

Timothy was somewhat taken aback by the blunt question. "We get along tolerably well." He again gazed aloft at patches of sky visible through freshly sprouted leaves. Reaching up, he broke off a small twig and intently studied its tender bark as if it held the secrets of the universe.

"My father and Gray's were brothers and very close. Indeed, so close that it seemed only natural that they and their wives should be together when they perished . . . in a yachting accident ten years past. As head of the Brandt family, Gray became my guardian. I've never doubted that his intentions are pure. I simply don't always agree or choose to comply with what he thinks is best for me."

Liz nodded, empathizing with Timothy's plight. Again she rhythmically patted the stallion's silky coat while her turquoise eyes narrowed on the slender man who, for all his fairer hair shared the Brandt family strength of jaw, high cheekbones, and grace of motion. Clearly Grayson had mapped out a less than appreciated path for the younger man much as her father had mapped out an unwanted course for her future. And only see where that had landed her.

"I understand rather better than you might think, Timothy."

Tilting a tawny head, Timothy met her claim with a look of mixed doubt and curiosity.

Certain she'd do well to have these two as friends in a family already commanded by two who disapproved of her, Liz decided to tell them exactly how things stood in her life.

"Come, let's sit down and then I'll explain." Attaching the stallion's reins to a branch, Liz motioned toward a small glade whose soft grasses had been refreshed by the morning rain and dried by the afternoon sun. Once the three had settled in a loose circle, feminine legs tucked demurely beneath skirts, masculine legs comfortably extended, Liz embarked on her story.

"My widowed father, as cattle rancher and owner of a railroad, is a very rich man." This admission of wealth apparently failed to impress these English, a refreshing change from the awe its mention usually brought from the average American. Pleased by this response, Liz felt able to speak openly. "I have always believed he loved me, yet he chose what he deemed best for my future and then by trickery saw me delivered here . . . while I had rather be elsewhere."

Liz saw that the concept of a woman preferring to be anywhere other than in the much-sought-after position of wife to a duke—a young and handsome duke—was difficult for the pair to comprehend. Doggedly continuing, she spoke of the Double H Ranch and told them the unedited tale of the shameful role her father had played in duping her into marriage and an immediate departure on a transatlantic voyage.

"So," Liz concluded, "the duke has what he sought in America. He has my father's wealth to use as he wills. But—and it's an unfortunate fact which I'm certain he finds distasteful—he also has me."

With innate loyalty Dru opened her mouth to defend her uncle, but a grimly smiling Liz lifted a hand to forestall the useless attempt.

"What I have in exchange is the undeniable truth that my bridegroom has consigned me to the rigid customs and company of what to me is a foreign countryside full of strangers and unfamiliar rules."

"We're not strangers." Timothy interrupted with a cheerful smile. "Not anymore."

Rarely one to wallow in either self-pity or gloomy thoughts, Liz pushed aside the bleak image her words had created and responded with an infectious grin.

"However—" Drusilla uncertainly began.

Liz immediately suspected this was the tentative opening to a gentle admonishment of the sort to be expected from a girl raised on compliance with a strict code of rules. She smiled, albeit wryly.

"There is one restriction you perhaps ought observe." Dru nervously plucked at her skirt as if the action might aid in plucking up her courage. "Don't ride astride elsewise you'll truly shock the countryside."

"I wouldn't have done so today if your uncle hadn't infuriated me." Liz sent Dru a contrite smile and motioned toward the fiery mane that had come loose during her wild ride. "I was born with a temper easily lit and quick to burn as brightly as my hair. But—although I much prefer to ride astride and on my ranch in Wyoming have several buckskin skirts split in the center to make it easier for a woman to take that far less awkward position—I wouldn't have flouted the rules to do the same here." An impish grin overwhelmed the contrite smile. "Leastways, not on this first day."

"We'll remember that quick temper and try to stay on your list of friends. Won't we, Silly?" Timothy suppressed a grin of his own while his eyes widened in mock fear. "For all we know, you may be as good a shot as you are a rider." He tilted his head toward the black stallion and the lighter streaks in his brown hair caught the sun. "I know few men and no women who could handle Midnight as you did."

"I am a good shot," Liz confirmed, shrugging to mitigate what might elsewise be heard as conceit. "I have to be on a ranch where cattle rustlers and other blackguards can be dealt with no other way."

This reference was enough to instantly rouse excitement. Not, as Liz might have expected, in Timothy but rather in the timid girl at his side.

"Have you fought with cattle rustlers?" Dru asked, awe in her tone.

"You've been reading those penny dreadfuls again, haven't you?" Timothy demanded, pursing his lips in feigned disgust. "If your stepmama finds them, you'll be condemned to remain in Ashleigh Hall for the *whole* season."

Dru glared at the man who'd interrupted but only for a brief moment. In the next she turned hopefully back to Liz.

Realizing she'd left herself open for this and knowing there was no option but to satisfy the girl's curiosity, Liz complied with good grace—and a measure of secret pleasure.

"I've personally tangled with rustlers only once. In the normal way of things, it's the responsibility of my foreman and the range hands to protect the Double H's stock. But on that one occasion I rode with them out to the south pastures to check . . ."

Liz spun a tale that soon had both listeners enthralled by the visions she painted of her beloved wide-open spaces where freely roaming cattle were a temptation to the unprincipled. Dru enjoyed the rousing account so thoroughly that when the story was done, she was no more than mildly disappointed that the villains hadn't been shot on the spot but rather rounded up, hauled off to the sheriff, and later tried in court.

"So, you see," Liz concluded. "Though I attended Miss Brown's School for Young Ladies, dutifully learning French and German, what utensils to use for every sort of formal dinner, and the intricacies of arranging such events, I'd far rather be on my ranch in Wyoming. There *I* choose when or if I go to town." She grinned. "And I ride astride with no one to tell me I mustn't. On the Double H I am free, subservient to no man—whether range hand or duke."

"Have you never had a stepmama?" Dru tilted a head of dark curls curiously to one side. Now that the exciting story was finished, Dru was far more interested in this apparent lack than in her new aunt's philosophy of feminine independence.

Liz was caught unprepared by the sudden question reviving the memory of her father lost in grief. A flash of long past but too well remembered childish confusion and deep sorrow shook her voice.

"My father was devastated by my mother's death when I was barely twelve. Still is, I think." She shrugged, but the shadow darkening bright blue eyes negated the seeming casualness of her gesture. "He has been pursued, as any man of his wealth must expect to be. But my father eludes feminine predators and privately tells me he hasn't the heart to remarry."

Pushing aside sad memories of home, Liz resolutely shifted the focus back to her companions. "Enough of me. What of you, Dru?"

"I've no memory of my mama." Dru concentrated on a single long blade of grass she'd pulled free. "She died while I was a toddler, and my father married Lady Euphemia within a year."

As if realizing this flat statement sounded like criticism, Dru looked up to gaze directly into still cloudy turquoise eyes while defending the result, if not the action.

"My story has nothing in common with those in childhood fairy tales. No natural mother could've loved me more than my stepmama has from the very first day. Truly my problems in no way reflect a lack of love for there's no question but that she loves me . . . perhaps too much."

Seeing Liz's faint frown and abruptly aware of what curiosity her odd statement must have aroused, Dru explained its meaning.

"Just as your father interfered in your choices, Stepmama is trying to force me into a choice she believes will be best for me."

Liz was surprised but not shocked. Although she'd shared her story thinking it paralleled Timothy's struggle for independence, now it seemed Dru also suffered a measure of the same difficulties. Why were all parents and guardians so certain they knew best, so certain that they had the right to alter another's chosen path?

"Silly is not to be allowed to attend any of the Season's social functions or to even visit the City until she repents of her wrong in refusing the aging marquess of Poxwell's suit last Season." Timothy made this announcement with obvious disgust.

Dru gently took over the telling before the young man lost his temper and said more than he ought. "It seems my stepmama has, with her famous tact and no doubt a large measure of flattery, convinced the offended peer to put my action down to the flightiness of youth. He has hinted at a willingness to not merely forgive me the affront but to again pay me his addresses."

In Dru's words Liz heard defeat but also a frustrated resentment subdued only by an honest affection for the one responsible.

Timothy's open face was robbed of its usual warmth by distressing prospects as he flatly voiced the specific list of ghastly requirements to be met. "Only after Silly promises to welcome the marquess's attentions, pretend to be flattered, and to accept if 'honored' with a second marriage proposal, will she be welcomed at Brandt House in Grosvenor Square."

"And if Stepmama knew that Timothy was here now, she'd have an apoplectic fit." Dru seemed to have taken a detour from the subject at hand, and when she realized how revealing it was, she blushed yet again and nibbled a soft rose lip.

While Liz had no doubt but that the refusal of a marquess's marriage offer was a major point of discord between Lady Euphemia and her stepdaughter, it seemed certain that in Dru's last statement lay the source of a deeper breach.

To test that premise, Liz asked a question with feigned confusion. "Timothy, as a Brandt, don't you have every right to be here?"

"The Ashleigh Estate belongs unconditionally to the title holder. Nonetheless, after Gray became my guardian I spent my childhood and all school vacations here. I've always been welcome . . . until last Season when both my uncle and aunt asked that I restrict my visits to occasions when I've been formally invited."

Timothy's mouth compressed into a tight line of hurt resentment, but the sight of fires beginning to simmer in brilliant blue eyes replaced it with a sheepish smile.

"Don't blame Gray. I don't. I don't even blame Aunt Euphemia. She takes her responsibility for Silly very seriously, and Gray feels it his duty to back his sister's decisions. My prospects are anything but what she desires in a match for her stepdaughter. Indeed, I have nothing . . . save for a modest income from my family stipend and the small measure of respect due my unpaid position as secretary to the House of Lords."

"But he *does* have prospects," Dru vehemently asserted, laying her fingers against his shoulder. "He's going to put his name up for M.P. of our local district. And he'll win, I know he will."

"Another *unpaid* position," Timothy interjected but Dru ignored him and went on.

"I've an inheritance from my father's estate pending my marriage and intend to use it in furthering Timothy's cause."

"No you won't!" Timothy quietly refused, gently patting Dru's hand. "The mere suggestion that you plan such a thing would put paid to any hope we have for a future together. Besides I wouldn't allow it." He softened the stern words with a small, tender smile. "You must save whatever you may inherit for our children."

Dru had at first looked ready to argue, but the mention of children transformed her mutinous expression into another charming blush and dreamy gaze.

After a few quiet moments, Liz gently prodded the two who, if left to their own devices, appeared more than able to slip into their own little world. "You've explained why you shouldn't be here . . . but not how and why you are."

"With Parliament's next session about to begin, because of my position with the House of Lords, my aunt and uncle believe I'm presently in London . . . making it possible for Silly and me to see each other, if only on the sly. For the past week I've been staying at the Tilton Arms in the village, and we meet here each day." His smiling eyes went blank and his expression morose. "However, by this time tomorrow I must be on my way back to the City. It'll be the eve of the queen's ceremonial opening of Parliament and the much anticipated night when Lord and Lady Cardington host the Season's first grand ball."

Liz stored this information regarding a ball and the opening of Parliament in one corner of her mind while pursuing the more important issue. "You've been exiled from the family estate because of Dru . . . yes?"

It was not truly a question, and Timothy grimaced yet immediately nodded.

"We're in love!" Dru hotly asserted. "But though I'm sure we could bring Uncle Gray around to accept our marriage, Stepmama won't hear of it. She is determined that because my father was a marquess, a title that has passed to a distant male cousin, I will never be allowed to wed anyone of lesser standing."

"While I as the son of a younger son possess no title at all." Timothy ruefully spread his empty hands wide. "Nor am I ever likely to possess one, despite my supposedly blue blood."

"Not as long as Uncle Gray lives to produce an heir."

Aghast at his beloved's artless inference, Timothy rushed to correct the potential poor impression given the new duchess.

"I wouldn't want a title at that price." He cast his beloved a censorious glare. "And I must say, Silly, it's a damn poor time to suggest any such possibility."

Dru's cheeks flooded with a hot color brighter than ever before, but her first words were a rebuke for Timothy. "Your language is atrocious and one reason Stepmama disapproves of you."

Though the delicate frown of dark brows earned an apologetic grimace from Timothy, Dru wasted no further time on the matter but looked to this recently discovered aunt with a plea for understanding in china blue eyes. "I love Uncle Gray. We both do."

Liz assumed the pair's guilt was born of the twin faux pas in suggesting the possibility of a groom's early demise to a new bride and mention of the heir she'd be expected to produce. She shrugged their unnecessary regret aside and diverted their attention with questions about the ball Timothy had mentioned. Before long she proposed a daring plan that surprisingly won timid Dru's immediate and wholehearted support. Timothy hesitated, no doubt weighing its possible danger to his career, but soon he also agreed to a plan that would free them all—for the length of one exhilarating night at least. Moreover, it was a freedom whose price in blame Liz gladly offered to bear.

Liz was once again ensconced in a luxurious ducal carriage. But this time she was enjoying every moment and every detail from the comfort of padded leather seats to the glow of gaslight on the vehicle's ebony finish.

For the first time in her life, Liz was deeply aware of what she wore and confident of her appearance. Before her arrival in Paris, Liz's interest in fashion had begun and ended in welcome for the American West's introduction of split skirts to make riding astride easier for females. But by the close of her visit to the Rue de la Paix, she had developed an awed admiration for Charles Worth. The great couturier had fulfilled Gray's prediction and given her his personal attention which, a multitude of seamstresses had assured her, was a signal honor. Monsieur Worth had waved his magic wand and—shattering all the rules by which Liz had been taught to abide for the sake of toning down her vivid attributes—a startling array of creations that did equally magical things for her appearance had materialized. Her new wardrobe hosted an array of unique hues from glowing peach to iridescent blue-greens and included outfits for every conceivable occasion.

Yes, Worth was truly a sorcerer. Had to be to have transformed a too healthy and highly colored country bumpkin into the beauty she felt in this extravagant creation—a black ball gown that he had termed the crowning glory of the trousseau he'd created for her. With her every step its brilliant turquoise lining flashed like lightning in a midnight sky. Paired with the Ashleigh sapphires, it was stunning.

Liz's wandering thoughts were summoned by the changing cadence of hooves, first from hard-packed earth to the city's uneven streets, and then to the smoother paving stones of squares where the titled resided.

"We've arrived." Timothy's bright announcement failed miserably to hide his anxiety over the deed he was about to commit.

Liz had seen the formal invitation he'd received. It was written in intricate copperplate on fine paper. The problem was that neither she nor Dru had received the same, yet Liz had convinced Timothy that he'd be forgiven for bringing two uninvited guests—in consideration of who they were. Plainly doubts over the wisdom of this stunt were assailing him. And unfortunately they relentlessly spread from Timothy to attack her resolve as well. To no good point. It was far too late to turn back. Heart in her throat and visions of Gray's likely furious response threatening to cloud her eyes, Liz leaned forward and peered through the window at their destination.

For the sake of the evening's entertainment, torches in ornate wrought-iron stands replaced outdoor gas lamps to pour golden light over the red carpeted walkway and sweeping stairway leading up to open double doors. This impressive sight further dampened Liz's initial delight in the planned revolt against unfair exclusions. She was forced to abruptly pull back as a liveried footman opened the carriage door.

Timothy stepped out and turned to aid the two ladies' descent. Then, with a lovely woman on each arm and growing dread, he moved down the torch-flanked path and ascended steps toward where Lord and Lady Cardington waited to greet their guests.

"Lady Cardington—" Timothy restrained the nervous tremble threatening his voice and exercised an inbred courtesy polished by a full year of political challenges to speak with mellow warmth. "Allow me to present the new duchess of Ashleigh, Elizabeth Hughes Brandt."

Small and still willow-slender, though well beyond middle-age, Lady Cardington caught her breath but was experienced enough both to hide her surprise and with a single sharp glance size up the unexpected situation. It required no more than a brief glimpse of the incomparable Ashleigh sapphires to know what direction to take.

"Charles, we are honored in being first to welcome a new addition to our little group." She smoothly completed Liz's introduction to her tall, distinguished-looking husband.

"And a lovely new addition you are." The host graciously acknowledged the duchess, a glitter of interest in otherwise dull eyes lending sincerity to his compliment, while his wife went on to formally welcome the duke's cousin and stepniece.

From their reception in the anteroom the trio moved forward, beckoned by a bright glow and the sounds of orchestral music and gentle laughter. Standing in the ballroom entrance, oblivious to the pleasant stir of appreciation their appearance caused among guests already thronging the glittering ballroom, Liz took in the splendid sight. She drank in the rich tones of many violins, gazed up to where chandeliers full of twinkling facets filled the ceiling, and then down to the colors swirling across a polished marble dance floor. And all the while the sweet scent of a multitude of flowers wafted through the air as footmen moved with elegance through the crowd, balancing glasses of champagne and fruit punch. Liz readily admitted that never before had she taken part in so lavish an event.

CHAPTER 5

The last of Lord and Lady Cardington's guests to arrive paused in the ballroom's arched, garlanded entry. Silver eyes surveyed men garbed in sober black and white evening wear leading ladies in extravagant, multihued gowns through the rapidly shifting patterns of the Prince's favorite dance. Gray personally detested the Triumph, thought it more suited to a dance hall than a nobleman's ballroom.

He was anxious to find Sir David, the old family friend who, before the close of Parliament's abbreviated mid-winter session, had expressed interest in lending support in the House of Commons to a cause near to Gray's heart. A variety of odd circumstances had prevented Gray from speaking with Sir David the previous evening, but he was certain the man would be here, a circumstance that lent this obligatory social appearance a worthwhile purpose.

Just as Gray decided his quarry must be in either the supper room on the other side of the corridor or in one of the withdrawing rooms, swirling patterns shifted again to leave one couple at the front of a line of laughing dancers. All thoughts of Sir David were driven from Gray's thoughts while his forced smile took on a grim edge.

An obviously enchanted Prince Albert Edward led a stunning beauty through a rollicking series of moves from the room's far side directly toward the entry . . . and Gray. Seizing lights from blazing chandeliers to glow in fiery splendor, red curls intricately entwined topped a head held with a regal poise that defied the ready laughter on peach lips. Gray watched as his wife, in Worth's startling black creation, executed the Triumph's energetic steps with the Prince of Wales.

When the royal personage, whom friends called Bertie, caught sight of this new charmer's ever-serious husband, he came to a full stop a single pace before the man. Once the prince stopped, the orchestra was obliged to do the same and as its last strains died away, an expectant hush fell over the entire room.

Curiously glancing up, seeking the reason for this abrupt interruption, Liz found herself the subject of a penetrating silver gaze. It seemed the visions she'd had of Gray's ominous reaction to her defiant arrival had come to life. Her heart set up a fierce pounding, but she couldn't honestly tell whether solely with shock at this sudden confrontation or in renewed awareness of her devastatingly attractive husband. It made no difference when she could do nothing but stand mute while the scene played out before her.

"I must congratulate you, Ashleigh, on your great good fortune in capturing such a delightful prize for wife." A neatly trimmed and slightly graying beard could go only so far in making a chubby face appear distinguished, not that it mattered, given the speaker's position in life.

"Thank you, Your Highness." Gray responded along with the requisite bow, knowing the whole room watched, ready, as ever, to pounce upon every nuance to fuel gossip and rumors for weeks to come.

As the Prince turned to motion for both the music

and the dancing to resume, Gray sourly acknowledged an unwelcome reality. In this brief exchange his American wife had instantly become the hit of the Season. Now he could not possibly dispatch her to the country again. Under the Prince's public endorsement, she was certain to be invited to every possible social event . . . hundreds of them. The prospect was demoralizing, for knowing Elizabeth as he'd come to, he greatly feared that somewhere, sometime during the coming weeks she'd do something—likely many somethings—to stain an old and respected name. He'd have to watch her closely, accompany her everywhere. It was a view of the future, Gray realized with disgust, not as unpleasant as he'd have sworn it would be.

Unsettled emotions shook Liz when at dance's end the Prince gallantly led her to the relative quiet of the corner where Gray had chosen to wait, looking carved of ice. She felt a sense of victory for, although she might not be totally up on the social system of the British aristocracy, Liz knew royal approval would prevent her husband from arrogantly dispatching her to the country once more. So, she'd won this battle. Hadn't she? But what exactly had she won? Her honest nature threatened to reveal the hollowness of her victory. She was stuck with a furious husband in the midst of a social whirl, the depths of whose treacherous waters Liz suspected would make those she'd tested and disdained in New York seem no more than a mud puddle.

"Now, Lizzy, my social duties require that I return you to your husband while I dance with others." An affable smile accompanied the Prince's pompous words. "But I hope to see more of you at future events. Perhaps at Lady Delmar's house party this weekend?"

Already frowning with displeasure that his wife had given their Prince the name she knew he disliked, when Gray heard the last suggestion his chin went up as if the recipient of an unexpected blow. To one of his worldly vision the invitation discreetly hidden within an invitation was crystal clear, but he knew his naive American bride could neither see nor understand its subtle meaning.

"I'm sorry, Your Highness." Gray smoothly deflected the offer's danger with a gracious refusal. "I regret that my *Lilibet* and I will be unable to attend. It's difficult for me to be away from London during the parliamentary session, as weekdays are busy in the House, leaving only weekends for negotiations on pending issues and important planning meetings."

Liz glanced sidelong at her incredibly handsome husband—by far the most handsome man present. Lilibet? She silently repeated the name, liking the sound, particularly in his deep voice. But it and the faint frown momentarily chilling attractive features emphasized his irritation with her for the Prince's use of Lizzy. That unjustified irritation stirred Liz's temper to life, burning a budding regret for her defiant actions to ashes. The earl of Hayton had led her through the first dance and it was he who had introduced her to the Prince. Moreover, it was the earl, insisting she call him Lawrence, who had told their royal companion the shortened version of her name used by friends. Under those circumstances even Gray couldn't have expected her to refuse the Prince permission to use the nickname—certainly not after the man had urged her to call him Bertie.

No matter, the fact that she'd flouted Gray's decision to leave her at Ashleigh Hall had undoubtedly convinced him that she was capable of any low trick. He need only consider her father's despicable actions to believe her wily response a family weakness and to find further justification for his poor opinion of a wife far different than he'd expected. This demoralizing thought endangered the flames of Liz's temper, but she whipped them to renewed heights with a refusal to feel bad that the husband who had abandoned her now unfairly blamed her for so small a wrong. Unfortunately she found that her determination was incapable of blocking the twinge of hurt caused by his having assigned yet another fault to her.

"Ah, well—" Bertie smiled benignly at the duke while raising his voice a trifle, the better to be heard by a painfully thin woman of middle years hovering nearby. "At least I feel certain Her Grace will be welcome to attend the tea party at Holson House tomorrow afternoon."

Before either the duke or his wife could respond, the eavesdropper stepped forward. Darting anxious glances toward the Prince, Lady Holson hurriedly issued an invitation along with the promise that early on the following morning a formal, written one would be forthcoming for Her Grace as well as Lady Euphemia and her stepdaughter.

The Prince beamed his approval and turned to lead Lady Holson into the dance forming. Liz was, at the same time, invited to partner a distinguished figure in a full dress uniform that Liz found impressive, although she'd no notion what regiment or even branch of the service it represented. Casting a quick glance at her grim husband, Liz nodded and graciously accepted the formally proffered white-gloved hand.

In the following two hours Liz danced with a dizzying array of men of every age and description. The faces of this ever-shifting flow blurred in her memory, leaving her worried that she might later shame herself by being able to recall the name of any save Lawrence, who had claimed her for a marginally acceptable second dance. But never in all that time did her dark husband bother to lead her onto the glowing marble floor. To Liz that lack seemed a pointed if subtle rejection.

Despite a wish that it was unnecessary, Gray remained on the dance floor's outer edges, keeping a watchful eye on the queen of the ball. Along parallel walls chairs were arranged for chaperones and dowagers, Lady Euphemia among them. Fortunately from his viewpoint, a number of other men also had reason to neither dance nor retreat into the relative peace of withdrawing rooms set aside for the kind of earnest discussions in which many men preferred to spend their time. Listening with one ear to a long-since-retired general's complaints about the handling of the Zulus, Gray saw a curious scene begin to unfold.

When the orchestra slowed to a less arduous tempo, a short, stout man of advanced age moved determinedly toward Liz. With one glare from black eyes nearly hidden in myriad folds of flesh, he sent into retreat the much younger man also approaching.

"I am the marquess of Poxwell," the victor of the wordless competition announced as his opponent faded into a crowd still large at this late hour. "And I pray Your Grace will honor me with this dance."

Amused by the ease with which this elderly but clearly influential man had sent the handsome youth fleeing, Liz acquiesced. He took her hand and Liz discovered it would be a new challenge to waltz with someone so much shorter that her chin was on a level with the top of his completely hairless head. Moreover, within two steps he began to wheeze under the difficult task of keeping up with even this music's gentle tempo.

"Last Season . . ." He surrendered to his physical limitations and slowed their steps to one quarter the pace. This adjustment made it possible for him to speak in pursuit of the goal behind his participation in an activity for which he'd nothing but disdain. "I paid my addresses to your stepniece and have been urged to renew them this year." A head tilted far back made it possible for narrowed black eyes to meet the duchess's stunningly bright gaze with serious intent. "That is, of course, her stepmother's opinion. I've sought you out to request yours."

Liz nearly stumbled. Oh, she'd recognized him for Dru's erstwhile suitor the moment he'd given his name, but she hadn't expected this forthright appeal from a stranger.

"I arrived in Britain only days past and have barely begun to find my bearings." She gave him a rueful smile. "I fear that as yet I've had little opportunity to form any kind of opinion about my husband's family."

"But surely you must've met the gel?"

"Yes, indeed, I have met Lady Drusilla . . . and her stepmother. But all I can tell you of a certainty is that Lady Euphemia supports your suit with the considerable weight of her influence."

The ancient peer nodded his head, setting jowls rippling.

The sight pushed Liz's often irreverent sense of humor down an off-center course that put her tenuous hold on a proper facade at risk. She looked at the man, bald but with rolls of loose flesh draped from chin to a chest resplendently garbed in the ornately embroidered waistcoat of an earlier era, and saw a turkey gobbler. Yes, a turkey gobbler just like those the cook on the Double H kept in a pen out behind the barn. She strangled a bubble of outright laughter in her throat but hadn't a prayer of suppressing the wicked grin that lit gleaming lights in turquoise eyes.

Lord Poxwell saw nothing untoward in her smile. He was satisfied with her answer and relieved by the ending of the dance. Then, as an old-fashioned, well-mannered man must, he led the lady back to her family's side, Lady Euphemia's side to be precise. But, finding that he'd hoped in vain for a glimpse of the young woman who'd been the subject of their talk, he soon excused himself and slowly wandered off toward another group.

After watching the marquess depart their company, Lady Euphemia's attention turned toward the unexpected and unwelcome duchess. Seated amongst a group of disapproving matrons, all veterans of an earlier and far more discriminating era, she lifted her ornate pince-nez to peer with ill-concealed distaste at the American girl's startling garb.

Liz's wicked smile deepened although she spoke in the most dulcet of tones. "I see you agree that your brother has remarkable taste. He and Monsieur Worth discussed the details of this gown at length."

After a glimpse of Euphemia's reaction—eyes going hard as granite and chest swelling with an indignation frustrated by their public situation against its corset—Liz trained an innocent gaze on the dwindling number of dancers.

Tonight Liz had discovered a surprising fact. This stuffy social scene could provide some wildly entertaining moments and a fair measure of enjoyment. Unfortunately, there were also periods of crashing dullness such as when one's partner droned on at great length about the specifics of how battlefield tactics in past wars could have been better commanded or lengthy descriptions of endless fox hunts.

"Gone wool-gathering have you, Lizzy?" Laughter underlaid the smooth question.

Pulling her thoughts back to the present, Liz sheepishly turned toward the earl of Hayton who stood uncomfortably near. And, no, not the earl of Hayton, for he'd insisted she call him Lawrence.

"I'm sorry, I was lost in admiration of the beautiful patterns made by the dancers." It was a lame excuse, but adequate.

"Come," Hayton enticed with practiced charm.

"Allow me to lead you onto the floor to add your startling accent to the design."

Hiding a feeling of helplessness behind a polite smile, Liz looked at his outstretched hand as if it were poison. By asking her for a third dance, he had put her in a most awkward position and he must know that he had. Her gaze narrowed, while at the same time she was terribly aware of the weight of Euphemia's spiteful disapproval. Liz knew she must refuse but was unsure how to gracefully do so. Gray smoothly saved her from the need.

"'Fraid not old chum. Lilibet's last dance of the evening belongs to her husband." Not waiting for the other two to respond, Gray took Liz into his arms and swept her into the opening strains of a slow waltz.

Intending to thank him, Liz looked up into the chill of accusing eyes. He apparently believed she'd meant to accept the earl's invitation. Liz reminded herself that Gray's poor opinion of her social graces was hardly news, but still she unconsciously gave her head a slight shake to ward off its hurt.

Seeing a bright head's despairing motion and the defeated droop to Elizabeth's shoulders, Gray felt responsible for stealing the fiery woman's spirit. He didn't like it; he didn't like it at all. His gaze softened to a rare tender smoke, and he gently squeezed the small fingers laid across his much larger palm until she again looked up.

Liz silently gasped and tumbled into the unprecedented warmth of a smoky haze while the crowd faded into oblivion. Yielding to Gray's lead and swirling through the dance, Liz could feel his heat through both her glove and the cloth of his jacket. Though barely touching, their bodies moved in perfect time. The heady power of his nearness wrapped her in exhilaration while palpable tension carried them deeper into a private realm and wordless communion. When the music came to an end, it was wrenching to stop and impossible for her to step away.

Gray was as thoroughly caught in the moment's magic as the beauty in his arms, but awareness of the sizable audience watching them abruptly broke him free of its gossamer tendrils. They'd ended very near where they had begun, within a few steps of his disapproving sister and the prying eyes of her friends. Feeling rudely jerked from a pleasant haven, Gray quickly decided it was time to escape the curious throng.

"It's time we take our leave from Lord and Lady Cardington." He looked down to find widened blue eyes still watching him. It brought a sardonic curl to his lips as he gently prodded her to turn toward the arched doorway where their hosts again stood.

When Gray placed her fingers in the crook of his arm, Liz realized she'd left one task undone and half turned toward his sister.

"Lady Euphemia, I nearly forgot to mention that Lord Poxwell told me how happy he was to find Drusilla in town. He mentioned how it would be a boon to more frequently see the gel . . ." Liz's perfect copy of the marquess's intonation and old-fashioned verbiage startled a spurt of laughter from a short, plump lady standing near and, despite turned back, obviously listening. ". . . particularly were he to again pay her his addresses."

Wondering if it could really be amusement she sensed bottled up in the man so near, Liz very properly ignored both the eavesdropper's chuckle and Euphemia's stony glare at the offender's broad back. What Liz had said was a lie, but only a little white one, and more likely to be believed when delivered with her impersonation's gentle mockery, which doubtless Euphemia heard as an insult to be expected from a rude American upstart. The important thing was that, if accepted, this tidbit of information might serve to lessen the lady's ill temper over her disobedient stepdaughter's arrival in the city. And, hopefully, convince her to allow the "gel" to remain.

Gray found himself lost between righteous dismay with his wife's succinct mimicry of a fellow peer and the difficulty of suppressing his own laughter. She'd perfectly captured the man's patronizing air of superiority. Too bad her audience had included Lady Oxley, the biggest gossip in all of London. His only hope for mitigating the damage was to get Elizabeth away from this too public stage for her antics. Then, once he had her in the privacy of the library at Brandt House, he would, again, attempt to instill in his irrepressible bride some sense of the respect, the dignity owed her position as duchess of Ashleigh.

Laying his hand over the one resting in the crook of his arm, Gray paused to speak to his sister, a flat announcement of the way things would be despite her expected dislike of it.

"Her Grace and I will take the carriage in which you and I arrived. That leaves you and Dru the carriage just up from the country to deliver Timothy to his lodgings before returning to Brandt House."

Like a cat sensing danger, though partially soothed by news of Lord Poxwell's renewed marital intentions, Euphemia's fur again stood on end. She glared at Gray, plainly put out by the pairing of Dru and Timothy within the close confines of a single carriage.

Liz knew the other woman dared not publicly deny her brother's command. However, in her fuming expression Liz could almost read the stern promise that after they were home she'd have a few choice things to say to him.

With her hand held tightly in the crook of Gray's arm by his much larger hand, when he turned, Liz had little choice but to accompany him toward the ballroom's exit even if she wished to do so but, truth be known, she didn't want to stay. Liz acknowledged another new discovery about the social scene. Events such as this could be every bit as tiring as a full day's work on the Double H. Her feet hurt and shoulders ached leaving her more than willing to depart.

While they wordlessly moved past dwindling numbers of merrymakers, a few lingering in small groups along the walls and others moving about the dance floor, she caught a reassuring glimpse of Dru. The timid girl Liz had led into rebellion was doing her part to mitigate her stepmama's ire. Over the course of the evening Liz had seen Dru take the floor with a wide variety of partners, but now she'd wisely broken the pattern of avoiding Lord Poxwell to join him for a last waltz. When the marquess took Dru back to Lady Euphemia, as he was certain to do at the dance's end, it would surely be another giant step toward securing Euphemia's consent to her continued London stay.

An unfamiliar voice interrupted Liz's thoughts while at the same time bringing the duke and, thus, her to a halt.

"Grayson, old boy. Where have you been hiding all evening?" A stocky man, little taller than Liz, had stepped directly into their path. Mock disgust arched black brows startling on one whose thick mane was a pristine white.

Gray was surprised. Here was the man he'd come to the ball looking for—until he caught his first glimpse of Elizabeth. That glimpse had driven thoughts of his father's old friend far from his mind . . . and considering the importance of the matter to be discussed, that was another wrong to be laid at her door.

"I tried to find you in all our usual haunts, don't 'cha know." The man plaintively claimed. "I visited the baccy tables set up behind the buffet in the supper room and the withdrawing rooms usually preferred for the political debates you favor. But you weren't in any of them."

Baccy tables? Liz frowned. The affable man must

mean baccarat, the game of chance she'd learned was a favorite amongst these aristocrats and very different from the occasional round of poker she had enjoyed with the Double H's hands. Perhaps the gaming tables were where this man had spent the evening. This distinctive stranger certainly hadn't been among the dancers or their audience in the ballroom. She hadn't been to the supper room, hadn't once escaped the ballroom, although many a partner had procured her a welcome cup of fruit punch.

"Elizabeth, let me introduce a family friend of long standing, Sir David Wrenwick. David, meet my bride."

Smiling politely and extending her hand, Liz was certain that, in the whole of this long evening, she hadn't seen this man before. His appearance was so unusual that he assuredly would have stood out among the crush of unfamiliar people Liz had learned proclaimed the evening a social triumph.

"Bride?" Sir David took the time to kiss Liz's hand with great aplomb before turning back to Gray. "I do believe I've been insulted. You didn't bother to send me an invite to the nuptials. Now what would your father say to such a slight of his old school chum?"

"It was a very small affair, Sir David." Liz took the initiative in answering, aware that her American accent would go a fair way in explaining the circumstances.

"I'm afraid, David, that you were on the wrong side of the Atlantic." A mocking smile tilted one corner of Gray's mouth as he offered the limited explanation, choosing to provide no further details at this hour and in this too public place.

Liz braced herself to withstand the narrowed gaze which the evening and its multitude of introductions had taught her to expect. In a moment assessing eyes would examine her from head to toe, taking the measure of her monetary worth. They didn't. Instead she was the recipient of a wide, pleased smile and hearty congratulations for them both.

Once Gray had accepted his friend's kind words, he hastened to broach the subject that had originally given purpose to his attendance at the ball.

"We need to talk about the proposed legislation, David."

"Precisely why I've been looking for you." Sir David nodded so emphatically his thick white hair fell forward to brush the black brows that gave his face its unique definition. "What say we meet early tomorrow? Even before the rooster crows."

"Oh—" Gray laughingly cringed. "Not as early as that, or we'd need to begin our talks right now."

"Oh, I say, you're right." Sir David glanced toward the full-length windows at the far end and seemed surprised to find night shadows beginning to dissipate. "All right. Let's allot ourselves four hours to sleep and then meet at our club."

With the matter settled and Liz between them, Gray and David moved to where their host and hostess stood accepting farewells and congratulations on a most successful event.

While the two men had discussed when and where to meet, Liz had glimpsed Euphemia herding Dru and Timothy from the ballroom. They, the marquess of Poxwell, and most of the remaining guests had departed. Dawn was not far off when at last Gray handed his duchess into an elegant carriage whose arms-emblazoned door was held by a footman resplendent in the ebony and scarlet of the Ashleigh livery.

Shut into the posh vehicle, alone with and directly across from her too fascinating spouse, Liz realized how easily on the dance floor he'd melted her sanity and strength with his wiles. In an earnest attempt to prevent a further exposure of her weakness to him, she sought some method to ward off the intense awareness he inevitably roused in her. While absently tugging a long kid glove from one hand, she again fell prey to the sorry habit of saying the first thing that came to mind.

"I'd never heard the name Lilibet until you called me that."

Gray, equally aware of his companion and the danger of that emotion, shrugged and gazed steadily into the darkness where the faint light of predawn had begun to give more definition to once blurry objects. "It's a common diminutive for Elizabeth."

Common? Liz stiffened. That, she felt, should tell her just how unimportant she was to him. Staring blindly through the window opposite the one out which he glared, Liz thought to confirm his belief of her commonness by making an admission. "Well, I liked it." After a brief pause she added, "Thank you." There, that ought to show him for the snob he was and prove what grace this *common* female possessed.

Surprised, Gray turned to study the totally unique woman whose vivid coloring not even the gloom of waning night could dull.

"It's what I called my maternal grandmother . . . before she died."

The softness in his voice caught Liz's attention, and she shifted to meet an unguarded gaze once more gone to gentle smoke. Nothing ever went the way she expected in her dealings with him. Her misreading of his meaning assailed Liz with guilt. She opened her mouth to apologize.

The next moment the carriage sharply tilted. A loud grinding sound filled her ears and she was thrown across the distance between herself and Gray. She landed hard against his powerful chest. Gray's strong arms sheltered Liz safely near while his head was smashed against an unyielding door frame.

CHAPTER 6

"I say, Ashleigh, are you all right?"

Liz heard the words but, they seemed to come from far away. Dazed, she stared at the warm darkness staining her hand and dripping onto the glove in her lap. Lifting her head from the reassuring steadiness of a broad shoulder, she uncomprehendingly studied the dark liquid trickling down a lean cheek.

Blood! Grayson's blood!

Liz shook her head, determined to disperse an unwelcome grogginess. The carriage's odd tilt complicated the goal. They lay together in one corner like toys in a box upended at an angle. Twisting about, she glanced behind to find a vaguely familiar face in the window now nearly above. She pulled from an ominously lax hold, struggled to lean forward and reach out to help release the jammed door latch.

Anxious to win immediate help for an unmoving Gray, the task seemed to take forever. In actual fact it required only a few minutes for the door to be pried open by Ashleigh servants . . . under Lord Oxley's unnecessary direction.

"We were turning the corner not far behind you."

Lady Oxley's plump cheeks trembled after she pushed her husband aside to stand on tiptoe and peer down at the trapped pair. "We saw the wheel come off. Come off as if there were nothing to hold it on."

"That accounts for this . . ." Liz paused and grimly smiled. Positive that Gray would not thank her for adding further fuel to the woman's avid conjectures, she suppressed her own dawning questions into a carefully measured response and finished, "for this mishap."

Concern for the unconscious duke's condition and location in the bottom corner led to a quick decision that someone should rush to the nearest stable or inn and return with a sturdy barrel. Next the menservants of both nobles would hoist the end of the axle lacking a wheel and rest it atop the barrel, thus bringing the carriage as near to its normal position as possible.

"But first, Your Grace," the Ashleigh coachman gallantly spoke. "If you can stand and reach through the opening, we'll lift you safely from the vehicle."

"No!" Liz instantly refused. "While the carriage is being raised there would be nothing to prevent the duke from falling sideways, perhaps worsening his injuries or sustaining others even more serious."

The fiery glare of her bright eyes was enough to deter further discussion . . . and enough to prevent anyone from noticing the slit of silver gleaming between his thick black lashes.

For safety's sake, the door opened with difficulty was lowered to rest lightly against its frame. And, as others made preparations to accomplish the agreed-upon deed, Liz cautiously settled back beside the injured man. She pulled Gray's tie lose, made the length of silk into a pad, and held it to the already congealing wound while at the same time wedging herself into a steadier position against the possible need to bear his much greater weight.

Fiercely concentrating on her goal, Liz failed to notice a faint smile testing the man's restraint.

"All right, men, after three." At the coachman's call from without, Liz tensed every muscle in readiness.

"One . . . Two . . . Three—Heave!"

The coach rose so high it briefly tilted Liz and her charge to a reverse angle. Grayson sagged limply against Liz, one arm falling to the far side of her waist. Unbeknownst to her, his open hand safely braced them until the vehicle settled with a thump only a small distance below its usual level.

Liz's heart raced while Gray's face lay buried between the ear exposed by upswept hair and sapphire strands looped across the expanse of shoulder and bosom Worth had decreed stylish. Surely it was a natural response to the expected but still difficult challenge of holding Gray safely upright. That was a lie, she silently acknowledged in a burst of honesty. She refused to look further for the source of "heart flutterings" like those the silly girls at Miss Brown's School had gushed about at the sight of every handsome man.

"Your Grace, if you permit, Stebbins and I will transfer the duke to Lord Oxley's carriage." The solemn Ashleigh coachman had reopened the vehicle's once-reluctant door. Despite missing top hat, torn sleeve, and muddied white gloves, he was the image of calm control. "His lordship has offered to drive you both to Brandt House while Stebbins takes a hansom to fetch the family physician. I will remain here to guard the carriage and arrange for its repair."

"We in America hear much in praise of unruffled English butlers and their ability to deal with any conceivable difficulty." Arms wrapped about her half-fallen husband and too aware of their position, Liz still smiled warmly at the servant who had not only suggested the method but had led in their rescue.

"Tonight you've proven it equally true of all English servants, and I heartily thank you."

Though the coachman nodded modestly, he couldn't suppress either a pleased smile or proud explanation. "I must confess that I *am* the butler at Brandt House. The coachman became ill this afternoon and, as the under coachman had been given leave for a sennight with his troubled family on the Ashleigh Estate, it was decided that I, who years past was trained as coachman, would take the reins for a single evening."

"I don't wish anyone to be sick . . ." Liz briefly bit at her lower lip before a grin even brighter than her hair defeated the momentary ruefulness. "Still I can't regard the the circumstances that put you here tonight as anything less than a blessing."

Lord and Lady Oxley were not in Liz's view but, hearing a disgruntled muttering, she became aware of the pair waiting impatiently. She instantly returned her attention to the goal of getting Gray home and under a doctor's care.

"Again I thank you for handling matters so well," Liz told the coachman-butler. "But now I would appreciate your help in seeing the duke moved into the Oxleys' carriage."

"Though already aware of your excellent talents, Ellison, I thank you, too."

Liz gasped as her burden suddenly sat upright with a mocking grin.

"I am grateful for the offer of assistance, but it's unnecessary as I'm quite capable of moving from this carriage to His Lordship's. Nor have I need of a physician. A dash of cool water and a few hours rest will suffice to restore me to my usual self."

"You need to see a doctor," Liz argued.

Gray waved the suggestion away. "Why bother the man over a simple bump on the head." Seeing a slender finger point to the dark stains on his shirt front while peach lips opened to further dispute his claim, he went on, smothering her unspoken words. "Cuts to the head bleed profusely—far more than justified by their insignificant damage."

"But you were insensible for some little time." Liz was not to be so easily silenced, not when she earnestly believed her cause important.

"Was I?" A dark brow arched. "Or was I merely enjoying your undivided attentions?" Gray waited for this deliberate half-truth to spark her temper. The impact of temple against carriage door actually had knocked him unconscious and left him dazed for a time after he regained his senses. But he'd rather Elizabeth thought otherwise. He hoped that misbelief would sidetrack her from a dangerous path he didn't want pursued.

Liz gasped then closed her mouth with a decided snap. The idea that he'd taken advantage of the situation to hold her so intimately set her temper on slow boil. This dastardly action reinforced a conviction that had begun to falter, the conviction that he'd been as much at fault as her father in trapping her into marriage.

"What's keeping you?" A querulous voice called from the darkness some distance behind Ellison's shoulder.

"Pray pardon our sloth, Oxley. I paused to convince my loving bride that I truly require no medical care."

"Ashleigh! Feeling quite the thing are you?" The aging lord moved forward to peer doubtfully into the carriage's gloom.

Gray stepped down into the street, forcing Lord Oxley to take a quick pace back and scattering the gathering crowd. With ill grace Liz accepted the hand extended toward her and then found herself unable to prevent her husband from tucking her fingers into the crook of his arm as he led her toward the waiting carriage.

Once both noble couples were settled inside and the vehicle was under way, Liz was terribly aware of the other pair's surreptitious scrutiny.

"You must speak smartly to your coachman and stable hands." Taking the position of sage counselor to the younger man, Lord Oxley blustered with self-important advice and mild reproof. "The wheel of a properly cared for carriage would never come loose, even less completely off. Must've been lax in their care of your carriage not to have closely checked every bolt."

"It's amazing that you reached the ball safely in the first instance, considering how quickly it came off after you left." Lady Oxley studied them for the effect of her suggestion that though all had been in good condition at evening's start, someone had sabotaged the carriage before their departure.

"Indeed," Gray nodded amicably enough but the steel in his eyes threatened with power enough to crush any question of either poor workmanship or possible underlying plot. "I'll look into it, of course. But I trust my staff far too well to overlook the simple fact that a piece of equipment often shows no external signs of wear when, in actual fact, over a time of excellent performance it becomes worn and suddenly fails." He shrugged. "I am certain I'll find the problem's source to involve nothing more sinister."

Liz was unconvinced. Nonetheless, she exercised a rare measure of discretion and held her tongue. Grimly polite smiles and silence marked the remainder of the blessedly brief journey to Brandt House. Gray helped Liz descend at their destination. She was so awed by the tall building's restrained elegance that she barely heard her husband again reassure their hosts of his health.

"Your Grace!" The door was opened by a young footman, startled by the vision of his bloodstained duke. "Where's Ellison? I—Sorry. I had thought he'd be with you." Flustered, he forgot all sense of decorum and leaned past them to study the unfamiliar carriage steadily moving away. "Where's the coach?" He stepped back inside and unceremoniously shoved the door shut before nervously turning toward the odd sight of his injured master and a strange redheaded woman. "What happened, sir?"

"I'm all right, Harris, but the carriage lost a wheel. Ellison and Stebbins stayed behind to oversee its repair and return to the stables." Under these unusual circumstances, rather than remonstrating against the newly appointed footman for his awkward welcome, inappropriate but understandable for someone left with duties far beyond his experience, Gray gave him a slight, reassuring smile. "Wake Mrs. Ellison to see that the blue suite is prepared for my wife and a bath is delivered to mine."

Harris audibly gulped but nodded several times before hastily turning to obey.

Gray's attention shifted to the woman at his side. "Before seeking rest, shortened already by my promise to meet David in a very few hours, I must ask you to join me in the library." As Liz's hand remained tucked in the crook of his arm, Gray enforced his directive simply by pulling her toward the room.

Liz could hardly refuse without making a scene, and even she preferred not to be more the brunt of the servant's gossip than already assured by her unexpected arrival. Nonetheless, the memory of what had happened on the two previous occasions when he'd insisted she meet with him alone roused her defenses.

The library was a gracious room lined with bookshelves on two sides. The third was taken up with windows from floor to ceiling and curtained in deep green velvet. On the fourth side was a huge marble fireplace flanked by chests inlaid with exotic wood. There was a massive desk in oak and green leather, its back to the windows and several large leather-covered armchairs before it. Gray motioned for her to take a seat in one while he moved to sit behind the impressive desk.

Though this elegant room bore no resemblance to Miss Brown's austere office, Liz had the uncomfortable sensation of having been transported back in time. She once again felt like a gawky schoolgirl, waiting hunched before her world's figure of ultimate and disapproving power. To defeat both that image and the sense of being relegated to the role of subservient wife, before Gray could speak, Liz renewed a subject she knew he wanted forgotten.

"You really ought to have sent for the doctor. The refined ladies of your exalted acquaintance might accept without question your easy dismissal of the danger in head wounds, but from my days on the Double H, I've too much firsthand experience to be so easily fobbed off." Liz inwardly delighted in the dark frown won by her words. So what if the claim was a bit exaggerated. It was true at the core. She had seen a ranch hand thrown while trying to bust a wild horse, and he'd died of the blow a hoof had dealt his skull. Restraining a shudder at the gruesome memory, she continued her effort to derail the duke's lecture.

"Furthermore, you can't expect me to believe that worn equipment could possibly be responsible for a wheel falling off a carriage as beautifully kept as yours."

When his face went as coldly unyielding as stone and his eyes to silver frost, Liz realized she'd hit upon a tender point. Seemed there was more to this story than she'd suspected.

"Neither of these issues is the reason I brought you

here. And, as we both need our rest, I can permit you to waste no more of my time on insignificant matters."

Liz froze and felt herself shrinking, just as he no doubt intended.

"I have repeatedly tried to impress upon you—unsuccessfully it seems—the importance of embodying the respect due our family name . . . and your title."

Liz's spine straightened, chin lifted, and eyes flashed blue flames. "Did I, in any way, defame either at the ball tonight?"

Gray took a deep breath to contain his growing irritation. No, she hadn't defamed either, but apparently she'd no notion how very near to the line she had come. While he mentally debated the wisdom of warning her about the dangers inherent in the Marlborough Set and their house parties, she spoke again.

"Even you have to admit that I've proven an ability to hold my own in your social scene. What would your Prince say if you exiled me to the country again?" Gray's brows met in an even fiercer frown, but Liz went on. "Indeed, what of the nosy matrons I've learned are as prevalent in London's society as New York's?"

"It's *not* my 'social scene.' " Only Elizabeth could so quickly pierce his calm exterior. "I detest the whole round of useless expense and sleepless nights. I participate only for the sake of my interests in Parliament and the obligations of my position."

Liz was surprised by the sincerity of the disgust in his statement. She remembered Dru and Timothy's talk of their uncle's dedication to certain causes but had suspected it would be more for public appearances than reality.

"However, it is true that you'll have to remain in

the city now that in a single evening you've managed to make yourself the season's darling. You clearly won't believe it, but I truly thought that by leaving you in the country I was providing you with the life-style you'd most appreciate." He could say that honestly although he'd also been anxious to keep her from disgracing herself and, in the process, him. "Now it's you who no longer have a choice. From tonight until the first of August, this is where you'll remain."

That was a dismaying thought which Liz had begun to face during the ball but had failed to adequately consider before setting out from Ashleigh Hall. She bit at her lower lip, irritated by her own folly. The vision of the weeks, months stretching out ahead was daunting.

"Because you're in London for the duration, it's imperative for you to accept the importance of our maintaining, both here in Brandt House and in the city as a whole, the expected image of a happy newly wedded couple." Gray knew it was the only way to both suppress gossip about their sudden marriage and, more importantly, keep her free of their discreet but ever amorous Prince's advances.

"What?" The word was nearer a hoot of laughter than a question. "You can't possibly except me to pretend to be a cherished bride. I've never been any good at seeming to be something I'm not and doubt I could start with a role so far from reality."

Silver eyes narrowing on Elizabeth, Gray silently acknowledged the truth in her statement. If there was one thing that could be irrefutably said of her, it was that she was utterly direct and honest. He slowly rose and the pleasure found in a tidy solution to the problem put a sardonic smile on his lips. He need only see that she became precisely what he'd asked her to seem: A love-besotted female. Elizabeth was unlike any female he'd ever known and therefore a challenge

—an amazingly tempting one—but he could do it. He'd overcome her defenses twice in the past and to repeat the process would be no difficult chore. Having seduced and won more than his share of feminine affections, he was confident of his ability.

A small, annoying qualm intruded. He irritably brushed aside the uncomfortable suspicion that seducing her physically might not be enough to appease the depth of his hunger. Behind thick black lashes Gray's eyes turned to ice. He'd suffered these pangs before. It had ended in a pain to which he had sworn he would never again be vulnerable. No, while he *would* seduce her, she would *not* weaken his defense against untrustworthy emotions.

Liz's eyes widened as Gray stepped nearer and nearer. She couldn't breath properly and her heart began a furious pounding. More of that silly fluttering she'd once disdained in females less sensible than herself. When he loomed above and reached down to draw her to her feet, she gasped. But, Liz was dismayed to realize, that reaction was less the result of alarm or aggravation than anticipation.

Gray saw her confusion and cautioned himself to go gently as he lowered his head, careful not to rush and startle the spirited woman into bolting. As he laid his mouth against peach-sweet lips, Liz's thick bronze lashes dropped against her cheeks. Swept full against a broad, muscular form, Liz went disgustingly weak while Gray proved just what a wicked danger he could be. He urged her closer into the curve of his body, and she helplessly melted as he moved his kiss from her mouth down her throat to . . .

"Gray! Are you in there, Gray?"

Lady Euphemia's strident voice pierced the soft haze shielding Liz from reality. The door burst open under the lady's less than ladylike shove.

"I wanted to discuss your ill-thought decision to put

Dru and Timothy in the same carriage, but Harris tells me the wheel 'fell off' the carriage you were in." Ignoring the woman still in her brother's arms, Euphemia stepped forward with a determined gleam in granite-hard eyes. "Now really, Gray, we must talk about Timothy's likely involvement in yet another accident!"

"Not tonight, sister." Gray released Liz from his embrace but retained his hold on her hand. "I've an early appointment with Sir David to discuss a most important matter—for which I need my sleep. Thus, we bid you good night."

"Well, I never . . ." Euphemia huffed, shocked by this response so unlike Gray. It must be the bad influence of this appalling American *female.* Duchess though she might be, Euphemia wouldn't term her a lady!

Without glancing at either woman, Gray led an unresisting Elizabeth up the stairs to private rooms on the level above. However, keeping in mind the plan to woo his bride, at the door to her suite he gallantly clasped her hand between both of his while at the same time bending to brush a heart-stoppingly gentle kiss across surprise-parted lips.

Liz watched dazed as a dangerously potent smile curved the duke's lips for long moments before he turned to leave her staring after him like some moonstruck fool.

Shaking her head to free it of mesmerizing mists, she stumbled into the assigned room aware that her best efforts to dispel the fog were doomed. Everything from ball to accident to passionate embrace had complicated the long day's emotional turmoil. The gentle kiss of moments past had thoroughly muddled her thoughts. Gloves dangling from one hand, she drifted into her new suite, hardly noticing its luxurious appointments or the young woman unobtrusively waiting to help undo the extravagant ball gown's many hidden fastenings and unlace a tight corset.

When eventually Liz fell into a large, four-poster bed draped in shining brocade, she tumbled into warm, misty dreams and whirled through an endless dance in the arms of a man who was adversary at one turn and lover at the next . . . on and on and on.

CHAPTER 7

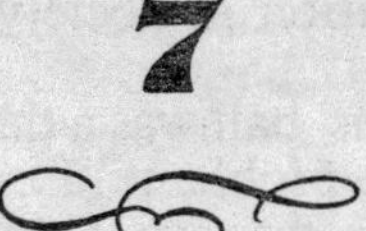

Lady Euphemia's mouth pursed as if she tasted something sour, an expression that did little to sweeten the atmosphere of the morning meal. But then not even the cheery sunlight falling through long windows lightly draped in sheer white and glinting over the array of silver and crystal dishes placed on a gleaming sideboard could brighten the breakfast room's mood. Three ladies sat in strained silence about a mahogany table whose center was graced by a crystal bowl of tulips while the outer edge was laid with delicately flowered china and highly polished silverware set on lace placemats.

Once the maid withdrew from delivering fresh racks of toast and a new pot of tea, Euphemia embarked on a mission she virtuously felt family loyalty obliged her to make. The newcomer must be made to understand the heavy responsibilities the duchess of Ashleigh's proper role entailed.

"I cannot emphasize strongly enough the importance of your duty to uphold the spotless honor of your husband's heritage." The stony glare accompanying this stricture fell heavily upon Liz.

Liz bore the weight well, silently lifting her chin to give the stern speaker a tight smile. She suspected her success at the previous evening's ball had deepened the older woman's fears that a new wife might attempt to assume the position in Society Euphemia held as the duke's hostess.

"The Cardingtons' ball was a delight." Liz immediately addressed the problem. "I marvel at the organizational skill required to see it run smoothly and fear I'd find it difficult to manage such a feat even on a smaller scale."

In actual fact, Liz was certain that, if necessary, she could meet that challenge. However, she chose to downplay her abilities for the sake of placating the noble sister-in-law gazing at her with what could only be termed dark suspicion.

"I'm thankful you're here, Euphemia, to plan what must be a wide variety of obligatory social events. Your experience and familiarity with important personages makes your lead in these matters invaluable." Idly nibbling at a narrow slice of toast, Liz peered through lowered lashes to catch the older woman's response.

Euphemia preened under the praise, and yet she was too realistic to permit a few complimentary words to allay her concerns. Only one hostess could stand beside Gray to receive guests. Convention called for that hostess to be his wife, the duchess. So long as the American remained in this house, she would always come before his lady sister. That undeniable fact turned gray eyes to granite.

Up to this point Dru had held her breath and remained as silent observer to a delicate balancing act on a playing field threatening to shift. But the antagonism now hardening her stepmama's eyes demanded she intervene before open conflict erupted.

Dru's uninvited arrival at the previous night's ball had been a rare example of rebellion against her stepmama and that success heartened her. She took action to disrupt growing tension, an action that would definitely not be appreciated. Dru introduced the one subject certain to shift the conversation's focus. It would anger Stepmama but also remind her that events had carried them too far to be reversed.

"Lizzy, last evening I was awed by your conquest of the Prince. Everyone knows he has a roving eye, but still, I've never before seen him so openly taken with a woman."

"Hmmph." Euphemia's disgusted growl made her opinion of the girl's observation plain. "Dru's experience is limited. She's only one year out of the schoolroom and wasn't in Society when the Prince's attention was caught first by Jennie Churchill, then Lady Consuelo Mandeville, Minnie Paget, and more —Americans all."

Liz heard the slur on her heritage but refused to be baited or even to acknowledge it by looking toward the speaker and instead stared at the gem colors of marmalade and jam gleaming in crystal dishes.

Dru went bravely on as if her stepmama hadn't said anything. She leaned across the table toward Liz and loudly whispered, as if imparting a particularly juicy secret. "And I did think Uncle Gray was going to explode when Bertie called you Lizzy, didn't you?"

Liz hadn't realized Dru was close enough to hear that exchange, but then whenever Gray was near, others faded. Despite Euphemia's fierce frown, Dru's grin was infectious and the soft, rich laughter of Liz's response drove the room's strain into abeyance and encouraged the speaker.

"Then when Uncle Gray called you Lilibet, I was that shocked." Dru snapped her fingers, an indelicate action that earned from Euphemia a "tch" of disgust. "It's what he called his beloved grandmama."

Having been told this much by Gray, Liz merely nodded.

Once more Dru loudly whispered, "She was a feisty old dear who detested being called 'grand' anything. Said it made her feel every year of her age—and she didn't like it." Settling back to lift a gleaming silver spoon, Dru absently added, "She passed on two years ago, full of life to the end, and I never thought Uncle Gray would use the name again. Indeed, I hadn't expected to ever again hear it."

A perplexed Liz frowned. "Gray told me it was a common diminutive of Elizabeth."

Distracted by the uncooperative shell of a boiled egg which refused to be gently cracked open, Dru gave a slight shake of unrestrained ebony curls. "Can't think why he'd say that. Li*s*abet is fairly common, but I've never heard anyone else be addressed as Li*l*ibet."

To hide her surprise—and thrill of pleasure—Liz bent her attention to the fragile burden resting on her own china egg cup.

The younger women's exchange had done nothing to improve Euphemia's mood. Moreover, the mention of the Prince's admiration for Gray's bride reminded her of another grave matter this American must be vigilant against.

"Earlier you acknowledged my familiarity with Society—" Euphemia met a turquoise gaze directly. "Supported by years of experience, I feel compelled to offer a serious word of caution. As charming as Prince Albert can be, when it suits him, he and the members of his far, far too fast Marlborough set are a group whose invitations to a closer friendship you simply *must not* encourage! All manner of . . . of . . ." Already thin lips pursed tightly for a long moment before Euphemia continued. "All manner of 'unmentionable' dangers lurk beneath their discreet facade."

Liz's brows rose and her spoon stilled a fraction above her egg. Unmentionable? What was that meant to imply? Lady Euphemia's lowered gaze and unbecoming flush accentuated the earnestness of halting words. Liz was intrigued and found matters growing, to quote Alice in her favorite childhood book, "curiouser and curiouser."

Whatever else the odd warning might mean, it provided an explanation of sorts for Gray's polite if immediate refusal of the Prince's invitation to a house party. Also, perhaps, an explanation for Gray's lecture after they'd arrived at Brandt House. Liz, no young and sheltered English girl, was not so naive or so foolish as to fail in heeding such an admonition. However, neither would she do anything to deflect the Prince's interest when it clearly irritated her arrogant husband.

Having done her duty to limit the American's damage to the family's good name, Euphemia redirected attention by holding up a promised and recently arrived invitation. "Midday has already passed us by, and if we are to attend Lady Holson's tea party this afternoon, either we finish this meal posthaste to begin our preparations or do without morning baths."

The three ladies found the notion of forgoing their baths was unpleasant and, wasting no moment more in conversation, the meal was quickly concluded.

Liz stepped from her suite into the corridor, smoothing the fitted waist of her cutaway polonaise overdress. For someone who'd once disdained the niceties of fashion, she took unusual delight in the gossamer texture of its seafoam-hued batiste and how the petticoats beneath a creamy satin round skirt rustled with her every movement. Air stirred by another's passing caught her attention. Liz sheepishly glanced up while recognizing the woman's identity by the faint clatter of a ring full of keys dangling on a chain from a belt nearly lost between ample chest and broad hips.

"Mrs. Ellison?" Liz quietly called after the straight back moving steadily away, anxious not to lose this unexpected opportunity.

The figure turned, presenting a pleasant face whose nearly smooth, plump contours declared the tidy hair below a starched cap prematurely gone pure white.

"Your Grace—" The woman responded with the requisite dip that passed for a curtsy. "Can I be of some help to you?"

"Would you spare me a brief moment? There is a matter I'd like to discuss with you." The answer to such a question from a duchess could not be doubted, and Liz reopened the door she'd just closed.

With years of practice, Mrs. Ellison hid her curiosity as she entered the new duchess's suite. Her husband, normally a moderate man and, after years as a butler, not given to profuse approval of the gentry, had been generous with praise of this American bride. Surprised by his rare effusive compliments, Mrs. Ellison had looked forward to an opportunity to observe the woman herself and now waited expectantly to learn the purpose of this visit.

Liz carefully closed the door to leave them in privacy and at the same time provide a moment to gather her thoughts. Sooner or later—too likely sooner—Lady Euphemia would try to foist off on her some lady's maid as prim and proper as her Mrs. Simms. Liz had rather that personal servant be someone of her own choosing.

"I understand Annie, the girl who since my arrival has been helping with my attire, is normally an upstairs maid?"

Mrs. Ellison nodded doubtfully, a slight frown on her good-natured face. Had Annie, who'd first come to Brandt House as a tweeny, somehow offended the duchess? She fervently hoped not. Childless, she and Mr. Ellison had become fond of the girl.

"I wanted to suggest that Annie be assigned as my

lady's maid." It was ostensibly a duchess's right to command that it be so, but Liz knew enough to clear anything affecting the management of Brandt House with its housekeeper.

Mrs. Ellison was, first, delighted by the position being offered to a favorite and, second, impressed that the American was aware of the way things ought to be and hadn't implemented such a decision without consulting her. She found the whole situation gratifying. Moreover, the fact that Lady Euphemia would not be pleased put a sparkle of secret delight in her small, dark eyes as she calmly agreed that the position would be a fine step up for Annie.

"Annie is a mite too high-spirited," Mrs. Ellison frankly admitted to Her Grace. "But still and all she's a good girl, and I don't doubt she'll earnestly work to be worthy of the honor and your confidence."

"Oh, I will, I will!" Annie burst through the door connecting sitting room and bedchamber. With strands of flyaway hair escaping pins and tidy cap, she dropped to her knees before a startled Liz.

"Girl, get hold of yourself." Mrs. Ellison was aghast. "Your eavesdropping and unseemly actions only prove how little you merit the duchess's trust."

"Oh-h-h." Annie sat back on her heels, hands clapped in horror over mouth in a belated attempt to stifle her wail.

"It's not Annie's fault," Liz rushed to reassure both Annie and Mrs. Ellison. "In my haste not to let the opportunity to talk with you slip away, I forgot that I left her tidying away nightclothes and straightening bedcovers."

"You've been very fortunate, my girl." The housekeeper wagged an admonishing finger at the trembling female. "Best you remember how near you came to losing this new position before it even began, and strive in future to maintain a proper decorum."

* * *

"Oh, my dear, have you quite recovered from that dreadful accident?"

Two steps within the flower- and greenery-filled conservatory of Holson House, Liz found herself swept into the effusive embrace of a heavily perfumed Lady Oxley.

"I was not injured, but—"

"You were so brave." The small, plump woman stepped back but in overdone comfort tenaciously retained her grip on Liz's hands while her gushing words drowned the disclaimer. "Trapped inside an upended carriage I would've fallen prey to the vapors and been of no good use to my husband. But you, you insisted on remaining with dear Grayson, supporting the unconscious man while the carriage was righted." Lady Oxley achieved the feat of both beaming at Liz and casting a patronizing glance at the curious women quickly gathering around. "So brave, so brave."

It was obvious to Liz that Lady Oxley had waited for this very public moment to brush aside their timid hostess and produce startling news of an event in which she could truthfully claim to have played an important role.

"Not really." Liz denied with carefully modulated civility, simultaneously pulling politely free of the smartly gloved hands patting hers in consolation. "I merely exercised commonsense precautions, the same precautions I'm sure you'd have taken."

"What's this I hear?" The speaker stepping forward was a woman of sizable dimensions in height, width, and—apparently—importance, for she sailed through a crowd seemingly parted by her force of will alone. "Another accident involving the duke of Ashleigh? Surely not!"

As the imperious woman stood directly in front of Liz, this demand for a denial was clearly addressed to her. Liz straightened to her own considerable height and met full on the scrutiny of this aging woman whose extravagantly plumed hat rode atop unnaturally black hair.

"Our carriage lost a wheel as we left the Cardingtons' ball last evening, but though Gray is looking into the circumstances, he believes it simply an unfortunate accident."

"Hmmph!" Plainly unconvinced, the older woman's attention remained fixed on Ashleigh's bride. "Isn't he always certain of that? Yet how many 'unfortunate accidents' befalling the same man can be accepted as only that before one begins to suspect foul deeds, what with anarchists and Irish rebels loose in the City?"

Turquoise eyes narrowed. Liz wanted to hear more on this subject of strange accidents to which both Euphemia and Lady Oxley had obliquely alluded the previous night. For her the question was how to secure further information from a woman she'd yet to formally meet without being seen to undermine her husband's well-defined position?

Liz needn't have worried, the speaker had no intention of losing this opportunity. She was a duchess herself, a leader in society, and—she was never loath to boast—a far more reliable source than even Lady Oxley for the latest tidbits of scandal to enliven any gathering. Having Ashleigh's young and likely naive American bride to herself for a time should provide a feast of succulent gossip. Not only was the duke's marriage utterly unexpected, but his startlingly unique bride had come from nowhere and, thanks to the Prince of Wales, become an instant success.

"Mildred, I'm so pleased that you could attend . . ." Lady Holson nervously attempted to intervene and dampen this possibly volatile situation, a complication she didn't need while still quaking with uncertainty over her unorthodox decision to host a tea in the conservatory. Really, she reassured herself for the hundredth time, it was the only place, short of the formal ballroom, to entertain so large a group.

Mildred was the second guest to brush the ineffectual Lady Holson aside. She then toned her forceful voice down into a murmur of soft concern to address Liz. "Has no one told you of the several 'accidents' from which Gray miraculously escaped during the past year?"

Much aware of Euphemia's dark frown and Dru's frantically widened eyes, Liz carefully sidestepped the potentially explosive issue. "I'm sure my husband wished not to worry me."

Liz, having read the other woman's desire to harvest a fresh crop of spicy fruit from a previously untouched field, then attempted to do what she'd insisted to Gray she could not. She played the false role of wide-eyed and unsuspecting ingenue, and her discomfort with the action added to its believability.

"Still, I'd like to hear enough to guard against possible dangers."

"And so you shall, so you shall." Preparing to direct Liz through the crowd, the overbearing woman took Liz's elbow but first cast a triumphant glance at a longtime rival. That look was the complete reverse of the gentle rebuke in her question. "Euphemia, why have you kept this poor child in the dark? It can be such a dangerous place to be—for both her and Grayson."

Mildred's mere presence set Euphemia's nerves on edge, and at the velvet-gloved attack she went rigid. Face going purple and voice tight with irritation for both Mildred and the American in her clutches, she returned the woman's assault with a sharp dig of her own. "Gray refuses to have the unfortunate series of accidents mentioned. No doubt to prevent busybodies from using them to drag our noble family name down into their slime."

"Hah!" The plumed hat perched atop flat black hair wobbled precariously as the woman threw back her head and fairly snorted—half in derision, half in pleasure for Euphemia's loss of composure.

"Come, my dear, we must talk. Others may fear to offend one of your rank but not I who, as the duchess of Etherton, am at least your equal." The emphasis on "at least" left no question that she, and doubtless everyone here, saw her as decidedly Liz's superior.

Hiding wry amusement with her gloating companion's avid smile, Liz allowed herself to be drawn to a small table in a fern-shadowed alcove which should have been private, but their persistent trail of listeners robbed it of that desirable state.

Mildred came near to crowing with delight. She need only win the silly twit's confidence by feeding her the spicy details of Grayson's near misses. Then the girl would be ripe and ready to be squeezed for all the juicy particulars of her courtship and marriage.

While settling into a graceful wicker chair far sturdier and more comfortable than its delicate curves suggested, Liz worked to maintain an expression of guileless innocence. She succeeded in appearing so ingenuous that anyone who knew her well would've been suspicious enough to see the sparkle of laughter lurking in turquoise depths.

"Now let's have our little chat," the duchess of Etherton invited. "Before the Prince and many of our husbands descend upon us. Their arrival makes such intimate tête-a-têtes as this impossible."

Like an obedient child, Liz folded gloved hands in the lap of her exquisite afternoon gown. By lowering her gaze, she hid her amusement over the woman's description of this as an intimate "chat" while there were so many people crowding in at the alcove's one open side. Not that everyone had followed. No, Euphemia, Dru, and a fair portion of the afternoon's guests made a show of remaining a distance away, but

Liz suspected that not all of them were as blameless as they clearly meant to be viewed. She suspected those holding themselves separate from others openly indulging in gossip would, in more intimate social gatherings, find self-righteous delight in examining every petty detail for signs of weakness or fault. Liz could easily imagine Lady Euphemia huddled with several ladies dissecting every word and glance of another and justifying their actions as a virtuous wish to prevent any offender's wrongs from sullying the purity of Society.

Hadn't the Knickerbocker matrons been doing much the same when they rejected Liz's harmless mother simply because her husband's wealth had been too recently earned? Thus, having firsthand experience of such sly and hurtful practices, Liz decided she preferred the duchess and Lady Oxley whose enjoyments, though hardly without sting, were at least open enough to be expected. With hands curled into tight balls in her lap, she nearly missed the first words as the duchess of Etherton embarked on the tale she'd promised to relate.

"Early last Season there were two incidents barely remarked upon. But when a third and more serious mishap overtook Grayson at the end of last July, just before Parliament recessed, well . . ." Mildred turned her shoulder to the hovering listeners, but the clarity of her whisper refuted any intent to truly exclude them. "Suspicions were roused." She nodded knowingly and the ostrich feather curving from her fashionable hat over one ear waved.

Before Liz could ask the duchess of Etherton to elaborate on the nature of that event, the woman spoke again.

"But what really caught everyone's attention was his riding 'accident' last summer. Hmmph!" Mildred's faint growl was full of disgust. "Riding accident? Gray? The suggestion of him *falling* from his own horse for no good reason was far too unlikely. Perhaps you don't know, but he's a top-notch horseman. Before his father died and he repented his wild ways to take up solemn duties, he excelled at that and well—" Eyes rolling and mouth twisting into a smirk made it clear to just what the duchess referred when she continued, "—a goodly number of other manly sports."

Liz was surprised by the woman's arch inference that the husband so concerned with the duty to keep the family name spotless had once cut a rakish figure.

Lady Oxley broke in, anxious not to be completely left out of the conversation. "More interesting still, the riding accident happened not in the City but while riding alone through the woodland edging his country estate."

"All in all—" Mildred's fierce glare stalled the other woman's voice, and it was she who finished the tale. "It seems an uncommon number of accidents."

Lady Holson approached and made a timid stab at regaining control of her own tea party. As it was, no tea had yet been served, though the time was past and her cook was fuming over cakes and biscuits allowed to sit beyond their prime. "One cannot help but notice how often envy and greed lie at the core of suspicious events. Just consider what happened to the little heir of Roydon." She nodded and, forgetting her purpose for gaining the women's attention, fixed Liz with a knowing eye. "While walking with his guardian he fell into a pond on the estate. His guardian, an uncle, is the new lord of Roydon."

Liz was initially perplexed by this seemingly abrupt shift in subject . . . until Lady Oxley spoke in defiance of the duchess of Etherton.

"Did you know that as your husband has no son, his nephew Timothy stands to inherit both the Ashleigh title and estates?"

Having known since the day she'd met Timothy

that he was the heir, Liz met the question with a serene smile and nodded immediately despite the barely hidden suggestion that the young man was responsible for Gray's mishaps. That possibility had startled Liz, but she certainly wouldn't reveal it to these aristocratic vultures. She glanced up and caught a glimpse of Dru across the room. Though unable to hear what was said, the girl was still anxiously biting her lip. Had Dru chosen not to warn Liz of these accidents in deference to her uncle's wishes? Or to protect Timothy?

"I say, ladies, why are you huddling in the corner. Trying to hide from your Prince?"

At the hearty call, those gathered in the alcove's opening scurried to greet Prince Albert and the men entering behind him. Some had come from a day at the track while others were making light of their early escape from Parliament and 'a deadly dull speech.' But Liz was disheartened to find not a single truly familiar face, not even the earl of Hayton.

"Bertie, you naughty thing, your timing is off," Mildred said and meant it. He'd come before she'd secured a single nibble of gossip. It was too bad of him.

Although the duchess of Etherton rose and curtsied in deference to her future monarch, it was clear to Liz that she was both familiar with him and secure enough in her position to risk a potential royal snub for having come perilously near to insolence.

"Bad timing? I think not. I've arrived in time to save this young beauty from your clutches." He returned the veiled insult with a measure of the same venom and equally close to the mark. He gave Liz a benign smile and genuine word of caution. "You've got to beware of this woman. She'll strip you bare of defenses and expose your secrets to the world before you know what's about."

Having curtsied to the Prince, Liz allowed him to fold her hand into the crook of his arm and lead her back to the center of the conservatory and into the circle of his closest friends. As focal point for the men's too personal scrutiny and the women's critical examination, Liz realized that here was the smart Marlborough Set with whom she'd been warned to deal warily.

During the next hour while tea and deliciously light cakes and scones were served, Liz exercised her dry wit to sidestep the veiled advances of not only her royal admirer but of his male friends as well. She managed at the same time to reveal amusing touches of the American openness that Bertie had found so intriguing the evening before. By the time rescue arrived, she was exhausted by the tension of guarding every word, nay, the inflection of every word to ensure it was utterly proper yet never dull.

"I hope you'll pardon me, Your Highness, for stealing my wife away." Gray gave the Prince a teasing smile that turned into a breath-stealing intensity when it shifted to Liz. "There's someone I want her to meet."

Shocked by his unexpected arrival, Liz blushed while again her heart fluttered foolishly under the potency of his smile. Placing his hand in the small of her back, Gray directed Liz to the same alcove, now deserted, that she'd earlier shared with the duchess of Etherton. She was so caught in his spell that she didn't hear the low murmur following them.

Ashleigh never attended afternoon events. His unanticipated presence gave life to an exciting new line of rumors and added the promise of additional enjoyment for the many whose pleasure lay in watching the ebb and flow of Society's foibles.

"I assume you forgive me for plucking you from the midst of such lofty company?" A mocking smile accompanied the question. "You *did* look a little desperate."

Liz immediately straightened and whirled to hiss at him. "I did no such thing!"

"Oh, then let me return you to the Prince's side." Gray reached for her hand. She jerked back and he laughed.

"I was handling the situation quite well, thank you very much. Still, I'd rather not resume the task . . . and amusing the Prince *is* a task."

"An indisputable fact." Gray nodded, forcing an exaggerated solemnity to his face.

Liz returned his teasing with an equally exaggerated glare and tight smile. "Now where is this 'friend' you wanted me to meet?"

"I lied." He shrugged. "But I'll be forgiven for wanting my charming wife all to myself."

Slipping away from Parliament at the first possible moment, Gray had come to make it publicly clear that between his wife and the royal ladies' man lay the most impenetrable barrier of all: an attentive husband. It was a vision that ever-curious gossip hounds were certain to lap up. Besides, this was a fine opportunity to continue down the path he'd sworn to pursue. By becoming an attentive groom, he'd see that Elizabeth would have no difficulty in convincing the world she was a cherished bride.

Again Gray's potent smile stole Liz's breath and impeded quick thinking. He stepped forward and she instinctively stepped back until brought up short by towering ferns. In one of the alcove's deep corners, flanked on two sides by thick greenery and blocked from the view of others by Gray's broad back, she gazed helplessly up into molten silver eyes.

It's only to convince the others they were the happy newlyweds he'd asked that she pretend to be, Liz sternly reminded herself, pulse pounding loudly in her ears. His actions were only that—an act. But as he moved so close his image blurred, she admitted his ploy would be a success. If in the next instant she could have formed a sane thought, she'd have been thankful for the strong hands holding her upright when his head bent and mouth claimed sigh-parted lips while her knees went mortifyingly weak.

CHAPTER 8

Liz threw open the armoire door and snatched down the first thing that came to hand. Her dressing gown wasn't where it ought to be, and she'd no time to waste either in looking for it or thinking about how inappropriate this extravagant silk dinner gown was while dawn's pastel hues had barely begun fading into palest blue. Gray could be heard moving about in his neighboring suite. If she were to speak with him privately, now was the time. She must throw on something—anything—and catch him before he'd departed for the day. Otherwise she wasn't likely to see him until evening and then not without at least family members or servants present.

Hurriedly stepping into the silk garment, she thrust her arms into its sleeves before the sound of Gray's door opening into the corridor sent her scurrying to her own door. She opened it only the smallest distance.

"Gray—" Liz called, peering out through the slight cleft between door and frame.

Surprised, Gray halted directly in front of his wife's suite.

"Can I speak with you for a moment?" After rushing to catch him in time, the request came out in an uncharacteristically breathless tone. It irritated her no end!

"Join me for an early breakfast?" Gray invited while consulting the watch at the end of a golden chain. Again this morning he'd an appointment to meet Sir David and had intended to do without a morning meal, but refusing her earnest appeal was unlikely to aid him in winning her affections. David had been late to arrive in the City for the Season, making Gray wait. It wouldn't hurt David to do a little waiting.

Liz's frustration grew. Gray's response was logical but it wouldn't do. It wouldn't do at all! She had watched for a chance to privately discuss the matter with him since the end of the previous day's tea party, but there'd never been an opportunity. Before dinner was done, he'd been summoned away to work out a compromise on some important bill, and she'd been asleep in her room before he returned.

A breakfast table would not be a suitable site to discuss this subject he most certainly viewed as private, one he'd already shown a reluctance to address. Servants, unobtrusive as they might be, would constantly flow in and out. Moreover, other family members might join them—unlikely at this early hour, yet possible.

Flustered beneath the unwavering attention of this devastating man, Liz rushed into words. "I doubt you'd welcome an audience for what I have in mind." The unintended implication sent a scarlet tide of heat to her cheeks.

"Really?" Dark brows arched in gentle mockery, but silver sparks flared in Gray's eyes.

Never one to retreat from adversity, Liz drove onward. "You've warned me, repeatedly, to hold private conversations in private. So . . ."

She'd no choice. Not really. Taking a deep breath for courage while with one hand holding the unfastened and very low-cut dress up in front, Liz nudged the door open before quickly stepping back. She stumbled over the bunched cloth of her dinner gown's long train and would have fallen but for Gray's quick action in reaching out to steady her with hands on both shoulders . . . bare shoulders.

Gray had initially been surprised by her call and next pleased by her request for privacy, but now he was startled by this unexpected vision of enticing beauty in a state of dishabille. His confidence in an ability to charm and then seduce his wife hadn't wavered. Rather, though daily he took more delight in his fiery, unconventional bride, he'd chosen to move slowly in consideration of both her innocence and the desired long-term result. The application of cool logic told him that this eager invitation to the unintentional temptress's bedroom was not an enticement to an apprehensive virgin's bed. A regretted fact, but a fact.

Blushing vividly beneath the appraisal of silver eyes, Liz's gaze dropped to the rich Aubusson carpet beneath unshod toes as she nervously shoved back the mass of brilliant curls threatening to overwhelm her face. Vulnerable in this flimsy, unfastened dress and lost in the deepest embarrassment of her life, Liz felt like the fancy piece who offered her favors at the bar in her small Wyoming hometown.

Recognizing the blush for exactly what it was, to reassure her threatened modesty, Gray lifted her chin with a gentle finger. Giving her an equally gentle smile, he diverted her attention by reviving the purpose behind her request for his attention.

"What is it that you want to talk with me about? Have I committed some further wrong?" The quiet amusement in his tone proved he didn't actually fear that possibility.

Liz felt overwhelmed by his presence as his finger

moved to stroke her cheek. He stood so near she had to fight to breathe and couldn't speak.

Gray saw her confused desperation and in a soft, deep voice he asked a question meant as a gentle jest. "Or have you decided you'd rather run back to the country and escape me?"

That slight on her courage shook Liz from dangerous fascination with the man. "No! I'm enjoying the Season and wouldn't dream of leaving now. My concern, odd as it may seem—odd as I've begun to believe it to be—is for you. I wanted to hear from you the truth behind all these 'accidents' about which everyone makes the most awful insinuations."

Eyes once molten silver went to ice, but Gray's voice remained calm. He didn't want others threatened by his choices, particularly not Elizabeth, and must dissuade her from pursuing this topic. The curs behind his danger, he'd find and handle himself. "You wanted to be alone with me for the sake of this boring foolishness?" He mournfully shook his dark head and the lighter hair at his temples glowed with the daylight growing stronger outside the window. "How disappointing."

His hand slowly slid from one shoulder down between the gown's unfastened edges and over her bare spine. Liz trembled under the intimate caress and gasped when he drew her near.

Taking advantage of her parted lips, Gray claimed a devastating kiss. Lifting his mouth a breath above hers, he whispered, "We have much more interesting things to occupy our private time—when the time is right."

In the next moment, with a wicked smile, he freed the innocent tease limply holding cloth against her breasts. He backed from the room, dazed turquoise eyes watching until he closed the door between them.

* * *

Liz's eyes widened as Ellison proffered a salver piled high with a great many formal calling cards and envelopes addressed in elegant script.

"Invitations I believe, Your Grace," Ellison stated the obvious, impressed by the duchess's genuine surprise.

Sunlight falling through the morning room's long windows burned the brighter on vivid hair as Liz nodded, accepting the bounty with wonder. "Yes . . . but so many."

"I am reliably informed that this is a mere taste—" Ellison permitted a small smile to crease his normally impassive face. "—of what's to come for the Toast of the Season. And attaining that accolade, if I may say so, is a signal accomplishment." The butler was pleased. This unconventional bride had earned his approval the night she'd insisted on putting the duke's safety before her own care and comfort. He was certain that, faced with the same circumstances, Lady Euphemia, her stepdaughter, or any of their noble and overprotected acquaintances would have either gone into hysterics or suffered a fit of the vapors.

Ellison's statement gave Liz a secret delight, but she nibbled her lower lip to still the curve threatening to betray something of which she felt she ought to be ashamed. After all, for years she'd found fault in women whose lives revolved around social events. How strange then that she had reached such an incredible pinnacle of social success—admired by a royal prince and sought after by the British aristocracy. Stranger yet was her guilty joy in it.

"Elizabeth—" Filling the half-open doorway, a disapproving Lady Euphemia curtly broke the warm exchange. "A respectable, experienced lady's maid has been at liberty since the countess of Nexton passed away last month. I contacted her after your unexpected arrival. She has agreed to serve you during the Season and perhaps, if you prove suited, will continue on after we retreat to the country."

Without waiting for the American to respond, Lady Euphemia opened the door wider and motioned another woman to join her inside.

Smiling automatically, Liz met the stony gaze of the prune-faced female who entered to stand primly before her. The woman was, as Liz had feared after arriving at Brandt House, nearly a clone of Euphemia's maid, Mrs. Simms.

"Elizabeth, this is Mrs. Smythe, who as I've just told you has excellent references and experience as lady's maid to a woman of impeccable background."

Liz politely nodded, but the woman gave the briefest curtsy marginally acceptable while examining a possible mistress as if it were she who would choose.

Beneath a gaze utterly critical of apparently the world in general and her in particular, Liz began to steam. Subjected to what could only be viewed as an insult, she accepted this action as Euphemia's demonstration of her intention to continue holding domestic control.

"Mrs. Smythe, as I have already engaged a lady's maid, I must apologize for the waste of your valuable time." Liz kept her voice soft, but its inflexible core was clear. "Had I earlier known of this plan, I'd have prevented this unproductive visit." Liz's excuse was a rebuke for the earstwhile mistress of Brandt House who immediately interrupted.

"Mrs. Smythe, would you be so kind as to wait a few moments for me to privately work out this misunderstanding?"

When Mrs. Smythe stiffly nodded assent to Euphemia's request, Liz thought it a miracle her neck didn't break. For a servant, the woman seemed able to match or exceed the proud condescension of any aristocrat.

"Ellison—" Livid beneath her icy self-control, Lady Euphemia's air of command was pronounced. "Please take Mrs. Smythe to the green drawing room."

Ellison led the prospective lady's maid into the corridor and quietly closed the door. Once they were alone, Euphemia stiffly turned on Liz and with harsh skepticism demanded further details.

"Pray tell, from whom and where did you locate your 'lady's maid'?"

"Why, here in Brandt House, of course." Turquoise eyes widened innocently but remained as unblinking as the slate gray they steadily met while Liz responded with cloying sweetness. "In attending to my needs since I arrived in London, Annie has proven to be precisely what I seek in a personal servant."

"Annie? How preposterous! She is in no way properly trained to fulfill such duties."

"Really? I'm amazed. I'd have thought you held her skills in some esteem as it was *you* who assigned her to me."

"Well, yes, but . . . but . . ." Euphemia fairly sputtered, finding herself in the unaccustomed position of having to defend her actions. Lifting her chin high enough to patronize her foe, she sneered an excuse. "It was a temporary arrangement."

And that, Liz realized, was meant to put an end to the issue. It did, but not the one neatly envisioned by the speaker.

"Your temporary arrangement provided an excellent trial period, and I thank you for the opportunity to test our compatibility as well as her skills. It worked out wonderfully well. For that reason, I discussed the matter with Mrs. Ellison. She agrees Annie is of an age for training to become the perfect lady's maid. Annie has no habits ingrained by years of service elsewhere, habits which I would have to see changed to conform with my preferences. Such a difficult task, don't you agree?" In reality, it was the likelihood of allegiances to others—to the one who'd secured her the position—that made the prospect of any maid chosen by Euphemia disagreeable to Liz.

"You've talked with Mrs. Ellison on the matter?" Euphemia inwardly seethed, and that angry disgust was apparent in her rigid stance.

"Of course." Liz promptly nodded. "Changing Annie's status without discussing the matter with the woman responsible for all female servants would be deplorable and as unacceptable as altering household arrangements without first consulting the one charged with their management."

Euphemia went white and Liz knew she'd struck an important blow. The other woman had plainly felt it unnecessary to consider the housekeeper's possible response to Mrs. Smythe's invasion of Brandt House.

"I'll tell Mrs. Smythe of *our* decision before sorting through the day's mail." Euphemia held her hand out in a silent yet imperious demand for the overburdened salver still residing on Liz's lap. "I can't imagine what Ellison was thinking to burden you with this duty of *mine,* but you may be sure I'll speak to him on the matter."

"Thank you for your concern, Euphemia, but as the majority are addressed to me and the others to my husband, Ellison took precisely the right action. And, although I appreciate your offer to relieve me of a task you seem to find onerous, I believe I'll give myself the pleasure of opening them."

Liz lifted one creamy envelope and slit it open with the silver knife provided for the chore. Her stated intention to leave Euphemia the position of political hostess had been, and still was, sincere. It was only that the woman would push her into the shadows, overwhelm her if she could. She couldn't and Liz meant for the woman to accept that as reality. But as a sop to her vanity and oblique reassurance of her unthreatened position, Liz added without looking up, "However, as I'm certain the invitations are meant to include both you and Dru, I'll gladly send them along to you once I've noted those I choose to accept and have entered them into my social calendar."

Liz glanced up with a sweet smile in time to see the older woman huffily leaving the room. Before she had accomplished more than sorting calling cards from envelopes of the most expensive type, she was interrupted again.

After peeking furtively inside, Dru slipped quickly into the room, motioning another to follow.

"We must talk with you . . . privately." The nervous girl dropped onto a corner of the nearest couch while Timothy settled with more grace into the chair on Liz's far side.

Dru's words were a repetition of those Liz had spoken to Gray that morning. She suspected the purpose of the pair's arrival and wished she could give them a more positive response than Gray had given her.

"It's about Timothy," Dru began, wringing her hands.

Liz nodded, accepting the expected subject before turning toward the young man in question. "You want me to believe you'd nothing to do with these 'accidents' threatening your cousin's life, yes?"

Timothy nodded, mouth compressed in frustration against an impending accusation.

Perversely, in Timothy's stoic expectation of her rejection of his plea Liz found reason to trust. A trust strengthened by his failure to immediately offer protestations of innocence in a neat package of believable alibis for each occasion. The answer she gave them was neither Dru's hoped for acceptance nor the refusal to believe that Timothy so clearly thought was imminent.

"If you are not responsible, then help me discover

who *is.*" It was a frank challenge for them to prove their claim, one she had reason to suppose them brave enough to undertake, considering their invasion of the Cardingtons' ball.

To Liz's satisfaction, without an instant's hesitation the pair enthusiastically agreed to do anything that might draw the culprit lurking amidst shadows into harsh light.

"But," Timothy grimaced regretfully. "I've already spent countless hours striving to do that very thing to no good purpose. Who, I've asked myself over and over, who would want to kill Uncle Gray? Who would benefit from his demise—besides me?"

The young man's bleak expression of defeat was another fine, unconscious defense. Only a talented actor could feign such sincerity. Perhaps that's what he was. Liz reminded herself that she barely knew Timothy, and though once proud of her ability to judge character, this matter was too important to risk complete faith so soon.

"Beyond a lack of specific villains, did you come to any conclusions at all?" Liz asked with an encouraging smile.

Sunlight picked out the lighter streaks in the young man's hair as he hesitantly nodded. "Only the unsubstantiated belief that, as Gray is an important member of Parliament and committed to several sensitive issues, these attacks might be politically motivated. But I have no idea specifically who is involved or even which issue."

"That possible motive makes perfect sense," Liz slowly agreed. "Five dangerous mishaps and yet Gray remains healthy. This surely means either our villains are remarkably inept or . . ."

"They were warnings," Dru calmly announced, certain of her conclusion.

Timothy murmured agreement.

"I'm thankful you see the situation as I do." Liz

smiled but added a sobering note. "As we believe Gray's enemies have thus far purposely refrained from seriously injuring him, we must remain aware that they may run out of patience."

The pair who'd come seeking Liz's help now looked more gloomy than when they'd arrived. Liz attempted to lighten the mood with a more positive observation.

"If politics are involved, and it seems a logical assumption, then we're fortunate to have a direct route to the information we may need to identify possible suspects."

"What?" Timothy and Dru looked at Liz as suspiciously as if the wicked witch from some childhood tale had just turned her into a horny toad.

Liz laughed. Her meaning was so obvious she was surprised they hadn't instantly caught it. "Not what but who. And that who is you, Timothy."

"Me?" Timothy's initial blank stare narrowed into disillusionment while a querulous tone strangled his response. "And I foolishly thought you'd begun to believe me innocent."

"You're right. I do believe you. Leastways, enough to ask you to use your position as secretary to the House of Lords to hunt through political records for clues to the source of Gray's danger."

Like dawn brightening the horizon, clouds of doubt cleared from the couple's faces.

"Anything, *anything* to help," Timothy promised, leaping to his feet. "I'll start today and spend every free moment sorting through transcripts from last session, listing the sensitive bills Gray was working on when the accidents began—and those who opposed his position."

"Then we're off to a great beginning," Liz said.

She beamed at Timothy's suggestion. Without such aid, her only source would've been Society's gossip mongers and their odd tidbits of questionable reliability. But even that limitation wouldn't have stopped her investigation, though it might have forced such slow progress that the answer came too late to protect Gray.

It wasn't as if she'd fail to also avail herself of the avenue opened by her social success. Her guilty enjoyment of the mad whirl of dinners, parties, and balls now had a worthy purpose.

"Once we've some sense of where to look, despite the battles my insistence may bring with Lady Euphemia, I will arrange our social calendars to put Dru and me into closer contact with our suspect's wives and daughters."

Liz straightened, determination glowing in blue eyes as she again emphasized their undertaking's importance and the need for haste. "We must hurry to find the culprits before they overcome their apparent ineptness, arrange Gray's murder, and see Timothy charged for their crime."

Liz's neophyte strategy to protect Gray by revealing the source of his danger received assistance from an unexpected quarter following her return from an evening at the opera and the delightful supper after.

"Your Grace," Annie nervously whispered while undoing the multitude of buttons and hooks fastening her mistress into a gown of heavy bronze-green silk.

"Yes?" Liz softly encouraged the usually cheery, talkative girl gone awkward. The silence lengthened and Annie's color rose before Liz added, "You can say anything to me, Annie?"

"Yes, ma'am." Lifting fingers whose fumbling had only succeeded in making the task more difficult, Annie took a deep breath and began. "When the wheel came off the carriage . . ."

Liz went stiff at mention of the accident. Pulling gently away, she turned to take Annie's trembling hands between her own. "You've learned something about the cause?"

A wisp of pale brown hair fell forward as Annie nodded. "The linchpin was loosened . . . apurpose."

It was what Liz had believed from the first, but having it confirmed could make a difference. "Are you certain?"

"That's what the coachman told my Jeremy. Although Mr. Ellison stood in as coachman that night, the missing linchpin was found. That discovery gave Mr. Durst a chance to look the linchpin over and he found it in right condition. So he says it was impossible for the linchpin to come off without a deal of help."

"Perhaps one of the grooms failed to fasten it tightly enough to prevent such an accident?" Liz didn't believe it but felt she had to suggest it if only to hear a denial.

Annie violently shook her head. "Couldn't be so. The carriages are checked over most particular like before leaving the stable. It would've been seen. Jeremy swears he checked it himself that night."

"You know this Jeremy well?" The heat of the expected denial and the warmth Annie gave the name betrayed a fondness for the young man.

Annie's blush deepened. "He's a groom—and being trained as a coachman. We've been walking out together for nigh on two months."

"Ah, then I'm sure we can trust his word." Liz flashed her maid a teasing grin.

Annie earnestly agreed then went on to underscore the meaning. "Thing is, to be so nearly perfect when found, the linchpin must've been thoroughly loosened afore it came out . . . so thoroughly that the carriage couldn't have gone far without it falling out."

In case her mistress had failed to catch the significance of this announcement, Annie added, "It means the duke's life wasn't ever in real danger."

Certain her maid had expected this reported fact to reassure her, Liz lightly squeezed the hands still in her own. And it did affirm the assumption made earlier. The "accident" so carefully planned had been meant as a warning.

"But how could the linchpin have been loosened between Gray's arrival and departure from the ball?" Liz murmured her thoughts aloud while turning to face a cheval glass and letting Annie return to the task of a half-undone gown.

"Don't know." Annie answered the rhetorical question not realizing one hadn't been expected. "But if I ask Jeremy quiet like I think he could figure it out . . . if you like?"

Annie's saucy grin was back as she leaned to the side and met Liz's eyes in the mirror.

"I would appreciate it very, very much." A slow smile warmed turquoise eyes.

CHAPTER 9

Pausing in the hallway just outside an open library door, Gray was surprised to find the room he considered his private domain already occupied. Afternoon sunlight drifting through massive windows was more brightly reflected by fiery hair than by the highly polished surface of the desk where Elizabeth's elbows were braced, steadying her head between slender hands. With face lowered, she looked to be either asleep or in prayer. Gray's customary stern expression softened at the sight of short tendrils which, though once properly upswept, had broken free to caress fingers and cheeks the hue of warm honey. She looked like an innocent child. But then, Gray wryly reminded himself, despite her two decades, his virgin bride was nearly that. However, if he had his way and he would, not for long.

Ill-timed thoughts of her had disrupted his concentration when he should've been addressing important issues or devising methods to defeat dangerous foes. He was certain rational perspective would be restored and the breach of his emotional citadel healed once he'd claimed her. And it must be done soon. Yet, though an even more serious danger lay in the unique beauty's invasion of his dreams, his experience lay in brief passionate affairs quick to flame but just as quickly reduced to cold ashes. He wanted, must have, a more lasting relationship with his wife. Despite a growing impatience to possess the source of a never before experienced delight, he hesitated to rush her.

Gray moved forward, footfalls muffled by the thick Aubusson carpet. A newspaper! She was poring over a newspaper. Not the section addressing Society's latest *ondits,* but rather the political pages. He was more surprised than he'd been in years . . . or at least since the night they'd met and she'd refused to wed him . . . or since he'd found her dancing with the prince . . . or . . . A sardonic smile tilted one corner of his lips. She'd delivered one surprise after another since that first dinner in New York, and it seemed a habit she was unlikely to abandon.

She twisted around at the sound of a cleared throat shockingly near. Eyes as startled as those of a hunter's trapped prey flew to a gaze softened into gray mists.

The man had come upon her unawares and caught her lost in the newspaper's contents, reading far more than the society pages acceptable for genteel ladies. Hands palm flat on the desk top, Liz rose, irritated by the heat flooding from throat to cheeks while she waited for another of Gray's cold rebukes.

Another? Of a sudden Liz realized her husband hadn't reproached her for anything since the night of the Cardingtons' ball. That fact, rather than comforting her, increased her uneasiness. He'd not only failed to censure her but, far more often than the constant flow of Society gossip would have her believe was the habit of the reserved man, he'd accompanied her on the hectic round of social events. Blocking a flattering number of potential escorts, including Lawrence, the Prince, and, amazingly, even the venerable Sir David, Gray had escorted her everywhere. They'd attended dinners and dance parties, weekend teas, and rides through the area of the park where aristocrats displayed beautiful horses or smart vehicles and the skill to manage them while curious crowds of onlookers of all stations watched.

Her uneasiness was roused not by his actions but by her own response to them. He'd been a most attentive, wryly amusing, gently protective partner—and a companion for whose company she found herself longing during odd hours of the day or night. Her fears for his safety had intensified in direct proportion to her increasing care for him. She worried that while distracted by his nearness, she might've missed any number of clues important to her investigation of past mishaps. Her only comfort lay in the certainty that Dru and Timothy continued the search for clues. The pair were so dedicated to the cause that a Timothy going through records was rarely seen, and Dru remained understanding of how seldom they could see each other, although she was often compelled to spend a deal of time with Lord Poxwell.

"I see you've been reading the *Times.*" It was a simple statement rather than question or criticism while, having noticed the important file one of her palms had rested on as she rose, he feigned unconcern as he bent to lift it. He absently tapped the file's edges to ensure no glimpse of its contents were revealed.

Liz observed his action and assumed the file to be a part of secret political documents. She lent it no significance beyond subconsciously registering the coarse grain of paper briefly glimpsed poking out from one side of the file and wondering that Parliament apparently used such poor quality.

"I read it most days." Her steady answer was a challenge for Gray to forbid the act.

Since the day her success at Miss Brown's School had won her an independence few women enjoyed, Liz had read every page of whatever newspaper was available. Her first morning in Brandt House, she'd asked the parlormaid to bring a current newspaper. Instead, Lady Euphemia had descended to deliver a scandalized lecture on the unsuitability of well-bred women sullying their minds with worthless publications circulating distasteful yellow journalism.

Liz had to admit it was true that the newspapers she'd read despite her sister-in-law's strictures were full of wild reports of anarchists, murders, and other foul deeds. But they also reported the political issues being raised and argued in Parliament. With exaggerated casualness Ellison—who'd become an ally since the carriage accident—had divulged the fact that newspapers, once ironed to set the ink, were deposited every morning in the library. Almost daily since then she'd crept into Gray's private haven to avail herself of them. In the beginning she'd constantly felt driven to glance guiltily over her shoulder, but after almost three undisturbed weeks of reading the newspaper from front to back, she'd grown careless.

"You seemed engrossed. What did you find to interest you?" Gray had perfect vision and could see exactly what she'd been reading but wanted to know how she'd answer. With feminine dithering? With the excuse of an unsuccessful search for the write-up of the previous night's dance and what lady wore which gown? A moment later he admitted he should have known better.

Once again color flooded Liz's face, irritating her no end. He knew what she was reading. Moreover, she was aware that he realized she knew he did.

Gray's name often appeared in the political pages, and Liz had found herself impressed by his views and the causes he supported. Today's newspaper contained the complete text of his most recent speech on one of the House of Lords' continuing investigations. She'd been reading that speech whose subject, she'd no doubt, every peer of the realm would go to great lengths to prevent his womenfolk from knowing existed. It was bad enough that they might one day be forced to accept the nature of the demimondaine's profession. Never would a gentlemen allow the sheltered females of his family to learn of the possibility that young girls were unwillingly sold into houses of ill repute. Raised on and fully involved in the management of a ranch, Liz was not so oversheltered as the women of the British aristocracy, but even she had been shocked by the report of a practice termed "white slavery."

"You're going to see that it stops, aren't you?" Liz waved toward the printed speech. Never one to avert her eyes from unpleasant truths or to cringe at the possibility of inciting anger, she figuratively leapt into the subject's midst and from there awaited his response, defiance in turquoise eyes.

She looked a stubborn child, and Gray couldn't help grinning despite the serious subject of her question.

"It is what I intend," he began, forcing control over his face, although nothing could smother the laughter in silver eyes. "But success depends on a great many more than me alone." That solemn fact quashed the last of his amusement.

"Other members of the House of Lords." Liz quietly expanded his statement.

"As well as the House of Commons and the police force. Even, I fear, public awareness of the problem will be necessary to bring the vile trade in human flesh to an end."

Liz looked at him quizzically. End the trade in human flesh? That sounded rather more encompassing than the description of the white slavery given in the newspaper. Did he mean . . . ?

"No." Gray read her unspoken question, amazed again by this unconventional virgin's awareness of matters no other would've been exposed to even in the abstract. "I don't purpose that it's possible to end a profession that has existed since biblical times. But I hope to be a part of rallying others to the cause of seeing that no one be physically forced into prostitution."

If anyone had ever suggested to Gray that one day he would hold a conversation on this subject with his wife, he'd have strongly suggested them ready for consignment to Bedlam. Yet, he was coming to expect the unexpected from Liz. And—he admitted for the first time without cringing at the danger to his efforts to remain emotionally aloof—finding his concerted effort to court his own wife remarkably enjoyable.

Listening to Gray speaking on a subject obviously important to him, Liz wondered if he'd ever shared such talks with his first wife. The silent question brought a stab of jealousy. In response to her curiosity, Annie had told Liz about Camellia, a sweet and fragile woman of pale blond hair and gentle brown eyes. Liz had instantly recognized Camellia as the reverse of herself. As Camellia came from an aristocratic yet poor family, Gray had clearly chosen the woman for what she was. Therefore, he must find delicate blondes most attractive and, as she was the direct opposite, Gray had spoken only the truth when he'd admitted early on that without trickery he would never have chosen her.

Suddenly realizing a hush had fallen, and certain he could tell her little more on the subject than had the eloquent words printed in the newspaper, Liz judiciously shifted the subject. "I read your speech on the Irish home rule issue last week. How do you propose to put your solution into motion?"

"First, it's not *my* solution, merely the one I support." Gray accepted the change of subject with a wry smile, acknowledging his wife's inexperienced attempt at diplomacy as he laid the file still in his hands aside and motioned her to join him on the small couch in front of long windows.

Soon he found himself earnestly debating the issue with her and discovered that she not only understood this and other issues but also that she had strong feelings on each. Although they did not agree in every instance, he couldn't help but respect her well-thought-out opinions and admire her sharp mind.

"Then shall we agree to disagree?" Gray asked the lovely woman. "Let's declare peace on the matter . . . at least within the walls of our home."

Liz, enjoying the rare opportunity to discuss important matters with a man as an equal, and feeling the invisible barriers between them fading, took the opportunity to pose a question she'd long wanted answered.

"Why have you spent years avoiding social events whenever possible?"

Dark brows arched in surprise. "Have I failed to escort you anywhere you wished to go—parliamentary sessions permitting?"

Liz gave a quick shake to the bright head glowing with sunlight falling from behind. "No, but it's the fact that you have which encourages so many to tell me how unusual it is."

Gray saw that he'd no choice but to share a part, definitely not all, of a very personal conflict he'd never discussed with another living soul. "I'm surprised your informants didn't also mention that prior to these last ten years, I cut a notable swathe through Society."

For the first time, Liz remembered the duchess of Etherton's broad hints of Gray's past reputation as a rake, but she didn't speak.

"As a young and untamed youth I lived so wild a life that I horrified my sainted father. . . ." Gray bit off words beginning to resonate with painful resentment. He would not continue, risking the revelation of a scene he'd spent years striving to block from his memory. "Suffice it to say, I disappointed him while he was alive, but after his too early demise, when I inherited the title and its responsibilities, I turned my energies to pursuits more productive than parties, hunts, and games of chance."

Liz had heard him earlier break off what he'd begun to say and knew there was far more to his story. But, not wanting to see this moment of private harmony ended by pushing for more, she impulsively set out to share her own reason for disdaining the social whirl.

"For my first ten years I lived a simple but very happy life with my parents on the Double H Ranch. Then my father's railroad made him an extremely wealthy man. Mama wanted to live in New York and we moved there. Then she wanted even more to become a part of its society. But no matter what my sweet mama did to impress them, the Knickerbocker matrons rejected her because Papa's money was too recently earned." Liz slowly shook her head again while her expression turned melancholy. "They may as well have aimed a rifle at her heart. Their rejection killed her."

In her voice Gray heard the depth of a long-repressed anguish. It seemed that, despite very different birthrights, their situations were strikingly similar.

"As my father said that first night, it was Mama who on her deathbed insisted that I take her place in the struggle to break through doors closed against her. And it was Mama's plea for Papa to see me properly wed that resulted in the trickery that landed you with me."

Her last statement made it clear to Gray that she'd absolved him of any part in that trickery. Yet his pleasure in her admission was tempered by both the girl's honest sorrow for the long ago loss of a loved one and the ache in words revealing suppressed guilt for resenting her mother's legacy of expectations. Seeing narrow shoulders droop just as did the corners of peach lips, Gray gently drew her against his broad chest.

Already burdened with increasing apprehension for Gray's safety and the tension of a constant struggle to fit into an unfamiliar sphere, Liz felt herself descending from contentment with this quiet time alone in Gray's company into a rarely permitted gloom. Sad memories of her frustrated mother joined to recent thoughts of what a poor substitute she was for Camellia proved too much for Liz. She snuggled deeper into the solace of Gray's embrace.

Gray rested his cheek atop the coil of her fiery mane and whispered, "Think how proud your mother would be of her daughter—the Toast of London Society."

Liz had repeatedly considered how surprised her fellow classmates at Miss Brown's School would be by her current position. But this was the first time she'd stopped to realize how she'd excelled at becoming the social success her mother had dreamed of for her. It brought emotional turmoil to a boil that bubbled over in hot liquid trickling from turquoise eyes.

Without thought, Gray bent to brush away each silent tear with his lips. Letting one hand cup her nape, while fiery tendrils clung to his fingers, his mouth shifted to lightly brush across petal-soft lips that parted on a trembling breath.

Suddenly aware of just how close they were, Liz attempted to pull back as the ever unwelcome rush of hot color flooded her cheeks. She didn't want his pity! For more than a fortnight they'd moved through the Season's whirl together—putting a brave face on what, he'd frankly admitted at the outset, he regarded as an unfortunate marriage. Since the morning she'd invited him into her bedroom to unsuccessfully insist he speak of his danger, he'd sought no closer contact with her than required by obligatory dances. It now seemed to her that he viewed the story she'd shared as no more than an effort on her part to appear pathetic and play so effectively on his sympathies as to win his intimate comfort. It hadn't been and she wouldn't. Liz renewed her struggles . . . to no avail.

"No, don't withdraw from me. You've been doing it for weeks and it's time to stop." Gray put a final end to his wife's unexpectedly fervent battle by shifting her to lay across hard thighs.

In this new and shockingly intimate position, Liz went still, but though turquoise eyes remained determinedly focused on hands joined tight together in her lap, heated memories of past embraces betrayed her intent to continue resisting.

With one strong hand, Gray gently nudged her chin to rise. "Lilibet, look at me."

Liz was a strong-willed woman but knew her self-control was in a sad state of disrepair when, unable to deny his dark velvet call, she glanced up at the fascinating man entirely too near and fell into glowing silver pools.

Even while sternly reminding himself that both the time and place were entirely wrong, Gray gently smoothed back the bright, escaped tendrils framing over-warm cheeks and heart-shaped face. Sorely strained patience had worn too thin, his actions were beyond control—and he couldn't lie to himself that he cared. Cradling the back of her head, he lowered his mouth to claim sweet lips for whose nectar he had continuously longed since his first taste.

Burning with fiery pleasures only this man could rouse, Liz melted into his powerful arms until, inhibitions scorched to useless ashes, she was driven to seek more and recklessly arched against him.

Lost to time and place, Gray crushed his enticing wife's generous curves more tightly to him while deepening a kiss that became long and slow and hard.

She moaned beneath its sensuous demand, and shudders of wild excitement trembled through her delicious, yielding body.

In helpless response to his wicked temptations, Liz instinctively writhed, brushing her bounty across the hard planes of his chest. Willingly sinking ever deeper into a dizzying whirlpool of fiery sensations, she wrapped her arms about its steady center, savoring the strength of his broad back.

His mouth left hers to rain fire across eyelids and cheeks. Head falling back, Liz laid the long, tempting line of her elegant throat vulnerable to a predator's threat. Gray's lips instantly followed its path, dazing his quarry with the wild sparks they left in their wake. While applying a burning torment of kisses to the underside of her chin and throat, he struggled with a multitude of tiny buttons, determined to unfasten the high collar and bodice to lay bare for him a measure of the silky skin beneath.

Liz mindlessly twined her fingers into cool black strands and tugged the wicked source of such hot pleasures nearer. At last Gray won limited success and opened the modest bodice wide enough for his hungry mouth to explore a severely limited expanse of never before sampled flesh. A small, sweet moan escaped Liz's tight throat while the sensation of a melting fire rushed through her veins, drowning the last shred of sanity. Overcome by an unfamiliar desperation, she clasped him more tightly to her shivering body.

"Well, I never!" Euphemia huffed from the open library door.

Feeling as if he was being rent in two, Gray pulled back and for the first time in his life looked at his sister with unshuttered distaste. "No, sister, I dare say you haven't."

"I know I've urged you to do your duty and provide Ashleigh with an heir, but really, Gray, I'd think you'd save your distasteful desires for the demimonde."

Saying nothing further, Gray sat up with a mocking smile but pity in silver eyes for Euphemia as he straightened his cravat and adjusted his sleeves.

Oozing disapproval, Euphemia stared at the woman next to him. That Elizabeth had clearly enjoyed what good women endured as their duty proved her low background.

"I assume you had a reason for coming into my study unannounced," Gray at last said in a cool challenge for her to provide an adequate excuse.

"We are expected at the St. Johns for dinner this evening and as no one had seen either of you for some little while, I took it upon myself to remind you of the commitment in time to see you properly attired."

Slate gray eyes moved from shamelessly disheveled red hair down a shockingly loosened gown to the toes of shoes inappropriate for evening wear.

From the pocket of his sober vest, Gray pulled the watch at the end of a glittering gold chain and solemnly consulted it. "We have more than adequate time to prepare, Euphemia. But to ease your concerns, we'll withdraw to our *private* rooms and begin."

As Gray followed his still unsullied bride up the sweeping stairway, he admired the gentle sway of her hips. Then, to his own surprise, he realized he was as drawn by her sharp mind and bold personality as by the fiery physical appearance he found all too exciting. He was growing ever more impatient with waiting to fully claim her as his wife. A reality increasing his irritation with the need to meet with Sir David again tonight after the dinner at the St. Johns.

Why the old family friend had become such a stumbling block to the passage of the bill most important to Gray was an annoying curiosity. David had earlier agreed to support the bill addressing white slavery only to first insist on so many meetings that its progress through Parliament had slowed to a snail's pace. Gray tried to exercise understanding of the aging man's old-fashioned views and patiently explain the same points over and over and over again. The thought of that repeated action's need, added to a months-long but fruitless search for a missing document, put such a dark scowl on Gray's face that it was a fortunate thing an embarrassed Liz did not look back before disappearing into her suite.

CHAPTER 10

The sizable ballroom at Kimball House was full to overflowing with the cream of Society. While in the background dancers revolved like a kaleidoscope of colors three people stood near a fountain of fruit punch—Lawrence, earl of Hayton, with the duke and duchess of Ashleigh. Gray, stern in impeccable black dress tails, was the perfect foil for his wife, a dream in peach satin moire that should've clashed with her hair but instead highlighted its brilliant hue.

"Then you'll come?" Lawrence asked with a charming smile as he glanced from Gray to the woman he persisted in calling Lizzy while taking joy in knowing it annoyed her husband. Considering how the enforced closeness of so many seemed to shrink the ballroom, no one could criticize him for standing near the radiant figure in peach.

An off-season weekend shooting party at Hayton Lodge was the last thing in which Gray wished to participate. He'd been politely trapped into agreeing and was irritated by that fact and by the man's contrived proximity to Elizabeth. It was this irritation that hardened pale eyes to ice despite the forced curve of his lips.

"Knowing what a stickler you've become, Grayson, let me calm your possible fears of impropriety." Hayton's eyes had taken on a taunting gleam. "My great-aunt Helena, the bishop of Wrexton's widow, will be acting as my hostess and lending her spotless reputation as a woman of irreproachable virtue to my little gathering."

"But what quarry can you hunt at this time of year?" Liz dove into the strain between the two men, as aware of her husband's growing vexation as of her own uneasiness in the earl's ever-hovering nearness. "Surely not ducks or pheasants during their nesting phase?" She rattled on while inwardly castigating herself for acting like a chattering simpleton. "Indeed, in Wyoming we don't go bird hunting in the spring at all." Liz was hideously aware that she'd shocked the men, suspected she'd even insulted them, but couldn't prevent herself from continuing. "But on a crisp autumn morning I do enjoy a good hunt."

"Our prey will be wood pigeons, a nuisance bird with the nasty habit of disturbing other birds' nests and feeding on their eggs." Lawrence smoothly recovered from his surprise and, amused by the woman's claimed experience in a man's sport, thought to call her bluff. "What gun do you use to hunt birds in Wyoming?"

Liz resented the note of condescension in his question, as if she were merely a precocious child playing at adult games. What depth of skill could this nearly effete man with his too-cultivated good looks possess?

"I've tried other rifles, but I still prefer the single-shot, breech-loading Springfield that's used by the U.S. Cavalry to fight Indians on the frontier. Indeed, used in my area of Wyoming." Liz said it for shock value and won what she sought. And yet it was perfectly true—though the Indian troubles had come to an end after the Sioux were driven out five years earlier.

Gray suspected her intention and repressed a grin for his feisty bride's tactics. He didn't for a moment believe her claimed hunting experience, but he'd come to delight in her talent for turning the tables on anyone she viewed as an opponent . . . a talent whose victim he'd been more than once. Unfortunately, the earl was not easily blocked.

"I hope you brought your favorite rifle across the ocean with you." Lawrence responded immediately. "I'm certain we men would be delighted to have you join us in the hunt—a woman's participation would be a welcome change to the boorish company of an all-male party."

The women of his class often participated in riding to hounds and a hardy—not to mention eccentric—few took part in bird shoots but never, in his experience, one so young and attractive. In the next instant, he realized the description "eccentric" fit Lizzy like a fine chamois glove. Beyond a momentary irritation with his failure to immediately see this truth, he found satisfaction in the many possibilities it offered.

Liz promptly answered with honest regret. "I sincerely wish I'd thought to bring my rifle when I left Wyoming in answer to my father's call, little knowing I'd be whisked into marriage and a transatlantic journey. Alas, it remains at the Double H Ranch."

Little knowing? Lawrence's eyes glowed. What a curious statement and deserving of further investigation. Better and better.

"I, too, am sorry your own piece is not here." Lawrence seized this unexpected opportunity. Were Lizzy to participate in the hunt, Grayson would be knocked off kilter . . . an ever welcome development. "But if you'd be willing, Lizzy, in my collection I've several rifles that sound the match of yours, and I'd be honored if you'd take them in hand to join us." It was spoken as a dare, one he suspected the American duchess couldn't resist.

Reading the unspoken challenge in the earl's smooth words and gleaming gaze, Liz agreed without hesitation. "I would love to see how you English go about the sport and happily accept your offer."

Looking between snapping turquoise eyes and the earl's half-sneer, Gray rued this escalation of tension in the coming event he already dreaded. Best get her away from this man before worse befell them.

"We've been here for hours, but her company is so urgently sought by so many that this poor husband has yet to be granted a turn on the floor." The blatant note of pride underlying this mock lament surprised even Gray. "I came looking for my wife to claim the privilege of leading her into the next waltz. As one has just begun, I pray you to pardon me, Hayton, for stealing my Lilibet."

Although at every social event she'd attended Liz had been mobbed by admirers—most amusingly fervent but others embarrassingly persistent—she was uneasy with this frank public statement of her triumph. Still, when Gray spoke that musical name in his deep voice, Liz's discomfort faded into insignificance as she sank into his thrall.

Gray looked down at Liz with a teasing smile that stole her breath. "Take pity upon your neglected spouse?"

Taken captive by a silver gaze, Liz flowed into his arms, her own eyes melting into misty pools as he twirled her into the dance. Though they'd danced together many times during the past few weeks, Liz still felt the same excitement in standing so close to him, held in his arms as they moved to the music. With one of his strong hands riding lightly at her waist, the other curled around hers and her free hand resting atop a broad shoulder, she could feel the warmth of his body, sense his intimidating strength.

But the cause of her heart's fluttering wasn't fear and she knew it. As he gracefully drew her with him into the waltz's rhythm, she lost the ability to block an alarming truth. She completely and unconditionally loved Grayson.

At that admission Liz stumbled, but Gray caught her close, and fortunately at that moment the music ended. Though she'd been struggling to suppress conscious awareness of her emotion for him, it so stunned Liz that she hardly noticed as he urged her toward french doors. They opened onto the porch, and the night coolness felt welcome after the stuffy warmth of a dancing crowd.

The flickering candles inside scattered Chinese lanterns cast interesting patterns of light and shadow over the flagstone terrace. In a gloom sweetly scented by roses blooming on the trellis to one side, they paused, leaned against a marble balustrade and gazed out across a small, walled garden moon-silvered and tranquil.

"Sometimes in the midst of all that festive noise and motion, I find a need to escape and seek a moment's peace to regain my balance." Gray's crooked smile was self-derisive, but Liz answered it with quiet understanding.

"From start to finish, I wish I could remain at home in peace and avoid the jostle, the necessity to constantly guard against . . ." Liz's words faded as she realized how naturally she'd spoken of Brandt House as home and feared what further such revelations might trip her into laying bare feelings she'd only just acknowledged to herself, feelings she certainly would not willingly betray to a man who rued their relationship as the sorry result of trickery.

Gray nodded and half turned toward his companion with a gently teasing smile. "Yes, you told me of your preference for the peace of country life—and I believed you only to be shocked by finding you at the

Cardingtons' ball. And look at you now . . . the Toast of the Season. Incredible."

Liz's laughter rang out like clear bell tones. If Gray could put aside the anger roused by that action to tease her, then she could respond in the same light vein. "You couldn't possibly find it more incredible than I do."

As she spoke, from the corner of her eyes she caught a furtive movement in the shadows behind the trellis. Instantly spinning full about, she leaned back against the balustrade, both easing her surreptitious examination of suspicious shadows and holding Gray's full attention while with a gay smile she made a bright plea.

"Come back in and dance with me again?"

"I thought we'd just agreed to share quiet moments together out here." Gray saw her abrupt wish to return to the ballroom as a desperate plan for flight just as prey sensing danger would try to flee the hunger. This he saw as a good sign, another welcome signal that his strategy to win her was near its goal. Tonight? Yes, tonight would see an end to the merry chase through which she'd led him.

"I promise you I can find pursuits far more enjoyable than dancing." He slowly reached out to pull her close and nuzzle her ear.

Caught between the thrill of his caresses and the sense of curious eyes heavy upon them, Liz's forehead dropped to a broad shoulder in embarrassment, not that many of those inside hadn't already seen Gray kissing her at Lady Holson's tea party.

She'd been aiding Dru and Timothy in their schemes to meet—in part, she admitted, to foil Euphemia's ghastly plan to wed gentle Dru to a nearly dead peer. However, the glimpse she'd caught of the pair behind the trellis, wrapped in a close embrace, proved them too infatuated for sanity.

If their play resulted in even a faint replica of the

wild sensations that the lips moving against temple, cheek, and throat sparked in her, then she must caution them against such closeness. That resolution was the last sane thought Liz had for some time. As his warm, ardent mouth descended upon hers, Liz sighed her surrender and drank in his strength and masculinity. She felt cherished and threatened all at once, and when he deepened their kiss an explosion of feeling again rippled through her body.

Aware of how common it was for women impressed with his position or anxious to win rich rewards for their favors to fake their responses, Gray found it heady to know that his wife's hungry welcome was no sham. The honesty of her passion deepened his pleasure.

The errant pair behind the trellis assumed Lizzy had drawn Gray into her embrace for the purpose of keeping him preoccupied. But neither Gray nor Lizzy noticed as Timothy led a slightly disarrayed Dru back into the ballroom.

"Ah, Gray, there you are. I've been looking for you. Never guessed you'd be in a private tryst with your own wife." Sir David tut-tutted in mock rebuke. "Better places, old boy, better places than this."

"That's very true, sir." Gray's smile was not a bit repentant. "But the flowers, the moonlight. . . ." He shrugged.

"And a beautiful woman. I know. I'm not *so* old as to have forgotten such sweet temptations." Sir David beamed, looking like an impish satyr. "But you know, I saw Hayton dancing with your wife and again later talking with the two of you by the fountain. Be careful of that man, Gray."

Sir David's earnest gaze shifted to Liz. "You too, m'dear. That man's interest is less platonic than ought to be true. Be vigilant against his wiles or he'll have what he wants afore you know it."

Liz suppressed the laugh his over-serious warning

had bubbling up in her throat. The earl was no danger to her virtue. Indeed, after her several experiences of even an incomplete measure of Gray's ardor, no other man could ever be a threat. Still, not wishing to insult this affable family friend, she nodded solemnly.

Gray knew precisely how practiced Hayton was in his dealings with women. There'd been a time—while both were much younger—when they'd been not only very much alike in their tastes but in semi-friendly competition to prove superior abilities. He'd moved beyond that immature phase. Hayton hadn't. And despite or perhaps because of that past similarity, he had a difficult time not viewing the man as a threat to his relationship with Elizabeth.

"But, Gray, I'd a more mundane purpose in seeking you out. I've been debating the Irish issue with Salisbury, and have come to beg you to join us at the club . . . if your good lady permits the dismal interruption of duty."

Gray strongly suspected that David used the Irish issue as a shield to avoid mentioning what was undoubtedly the actual subject for this evening and so many past: the issue of white slavery. He glanced regretfully at his wife. "I must go, but since Sir David, in recompense for his interruption of my evening amusements, *will* take me into his carriage and later deliver me to Brandt House, I'll leave ours for you, Euphemia, and Dru."

"Of course, my boy." A beaming Sir David agreed. "Of course I'll give you transport."

Liz graciously nodded her agreement to Gray and smiled at Sir David. There'd never been any possibility of her doing elsewise.

Exhausted by another busy day and long evening out, Liz's lashes felt weighted as Annie stroked a silver-backed brush slowly, rhythmically through her thick red mane. The city was dark, but in the country cocks would soon be awakening to crow in the dawn's arrival.

"Tonight in the servant's hall at Kimball House I heard interesting gossip about certain events leading up to your carriage 'accident' after the Cardingtons' ball."

Bright blue eyes abruptly opened wide, sleepiness scattered by this unexpected news on a subject rarely far from Liz's thoughts. As was the practice for all lady's maids, Annie, with the woman serving both Euphemia and Dru, had followed Liz to the ball in the servants' carriage. Liz was certain Annie had quizzed the groom she was walking out with as promised but until now had not broached the subject.

"What was said?" Liz softly demanded, too anxious for the news to waste time in the tactful niceties Annie would excuse her for forgoing.

"Mr. Ellison was summoned by Mr. Beaton, the coachman who drove you and the duke's stepniece and cousin to London, to help calm a horse unaccustomed to city crowds. The footman was left to watch over the equipage, but he was lured to an inn to share a pint of bitters with the footmen of three other nobles."

"Do we know which three nobles employ the footmen who 'lured' Stebbins away?"

"That we do." Annie anxiously bobbed her head. "But first, ma'am, I must convince you that Stebbins is a good man who works hard and would never have willingly done anything to harm the master."

Liz knew her maid feared this honest report might bring woe to a fellow Brandt House servant. "You've done a wonderful favor for me, Annie." She smiled reassuringly. "I won't forget it. Nor would I allow what you've told me to cause problems for Stebbins."

Annie released the breath she hadn't realized she was holding. "They're servants to the marquess of Blaise, Viscount Deerborn, and earl of Hayton."

Light brown eyes met turquoise in the gilt-edged mirror Liz sat facing, and a proud smile bloomed on the maid's mouth, a warm echo of the grim upward tilt to her mistress's lips.

"I tried to win news from my Jeremy, but this kind of information is more than Stebbins's job is worth, and I'm certain he hasn't shared it either belowstairs or in the stable."

"No doubt that's true," Liz promptly agreed, wordlessly reassuring her friend of continued trust as she sought a further favor. "I mean to go on doing everything I can to unmask the culprit behind these suspicious accidents befalling my husband, and I thank you for helping me move closer to that goal. Now I've another boon that I pray you'll give me, one that may carry me even closer to the truth." Liz saw the excitement starting to build in pale brown eyes and knew she'd set the right tone to intrigue the adventurous girl. "I would greatly appreciate it if you'd continue reporting to me anything of interest you overhear in the homes of people I call upon."

Annie unabashedly grinned. "I might even be able to ask a few innocent questions, nudging my hosts in the servants' hall and the other servants awaiting the conclusion of their mistress's visits into revealing further useful bits." She rubbed her palms together in obvious delight. "Never thought I'd be involved in something more exciting than any penny dreadful's tale."

Absently smoothing a precisely tailored riding jacket, Liz urged her beautiful chestnut to canter past the Albert Memorial and enter the Row. It was nearly noon but early to begin a lady of Society's traditional "morning ride."

"Timothy and I always appreciate your help in arranging opportunities for us to meet, particularly now when he's so busy poring over old records." Dru hesitantly began, casting a sidelong glance at the handsome young man riding on Lizzy's far side. "But why were you anxious to be out so uncommonly early today?"

"To ensure our privacy for the serious talk you must have known would come." Though Liz rode between them, neither the shamefaced Timothy nor blushing Dru would look her way. She first addressed the latter. "For days I diligently strived to persuade your stepmama she might safely leave you in my charge when you know she believes I'm unworthy of that trust . . . possibly rightly so if recent events are any proof." Liz's tone held a strong thread of rebuke never before heard by either of its targets.

Dru was startled into abruptly turning to peer more closely at Lizzy. The action threw her off balance. Although she instantly restored her seat, ruined was the much-sought-after image of a rider totally relaxed while keeping her mount under perfect control. The epitome of the Grecian Seat, a method taught for decades to the well-bred by Rimmell Dunbar.

"It's because of what you saw last night, isn't it?" Dru asked anxiously, by long-ingrained training transferring reins and whip from right to left hand, a delicate maneuver difficult to perfect, and leaned forward to pat an equally well-trained horse for not flinching under the unusual shift in position. "You're going to berate us for our behavior and taking of a foolish risk."

"I'm going to point out the undeniable fact that such future actions will make it impossible for me to help you continue meeting." Liz didn't bother to warn them of the punishment certain to follow such near-public actions. They knew as well as she that Lady Euphemia wouldn't hesitate to exile the girl to the country for the rest of the Season, and this time keep her there closely guarded. Liz permitted the long silence following her quiet warning to continue as their small party reined to a halt beneath the spreading limbs of a towering elm.

It was Timothy who at last responded to the justified lecture. "I assumed that this was why we'd been summoned. And it's I who take responsibility for our foolishness. I, an aspiring M.P., should've had sense enough to prevent it."

"You understand? Good, then we need speak no more upon the matter." Liz nodded and the tulle delicately swathing her appropriately small hat trembled in a slight breeze. "Now on to more important matters."

Timothy exchanged a startled look with Dru.

Paying no attention to their reaction, Liz carefully repeated the information Annie had provided the previous night or, rather, very early this morning.

"Thus," she concluded her recitation, "I suggest a spot of discreet sleuthing whenever we find ourselves, as we inevitably will, in the company of these nobles or their families. Perhaps even a quiet search of their homes on those occasions when we're invited inside."

Relieved to have been let off with no more than a warning, serious as they knew it was, the prospect of continued sleuthing was welcome to the pair. That chore, as always, was lent particular importance by the need to prove Timothy innocent of ill-founded rumors and vicious lies.

CHAPTER 11

The mellow sound of a hunting horn filled the late afternoon air. Its signal of an end to the day's last stand was welcome to Liz. She relaxed her stiff stance, allowing the barrel of the rifle still in her hold to drop and point toward the ground while Gray, several other gentlemen guests, and their host, the earl of Hayton, did the same.

Lawrence—calling her Lizzy, to Gray's annoyance, and insisting she use his first name—had boasted that this final site in a hollow with good cover at the base of a long wooded hill was perfection. As nothing about this "hunting" experience was familiar to Liz, she could only accept his claim.

Despite the fact that his lecture had prevented Liz from making final plans to put into motion a scheme that should lessen Gray's danger, she was thankful that Gray had saved her from arriving for a weekend at the earl's "humble" ten-bedroom hunting lodge completely unprepared for practices alien to her. Her husband had provided a detailed explanation of a British bird shoot's mechanics. And the difference in terminology between an American bird *hunt* and a

British bird *shoot* was, she felt, most appropriate and the very crux of the reason for her distaste.

Yesterday in their private car on the rail trip to the village nearest their destination, Gray had described how beaters, men dressed in long white coats, moved through the woodland tapping sticks against tree trunks to drive birds from their coverts up into the air. The hunters waited until the sky was filled. Then they, flanked by two servants, worked with three rifles. The man on the right handed the shooter a loaded gun which once emptied at feathered targets overhead was given to the man on the left. The shooter's eyes were never to shift from the sky until a second horn blast signaled the beaters' arrival at the end of the current stand.

Driven by a need to prove her marksmanship equal to any male's, Liz had participated without quibbling at what she could only see as an unnecessary slaughter. Each of the day's three stands had netted several hundred birds, a massacre which couldn't be justified by Lawrence's excuse of ridding the countryside of destructive pests. Although each kill included wood pigeons, many other species had also been among those lined up for the shooters' inspection at the end of earlier rounds.

Watching loosed dogs sniff out every bird fallen in the most recent fusillade, Liz was disgusted. English huntsmen practiced a mindless destruction that she could never call sport.

"Pardon? Not sport?" Lawrence's brows arched upward in disdain for the unexpected insult from a female standing here in a lush glade amongst some of the best shots in Britain and only on sufferance permitted to participate in a man's game.

Unaware that she'd spoken aloud, Liz blushed but refused to recant. "Where's the sport when with so many birds in the sky it would be hard to miss? What enjoyment is there in senseless carnage?"

Gray was delighted by Elizabeth's frank assessment and the earl's chilled response. Yet, uncertain of Hayton's reaction to so public a reproach from a woman, he moved to stand protectively near even as the other man spoke.

"I'm sorry, Your Grace." Mockery lay behind Lawrence's wry smile while he made a show of consoling the woman, attempting to make it clear to their onlookers that the problem lay with her. He plainly meant for them to believe that she'd proven herself not so impervious to blood sports as claimed nor, though she'd proven herself a crack shot, up to participating in this manly pursuit. "I believed it when you said you enjoyed the sport of hunting."

"Surely to be sporting, there must be an honest challenge." Liz immediately straightened, turquoise flames flashing against the earl's condescension. "By that definition, hunting should directly pit the hunter against the hunted." She wouldn't permit the man to treat her like some simpering debutante suffering an attack of vapors at her first glimpse of blood. "You play the sport unfairly, paying someone else to hunt the quarry and drive it forward for you to kill and then take the credit."

With Gray at her back, Liz unflinchingly met Lawrence's gaze as a collective gasp rose from the three other shooters and even from the loaders standing on the forest edge, a discreet distance from their masters.

Liz glanced defensively behind when Gray gently clasped her rigid shoulders. On his face she found an expression of honest admiration, and the sight accomplished what the horrified response of most others had failed to do. It stole her voice.

"I see." Lawrence smiled, but his narrowed eyes moved consideringly between the outspoken woman and her husband. There were possibilities here, interesting possibilities. "You believe your ways more sporting than ours?"

Liz gave a nod that ended with chin defiantly tilted upward. "I and my countrymen find that the thrill lies in searching out one's own prey and bringing down a flying bird or elusive buck without anyone else's help. True sport is a contest between an animal's natural instincts and a hunter's skill."

"Here, here," Gray dryly agreed with his wife's fervent yet logical argument. Hunting was not his favorite pastime, but he saw more to interest him in her method than the one he'd been raised to employ.

Liz was further surprised by this supportive comment from the husband she would've expected to be appalled by her bold action, surely the epitome of all he'd asked her to eschew.

Amused by the confusion his uncharacteristic response roused in his wife, Gray silently admitted it was only to be expected. There was no way for her to know about the deeply buried but ever-burning antipathy between himself and the earl who'd begun speaking again.

"Each 'man' for himself, hmmm? No masters, no servants? Certainly a very democratic view." Lawrence still smiled, but a new grimness pulled at the edges of his mouth while a strange exaltation glowed in his eyes. "So, tell me what tactics you Americans employ on these hunts you claim are more challenging."

"In Wyoming we set out before dawn," Liz began, despite an odd sensation of danger. Having rarely turned aside from a challenge—and this was one as surely as was the sort of hunt Lawrence asked her to describe—she wouldn't do so now. "Each hunter carries a single rifle. The party is accompanied by good hunting dogs but, as hunters load their own guns, no servants. They rely solely on personal skill and experience to find the most promising places to locate their quarry. Rarely is it so tidy as your prearranged stands, and never do hunters return so nearly untouched by nature's grime. Also, we take no more game than we can carry home ourselves and put to good use."

"All right, on behalf of good Englishmen everywhere, I accept your challenge." The strange pleasure adding bite to Lawrence's words frightened Liz. Seemed she'd seriously offended him. "Tomorrow we'll make a contest of it and hunt like your compatriots in the Wild American West we hear so much about . . . and still we'll prove ourselves the better huntsmen."

This proposed resolution to the conflict between Hayton and the Ashleighs caught the other three noble guests unprepared and less than enthusiastic. However, there wasn't a man present willing to admit that a woman, even less an American woman, could possibly be superior in a sport generally reserved for aristocratic males. Uniquely beautiful and the rage of the Season she might be, but . . .

Liz drank in the pungent odor of the dew-damp earth beneath her boots as well as the scent of new foliage and spring flowers. Little more than an hour had passed since the challenged hunters had set out in predawn gloom and already both she and Gray had brought down four birds. They were off to a good start.

Following a lengthy dinner the previous night, Lawrence had led in establishing this hunt's guidelines, paying strict attention to Liz's American standards. For safety's sake divided into pairs, the six contest participants had departed from the lodge at the same time. They'd agreed to shoot only birds on the wing—to prevent accidental injury of other hunters. And the winner would be not the shooter who bagged the largest number of birds but the first to bring ten down and deliver them back to the lodge where Great-aunt Helena and the hunters' wives, except Liz, waited to confirm the victor. With the spouses usually left to a day of solitary boredom given a role to play in the competition, their infectious anticipation had spread to initially reluctant huntsmen and the event had begun with laughter and high spirits.

While stealthily moving forward, exercising both the vigilance and patience required for success, Liz's thoughts drifted back to memories of the past two disappointing evenings. After their arrival and light dinner the first night, Lawrence had led the men into the billiard room, leaving Liz amazed by the inclusion of such a thing in a hunting lodge. Once the men had withdrawn, guided by the firm hand of Lawrence's prim and exceedingly proper great-aunt Helena, the women had made an early night of it, retiring to individual rooms. A circumstance that had thwarted Liz's hopes for implementing her plan to lessen Gray's danger.

Last night she'd intended to pursue that goal and a small thing more. With the dinner and discussion of the coming hunt done, she'd wanted an opportunity to privately thank Gray for his support during the confrontation with Lawrence. But again Great-aunt Helena's interference smothered Liz's hope for private time alone with her husband. As the weekend's hostess, Great-aunt Helena had made plans to fill the guests' second evening. Following a lengthy game of charades, featuring figures from Greek tragedies and biblical stories, it had been her intent to see the evening concluded with edifying readings—a daunting prospect that had inspired the ladies to plead weariness and flee to their beds.

Although the hour was hardly late, Liz had had no option but to join them in retiring. The men, however, had remained in the drawing room to play games of chance and discuss the politics of serious subjects rarely mentioned in the company of virtuous wives they earnestly believed must be protected against sordid realities.

The screech and churr of startled birds completely overshadowed the rustle of footsteps nearby and sent Liz's full attention to the sky. The barrel of her rifle rose and the sound of shots fired near simultaneously was followed by the sight of two birds plummeting toward earth.

"Five each, Gray!" Liz was thrilled. "We're halfway there!"

The answering groan and thud of something much heavier than a bird hitting the earth startled her into immediately whirling about. Gray sat amidst a clump of ferns, clutching the outside of his thigh halfway between knee and hip while blood oozed over fingers whitened by their tight grip.

"Help! Hunter down," Liz loudly called as she reloaded her gun to shoot once more. Then, while repeating her cry, she sank to her knees at the fallen man's side, pulling her scarlet ascot loose. Brushing his hands aside, she wrapped the bright strip of silk about his thigh in a rough bandage for the wound.

"I hadn't thought the aim of our fellow hunters so poor," Liz muttered in disgust, quivering inside yet working to tie scarlet ends with a calmness she didn't feel. There was no answer and she looked into eyes suspiciously void of emotion.

"How foolish of me." Liz gritted out the admission that she'd misinterpreted an obvious assault. "Of course, they're not." But, she silently wondered, did that mean one of them had knowingly shot Gray? Or was there a stranger lurking about and using this contest as cover to do the dirty deed?

"It doesn't matter," Gray quietly stated. "The damage is negligible." As if to prove his statement, he made to rise.

"Don't be a nitwit!" Liz would have none of it and launched herself at his chest, forcing him back down.

"I agree that as the bullet passed cleanly through, the injury isn't life-threatening as it is, but without proper treatment it could become so."

Finding himself laying comfortably atop soft ferns with the fire-haired beauty snuggled against him, Gray agreed that he would indeed be a 'nitwit' to struggle. Rather, he slid his arms around her back and cradled her near while nuzzling the vulnerable spot beneath her ear.

For a brief moment an unprepared Liz melted but then attempted to pull away. "The others are coming."

"Eventually," Gray agreed, refusing to release the woman, his by the laws of God and man. Instead his lips moved across a cheek rosed by crisp morning air to claim her mouth. At first he merely brushed its soft contours but silently admitted he couldn't take much more of this. For weeks he'd patiently wooed his bride but that patience was nearly exhausted—and his control sorely strained. He was determined that soon, very soon, he would see an end to the waiting. Even now in this utterly inappropriate time and place, too familiar with the sweet wine inside soft lips, an unintelligible noise escaped his throat as he deepened the kiss into a blazing hunger.

"Hunter down, indeed!" An elderly noble's high-pitched tittering pierced the couple's absorption. "But I don't see as our help is needed, eh what?"

A chorus of chuckles and ribald banter, muffled in respect for the lady involved, rolled from the four men who'd broken through what earlier had been a solid wall of vegetation.

Gray instantly released his wife but in one brief moment caught an expression of bemused pleasure, almost awe, on her face before embarrassment flooded it with a hue near as bright as her hair. The sight offered welcome proof there was little reason to be patient much longer.

"You heard right. I've been shot." Gray put Elizabeth aside to sit up while wry humor tightened his next question. "Any of you care to own up to the deed?"

Teasing laughter stopped abruptly, leaving the air instead filled with a shocked silence.

"Sure you didn't shoot yourself?" Lawrence's lightly spoken words broke the awkward moment.

Liz leapt to her feet and heatedly confronted the earl. "He and I both shot into the sky and I saw two birds fall, the fifth for each of us."

Lawrence shrugged. "We all heard the shots fired and, as we were hunting in pairs, our positions can easily be established. Therefore, whatever nasty 'accident' occurred here, it can be proven that none of us could be the culprit behind the action." He purposely used the term Gray inevitably applied to such events.

"Of course you're not," Gray immediately agreed. "Perhaps we had the misfortune of stumbling across a poacher's path." He shrugged before shifting the focus with equal haste away from culpability. "I'm more concerned with getting back to the lodge and having a doctor deal with this inconvenient wound that will keep me from proving myself the better hunter."

The other men answered this mocking taunt calculated to revive their good spirits with exaggerated claims of their own superior prowess. While they laughingly argued the issue, Gray acknowledged that by suggesting himself incapacitated, he paid the cost for diverting their attention with his prized independence. Gray believed he was perfectly capable of walking back to the lodge and treating the injury without anyone's help. But then, he'd put himself into this dependent position not only for the sake of harmony but also to please Elizabeth by submitting to the treatment her gratifying concern for him demanded.

When, after what Liz considered an unconscionable

delay, Lawrence and the others hurried off to arrange Gray's transport, she anxiously remained with her husband, alone. Too aware both of what had passed between them before help arrived and the fiery, tactless defense that had required Gray to calm the waters she'd agitated, Liz couldn't find words to apologize. The man had gone white and laid back, eyes closed while blood seeped through the makeshift bandage. Waiting in silence, Liz could only be grateful that the lodge was not far distant, for either minutes passed quicker than she deserved or a mounted earl truly returned in an amazingly short time. He was accompanied by a farm wagon driven by two husky servants he directed lift the injured duke onto the vehicle's blanket-padded bed.

Although offered a position on the driver's bench, Liz refused. Instead, ignoring the decorum proper for a genteel lady, she scrambled into the wagon and again settled beside her husband. Before the wheels had twice turned, she was disconcerted to find herself the focus of a steady silver gaze that remained upon her throughout the whole of a rough and blessedly brief trip.

The hunt had begun at so early an hour that it was barely noon by the time a doctor had treated Gray's injury and he was tucked into bed in the guest room allotted him. This room, like the other nine, had been decorated to enhance its rustic appeal with thick plank floors granted a meager few rugs, candles in pewter holders rather than gas lamps, and a thick embroidered counterpane on the heavy iron bed.

Though Liz was excluded while the doctor was at work, giving her time enough to be rid of her hunting suit's tight-fitting jacket, she was allowed to return to Gray's room once the doctor had finished. Finding her husband modestly attired in a white nightshirt and propped up by a multitude of pillows, she remained at his side as the afternoon wore on, disgusted by the fact that they were afforded no privacy. There were pointed questions she wanted to ask about the source of a threatened danger he could no longer deny. She wouldn't be fobbed off with inane talk of accidents. Not this time . . . not that she'd accepted such a weak excuse for previous incidents, only that after her first attempt she hadn't tried to discuss the matter with him.

Her impatient wishes mattered not at all. Never were they left alone. Great-aunt Helena hovered at the edge of a constant crowd of visitors flowing in and out of the sick room, determined to cheer the duke with silly games and even sillier chitchat. The men soon became bored and excused themselves, but their wives were far more persistent in their attentions.

Particularly Deidre. Liz's eyes had begun smoldering the moment the flighty but very pretty young woman had entered the room. The previous evening Deidre had wasted no time in letting Liz know that her name had once been romantically linked with Gray's. That had, of course, been before her marriage to "dear Arthur," a man nearly triple her age and whose title, though not as exalted as Gray's, had doubtless made him a sterling catch. A circumstance which made Liz think of poor Dru and the marquess of Poxwell.

Liz had been able to find amusement in, even pity for, the woman the night before. But this afternoon when the woman had insisted on drawing a chair up next to Gray's bed, as if she'd the right to remain as near to him as the wife opposite her, Liz's patience had begun to fray. A fact accelerated by every word the woman cooed and her each consoling touch, infinitely nearer a caress.

"Deidre, seems this wound has affected me more than I'd thought. I find myself growing weary." Gray had initially found the signs of Elizabeth's jealousy both amusing and flattering. However, also familiar with her unpredictability, he knew the wiser course was to put an end to the scene. Besides, despite Deidre's inferences to the contrary, he'd never been able to put up with her mindless chatter and cloying adulation for long. "I trust you won't be offended by an injured man's wish for privacy and a few hours rest—in his wife's care."

Liz wasn't certain whether he'd added the last for her sake or simply to be rid of someone he found irritating. Whatever the reason, she was pleased. The safely married Deidre had made it plain that she intended to revive her past association with Gray, and if Liz had been forced to watch the woman bat her lashes or stroke dainty fingers down a powerful masculine arm one more time . . . Well, thank heavens she wouldn't!

The thick door closed behind both Deidre and the ever lingering Great-aunt Helena, shutting Liz into a small space with Gray for an indeterminate amount of time. It was then that she realized this was the opportunity for which she'd been waiting. To demand answers, she firmly told herself, only that. But though she tried to shut her mind against the insidious memory of her second reason for longing to be alone with him, her heart again began a foolish fluttering.

"Gray." Firmly suppressing errant thoughts of past intimacies, Liz turned toward her husband with a determination reinforced by lingering anger over Deidre's advances. "Why is someone trying to kill you?"

"Kill me? I hardly think so." Gray absently answered, reaching behind to rid himself of all but one of the pillows used to prop him up. "Apparently you've forgotten the last time you sought to discuss such a matter with me, demanding privacy to do so."

Turquoise eyes widened on hands beginning to unfasten buttons down the front of his nightshirt.

"I assured you then that whenever we found ourselves alone we'd have better things to do with our time." In a single smooth movement Gray pulled white cloth over his head and with a disgusted grimace tossed it aside, powerful muscles rippling with the action. "Hate those things."

Stunned by this first sight of his nude torso, Liz's breath caught somewhere between lungs and throat. Plainly the man perfectly at ease sitting half if not completely nude on his bed did not spend all his time seated in Parliament or behind an estate manager's desk. She'd been in his arms, held against his body often enough to know his strength. Still, her heart skipped wildly at the devastating display of blatant, frankly threatening masculinity. Her gaze strayed from a broad chest with its wedge of dark hair arrowing down over a firm belly to where covers lay haphazardly across narrow hips.

Gray watched fear war with fascination in brilliant blue eyes. The inevitable victory of the latter put a potent, knowing smile on his mouth. Nonetheless, Gray purposely misinterpreted her reaction. With brows mockingly arched over a glittering silver gaze he asked, "Shocked that I prefer to sleep without useless encumbrances?"

Struggling through a sea of unsettled emotional and physical responses, Liz caught and clung to the idea of her surely virtuous scheme to provide him with leastwise a measure of protection. She ignored the battle between longings and apprehension of the unknown to boldly step forward.

"You're right. There's little point in wasting time discussing the danger when there are actions we can take to lessen it."

Gray's eyes widened, once again startled by her unexpected response. "Lessen it?"

"Yes." Liz moved to within a pace of the bed but

kept her gaze safely on his face rather than on the intimidating, exciting width of shoulders and chest. Earnestly she began her appeal.

"Having given the problem considerable thought since the night our carriage lost a wheel—" Liz was amazed at the steadiness of her voice when inside she was trembling. "—I've come to the conclusion that as a first line of defense you must have an heir."

Sunlight glowed on the lighter hair of Gray's temples as, thunderstruck, he slowly shook his head trying to find sense in her words.

"It's not," Liz hastened to add, fearing she'd be misunderstood, "that I believe Timothy is in any way responsible for these 'accidents.' But it might slow the true aggressors down if there was no one convenient to bear the guilt for their deed." In Gray's continued negative motion, Liz read denial of her plan's logic and earnestly attempted to restate it more clearly. "Don't you see? When you've an heir, or the visible promise of one's imminent arrival, your foes can't expect Timothy to be blamed for your demise. You do see, don't you?"

Amusement growing, Gray watched Elizabeth dither in a manner he knew she would normally despise. For days, weeks, he'd gradually, gently wooed his bride, growing ever more impatient to fully seduce her. Now here she stood, offering herself to him. How like his straightforward bride to do what no other well-bred woman would—proposition a man, albeit her husband. Rich laughter suddenly filled the room, and Gray reached out to pull Liz down next to his uninjured side.

"Then—" Gray grinned at the woman in his bed at last. "By all means, let's implement your plan to see me protected."

He slowly slipped the pins from her hair and, once unbound, threaded fingers through its thick fire. The lingering mockery in his smile was burned away by memories of nights spent dreaming of her. In his fantasies the brightness of her mane provided a perfect foil for her body's lush enticements while she hungrily reached for him. Intent on seeing that vision fulfilled, Gray spread the mass of vivid hair, silkier even than he'd imagined, across his pillow, gently pushed her back to lay atop its blaze, and in a haze of growing desire started painstakingly unbuttoning her prim shirtwaist.

He had embraced Elizabeth often enough to know she hated, rarely wore and, with her tiny waist, had no need for a corset. Thus, once he'd dispensed with buttons there would be nothing between him and her lush bounty save one of the fine, nearly transparent undergarments he'd chosen for her in Paris. Lightning seemed to flash from his eyes, as that fact painted dangerously potent pictures in his mind.

Overwhelmed by the devastating man's nearness, Liz couldn't move. Soon she was lost in a fog of wild excitement, tingling with the consequences of her bravado while with each button released, Gray's lips brushed short, tantalizing kisses over what lay beneath. He began by lightly touching the flesh just below her throat, then moved down to more firmly caress the narrow strip barely covered by a thin chemise exposed between the open edges of her blouse. Despite flimsy cotton ostensibly shielding her flesh from his lips, tendrils of fire spread through her body from wherever he rubbed teasing kisses until she shook with their heat.

His bride's involuntary response put a pleased curl on Gray's mouth. Determined to see her as hungry for him as he was for her, he silently commanded himself to damp down the flames setting his blood to coursing and hold impatient desires in check. Toward that goal, rather than tearing off her garments as his passion demanded, he nuzzled into her cleavage. Yet every passing moment deepened his awareness of unrestrained, barely shielded breasts. It created a too vivid vision of her bounty straining against the fragile bonds of dimity and lace. Suddenly he wanted to caress and grab at the same time, an unruly urge so far outside the experience of a man famed for his icy control that it shook him to the core. This woman affected him in ways no other had . . . or likely ever could. He went still, struggling for control.

While she sank into a blaze of sensations, Liz heard his labored breathing. It broke the invisible bonds holding her motionless. Without conscious thought, her hands lifted to explore the muscled contours of his shoulders, delighting in their strength before her fingers twined into the cool black strands at the nape of his neck.

The feel of Elizabeth's curious caresses weakened Gray's restraints. He had intended to gently nudge back the shirtwaist's edges but now pulled free to hastily tug the garment from her body and toss it across the room. And although it was a more dangerous threat to his control, he couldn't close his eyes against the tempting sight of the dainty, almost sheer chemise, an incredibly erotic impediment to the view of breasts which even laying flat were luscious and full. He bent to brush his lips over the supremely soft flesh swelling above while slipping his hands beneath the lower hem to cup their generous weight. A strong shiver passed through Liz and she moaned, unconsciously twisting more completely into his hold. Gray leaned back to ruthlessly remove the barrier and allow glittering silver eyes to feast upon the prize he firmly clasped while his thumbs lightly traced circles around outer edges.

As his touch slowly, gradually moved closer to the center, Liz helplessly watched, wanting it to stop, wanting even more for it to continue to some unknown end. The sensual torment incited such wicked delights and aching needs that a small, desperate whimper escaped her tense throat.

It was the same wild sound Gray had never stopped longing to hear again since the first time. Still looking down at the enticing woman in his bed, his mouth went dry as he watched her arch in response to the pleasure of his caress, watched her dragging in deep breaths as his thumbs moved over her breasts and ever nearer their summits and tight crowns.

The scorching touch had roused in Liz an unbearable, burning need, and with every sense focused on the fingers now lifted to hover a whisper above sensitive curves, she couldn't help but reach out to pull his hands down to fully clasp aching flesh. Her head turned restlessly from side to side as he firmly pressed and with his palms caressed her satin softness. Under this small, recklessly sought climax she moaned out his name.

Gray felt himself sinking fast through the perilous depths of uncharted liquid fires and into a hungry passion beyond even his experience. Rolling away, he completely separated them to lay on his back, eyes clenched against her temptations, struggling to control the dangerous need to take her instantly and so roughly that it likely would kill the flower of her unexpected, deliciously wanton passion before it had truly blossomed. Unfortunately, haunting the darkness behind closed lids were equally dangerous visions, memories of his recent taste of sweet flesh that felt like warm silk to touch.

Feeling deserted, Liz flowed toward the master of these aching desires as naturally as water downhill. She pressed lush curves against his side, while burrowing slender fingers into the wedge of dark curls across his chest. Using his actions as her guide, she explored him, taking pleasure in the steely muscles of a chest rising and falling with deep, uneven breaths.

Gray went rigid under her touch but did not deny the hands stroking his body's hard planes with delicious torment until soft lips moved to follow their path and settled with innocent seduction on a flat masculine nipple. Shuddering as a harsh groan was torn from his throat, he rose up on one forearm to claim eager lips with his own. As his mouth opened on hers, Liz wrapped slender arms about his neck, pulsing with excitement while his tongue teased and stroked and explored.

She hardly realized that during the devastating kiss his lean hands had unfastened her skirt and petticoats until he sat up to rid her of them. Then while he hastily pushed the bedcovers to the floor, she caught her first glimpse of a totally nude male and, reminded again of a panther, was stunned by his grace and power. The next instant he reclaimed her mouth with gentle persuasion.

The lingering kiss once more drove rational thought beyond her reach, although she was breathlessly aware when he gently slipped his hand beneath a lower edge of cambric drawers and up one quivering thigh to tug at a dainty satin and lace garter. He deepened their kiss, slowly building the pressure into something wild and deep and so overwhelming it swamped her momentary apprehension and drained strength from trembling limbs while he began sliding the garter down a slender, finely shaped leg.

By the time he abandoned her lips to finish the chore, she was dazed by new sensations and lay in willing surrender as he sensuously caressed and lightly taunted silk-covered flesh all the way back up until he had the top of her stocking in his hand. With passion-heavy eyes, they both watched as the filmy cloth was removed. He immediately began the process over again with the other leg, inching his hand tantalizingly up under her drawers while, burning all over, she began to shake with unfamiliar needs intensified. And once the second stocking was gone, she clenched her legs together against an unfamiliar burning emptiness.

Face taut but for the sensual curve of his normally firm lips, Gray's eyes flared with silver flames at this demonstration of an innocent's passionate need. His goal was very near and he would do nothing that might possibly frighten her from the spiral of mindless, blazing hunger. Rather he returned to stroking her breasts, lightly teasing their tips with his lips until with a hungry groan she pulled his mouth tighter. When at last he drew the nipple into his mouth and began suckling she cried out, urging him to deepen the contact. With one hand he cupped and gently squeezed the other breast while his free hand unfastened her drawers and began an invasion over the sleek skin below. Soon, driven even further beyond the restraints of innate modesty, burning with tremendous heat, she arched upward.

Moving her to lie facing him, his hand swept down the arch of her spine, then slipped lower to cup the perfect curve of her derriere and pull her hips to his. She pressed even closer as he began to rhythmically move her against his arousal. She gasped but wanted an even closer contact, wanted something unknown, something more. With nails digging into his shoulders, she arched and then writhed against him. A groan reverberated in his chest, but he did not break their ravenous kiss. When at last his mouth left hers, a soft, involuntary sob of protest escaped her throat. Gray was pleased by this proof of a need spiraling as deeply into desire's fiery riptide as his own.

Feeling empty and aching for something only Gray could give her, Liz struggled to pull him fully atop her and was annoyed when he took time to remove her last remaining garment, an impediment to what they both desired. When he leaned back, gazing down at her body yearning upward, she urgently tugged at his shoulders, striving to bring him to her wanting body.

Here in enticing arms, blue eyes gone nearly black with hunger and soft, trembling lips silently pleading for his, Gray saw the fulfillment of his dreams, a reality infinitely more exciting than any fantasy.

"I've been patient too long," he growled, voice a low burr. "I can't wait any longer."

He speared a hand into the rich tangle of her fiery hair, slid one leg between hers, and shifted to stretch out on her slender form. Loving the feel of his aroused body pressing down against hers, Liz trembled with pleasure, desperately wanting, needing more. Again she helplessly writhed beneath him. Her unconscious movements roused him into equal desperation and he lifted her hips to ease their slow joining. She instinctively twined silken legs about him, bringing him to her. Her moment of pain was lost in a mindless need to ease the throbbing ache inside. He stilled for a moment to allow her body to adjust but she surged upward, sharing the ever-building heat in their depths while he began to move again, rocking her deeper into a fire storm of intense pleasure. Afraid she couldn't bear more of the sweet anguish, still she moved with him, matching his rhythm, striving to reach its blazing core. It was madness and heaven while together they clung until Gray groaned out her name, Liz's fingers dug into his hips, and the flames of an almost unbearable pleasure consumed them. It left them sated and trembling adrift in the gentle smoke of a passionate explosion's aftermath.

While other houseguests surely spent another deadly dull evening below, Liz lay warm and content with Gray's head pillowed against her as she slowly stroked through the silver hair at his temple. Some time earlier Great-aunt Helena had disturbed their contented slumber by loudly knocking at the door and primly suggesting Elizabeth, at least, ought to come down for dinner. In a sleep-rough voice, Gray had sent her away with the news that he required his wife's attention—and privacy for her healing powers to be effective. The memory put an amused gleam in her eyes and a warm smile on the lips she brushed across her devastating lover's black hair.

Gray lazily pressed his mouth to one creamy globe. "You have the world's most beautiful breasts—incredibly soft, wonderfully full and, oh, so responsive." He nuzzled more firmly against yielding flesh. "I hate the thought of sharing so much as an innocent glimpse of their perfection with any other man, no matter what Worth has decreed fashionable. If I had my choice, you'd wear only dresses with collars that wrap about your throat."

"Oh?" Amusement vibrated in the mock question as Liz teasingly tweaked one of the dark locks she'd so recently kissed. "We could set a new style with high collars on ball gowns. But, regrettably, it would be a waste of all those expensive creations by Monsieur Worth."

"Perhaps, but to coax you into adopting that style a little more often, I've a special gift for you."

Despite a reluctance to leave his comfortable position and ignoring the slight discomfort of his negligible wound, Gray pulled away, rose, and went to a chest beside the door. Liz watched, loving the masculine perfection of his strong body, the play of powerful muscles as he first lit a new candle against the nearly guttering stub of the last, and then rummaged through a small travel bag.

Gray had risen without considering the possibility of lingering inhibitions that might make a woman so recently a virgin uncomfortable with a man wandering around nude. An abrupt tension in the room and feel of her gaze reminded him and it was with anxious hesitation that he turned toward her with something clasped in his closed hand.

The burning admiration in eyes gone near to black

quashed his fears. Smiling broadly he moved to sit beside his exquisite wife, and with one powerful arm drew her up to meet his kiss. Her mouth instantly responded to his, and several minutes passed before he pulled a brief distance away, solemnly lifted one hand, and opened his fingers. On his palm lay a lovely charcoal-hued cameo. Intricate silver filigree edged the oval in whose center was an exquisitely carved pair of lovers embracing.

"This keepsake is not as monetarily valuable as the Ashleigh sapphires, but it's priceless to me. Moreover, unlike the impressive family jewels that are entailed to future generations, this is now yours alone."

Liz was almost afraid to touch the delicate piece, but Gray lifted her hand and put the keepsake inside while he told her of its history.

"On their honeymoon in Venice my grandfather gave it to my grandmother, the first Lilibet."

Liz heard the love in his voice and gazed up at him with her heart in her eyes, wishing he felt the same about her.

"As you see," he said, turning the piece over. "Their initials are entwined on the back."

Liz looked down and saw etched into the charcoal onyx the tiny letters *G* and *L*.

"Our initials, too." Gray wryly smiled. "Perhaps it was fate that sent a second Grayson, his own Lilibet." Though Gray had made the suggestion in jest, his eyes went to smoke and, despite the self-mockery it brought, he seriously wondered if what he'd said was true.

For Liz's part, the mere fact that Gray had given her something that had once belonged to his beloved grandmother blocked her throat with so much emotion she couldn't speak. Surely it meant there was a chance for them, a chance that he might someday feel for her some small part of what she could no longer deny feeling for him. Hand gently closing around the keepsake, a talisman of hope, she brought it to her lips.

Gray saw the golden glow of candlelight on thc path of a single crystal tear. Like some personal charm against danger, he'd carried his grandmother's cameo with him since she'd pressed it into his hands as she lay dying. On surrendering to the compulsion to give it into his fiery wife's keeping, the last thing he'd expected were tears. The thought brought a crooked smile. How else but that his Lilibet again do the unexpected?

"Hey, now." With a gentle forefinger he traced the liquid trail. "What's this?"

Shaking a cloud of bright curls, Liz bit her lip but couldn't speak as an embarrassing rain of more salty droplets followed the first.

Gray truly wished he understood but though he didn't, carefully took the keepsake from her hands to set it safely aside on a bedside table before sweeping her into his comforting arms. Solace soon yielded to pleasure, and as lush curves first held tenderly near pressed closer against him, the motion revived the earlier shocking delight of her bare skin crushed to the heat of his broad chest. Urgently pulling her even tighter, Gray claimed her mouth in a kiss already full of renewed passion. Banked embers ignited to flare anew and set ablaze a vortex of fire the hotter for the tenderness feeding the flames. Before dawn broke, Gray, with Liz's unrestrained cooperation, did his best to see conceived the heir she'd come to his bed suggesting would be his protection.

CHAPTER 12

"A shooting accident?" Euphemia fairly snorted. "Oh, really, Gray. When are you going to talk sense?"

Standing at her husband's side, Liz felt him go rigid. The front door of Brandt House had barely opened before his sister descended upon them for all the world like a strict mother coming to sternly chastise her errant children.

"I'm told a woman joined your shooting party." Disgust coated Euphemia's announcement. The day after the pair's departure gossiping callers had told her the identity of that female. "No doubt it complicated the field considerably . . . and possibly offered dangerous distractions." The hard glare of slate gray eyes bored into the American whose conversation with Hayton had been repeated nearly word for word, confirming the fact that she'd wangled from him an invitation to actually participate in the manly pursuit.

Liz heard the implied accusation in the other woman's sneered words. Already feeling at fault for having suggested the hunting style that had put them alone in the forest, she shrank away, but Gray wrapped an arm about her shoulders and pulled her close.

"That's enough, Euphemia!" Beneath Gray's infinitely more powerful silver glare his sister fell back. He'd been appalled by the depth of venom behind her insinuations. "First Timothy and now Lilibet? It's not only enough but too much."

Though her gaze had fallen to the entry's polished floor, Euphemia's eyes remained as shiny and hard as small clouded agates. By Gray's immediate defense and use of his grandmother's name for this woman, she recognized precisely where matters stood between him and his wife. She was *not* pleased!

"I thought you had better sense than to initiate such a discussion in less than strict privacy." A steely thread of irritation flowed through Gray's words as he meaningfully tilted his head toward the discreet, properly solemn Ellison. The dutiful butler still held open a door through which the returning couple had yet to fully enter, though just behind them a steady rain fell.

An unlovely flush swept over Euphemia's grim face as she whirled to stomp back up the stairs. This was the first time in memory that she'd made such a social blunder . . . and she blamed the uncivilized American for causing the scene.

"Ellison, in addition to the usual trunks, have Harris carry the private cases to our rooms." Outwardly Gray was calm, but Liz sensed his lingering irritation as he led her toward the vacant morning room.

"I'm sorry," Liz murmured once the door had closed them alone inside a room lit only by the watery sunlight falling through the long windows of one wall. They'd departed from Hayton's hunting lodge shortly after dawn to arrive at Brandt House with the morning only half gone.

"For what?" Gray's irritation with Euphemia carried over into the crisp question.

"For egging Hayton into hunting by my rules, rules that made it so much easier for the attack on you." She nervously removed a small hat and laid the stylish creation atop the table used for family games, wasting no concern over the fact that the action had loosened a carefully constructed chignon. Instead she leaned back against the table and tightly curled her hands about its edge.

That she'd called the earl Hayton rather than Lawrence lightened Gray's temper, and he smiled while shaking his head in denial of the need for her apology.

"It was an impromptu change of plans and not what caused the shot to be fired. Indeed, if it hadn't taken place there, it assuredly would've happened elsewhere. You no more caused the assault than you could've stopped it."

This was as close to a discussion of the danger as her husband had ever willingly permitted her, and Liz opened her mouth to pursue the subject. Gray guessed her intent and bent to put her sweet mouth to better use. Liz trembled as his firm lips brushed hers in a touch so tantalizing hers immediately opened, seeking what Gray was more than willing to give. Minutes later he lifted his head and, to block the sight of the alluring figure before him, lowered thick black lashes over the clouds of passion and hot silver sparks in his eyes. This was the wrong time and place for the kind of embrace his unruly senses demanded. His icy control seemed to have little power against Lilibet's inexperienced wiles.

Clinging to him for support, Liz fought a fog of desire to restore sufficient rational thought to continue her quest for withheld information. "But who could know enough to . . ."

Gray's mouth descended and again drank the heady wine of Lilibet's lips before moving to nudge aside bright ringlets to nibble her ear as he whispered, "Let's waste no time worrying about what was or might be but rather put our energies into fulfilling your welcome suggestion of yesterday, a line of defense I'm anxious to zealously pursue." His mouth slid down from her ear, around to graze the proudly worn cameo at her throat, and then dipped lower.

Liz shivered, memories of recent intimacies lighting fires until she ached with the intensity of her hunger for his touch. Running her hands over his shoulders and twining her fingers into the hair at his nape, she arched up against the handsome face taut with desire nuzzling her breasts. With a deep groan, Gray urgently lifted her completely off the floor, giving him greater access to the unbearable enticement of her generous curves.

"Fie, woman." Gray abruptly put her down, dragging deep breaths through clenched teeth. "You could tempt a monk from his vows and me to desert vital duties."

While continuing to hold her upright, he leaned back and gave a glare of feigned reproach to the passionate woman who since the moment they'd met had proven able to tumble his well-ordered life into complete disarray. She simply stepped through or around all the sensible barriers he'd erected over the years to protect him against the assault of dangerous emotions or invasions threatening to reveal the hidden core of those in his past.

"You've got to stop tempting me to stay when I truly must not." Uncomfortable with thoughts that were nearly admissions of dangerous emotion, Gray determinedly turned his attention to the immediate problem. "One can lose track of days after a weekend in the country, particularly one as eventful as the one just past." The glow in silver eyes nearly melted Liz. "But it's Monday. Parliament is already in session, and I've got to hurry off and take my seat in the upper house."

Despite the honest need for haste, Gray bent to claim one more burning kiss before pulling from her enticing arms to back away. From the open doorway he gave her a potent smile and softly called, "Until tonight, tonight. . . ."

Liz gazed after the man who the past twenty-four hours had taught her was even more devastating than in her innocence she'd dreamed possible. Weakened by the passion he'd so easily stirred, Liz drew one of the chairs out from the table and sank down. She buried a burning face into arms crossed atop the table's polished surface. As cool sanity returned, she realized how effectively he'd distracted her from the important questions she'd meant to ask. It was disconcerting to find herself caught between justified resentment of his ability and delight in its welcome pleasures. The latter thought brought to mind something else that needed doing. She must write to her father that she forgave him the trickery which had brought her this happiness—but Liz lingered unmoving while warm memories put a slight smile on her lips.

An uncounted time later, Ellison cleared his throat to win the duchess's attention.

Liz glanced up, feeling foolish for having been found alone still in her traveling clothes and more than slightly disheveled by Gray's lovemaking. As Ellison spoke she wondered if, considering his experience of human nature, he'd guessed what had caused a bride's embarrassment?

"Your Grace, Annie and Davis have already unpacked the trunks containing your gowns and the duke's apparel."

Liz nodded. That her maid and Gray's valet had taken care of the chore part of their normal duties couldn't be the reason for this visit. She waited for Ellison to explain where the problem lay.

"Unfortunately, the personal cases which the duke

also bade Harris carry up are identical. Harris doesn't know which belongs where. Would it be acceptable for him to leave them in your suite pending the moment you have time to sort out their proper places. Then if you will ring, the proper one can be moved to the duke's rooms?"

"Certainly," Liz immediately agreed. While servants packed and unpacked for their masters, it was common for members of the nobility to carry personal cases that no one but themselves were permitted to go through. She would never have invaded Gray's privacy under normal circumstances, but in the face of this dilemma either he or she would be bound to see the contents of the other's bag. By that eminently logical rationale, Liz decided it might as well be her.

Smiling brightly, Liz rose. "I'll go right now and determine which belongs where."

"Thank you, ma'am." Ellison nodded, allowing his usually impassive face to give way to a warm smile as she passed him on her way out the morning room door.

Upon entering her boudoir, Liz found the matching cases waiting neatly lined up along one side of her bed. As she absently moved toward them, thoughts wandering far from the present, a thrill of anticipation brought a soft curve to her lips. Would Gray come to her bed tonight or would she be carried to his?

More bright tendrils were freed from restraining combs unequal to the chore of keeping fiery hair upswept when Liz shook her head and determinedly turned her attention to the task at hand. The straps normally holding these cases closed had already been unbuckled, but she was certain the lids had never been lifted. Taking into account both the tempest of actions surrounding the shot that had wounded Gray and the bemusing pleasures of the hours that followed, it was little wonder that neither case had been packed with any great care.

When she simultaneously opened them, a crumpled bit of paper tumbled from Gray's over-full case. Liz bent to retrieve it and frowned slightly. The paper was decidedly not the fine quality favored by the gentry. Rather, it was coarse and had plainly been torn from a larger sheet, possibly of the sort used to wrap marketplace purchases. Placing the scrap atop the hard surface of a book laying flat in a near corner of Gray's case, she smoothed its surface with her palm . . . and went cold.

Stop or next time our aim will be better.

Cryptic but brutally clear, the crudely written threat struck Liz with the same stinging force Gray must have felt when the bullet pierced his flesh. She sank to her knees, dazed with fear for her love's life. A moment later the memory of similar jaggedly torn fragments of paper flashed through her mind. Liz scrambled to her feet. Despite trembling legs she rushed from the room, down the sweeping staircase and into the library.

Liz began a thorough search of Gray's desk to the unspoken dismay of Daisy, a plump, pretty girl only recently promoted to replace Annie as housemaid after Annie had been granted a housemaid's dream and become the duchess's personal maid.

Through the haze of her single-minded pursuit, Liz became aware of the surreptitious scrutiny of a maid industriously dusting the bookshelves. Believing it was best to face down any challenge, Liz paused and glanced up to give the other a bright smile.

"Are you happy in your new position?" Liz suspected the reason for this new face in the front of the house.

"Oh, yes, ma'am." Daisy bobbed a quick curtsy but, standing too close to the movable ladder used to fetch books down from the top shelves near the high ceiling, she nearly fell. As was true of very fair complexioned people such as she, Daisy blushed easily. And under the startlingly beautiful duchess's gaze, her round face burned brighter than ever before while her eyes instantly brimmed with liquid shame.

Liz was appalled to think she'd caused such distress. "I swear those ladders were created just to trip people." Knowing she was babbling again but unable to stop, she added. "I mean, no woman could use it with any propriety. Do you suppose that's why men invented them?"

A spurt of laughter miraculously wiped away threatened tears and left on chubby cheeks only an attractive blush.

"It's why I dust here when there's never—I mean rarely—anyone likely to come in."

"A wise choice. I'll be gone in a moment, and I promise I won't watch you if you promise me the same. Pact?"

Daisy nodded earnestly, thinking the talk in the servants' hall was true. The American duchess was a special sort and more likable than most of her class.

Feeling secure in her oddly arranged bargain, Liz returned to her quest. Just as she wouldn't have invaded her husband's case were it not for the problem of identifying owners, she wouldn't have searched through the hallowed sanctum of his desk without pressing cause. But surely finding information that might prevent someone from carrying out the death threat against Gray superseded the niceties of polite social rules.

Buried beneath a pile of paid bills in one of the lower drawers of a fine pigeonhole desk, Liz found what she sought: five more warnings in the same poor handwriting. They were worded in such a way that it was clear one had been delivered following each of Gray's previous "accidents." Equally clear was the fact that her husband refused to knuckle under to threats although he knew precisely how dangerous was the course he seemed intent upon following. Liz was on the one hand proud of his courageous determination to stand firm against intimidation, on the other more frightened than she'd ever been in her life.

It took but an instant to dismiss an urge to confront Gray with this evidence of his peril. He'd refused to bend to the villains' threats and certainly wouldn't weaken under any pleas she made. No, she had to work on her own—with a little help from Timothy and Dru. Carefully replacing things just as she'd found them, Liz rose and left the room with a parting smile for the maid, which she hoped would be interpreted as proof there'd been nothing exceptional about her actions.

Walking blindly past Ellison, Liz moved to the sweeping staircase. She was unaware that as she climbed, the butler motioned Harris into silence when he would've intercepted her to ask if the duke's case was ready for delivery to his room.

Entering her suite, Liz silently acknowledged a new challenge. In the same way and likely for the same reason—protection of the other—she must keep him uninformed. She daren't allow Gray to discover how much she knew. If that were to happen he was certain to forbid whatever plans she laid. A brief flash of wry amusement lightened concern-darkened eyes. Considering the fact that forbidding her anything had already proven a waste of his time and motion, she didn't view this as a serious barrier.

Worse and possibly more successfully, however, he'd do his best to prevent her from continuing the desperate search for his potential assassin. It didn't matter, using whatever means were necessary and no matter the danger, find that villain she would.

"You swore Gray would *never* be harmed and you lied!" In the stillness of a night-shadowed garden Euphemia's voice vibrated with disgust for the betrayal she felt had been dealt her.

"No, my dear lady." A soft, cold laugh utterly lacking in humor accompanied the immediate reply. "You asked it of me, but I swore only that Gray would not be seriously injured . . . nor was he."

Euphemia disdainfully sniffed her immediate rejection and opened her mouth to refute the claim. However, the dark-clad visitor blending into the gloom between tall hedge and an unlocked gate opening into the mews behind Brandt House allowed her no opportunity to argue the point.

"Moreover, if it's your wish to see your brother remain healthy—" He let the silence deepen before adding an ominously gentle warning. "I advise you to exercise greater caution in your actions. By sending a message to me, demanding this meeting, you took a terrible risk that endangered not only you but your partners."

"We are not partners!" The woman's hissed response was perilously loud.

"Be quiet!" The visitor's command was emphatic despite its softness. "Remember the bargain we struck to see an end to both your problem and mine; remember that in it you are as culpable as I am. By virtue of that undeniable fact we are indeed partners."

Certain that after a heavy rainfall no one would be so foolish as to venture into the midnight garden, Euphemia had chosen this site as a rendezvous point. Lingering clouds hid the moon, and though the once drenching rain had faded to a drizzle, the ground was sodden. It squished beneath her feet as she shifted in rare discomfort with a decision she'd made. Should she take the whole sordid mess to Gray? No. It would destroy her pride, shame the family name and Dru. . . .

"I've watched you," the visitor continued in a frighteningly intense whisper. "And I have discovered that the fraying ends of your nerves are showing. It worries me that you might be foolish enough to confess our bargain. Although I admire your sisterly concern for Gray, out of my sincere concern for *your* health, I advise you to keep your tongue quiet."

Euphemia lingered in the cold garden after her visitor had slipped away. The misty damp soaked through her dark shawl and dress, chilling her to the bone. But, overwhelmed by the truth in bleak facts flatly stated, she didn't notice.

CHAPTER 13

"So, Timothy, there is tangible proof that you are not responsible for your cousin's accidents." Liz felt this reassurance necessary to compensate for the initial uncertainty on the matter.

While the majority of upper class London slept, she had accompanied Dru out on an early morning drive about the park. Lady Euphemia had yet to rise, and when she did would be unable to find any apparent impropriety in the action, although within blocks of Brandt House they'd rendezvoused with Timothy. The young man now sat with the two women in the richly upholstered carriage's comparative privacy as it circled and recircled the sizable plot of rain-washed greenery near the City's center.

"But what do they want Gray to stop? And who are they?" Convinced of Timothy's innocence, Dru gave her attention to the still unsolved puzzle of what and who was responsible for her uncle's growing danger. "Unfortunately these wretched threats don't seem to provide any real answers."

"You're right." Liz's soft mouth twisted in a grimace for the truth of Dru's words. "The words don't tell us specifically what their writers want stopped. All we can assume is the obvious fact that it must be a matter over which Gray has at least a measure of influence."

Though the carriage windows were open to the fresh air, as it moved steadily onward there was little chance that Liz's words could be overheard. "I think it must be, as Timothy suggested, a political issue. However, according to speeches printed in the newspapers, Gray has taken firm stands on a variety of volatile issues from Irish home rule to revisions of the Poor Law. It does seem impossible to discern which one is the subject of these threats—a stumbling block, which only means we must try harder."

"I may have the answer," Timothy hesitantly suggested, then faltered under the hope on both women's faces. "I can't be certain it's the correct one." He retreated in an attempt to dampen their hopes to manageable levels. "In my search through House records, I found a weak yet common thread apparently connecting the timing of Gray's accidents."

The two women still stared at him expectantly. He shifted uneasily. "Each followed an eloquent speech made by Gray addressing the same issue, speeches rousing ever greater support for his view and recommended cures."

Timothy was flustered by the subject of these speeches, one which no well-bred man would so much as allude to in front of genteel ladies. Moreover, a subject whose nature he particularly disliked discussing in his sweet, naive Dru's presence. He took a deep breath, preparing to dive into the difficult statement's perilous waters.

"The white slave trade?" Remembering the speech Gray had caught her reading and discussed with her, Liz saved the young man from having to take the first plunge into the shameful topic.

"Yes." Timothy agreed, and while he nodded with

heartfelt relief the morning's weak sun picked out the lighter streaks in his hair. "Yes, exactly that. Or, more precisely, the trade flourishing between Britain and the Mideast."

Liz realized not only how difficult bringing up the subject had been for this impulsive yet very proper male companion but how hard he must have worked poring over the records to trace it. She gave him a brilliant smile. "Thank you for being so persistent in your search. I'm sure it required a great many hours to cross-check speeches and dates."

"Oh, yes, Timothy," Dru immediately added, admiration for her gallant glowing in a fond gaze. "It was wonderful of you, and now I forgive you for attending so few of the social events where I searched in vain for a glimpse of your face."

The interruption gave Liz a moment to wonder, despite her sincere gratitude, how long he'd had the information but hesitated to discuss the issue with his feminine allies. No matter, she pushed onward.

"If the white slave trade is the only political issue correlating with dates of the accidents, then I think we can be fairly certain our villains' motive is to see Gray's proposed rules for restraint defeated. Unfortunately, even if our assumption is correct, it does little to identify the villains."

"It's almost but not quite so bad as that."

Timothy's announcement startled Liz. Dark bronze brows arched in silent demanded for an explanation.

Attempting to appear nonchalant, Timothy shrugged. "A single name is repeatedly mentioned."

"A name? These speeches included a name? Oh, Timothy, why didn't you tell us immediately?" Dru gave her love's arm an urgent shake.

"Not in speeches but supporting documents—police interviews and such like. And I didn't tell you immediately because I didn't want to raise a possibly false hope." The stern rebuke of dark eyes was softened by the love in their depths for the dainty girl at his side.

"How could it be false hope if we have a name?" Liz quietly enquired, calmly exercising a sharp mind and demanding the attention of the couple on the seat facing hers.

"Because it's not precisely a name. Nor is there a particular address known for 'the Badger.' It's merely reported he lives somewhere in the warrens. A place, Lizzy, which you may not know is a dangerous labyrinth of dirty streets and disease-ridden alleys, a place even constables fear to enter."

Liz nodded. She heard the warning in the statement but refused to be hindered in questioning further. "No address? Surely the police insist on being provided some method to trace anyone suspected of criminal activities."

Feeling more than mild disgust with himself for having mentioned the creature at all, Timothy reluctantly answered. "The report states that according to their informants, the Badger negotiates his deals at the Gaiety Hall in the Haymarket area."

"Gaiety Hall? What is it? An inn? Some kind of club?" Liz was puzzled by the frivolous name for a criminal's base of operations.

Timothy turned bright red, a response that Liz thought provided her answer.

"A brothel." She said it matter-of-factly.

Dru gasped while Timothy quickly spoke to correct this mistaken impression that had made an uncomfortable situation worse.

"No! Though I guess it's not much better. Gaiety Hall is a music hall—one with a particularly unsavory reputation."

"A music hall? Is that all?" Liz was disgusted with the young man's too circumspect attitude. In Wyoming good women knew all about the fancy ladies who entertained publicly on tavern stages and privately in the rooms above. It was accepted that such females protected good women from the random assaults of cowboys and miners. "Fine, then there's nothing to prevent you and me from going there tonight and talking with this man who sports an animal's name."

"No!" Timothy cried out again, vehemently shaking his head. "Absolutely not! The Haymarket is notorious and the Gaiety Hall a dangerous place for gentlemen to visit, for a lady it would be . . . a . . . it would . . ." Surrendering to the impossibility of describing a prospect so horrifying, he weakly waved his hand.

Liz's lips firmed into a grim smile. Clearly, Gray hadn't warned Timothy about the American bride's stubborn nature. Moreover, it seemed the younger man had forgotten her single-minded resolve to—and success in—joining the London Season despite Gray's command for her to remain in the country. Too bad because otherwise she wouldn't have to waste time convincing him that, as she'd sworn nothing would be allowed to block her determined search, there was nothing Timothy could say to change her decision.

Timothy hadn't forgotten the lesson of the Cardingtons' ball and saw the obstinate glow in turquoise eyes, but he tried to reason with her. "No one will even admit to knowing what the man looks like. Apparently the Badger wields such dreadful power over those who know him that they live in grave fear of the consequences of offending him."

It was a desperate plea for sane reconsideration but, by the look on her face, one doomed to failure.

"With or without you," Liz calmly stated, meeting dark brown eyes directly. "I *will* go."

Despite a growing sense of defeat, still Timothy shook his tawny hair.

"You can't." It was Dru who nearly wailed the

alarmed protest. Though on one side she was awed by Lizzy's wild bravado, on the other she was truly terrified by a too likely dreadful end to the mad scheme.

"Forget, if you must, the dangers of Haymarket but remember precisely what business the Badger is apparently in!" This plea made it clear Dru was not so cocooned from the harsher side of the world as the other two had thought. "Remember, otherwise you may find yourself sold into some barbarian's harem!"

A shiver of fear went down Liz's spine at the image painted by the younger woman's warning. Still, she wouldn't be deterred from the planned visit when Gray's life might be the price for her cowardice.

"I won't be alone." The growing sunlight of midmorn fell through the carriage window to burn on vivid hair, a visual reinforcement of Liz's determination. "Timothy, if you refuse to protect me, I'll order Harris to accompany me."

"Before you can even depart, Harris will report your unbelievable command to Uncle Gray," Dru calmly stated. With honest regret she listed another unpleasant fact. "You'll be packed off to Ashleigh Hall posthaste."

"Not so, not so!" Soft laughter burst from Liz. "Gray won't be home until after I and whoever goes with me have gone and returned." She chose to see a good omen in the fact that at least one circumstance worked in her favor. A circumstance greatly rued when, after being gently awakened by a lock of her own hair used to tickle her nose and cheeks, with exaggerated sorrow Gray had warned her of the unhappy prospect. "Tonight Gray has a meeting at the parliamentary offices. He warned me it would likely run into the early hours of tomorrow. So, Timothy, we'll have plenty of time."

A sinking feeling assailed her chosen escort. How could he refuse, abandon his cousin's wife to enter the slums with only a servant for questionable protection? Yet, how could he be the one to take her there? He was doomed one way or the other.

"Uncle Gray has plans for the evening and so have you. Or have you forgotten the dinner at Sir William and Lady Anesty's home?" Dru demanded. "All of Society vied for invitations. Stepmama and I were among the honored few only because they wanted you to attend. You can't simply bow out at the last moment."

"Have I mentioned—" Liz began in a weak voice while rubbing her temples and frowning in apparent pain. "I feel a sick headache coming on." She limply slid sideways against the upholstery's soft red leather. "We must return to Brandt House where I mean to retire to my bed." She peeked mischievously at them from beneath the hand now rubbing her forehead. "Yes, return . . . as soon as we finalize the details of our adventure."

The pair looked at her so dubiously that Liz abruptly sat upright and glared at them. "Now that there's proof to absolve you, Timothy, will you go back on your honorable oath to help find the villain behind these threats against your cousin? And you, Dru? What happened to the great concern you so recently expressed for Gray? I thought you both more courageous than this."

"Of course, I'm not going back on my oath." Timothy would never have claimed to anyone that he was the bravest man alive, but he certainly wasn't about to look a pigeonheart before this brave woman or, more important still, the woman he loved. "It's just that it would be better for me to go alone."

"No!" The denial came from both women simultaneously.

"You're wrong, Timothy," Dru heatedly responded. "It would be better if we all three go together."

Liz hadn't expected the timid Dru to suggest, let

alone demand, to go this far. Thankfully, here also there were fortunate circumstances that first, placed a barrier against Dru's demand, and second, offered an important task to keep her otherwise occupied for the evening.

"Now it's you who are forgetting the dinner at Sir William and Lady Anesty's. No matter the reason you think you and your stepmama were invited, Lady Euphemia assuredly regards the invitation as a social coup. Your part in our scheme is to convince your stepmama of my illness. Then see she arrives at the dinner party and remains the entire evening to enjoy their hospitality."

Dru couldn't deny the need for this action, but a slight pout turned rosy lips down as she reluctantly nodded acceptance of the charge.

Filled with growing confidence in her plan, Liz shifted her attention to Timothy. "Once the others have departed, with my reliable Annie's help, I'll slip out and through the gardens to meet you just outside the back gate into the mews."

When Liz returned through the unlocked garden gate, her shoulders slumped, weighted down by disappointment. The adventure begun with great hope had ended with precious little to show for the size of the risk taken. Her foray into the Haymarket area and notorious Gaiety Club had provided only a frightening view of the dark, fetid realities of life among the dregs of human existence. Sad to say, the questionable good of that demoralizing lesson had been the evening's high point. She and Timothy had completely failed to secure even the tiniest clues regarding the subject of their quest. The substantial bribes offered rough characters crowding the Gaiety Hall had won nothing but irritable shrugs and stony stares and resulted in Liz's growing frustration. Seemed even this most desperate of measures had only proved the unyielding strength of the wall of secrecy barring Liz from her goal.

Liz carefully skirted the stone-laid path, afraid the noise of her booted feet would draw attention. It was late, much later than she'd expected to be. However, the house's inhabitants seemed to be sleeping, giving her reason to assume the servants were abed and making it possible for her to slip unseen through their entry at the house's rear.

The well-oiled door opened and closed silently as a heavily veiled Liz moved through it. Lifting the hem of a dark cloak and gown with black-gloved hands, she ascended three steep steps into the back passage, heartened by the belief that at least her identity remained as much a secret to underworld denizens as the Badger's was to her.

"Oh, thank the good Lord!" Annie reached out and pulled the duchess into the servants' hall. "Ma'am, the duke's home and looking for you." Desperate anxiety filled whispered words while shaking hands began quickly removing and tossing the dark cloak aside before starting to unfasten buttons down Liz's spine. "I brought your nightgown here, praying you'd soon return. We've got to get you into it and up to him straight away."

"What did you tell him?" Heart pounding so hard it threatened to choke her, Liz fumbled with the tiny catches on kidskin gloves. She was oblivious to the bizarre picture she presented, standing in a dress nearly undone while her gloves remained demurely in place, and insistently repeated her whispered question. "What did you tell him?"

"I lied." Though Annie's words were barely audible, their terror was crystal clear. "When he found your bedroom empty, he sent for me. He asked me where you were and I lied. For that he could dismiss me without character." The last was the soft wail of a tiny mouse trapped by a cat—a panther.

"No, he can't," Liz whispered back, stripping off one glove and turning her energies to the other, striving all the while to be hastily rid of her clothes. "Even if the duke dismissed you without my consent—and I'd make his life miserable if he tried—it's I who would be asked to supply references for you, and I would give you a sterling recommendation."

Annie's trembling fingers steadied a little in response to her mistress's encouragement. "I told him you came down seeking a tisane for your headache. Then, feeling faint after taking it, you sat down for a moment . . . and dozed off here in the servants' hall."

The maid's weak smile was an admission of how very lame this excuse sounded. Liz gave Annie a reassuring smile, struggling all the while with straps, laces, and garters, thankful that with the prospect of being swathed in shapeless black, she hadn't worn a corset. A corset would've been difficult to be rid of and would've left its impressions on her skin for some little time to come.

"My nerves were making a meal of my thin courage. I was certain His Grace would see the truth on my face, so I foolishly picked up your pretty china bowl—the one you keep odd bits and pieces in on your dresser. I told him I hadn't liked to wake my poor lady when, after enduring a difficult day, she was finally resting."

A drift of soft, white cambric descended over Liz's head while the last of her dainty underwear dropped to the floor. She slipped her arms into sleeves whose cuffs, like the neckline, were delicately tucked and embroidered.

"'Course," Annie continued, "the duke wanted to know where you were sleeping so as he might carry you to your own bed."

Rather than hearing danger in the statement, Liz's turquoise eyes softened to a gentle haze. That Gray had wanted to care for his ailing wife warmed a soul chilled by the evening's defeat. Even in the midst of this moment's urgent predicament, the prospect of him carrying her upstairs reminded Liz of their previous night. Yestermorn, on their return from Hayton Lodge, she'd wondered if he would come to her or if she'd be summoned to him. In actual fact, cradling her close, he'd carried her into his chamber where he'd lowered her into the fiery welcome of his huge bed.

"Well," Annie added, interrupting thrilling memories with reminders of their present desperate plight. "When he said that, don't you know I was so startled I dropped the china bowl. Not apurpose, but I used its crash to keep him from coming in search of someone who wasn't to be found. Told him that he was never to mind 'cause my clumsiness had surely awakened you."

Annie finished tying a narrow ribbon into a bow at her mistress's throat. "You made it back but just barely as it was only minutes ago that I assured him I'd come tell you he'd returned."

Liz took one last moment to be sure that the delicate gown's folds were properly arranged before turning toward the door . . . a door swinging open.

"Lilibet, are you feeling better?" Gray quietly asked, concern lowering his voice to dark velvet. News of his wife's illness had shocked him with unpleasant memories and fears that the unhappy past was repeating itself. He'd have sworn Lilibet wasn't prone to the same fragility as Camellia. He couldn't bear to think his fiery, wanton innocent would, as the delicate Camellia had, begin to sicken and fade so soon after their marriage. Most of all, he didn't want to believe, refused to consider, the possibility of a similiar ghastly end.

Praying Annie's skirts and the shadows behind

would hide carelessly discarded clothing piled in a corner of this most inappropriate room, Liz rushed into Gray's outstretched arms.

"You're cold." He wrapped her closely in his embrace while sending Annie a look of faint reproach. "Shouldn't have been allowed to sleep here."

"No, Gray, don't blame Annie." Leaning back, Liz gave Gray a pleading smile of such innocence he'd have been suspicious were his emotions not already in turmoil. "She knows how poorly I've been feeling today, and I'm sure her actions were born of the noblest motives."

Liz hid an impish smile against the scarlet velvet of her incredibly handsome husband's dressing robe. She could hear his heart pounding with an unnaturally rapid beat. Did he suspect something? Was he angry with her?

"Are you upset with me for falling asleep down here?" She rubbed her cheek against the broad planes above that too loud thumping.

"Upset with you for that? Why ever would I be?" Gray was amazed that his seldom repentant wife sounded so sincerely fearful of irritating him, he held her back and gazed down to see her anxiously nibbling a soft lower lip. "No, the truth is I feared for your health."

Of a sudden Liz remembered the first wife who'd been so fragile and often sick. "Don't worry about me, Gray. I'm healthy as any sturdy American girl ought to be." Guilt flowed over her. She'd just used the same shameful pretense her father had inflicted upon her and caused pain in the man she loved.

"It was a simple headache and gone now that I've slept." Her bright grin turned to a mock frown of regret. "Indeed, I'm in such fine shape that my only problem will be the hours it'll likely take for me to fall asleep again."

Her energetic claim of good health soothed Gray's

worry so thoroughly that in answer to her last claim, a sardonic smile curled his lips. "A problem sleeping? Let's see if I can help you while away those night hours and ease you into slumber."

Gray swept his wife off her feet and, to the maid's delight, carried her from the servants' hall, up the stairway's wide curve, and into the master's room. There a freshly stocked blaze roared but not so hot nor bright as the pyre of pleasure he and his fiery mate built to consuming heights and then rekindled to burn again and again throughout the remaining hours of night.

At an hour nearer dawn than midnight, the front door to a palatial house opened, admitting the entrance of an extraordinary pair no one would've expected to be permitted within miles of so fine a residence.

"Git in ther', 'Lil Tom," a burly man hissed, shoving a boy of perhaps ten. "And don't give the gents no sass or I'll see as you regret it. You an' yer brother, too."

'Lil Tom nodded earnestly, staring at an impassive man dressed in the impeccable garb of a butler. It tickled him when the butler began leading them toward the light glowing through an open door for all the world like someone important come to call. He stared at the elegant surroundings, awed by the beauty of a home someone of his station was unlikely to ever see—lest he was to take to thievery.

A fire burned in the book-lined room where their two hosts silently waited, backs to the flames and faces in shadow.

"Tell 'im wot you see'd, brat." The man smacked the boy's ear.

"Ther' were a gent and a loidy come t' ther hall t'night, askin' questions 'bout the Badger."

"Names?" The single-word question was a rough whisper.

"Nah. But I follered 'em home. Leastways, ther loidy. Then ther gent got a hansom an' I lost 'im."

The host gave a brief growl of acknowledgment then added another single-word question. "Where?"

"Ther loidy, yer mean?"

A deeper, disgusted growl urged the boy to waste no more of the man's time.

"Follered 'em a nasty long ways through ther mews then ther gent slipped round ta ther front and down 'ta wher' 'e got a hansom. Once 'e got took up, I went back and see'd ther sign. Don't read ner write, but I's good wit' mi 'ands." 'Lil Tom held stretched out the grubby instruments of which he boasted.

"I carries a bit a coal in mi pocket, see, an' I found an ol' newspaper so as I could copy ther marks down." 'Lil Tom was plainly proud of his initiative as he pulled a grubby scrap of a paper from inside his shirt and traded it for a shiny sovereign.

Across a piece of torn newsprint so old it threatened to disintegrate, badly formed characters were scrawled:

Brandt House

CHAPTER 14

Despite its position in the midst of the City, the garden spreading out behind the duke of Alerby's residence was remarkable. Plants nurtured in hothouses throughout the winter had been carefully restored to neatly tended beds. There, under a clear sky's welcome sun, the profusion of blooms in many hues filled the air with heady scents and supplied an appropriate background for the array of noblewomen exquisitely garbed in rich laces, ribbons, and gossamer fabrics. The few men available to attend a midafternoon garden party seemed to be present for the sole purpose of providing lovely women with the admiration due them.

Beautifully dressed in a confection of ivory laces and delicate fabrics in various shades of pink, daring for one of her coloring yet a perfect complement, Liz stood with a charming smile on lips that murmured appropriate words. Almost oblivious to her surroundings, she hardly saw the people milling about the garden's center and near edges of paved paths. Like some well-oiled machine, Liz inwardly mocked herself, she moved through the motions required of her as one of Lady Alerby's guests. Somewhere in the back of her mind she registered surprise that this was possible when her thoughts were so far removed from the present time and place. Her thoughts were memories of the late hours spent in Gray's arms and the growing tenderness that had pillowed their heated play, memories that deepened both her fears for his safety and her despondency over the failure to learn anything of value in the Gaiety Hall.

"My dear, you're so white you look ready to collapse."

Shaken from bleak thoughts by another's perception, Liz's attention dropped to find, standing directly in front of her, a petite woman of an age to be her grandmother, possibly even great-grandmother. A woman who, despite her frailty, proudly bore a confidence earned over many years.

"Come sit with me." When the stranger gave an appealing smile and tilted her head, sunlight glowed on the thick silvery hair revealed by a tastefully small hat. "We'll share a brief chat and relax."

Caught with worried thoughts all awry, Liz had no quick response. The only thought that came clear in the muddle was a useless recognition that the understated elegance of this woman's purple-gray gown was the perfect foil for an ingrained hauteur as surely a part of her as the penetrating darkness of unblinking eyes.

"If you won't admit to that need for yourself, then take pity on me. I'll willingly admit I am that weary and in need of a few moments rest."

The light touch on Liz's arm was far too weak to force anyone, least of all someone as headstrong as herself, into an action she'd rather not take. But, perhaps because of that weakness or because of the woman's plea of fatigue, Liz yielded.

Once they reached a sturdy wicker bench in the shade of a towering elm in one corner of the garden, the charming older woman settled on the seat's edge and half turned to face Liz with a bright knowing gaze.

"I'm Lady Charles and your husband's grandmother was my dearest friend. When I saw my friend's most prized possession at your throat, I knew I must make your acquaintance."

Faintly scowling, Liz's hand spread protectively over the delicate piece nestled in ivory lace. Did the woman mean to challenge her worthiness to wear it?

"Lilibet treasured that cameo brooch above all other possessions, save the grandson who bore her beloved husband's name." A faint smile gentled the facial lines of an inbred arrogance unable to steal the warmth of her nature. "She entrusted the keepsake of her happy marriage to Grayson, telling him to give it to the woman he would one day love."

Having regained a firm hold on the present, Liz sensed there was a purpose behind Lady Charles's desire to speak with her and wished she knew what it was or even what was expected of her. She settled for the one fact she could state with absolute honesty.

"I can assure you that I prize this brooch as dearly as your friend must have done."

"I'm pleased, the cameo should be treasured by its owner." The older woman smiled in genuine pleasure but still did not settle comfortably against the bench's high back. "It should also continue to be the symbol of a successful union."

While returning the smile, Liz's eyes went soft with thoughts of the unexpected happiness she'd found in hers.

"I was worried by your apparent distraction." Lady Charles's face took on a regretful expression, truly sorry for the young American doubtless struggling to adjust to unfamiliar ways. "And as you are new to our social circles, I thought it my duty to counsel you on its practices, in particular one which astute wives choose not to see."

Liz knew how extremely unlikely it was that Lady Charles had any notion what had actually distracted her. Therefore, it wasn't that statement which shook her. Rather, the moment the word "duty" was spoken, a stab of apprehension scattered her haze of comforting warmth. Never in Liz's experience had another's use of the word been a precursor to welcome news.

"It's a practice well-bred Englishwomen have learned to dismiss, but one which I fear you may not be prepared to meet." Suspecting that the young duchess had already heard hints of unpleasant rumors, Lady Charles raised a subject she was certain would be easier to digest coming from a sympathetic voice. If she did not warn the girl, she'd no doubt these facts would be fed to her in cruel bits and pieces by spiteful gossip mongers always anxious to stir half-truths into the kettle of happiness and brew a fresh tea of scandal.

"Your husband and I share the same solicitor. Though our Mr. Stevens is the soul of discretion, until very recently he employed a clerk of somewhat less admirable qualities. That person let it slip to several nosey parkers that Grayson has recently altered his will to include a bequest that ensures the occupant of a home in St. John's Wood remains in comfort till the end of her days."

Confused by this odd bit of information seemingly of little interest to her, Liz said nothing.

"She is Grayson's 'kept woman.'" Caught between amusement and pity for the young duchess's naïveté, Lady Charles leaned forward to whisper the acceptable term for a vulgar reality. "As I understand it, she's inhabited the home for a number of years, since long before he traveled to America."

Liz felt like a fool for not having understood the woman's meaning from the first. But even understanding it now, she felt numb, stunned into silence.

"I can see this has come as a shock to you, my dear." Lady Charles gently patted dainty hands gloved in fine white kidskin. "I hate to be the bearer of unpleasant tidings, but I feared it would be necessary to see that you comprehend Gray's position in a society that perhaps deals with situations such as this in ways unfamiliar to you."

Liz heard the words and in her mind saw pictures of Gray with another woman in his arms. All those nights he'd claimed he must work late to resolve differences and make compromises with his fellow politicians had he been in some little cottage cavorting with his mistress? Painful hurt fed a smoldering anger. Englishwomen might choose to look away and pretend they didn't know, but she'd warned Gray of her inability to pretend to be what she wasn't. He couldn't expect her to turn a blind eye to his games. The only option she saw for dealing with the "situation" was to confront him with it face to face.

Lady Charles was alarmed by the fires kindling in turquoise eyes. "Perhaps, now that you're wed, he'll have no desire to continue his visits to St. John's Wood. Perhaps he has already broken it off but, as an honorable man, finds himself unable to cruelly pitch into the street a woman who's been loyal to him for so long, a woman who must be past the age to secure alternate support."

"Lady Charles, there you are."

The unexpected call shattered the uncomfortable tension between the one called and the younger woman who had said not a single word since the unpleasant disclosure was made. They both turned to see the afternoon's hostess rushing toward them.

"Ellen has been searching for you. I believe she wants you to meet the Honorable Colin Benhurst." Blond brows so pale they were almost invisible arched knowingly.

Giving Liz a resigned smile, Lady Charles stood up. "My granddaughter wants me to support her wish to marry the young man although my son disapproves." She hadn't had time to give this Lilibet the advice she'd meant to impart but willingly abandoned the effort.

Liz politely rose also, watching while the other two moved toward the garden's center and melted into a crowd gathered about tables laid with tasty delicacies encircling a massive punch bowl. In the past days and weeks Liz had become aware that the price for being the Toast of the Season was to rarely be permitted a moment's peace. She was grateful to find that with the others' attention bent on the proffered meal, it was possible to slip unnoticed into the relative privacy of an ivy-draped gazebo. It was hidden in a grove of trees behind the wicker bench she'd shared with Lady Charles. By some miracle—likely the fact that the female guests had come to show off their gowns, exchange gossip, and review the details of recent social events for which privacy was useless—it was empty.

Hoping that in the sizable crowd she wouldn't be missed too soon, Liz welcomed the shadowy peace to assimilate the painful revelation of Gray's mistress. She sank forlornly down on the bench lining five of its six sides. Sharp pangs of jealousy punctuated anguished clouds of betrayal. How could it be that the man alternately so tender and so passionate with her could want to be with another woman? And not merely be with but also thought so much of her that he'd kept her for years.

Another unpleasant thought struck a further blow. Obviously Gray had chosen that woman because she embodied what he actually wanted. On the other side, despicable trickery had landed him with her, a female he'd early made clear was the opposite of what he found either alluring or admirable. The memory of

Annie's description of Camellia, the frail and pastel wife he'd chosen, underlined that sad truth.

Never before had Liz felt so worthless or despondent.

The velvet petals of a single pink tea rose brushed against Liz's cheek. Startled, she pulled away while turquoise eyes brimming with liquid crystal gazed up at the man holding its stem.

"Lawrence." It was an unsteady and none too welcoming gasp. Liz wanted, needed to be alone.

"I saw you sneaking into this hideaway, looking like a little lost child." Lawrence ignored her unspoken request for privacy and settled beside her, putting the rose whose thorns he'd removed into her limp hands. "I had to come and see what I might do to help you find your way again."

With the back of one hand, Liz dashed away the single tear that defeated her will to roll down an emotion-brightened cheek. "I'm fine. I just needed a moment to catch my breath."

"Fine? Of course you are." Lawrence quietly agreed, dark eyes softening while at the same time laying his open hand against the side of her neck and using a thumb to gently rub away yet another escaping tear.

Liz ducked to free herself and turned her back on the man, hoping he'd accept the action for the demand to be left in peace that it was.

"Don't worry so. I'm told even the happiest marriages must endure rocky paths at the start." He squeezed her stiffly held shoulders reassuringly. "Surely this tempest can be no more than the storm brewed by one of the little tiffs to which newlyweds are prone."

To Liz's eternal mortification, his consignment of her pain to matters so trivial released the floodgates. She silently wept and the drenching rain washed cheeks burning with shame.

Lawrence gently turned the bride, whose will had weakened, and took her into a platonic embrace. "I'm sorry, Lizzy. Sorry, sorry, sorry." He whispered the comforting cadence into her ear, dislodging a smart bonnet crowned with silk roses. "I ought to have known it would be more serious than a lovers' tiff when you've a bridegroom so crass as to suggest, as Gray did during our transatlantic crossing, that he could easily seduce you into providing him an heir."

Under the sharp blow of this further revelation, Liz cried the harder. Recognition of her gullibility rubbed salt into the wound and stung her temper to renewed life. Hadn't she warned herself from the first of the danger in any man so stunningly handsome as Gray? He'd proven the harsh truth of her worst fears. She had fallen to his wiles as easily as he'd no doubt expected. Oh, hell and damnation, easier, for hadn't it been she who'd gone to him offering to provide his heir? She had been a fool; she *was* a fool to still love him so deeply she could almost forgive him the justified boast. But she could not, indeed, *never* would forgive him the other woman. Fine English ladies might turn blind eyes to such arrangements, but not this American!

"A man so unfeeling as Gray," Lawrence whispered again into the ear buried in red curls escaped from inadequate restraints, "is unworthy of so wonderful a wife as you."

Suddenly conscious of her compromising position, held tight in the arms of a man not her husband and thus almost as guilty as Gray, Liz pulled away and attempted to restore a semblance of normality. That it was a doomed cause became immediately clear. A number of necessary hairpins were lost forever in the narrow cracks between the boards of the floor, the straw reinforcing her bonnet was bent beyond repair and though tears had slowed, they refused to completely halt their irritating flow.

"Let me help—" Lawrence began, dark eyes warm and sympathetic.

The firm shaking of an already loosened chignon saw the last pins fall away and a wealth of fiery curls descend to cloak slender shoulders in wild disarray.

"You must, Lizzy. Since you can hardly return to the party with your hair unbound, charmingly lovely though it is, you've no choice. So, allow me to see you back to Brandt House and safely inside."

Liz firmly shook her head and tried to speak but couldn't get words beyond a deeply resented lump in her throat.

"Hush while I go leave a message to later, much later, be delivered to Lady Euphemia. A simple message saying you've a fierce headache but didn't want to interrupt the afternoon's enjoyment for her or Lady Drusilla."

He was right and Liz knew it. She had no choice. While he was off on his errand, she renewed the search for lost hairpins and recovered enough to pile fiery tresses in a less than stylish knot atop her head. It was hopelessly unsteady, but she prayed it would see her into Brandt House without rousing suspicion and starting too many backstairs rumors.

By the time Lawrence reappeared, Liz had her tears under control, but beneath the ominous composure lay simmering emotions beginning to boil. She'd been foolish to be jealous of his dead wife when Gray had apparently been unfaithful to her as well. Liz's savior led the way between greenery and garden wall to a servants' gate at the kitchen side of the house. His carriage already awaited them there.

The journey to Brandt House passed in silence, but once they stopped in the mews behind the back gate, the same back gate Liz had crept through the previous night, Lawrence spoke.

"I'll be at Hayton Lodge for the next several days—problems have arisen concerning the police investigation of Gray's hunting accident. But if there's anything I can do, anything you need, send a message and I'll instantly return."

Anxious to get safely unseen into the house, Liz absently nodded before nearly falling out of the carriage, in her haste ignoring a footman's offered assistance.

"Your Grace," Annie hesitantly interrupted the duke's progress down the corridor toward his own room. When he stopped and turned penetrating silver eyes to her, she nearly faltered. "Your wife asks that you come to her."

"What?" Gray had plans for this evening, dangerous plans, and he'd hoped to depart without having to lie to his wife about it. "I thought Lilibet was to be at a garden party this afternoon."

"She did go, but her headache returned and she came home early." Annie was so nervous she bobbed another curtsy, intending to flee only to find herself frozen in place by his icy glare.

Gray nodded but swept past the maid, worried by this sign of a more serious illness than Lilibet had admitted last night. Quickly entering the room and expecting to find her in bed, he strode in that direction.

"Grayson." Still in her pink garden party gown, Liz spoke from the doorway connecting bedroom and sitting room. "I sent Annie to ask you to join me here where I can be certain of privacy for an honest talk."

The lingering daylight falling between heavy velvet drapes highlighted the silver at his temples as he nodded a dark head, trying to make sense out of this vision of an unexpectedly healthy wife babbling about honesty.

"You know I have a distaste for lies and half-truths—" Having just glimpsed her devastating husband's unquestionable fear for her health, Liz found it more difficult than she'd expected to raise a subject almost certain to end in harsh discord. "That being so, you won't be surprised by my demand to know if it's true that you keep a woman in St. John's Wood."

Gray was stunned. This was his ailing wife? This harridan making demands for truth from him was the woman he'd been terrified of losing? Her attack was all the more upsetting after he'd spent a decade striving to atone for his youthful follies. Now when he was innocent she condemned him.

The warmth Liz had of recent days found in Gray's eyes was gone, turned to ice. To fight back a growing panic over whether it was right to question him, she wielded thoughts of another woman in his arms and demanded an answer. "Can't you tell me the truth?"

"Truth?" Gray roared. "What would a woman prey to wicked headaches conveniently cured know of that? You want the truth from me? I want the truth from you—where were you really last night when I so inconveniently returned earlier than expected?"

Liz felt as if the wind had been knocked out of her, certainly the ground beneath her self-righteous virtue had been shaken. Unable to give him the answers he demanded, she'd no right to expect truthful answers from him.

While she stood, gripping the door frame until her fingertips turned white, he turned without another word and walked out of the room and out of the house.

The two ladies Liz had left at the garden party had returned as Grayson entered his bride's suite. In his concern he'd forgotten to close the door behind him, unintentionally defeating Liz's goal of privacy and his own demand that family matters be held in confidence. The entire house had heard their dispute.

Satisfaction lent an unpleasant glow to otherwise

dull gray eyes. Euphemia had heard every word of the loud altercation, proof of the American's lack of breeding. All well-bred Englishwomen knew better than to mention, much less question, their husbands' private lives. Dru left her gloating stepmama on the landing and hurried to Liz's room.

That night was the first time Liz ate a family dinner in Brandt House. She was sorry for having sent her regrets, pleading a headache, to the hostess of an assuredly more pleasant event but with Dru's silent, unbending support made it through the meal. Then Annie was there to nurse the headache which, by the evening's end, had become a reality.

In the back of a large room Gray and a friend sat at a small table across from two rough figures who were more than half drunk. Bright light from the stage at the room's opposite end revealed tiers of boxes and balconies on three sides while in the center of the floor were numerous tables. Now that the jugglers, jesters, and contortionists were done, the place resounded with bawdy songs and the loud revelry of its patrons —ladies in gaudy dresses with flounces low off the shoulders and men of every station from the crude and roughly garbed to the rich and dressed in formal black and white. In this meanest of all music halls the former were far more common than the latter.

"Nah, m'lor." A gaunt man with a disconcertingly blank gaze that nonetheless left the impression that it was sizing up every possibility for self-interest. "Ain't no one name o' Badger here, but 'e sure mus' be somethin' big 'cause ther were someone lookin' for 'im last night too."

Gray peered through greasy atmosphere that included a foul odor of gin, sweat, and bad perfume one could nearly see. "Someone asked about the Badger last night?"

"'At's roit, guv." This answer came from the shorter, even less steady of the pair who'd slipped into seats at their table as if some bizarre welcoming party.

"What did he look like?" Gray was disconcerted to think that someone else was scraping the same filthy pot as he. Friend or foe? It didn't really matter. Either way it would likely muck up the whole, making it important to see that the others stopped.

"Ther was two 'o 'em . . . one a loidy and one a gent." The first speaker took over again, plainly put out at the other's participation.

"And . . ." Gray restrained his impatience, silver eyes demanding more. A lady? Well, a female. It startled him to think of a woman involved in this nasty trade, but on second thought realized the foolishness of that logic. After all, women had been dealing in the misery of others of their gender for centuries. The madams and procuresses in London alone were innumerable.

"Ther loidy was draped 'ed to toe in black, couldn't say wot 'er look'd loike. But ther gent gots dark oiyes and loight 'air."

"How tall?"

"'Bout ther size o' yer mate. Yer agree, Stan?" The blank gaze shifted to the drunk beside him who didn't look able to remember much of anything from day to day.

"Aye." When the man sharply nodded, several lank strands of hair fell around his mottled face. The action nearly overset Stan, and his companion was forced to catch and again prop him up with arms folded on the tabletop.

"Thank you," Gray smiled grimly and gave each a shiny coin which they immediately tested between the few brown teeth they still possessed. Their description fit two men of Gray's acquaintance. Neither seemed likely but both could be ominous. Timothy surely had no reason to desire a meeting with the Badger. And even more surely Hayton already knew the man.

Gray and Sir David departed from the Gaiety Hall's raucous din, welcoming even the acrid smell in the darkness beyond. As they wound through the unsavory streets of the Haymarket, Sir David had to take twice as many steps to keep pace with an irritated Gray's much longer stride. There were few gaslights in this part of the City, a stretch of bawdy houses, sweatshops, and gin mills bordering the bleak misery of the tenements in the warrens beyond. The only consistent illumination came from a moon barely cresting the ragged skyline of dilapidated buildings that would likely collapse if decades of filth were removed. Wretched as the buildings were, the inhabitants paying a pence for a strip of floor to sleep on were fortunate. From every shadowed corner they passed came the sounds of dogs, rats, and pitiful humans struggling for survival.

"Don't see why we had to slog through such nasty surroundings, old boy." The always contented, pleasant Sir David sounded sincerely befuddled by the journey and a touch disgusted that Gray had as well have led him into the sewers.

"Sorry, David." Gray did regret bringing this friend of his father's down into the kind of human desperation the man had likely never seen nor cared to permit disturb his comfortable life. He hadn't wanted anyone to accompany him on this ill-fated trip during which he'd learned nothing of what he'd wanted but too much of what he didn't.

"See the glow to the right. Those are the gas-lighted streets where we'll be able to hail a hansom to take us to our club with its warmth, cleanliness, and good food to eat."

"Let's hurry and be shut of this horrible place." Sir David renewed his efforts, forcing his stubby legs to move faster.

"'Orrible place, guv?" A huge brute of a man stepped directly into Sir David's path, broken-toothed smile gleaming with malice. "Fer tha' insult ter our fair 'ome yer'v got ta pay us toll ta pass."

Blustering, Sir David fell back and nearly lost his balance on grimy cobblestones. Gray stepped around his companion, activating the catch on his stylish walking stick. A hidden sword hissed free. Moonlight glinted off steel as, with the easy grace of a cat, he advanced on their accoster, an equally deadly intent glittering in silver eyes. Like an overmatched rat, the man turned tail and scuttled back into the sewers from which he'd come.

His opponent fled, but at the ominous sound of a body falling Gray spun about. Sir David lay crumpled, stunned, in the filthy street while poised above him, a wiry assailant aimed a foot at his ribs.

"Stop!" Gray yelled before the blow could land.

Startled and off balance, the man stumbled, but as he fell managed to lash out, striking Gray's wrist a numbing blow.

The sword knocked from Gray's hand skittered across cobblestones to stop against the wall behind a foe rising to his feet with the amazing agility of desperation. Facing the other, armed only with fists and sharp wits, Gray waited, cool and confident.

The second assailant, with a stirring Sir David behind and this daunting target proven dangerous foe ahead, launched a rash assault, swinging fists recklessly. Gray ducked and whirled, so successfully dodging poorly aimed blows that only one landed, grazing his jaw. Increasingly frustrated and huffing breathlessly, his opponent's guard slipped. Gray's fist sank into an unprotected stomach and fetid breath exploded in his face. Then Gray's other fist deliberately smashed the man's chin, laying him flat.

"Gray . . ." At Sir David's weak call, Gray turned toward a shaken friend's faint accusation.

Sidestepping the man who'd thought to extort money from them but had instead been robbed of his senses, Gray helped Sir David to his feet before scooping up the sword and sheathing it in his walking stick.

When the older man, grimacing in distaste, began brushing away the worst of the dirt, Gray urged him to hurry. "We've fresh reason to believe what I already knew—the dangers lurking in these streets."

Nerves taut with awareness of those dangers, likely growing each moment they delayed, and despite Sir David's feeble protest, Gray hustled his companion through the last of the grimy streets. Only when they reached the safety of well-lit and patrolled streets did he slow their near-running pace. And only after he'd hailed a hansom and they were safely inside did he permit himself to consider the question: Had they merely been the victims of another of the many attacks common to the area or had their assailants been ordered to specifically attack him?

CHAPTER 15

Having waited until Gray departed from the library and the house, it was midmorn when Liz quietly slipped into the book-lined room, laid the freshly ironed newspaper across the desk top, and began scanning its pages. Finding what she sought, Liz sank down into a chair and carefully read yet another of her husband's speeches urging action to end the horrors of the white slave trade.

Upon arriving at the morning room for breakfast, she'd been surprised to find Gray still there . . . though not for long. He'd risen the instant she walked in and, with an icy glare, had silently left her alone with rashers of bacon, lightly buttered fingers of toast, and marmalade. But that instant had been long enough for Liz to see the purple bruise discoloring one strong cheek. Plainly he'd been assaulted and this speech confirmed Timothy's theory that these attacks inevitably followed every action Gray took to see the despicable practice halted.

Gray was furious with her, but then she was none too pleased with him. However, Liz could no more stifle love for her apparently uncaring husband than she could suppress a growing alarm over the dangers threatening him. She was determined to plow onward with her attempt to unmask the face of his enemy the better to protect his safety.

Turning her attention from newspaper to the bottom desk drawer, Liz quickly found the file she sought still residing beneath paid bills. A new scrap of paper had been added and the words scrawled on it read: "Two of my minions this time. Next time more and you won't walk away."

"Your Grace—" Annie softly called from a barely opened door.

Liz glanced up and knew by the excited glow in her maid's eyes that something was afoot. "Come in."

Annie stepped inside, freshly starched uniform crackling. She was careful to close the door silently behind while Liz exercised equal care in returning the file to its position in the bottom drawer.

"Like you suggested," Annie began, "I've listened to servants' gossip everywhere you've visited. Mostly they babble over silly backstairs entanglements and suspicions of what mischief their betters are about." Her hand made a rapid fluttering motion as if shooing away a pesky fly. "But just yesterday, while you were in the garden and I was in the servants' hall, I heard something strange, something I thought you might like to know. I guess it's as well you left me behind when you returned home, as I'd not have heard it elsewise."

Liz recognized the hint of justified censure but, unwilling to impede the flow of Annie's words with an apology that would be as sincere when given later, merely nodded encouragement. This was apparently her morning to learn new things . . . only fair considering all that she'd learned from Lady Charles and Lawrence the previous afternoon.

"There's talk of a rough character making repeated

late night visits to Hayton House . . . and last time a street urchin was with him."

"Did your babbler know this rough character's name?" Waiting with breath held for an unlikely answer, Liz nibbled her lower lip.

Annie shook her head mournfully. "Unfortunately the source in the earl's home can't remember but claims it matters little as it wasn't a proper name, just some sort of animal nickname."

This information, which Annie thought unsatisfactory, pleased Liz, and turquoise eyes glittered although she stared blindly at the newspaper still laying open across the desk. Seemed certain that the "rough character" making midnight visits to the earl was the Badger. Despite Lawrence's practiced kindnesses a day past, Liz had for some time suspected him of having a part in Gray's danger. Now she was certain that he did. However, suspicion was not enough. Physical evidence would be necessary.

"Thank you, Annie." Liz refocused her attention on the earnest young maid. "Once again you've been a great help to my cause. Moreover, I assure you there were reasons for my hasty departure from the garden party without calling for you to accompany me. But still I apologize for not leaving you word of my leave-taking."

Quick to forgive, Annie's cheery smile flashed. Then, having said what she'd come to say, she bobbed a quick curtsy before slipping out the door.

While Liz returned the newspaper to its usual position, carefully draped over a waiting stand's horizontal brass rod, her mind began quickly devising and discarding possible methods to obtain the needed physical evidence. Purpose straightened her spine and tilted her chin as she, too, slipped from the library. She must find Dru and win the timid girl's cooperation in a daring scheme.

* * *

"Can't believe you talked me into this," Dru dramatically whispered to Liz—as if anyone were likely to overhear a conversation held in a closed carriage.

"We'll be safe, Your Ladyship." Annie promptly offered reassurance to the noble girl roughly her age although of infinitely higher status. "Jeremy knows what to do to make it seem an accident without injuring us."

Dru grinned at the maid as likable and almost as prone to quick, bold action as her mistress. At Liz's behest, the girl had wheedled her young man to borrow the still absent under coachman's uniform and, obeying the duchess's command, bring the coach around for the three of them to use on an after-tea ride.

"But how can you be so certain when your Jeremy isn't even a coachmen?" A born worrier, Dru was sincerely concerned, and yet she enjoyed gently teasing the girl.

"He *has* been trained," Annie heatedly defended her particular friend, country accent showing through the careful discipline of her voice. "An' since Beaton has stayed with his family at Ashleigh for more'n three weeks and don't seem inclined to return to the City, likely Jeremy'll soon be officially named under coachman."

While the other two debated the opening stage of this shaky scheme, Liz mentally cringed. Annie's innocent statement of her beau's ability to "make it look like an accident" too vividly reminded Liz they were about to employ the very same trickery that the foe they stalked had used against her and Gray that first night in the City. With the righteous claim that it was only just that they should return trickery with trickery, Liz bolstered a courage whose wavering she daren't admit even to herself. She also dare not admit how weak the plan was for fear of undermining her resolve, and, to steady her nerves, lightly ran a gloved hand over the silvery gray suit whose hue so closely matched her husband's eyes. It was her favorite, and she didn't care if it wasn't stylish to be seen in the same outfit more than once during the Season.

After reinforcing her own courage, Liz addressed the challenge of seeing to it that Dru's unsteady bravado took on the same firm valor possessed by the characters inside those penny dreadfuls in which she secretly delighted.

"Dru, remember how impressed you were that I'd actually faced cattle rustlers on my ranch in Wyoming? Timothy accused you of reading more penny dreadfuls."

Dru's chin tilted defensively, but she wordlessly nodded while Annie gasped in amazement. This was the first time the latter had heard tell of such thrilling exploits.

After casting Annie a quick grin, Liz returned her attention to Dru, steadily meeting the other's azure gaze. "Now it's you who've got a chance to face down an even more menacing foe."

"I confess an enjoyment of exciting stories and an admiration of your adventures. But never in my wildest dreams did I ever claim to be fearless or in any way able to perform the same feats." The fingertips of Dru's palm-joined hands momentarily pressed against her lips with little regard for any smudges the action threatened to leave on white gloves.

"Nonsense," Liz immediately refuted Dru's statement. "You defied your stepmama and Gray to come with me uninvited to the City and the Cardingtons' ball."

"That's a far different matter." The two of them had been debating this scheme for major portions of past hours, giving timid Dru more confidence to argue against an opposing idea than was usual for her. "It's one thing to risk a small social gaffe by being turned away from a ball or being sent into country solitude after an attempt to flout another's will, but quite another to risk becoming a social outcast by losing one's pure name visiting a bachelor's home. Anyway, Timothy was with us when we came to the City."

"Ah, Timothy. That's what all this comes down to, is it? Well, my girl, you know as surely as I that Timothy will love you no matter what happens."

A delicate blush reflecting the hue of crimson feathers atop a smart poke bonnet caressed cheeks framed in dusky curls.

"Besides," Liz went on while Dru's voice was held forfeit to happy thoughts. "As I told you, Lawrence won't *be* home! He told me only yesterday that he'd be at Hayton Lodge for several days, working with the police to resolve the question of Gray's gunshot wound. So, obviously we're *not* visiting him. We are simply genteel ladies out for a ride but who've met with an unfortunate mishap."

"Whether the earl is there or not," Dru said, demonstrating a stubborn streak almost as inflexible as Liz's. "I fear it won't lessen the stain this visit will cast over our reputations."

Liz would've spoken, but Dru lifted both hands, palms out, to signal a request for an uninterrupted moment more.

"Who knows what kind of people he employs? Mightn't our actions risk consequences far worse?" The last words were darkly shadowed with indistinct specters of whatever hideous meanings lay behind the term *white slavery*.

This was a depressing possibility that had already assaulted Liz. For the sake of the husband she loved, no matter his feelings for her, she was willing to take the risk, but guilt nibbled at her confidence. She'd no wish to be responsible for leading her friends into even an unlikely danger. If necessary she could somehow revise the plan and go alone.

"Dru, I'll have Jeremy see you safely home if you'd really rather not join me in this search for proof of Hayton's complicity."

Having uselessly argued many of the same points before, Dru was startled by this last minute offer of reprieve. Knowing she need not go, Dru realized she'd been arguing for the sake of doing a thing seldom done. A remarkably free laugh bubbled out, and she hesitated no longer.

"What? And miss my one opportunity to live out my fantasies? I wouldn't permit you to have all the excitement. But, bear with me and please tell me the plan one more time to be certain I've got it right."

Liz hardly had to think as the words had been repeated often both before and after an afternoon spent with Lady Euphemia making obligatory return calls.

"Our carriage will break down not far from Hayton's London house. It only makes sense that we go there seeking shelter while our coachman hastens back to Brandt House, intending to return with an alternate conveyance. We're sure to be admitted. Once inside, you pretend to be taken ill and swoon. An action making it possible—we can only pray likely—that you'll be carried to a bedroom in the house's private area. I, as your companion, will naturally accompany you and thus, when left in privacy to await developments, be free to poke about for evidence."

"I still think your scenario extremely *un*likely." Dru shook her head doubtfully then sank back to strike a sickly pose and in exaggeratedly fading tones continued. "But I'll pretend I'm Violetta from the opera we saw the other night and swoon so believably that the servants' hearts will be wrenched with pity." Sitting up and straightening the bonnet knocked slightly askew by her antics, she matter-of-factly added. "To me it seems far more probable that an ailing woman will be comfortably laid out on the nearest couch until a servant fetches smelling salts."

"Smelling salts in a bachelor's home?" Bronze brows arched in teasing disbelief.

Dru shrugged. "I grant you the improbability of that. But failing such an easy response, surely a doctor will be fetched while I remain stretched out atop the couch."

"Yes." Liz knew how implausible the scheme was and readily conceded the point. "But it's the only plan I could come up with and you offered no alternatives."

"True." Dru's grimace became a grin. "At least we two are in it together."

"And me," Annie boldly added.

Liz warmly glanced at the plucky maid who was possibly daring even more serious reprisals for her part in this scheme than two well-bred ladies. It was Annie who had wheedled Jeremy into bringing them here. Thus, while Liz and Dru risked becoming social pariahs, if anything happened to the noblewomen she accompanied, Annie would likely be blamed by the Ellisons or, worse, the duke and his sister. Liz had read enough bleak news reports to know that a servant dismissed without character had no future and all too often ended brief lives scrabbling for survival in workhouses or tenements. Under growing dread, Liz's vivid imagination provided pictures of even more dire consequences. Images of Hayton's servants not as the respectful well-trained group they probably were but as rough thugs ready to act at his command to further his business in human slavery. They'd less to fear in selling a servant or using Annie as a gruesome example of what would happen to the ladies . . .

Forcing back conjectures so wild they'd be fodder for the penny dreadfuls her two companions seemed so fond of reading, Liz nodded out the window. "We're nearly there. Prepare yourselves."

Suddenly the coach tilted. Liz felt as if she were reliving the earlier experience except this time all inside were ready for both the impact and awkward angle in which they landed. No one was hurt, thanks in large measure to the precaution she'd taken in warning her companions and insisting, once in the carriage, that they practice ways to brace against what was to come. Liz prayed that they'd be as unharmed at the end of this adventure.

The door almost directly over head was wrenched open by Jeremy, looking natty in the under coachman's gold-braided uniform which, unlike Ellison's at the first such accident, had escaped noticeable harm. While handsome enough to be a footman, he lacked the height though fortunately not the strength. He lifted first the duchess and next Lady Drusilla from the lopsided coach before turning to Annie. With a wink he offered Annie a brief glimpse of the errant linchpin surreptitiously recovered from the ground while making an exaggerated show of examining the damage. The damning evidence was then safely pocketed where no curious searchers might find and use it to expose the truth of their mishap.

Annie returned his grin but had her features schooled into lines of a respectful humbleness by the time arms she thought wondrously strong pulled her from the carriage and settled her firmly on solid ground.

The three ladies, Liz leading the way and Annie following demurely behind, approached the earl's home. The door opened before they could knock.

"We seem to have had a small mishap," Liz ruefully began. "Your master is a friend who in the past has offered to lend me his aid. Might I, my companion, and maid rest inside while our coachman hastens back to Brandt House and arranges our rescue?"

The butler said nothing but stepped back and bowed them into a marble entry hall. Door closed again, he led them toward what Liz assumed would be the front drawing room. She was pleased. Things were going much easier than she'd expected. Indeed, all went swimmingly until . . .

"Lizzy, I'm honored that you've accepted my offer of assistance." Lawrence stood in the middle of a room elegantly done up in highly polished cherry wood, plush gray carpets, and subtly patterned couches and chairs. "Come in, ladies. Please have a seat."

Lawrence had seen the ladies approaching and, doing his best to ensure their visit would go unnoticed by passersby, had instructed his butler to hurry them into the house. He was curious about their purpose for descending upon him, but in the end the only important fact was the need to see them gone without attention-drawing scandal being attached to anyone involved. Though he'd been a party to more than one indelicate situation and certainly wouldn't mind creating one with the fiery Lizzy, the timing was awful. Matters were coming to a head, and he must not jeopardize the whole for a few hours play.

When Hayton half turned to motion them toward comfortable seats, Dru's brows lifted in mock disgust. Liz caught the gently accusing expression and returned it with a rueful grimace.

This was certainly not what Liz had expected. Alone for all intents and purposes with a gentleman in his house, they dared not risk forgoing what marginal propriety they could claim by faking an illness. No, their scheme must be abandoned and their every effort focused on getting safely free without being seen. Liz knew that while they might've been able to excuse a visit to an *absent* gentleman's home, though a lady *never* visited a bachelor's residence, Society in general and Gray in particular would never forgive her this—were it to become known. And it must *not!*

Lawrence shifted his attention from Lady Drusilla

perched at the edge of a sofa and the maid stiffly upright in a high back chair against the wall to the still-standing Lizzy.

"Lizzy, please sit down while I arrange for my carriage to see you safely returned to Brandt House."

While the earl gave instructions to his butler, Liz took a seat on the delicate, barely padded chair toward which she'd been motioned and struggled to stabilize unsettled responses—not the least of which was a sense of anticlimax. That, she assured herself, was simply a normal reaction to having her scheme to search for evidence neatly turned back by the earl's presence and chivalrous action. The next instant she became aware that chivalrous action threatened to deepen the breach between her and Gray. If Gray saw or even heard of her return in a carriage bearing Hayton's coat of arms, Liz feared he'd believe it was the answer to his previous day's demand to know where she'd been the night he came home to find her in the servants' hall. The thought added a layer of unhappiness to the burden of her distress over Gray's relationship with another woman.

Nonetheless, as their host faced Liz again, she gave him a brilliant smile. "I'm glad you are here, Lawrence. When our carriage developed difficulties and I realized your home was so near, thinking that you were at Hayton Lodge, I hesitated to come seeking help."

Lawrence returned Lizzy's smile with one equally bright, equally false. Seemed she hadn't forgotten the excuse he'd given to explain a lengthy absence halfway through the Season. He had thought her too upset to clearly remember. That she did increased his curiosity and roused a new suspicion.

"I will soon be off to the lodge, but certain matters delayed my intended departure." His too charming smile moved from Liz's carefully blank expression to Dru's polite social smile. "Recent fluctuations in the

'Change have my man of business rather concerned. He asked me to put back my visit to the lodge." He shrugged, smile deepening, and added, "Then, too, the Prince asked my advice on a new filly he's considering for his stables. And you know we none of us leave a royal summons unanswered."

Liz listened attentively. The man seemed oddly uncomfortable. Uncomfortable with the unexpected visit of genteel ladies? Perhaps. Perhaps more. The possibilities raised by his discomfort bought up her hunting instincts, instincts stymied by his presence.

Strangely, Liz thought, were it not for Gray's ever so much stronger image, she once might've thought the pale, slender man attractive. Now, knowing what she did, it was difficult to imagine that this clearly conniving and decidedly too flattering creature was capable of wielding sufficient power to be the source behind Gray's danger. Still she believed it to be an absolute fact.

In a remarkably short time the butler reappeared in the doorway. An odd flash of relief crossed Lawrence's face as he motioned his guests toward the door.

"Your Grace . . . Lady Drusilla," he affected an overdone gallantry. "The coach awaits only your delightful presence."

And thus yet another of Liz's bravely begun schemes fizzled to a frustrating and utterly unsatisfactory end. She'd lost this battle but not the war and, with her beloved at risk, would neither retreat from the conflict nor surrender.

CHAPTER 16

Gray marched in growing frustration from one side of the front drawing room to the other. The thick carpet beneath his feet couldn't muffle the sound of his heavy tread enough to ease the anxieties of servants whose duties required them to pass by on the door's far side. Even Mr. Ellison seemed anxious to avoid unnecessary approaches to the library door and refrained from casting frowns of disapproval upon those forced by duty into the entry hall and walking on quiet but less than dignified tiptoes.

One of their number had delivered the report that resulted in deepening the anger of an already scowling duke. Though the duke hadn't said a single word in response, never before had anyone seen him in such a dark temper.

While beyond the drawing room's walls servants exchanged nervous glances and others behind the green baize door of their own world whispered about odd happenings, the subject of their conjecture, a man famous for his icy control, simmered.

For the first time since taking his seat in the House of Lords, Gray had left Parliament in the midst of an important debate on a sensitive issue. His conscience had been beating him from the inside out over his unjustifiably harsh response to his wife's understandable distress. He should have trusted the fiery woman who, though unpredictable, had given him no reason to suspect her of being disloyal. Under the weight of guilt, he had abandoned his duties and returned to Brandt House intent on setting right the wrong he'd committed against Lilibet. No matter the painful memories the deed aroused, he had come home intending to provide her with the simple answer she'd demanded.

Yes, he'd thrown important responsibilities aside to return—only to find she wasn't here. There was nothing on her social calendar. Gray knew because he'd found it laying on her dainty escritoire, neatly open to the current date. Adding to his resentment of the situation, he'd been left no option but to humble himself enough to ask his sister for the whereabouts of his wife. With gritted teeth, he'd withstood Euphemia's disapproval of an early return to hear her explanation of Elizabeth's proposed quiet carriage ride around the park with Dru. It had calmed him for a time. But with every passing moment growing irritation had tangled with an increasing fear that his enemies might've shifted their vile attentions to Lilibet. He should've realized, as they likely did, that such a tack was far more likely to win their objective than any threat against him.

Then the groom, Jeremy, had appeared with an unwelcome, infuriating report playing such havoc with Gray's emotions that his fears for Elizabeth's safety somersaulted into renewed suspicion and distrust. Gray stomped toward the door determined to do something, anything. Stopping, hands clenched into impotent fists, he whirled about and strode in the opposite direction. Never before had he experienced such a maelstrom of wildly shifting feelings. Being subject to it now did nothing to improve his foul temper.

Forcing himself to pause at the fireplace and regain control, Gray gripped the charcoal-streaked white mantelpiece so tightly his fingertips paled. He had succeeded in wrapping a thin veneer of ice about the fires raging inside by the time the quiet was broken by the sound of the front door opening and the gentle swish of silk skirts and taffeta petticoats. In three long strides Gray reached the door and loudly threw it wide to stand, a formidable figure, in the opening.

Liz felt his freezing glare but proudly refused to look toward the man radiating cold accusations. What unwelcome imp of fate had brought Gray home early on a day when she'd counted on him being kept occupied in Parliament until much later? What of the important matter which the newspaper reported scheduled for today's consideration? By his mood it seemed clear that he'd already been given an account of their carriage's problem. Battered by the defeat of her purpose in embarking on the outing, Liz felt unequal to a confrontation with the dark man intimidating in his anger. Attempting to ignore him, she began steadily climbing the curving stairway, weakening the hold of her chignon by roughly jerking a smart bonnet from her head as she went.

Gray was livid! He'd been stricken with fear for Elizabeth's life only to discover she'd been with a single man well known as a rake . . . and, he privately suspected, a man guilty of something far, far worse. Now she had turned her back on him as if he and his reaction to her misdeeds meant nothing. Gray strode after her, expression thunderous while his eyes flashed like lightning.

Liz swept into her suite, tossing the bonnet onto the escritoire where it sent a flurry of papers and one quill pen flying. She didn't bother to close the door behind as Gray would obviously be denied neither entry nor his planned scathing rebuke. Her one defense was to march to the room's far side and stare blindly at a delicate floral watercolor while her stiff back remained turned to the open portal.

Her peach and pale green boudoir had been designed as a restful haven, but when Gray stepped inside his temper shattered that illusion with the same force he employed in kicking the door shut.

"Hayton!" He snarled, making himself stop one step into the room for fear he might otherwise completely lose control. "You tossed your good name—*my* good name aside to go in pursuit of Hayton!" He gripped the back of a graceful Queen Anne chair so tightly it seemed in danger of snapping in two, an action lending him a tenuous measure of composure. "Had you just returned from an assignation with the earl the night I found you in the servants' hall?"

To Liz the enquiry seemed spoken in an icily controlled voice that could've chipped stone.

"Certainly not!" She whirled, flaring back at him to return ice with fire. "I know how little you think of me, but surely the aspects of my character which you find most distasteful—my temper, my willful independence—are proof of how unlikely I am to act the silly twit and be taken in by that toad's slimy advances."

Gray was momentarily knocked off kilter by her contemptuous description of Hayton. But only for a moment. The mere hint that any other man, Hayton worst of all, had supplanted him in his wife's affections—and bed—drove Gray so far from his usual restraint that the full meaning of her response failed to penetrate and relieve his dark fury.

"Under duress, Jeremy admitted that you waltzed up to Hayton's door before he was out of sight. Not even an ill-bred American female would so boldly approach a bachelor's door without knowing him well."

"No!" Losing her temper completely in the face of his unyielding wrath, Liz defended her action without pausing to think rationally. "I wouldn't have done it at all if I'd thought the man would be there!"

"What?" Black brows arched in exaggerated amazement. She made no sense, no sense!

Liz drew in a deep breath, striving to suppress angry fires while joining her hands tightly together. "At yesterday's garden party Lawrence told me he would be at Hayton Lodge for a visit of several days duration. He claimed the local constabulary were seeking his help to settle the matter of your hunting injury."

The word Gray heard most clearly was "Lawrence" and with that intimate title the news that the man apparently had reason to believe she'd be interested in knowing his whereabouts. Gray shook a head and softly scoffed at her explanation.

"So you'd have me believe that after accepting the truth of a 'toad's' statement without question, you blithely went alone to a *bachelor's* residence? A trust given him, I might add, you've rarely given me."

"I was not alone! Both Dru and my maid accompanied me. And only after our carriage became disabled did we seek refuge at Hayton House. With Jeremy off to fetch help, as the proper ladies you would have us always be, we sought shelter to save us from standing aimlessly on the street like common trollops."

Silver eyes narrowed. A disabled carriage? Here was an event requiring closer investigation, but there was no time now to waste pondering the matter.

"Moreover—" Liz added, gaining confidence and believing the worst was past. "You needn't be concerned about the earl's actions after we unexpectedly arrived. He was the soul of propriety and arranged for our immediate return to Brandt House."

Her tone held a tinge of disgust that raked across

Gray's nerves. "You sound disappointed by his failure to advance a 'slimy pursuit.'"

"Disappointed? Yes!" Liz took two steps toward the intimidating image of cold condemnation while sparks blazed anew in her eyes. "Disappointed that he was there, disappointed in myself for believing what he'd said about his departure."

Gray released his punishing hold on an innocent chair, moved around it, and took two steps toward his fiery foe while abruptly shifting the direction of his questions, hoping to startle her into a truth he felt certain he'd yet to hear.

"What were you doing in Hayton's neighborhood? Setting out from here, it's the opposite direction from the park you assured Euphemia you'd be visiting."

"We weren't going to the park." Temper quashed by the need for quick thinking, Liz inwardly scrambled for some alternate excuse and came up with a bold counterclaim. "All right, Gray, I confess that the earl's home was our destination."

Ice-layered steel glittered in silver eyes. He'd challenged her but at the core had not expected, had not wanted to confirm, that his suspicions were founded on fact.

"We set out," Liz continued, "to steal a glimpse of his gardens. The duchess of Etherton never stops boring everyone with complaints about how the earl stole her gardener. A treachery, to hear her tell it, that has resulted in Hayton's gardens, particularly those in front, supplanting hers as the loveliest in London."

Listening to her disjointed tale, Gray's thick lashes fell while his face went emotionless, hiding both relief and disgust at finding so foolish a cause at the root of his distress. He found it easy to accept this account, which sounded just the sort of useless tittle-tattle bored Society ladies wasted their energies upon. He was only surprised that the same Lilibet who could and had intelligently discussed important issues with him allowed herself to be swept up in such silliness.

"Did you see these gardens?" Gray asked, as his too potent half-smile appeared for the first time that day.

"Too closely." Liz grimaced, disconcerted by a sudden awareness of his nearness. "And they're nothing so spectacular as Mildred would have us believe." Liz was pleased by Gray's sardonic smile. He plainly believed her excuse—and his ice had begun melting. In the next instant she berated herself for caring when it was no matter if an adulterous husband warmed to her. She would not warm to him.

Gray saw a turquoise gaze momentarily glow only to go blank, and bronze lashes fall as sweet peach lips compressed into a bitter line. The winds of unpredictable emotions shifted again and guilt returned. He had demanded she be honest with him but had not been as frank with her despite his purpose in an early return to Brandt House. It was a duty good conscience insisted he fulfill.

"You haven't asked why I'm here while Parliament remains in session and we've no social commitments demanding it."

Liz had wondered about it upon entering the house to find him already there but, fearing his ability to charm her into compliance regardless of her continuing sense of betrayal, refused to look up at the too attractive man.

"In my jealousy of your relationship with Hayton, I've wrongly accused you . . . but I will not apologize as you are guilty of the same fault."

Startled, Liz's eyes flew up to meet his penetrating gaze.

"Yet—" Gray continued, pleased with having drawn her eyes to his. "Just as I've demanded explanations from you, I owe you the answers you demanded of me yesterday." His strong jaw firmed and smile faded. "It's a subject I've discussed only with my solicitor since the day it was thrust upon an unwilling me."

"No." Swamped with guilt for having convinced Gray that a lie was the truth, Liz quickly moved forward, placing one hand against his chest and the fingertips of the other over his lips. "You needn't tell me anything you'd rather not share. I *should* trust you. You were right in saying I've failed as a wife to give you the trust owed a husband."

"Hush." Gray took her much smaller hands in his and gently tugged her toward the loveseat comfortably placed before a low-burning fire. "No wife owes her husband a trust he hasn't earned. And I cannot rightfully ask for yours until I've shared with you all the bleak tales of my past."

Liz said nothing but her eyes widened. Was there some hideous secret in the Brandt family? Some mad aunt locked in a tower on the Ashleigh estate?

Gray saw the fleeting expressions racing across her face and knew that her imagination had taken flight. "No." A measure of the bitter grimness strangling old memories was released by the warmth her bright company inevitably brought, and he smiled. "It's nothing so bad as you apparently fear. Only the secret of the house in St. John's Wood."

Liz forced herself not to stiffen or pull her hands from those still holding them. She'd promised trust and meant to give it no matter the cost.

"That morning I found you reading a newspaper in the library I told you how I horrified my father with my wild ways. I'm afraid that was a serious understatement. In reality he was furious . . . but so was I." Gray's attention shifted to the fireplace and in battling flames he saw the past reflected.

"I loved my mother dearly, as dearly as I loved *her* mother—the first Lilibet. I was a youngster barely out of short pants when I first discovered that the father I idolized as the perfect example of what a gentleman ought to be kept a mistress. Mother maintained a near-perfect facade of ignorance on the subject. But in rare flashes of deeply hidden pain I saw that she knew of the woman, though for love of an unworthy man, pretended she did not. She forgave him the insult and the aching wound—but I couldn't. He thought I would grow out of my unreasonable attitude, thought I'd follow along in this common practice of men of our station. After seeing the pain it caused mother, I couldn't, didn't, and won't." Smoky eyes stroked the woman who looked like a single bright flame frozen in time.

Sighing under the intensity of his gaze, Liz opened her mouth to speak but found no words adequate to express the myriad emotions he'd roused—sympathy, admiration, appreciation, and most of all love. Gray continued before she could put her thoughts into rational order.

"Despite my father's image of rectitude and the impossibly high standards he sought to impose upon me, he hurt mother, not once but constantly throughout their lives. The disillusionment sent me wild. I figured if he could be so vile despite his well-guarded reputation of moral purity, I would never hide what I did. And I was determined to do a good deal, enough to bring the shame he deserved but carefully evaded. It had the initial effect I sought, infuriating the father so proud of our noble family name, terrifying him of the stains I purposely attempted to put on it."

Liz found it mind-boggling to learn that this man had once purposely set out to wreak the kind of damage he'd feared she might and couldn't restrain a soft smile. She shook her head in mock regret, trapping flickers of golden firelight in the bright curls on one side of her head while fading sunbeams from windows on the room's far side danced over those on the other. "Only think how often you've accused me of coming too close to that mark."

"Ah, but you would've been blamed whereas I was not, despite my earnest attempts to earn dishonor. What I learned instead was how amazingly forgiving Society is of a man with even the promise of a title as important as mine."

Looking up at Gray, Liz saw that his face had taken on the same cold, arrogant lines it'd had the day she met him. Seeing that expression again, she suddenly realized how his frozen facade had gentled during the intervening weeks. It occurred to Liz that her ability to so often rouse Gray's temper had likely played a part in melting his ice. In that moment she so badly wanted to wipe the coldness away once more, she nearly caressed the strong lines of his face.

"But no matter." With a shake of his dark hair Gray freed himself of a bitter chill's tendrils. "Just before setting off on another of his beloved yachting adventures, my father summoned me to Ashleigh Hall for what I expected would be a repeat of the usual lecture. I was wrong." Cynicism lent a hollow echo to his humorless laugh. "He had just rewritten his will and wanted to make me aware of its provisions."

Long-repressed memories of an unpleasant scene filled Gray's vision while he went on, determined to finish his narration with hopes it would never need be spoken of again.

"The title and property were entailed to me as his heir. Also, save for bequests to loyal servants and close relations, he settled on me what income is earned by the Ashleigh estate and investments. However, that income was given with the stipulation that to receive it I must promise to see his mistress kept in luxury for the rest of her life. We had a blazing row and I stormed back to London . . . it was the last time I saw him alive."

Liz saw Gray's eyes darken with an odd combination of sorrow and resentment that she would've paid any price to ease.

"He was a hypocrite!" The words were a soft growl aching with pain. "But so am I to rue the death of a man I couldn't respect."

"No," Liz instantly refuted his self-blame. "No man is perfect, and there is nothing shameful about loving an imperfect father. After all, he loved you despite what he saw as your faults. And one day, if we are blessed with sons, I've no doubt you'll love them no matter what mischief they get themselves into."

The thought of a child created with this woman as compassionate as she was willfully independent put a warm smile on Gray's face, a warmth able to drive cold bitterness into abeyance. It was not and possibly would never be completely gone, but it ached less in the midst of her warmth.

"Because you ask it, I'll try to forgive my father just as I long ago forgave yours for the deception that gave me you. More than forgiveness, I owe Samuel Hughes gratitude." He pulled her close and rested his cheek atop blazing hair while adding one last statement.

"Now you know who inhabits the house in St. John's Wood and why she's a part of my will. I couldn't believe my father wanted me to perpetuate his insult to my mother, but he had me firmly trapped. Distasteful action was twined tightly with the income necessary to see the people of Ashleigh Estate survive. He left me no choice."

Gray held his Lilibet a breath away and gazed down at her with molten silver eyes. "Although I confess to not having lived the life of a saint, even to having kept a series of mistresses, I privately swore I'd never do that to my wife and I never have . . . not to Camellia and not to you."

"I'm sorry for doubting you, Gray." Liz tucked her head beneath his chin and, radiating the compassion of her loving heart, slowly stroked solace across his chest. "I'm so sorry."

Liz berated herself for not having had more faith in Gray's honor after reading his impassioned speeches and knowing how courageously he had withstood dangerous threats for the sake of what he believed. Without fore intent, she sought to heal this invisible wound of her making with small kisses placed against firm throat then up faintly abrasive chin to cheeks. These actions honestly intended to ease the distress she'd caused him kindled in her a reckless desire to tempt the incredibly handsome man back into her bed, a desire she struggled to tame with reminders of poor timing while nearing the dinner hour. It was a chore made more difficult by memories of the touch and taste of hungry kisses, firm flesh, and exquisite delights.

Welcoming her sweet comfort, Gray lightly brushed his lips across thick, bright hair from which he soon pulled the few remaining, inadequate pins. Released, the rich mass flowed like a cascade of fire down her slender back.

Feeling freed by his action, Liz pulled a whisper away to lift her lips in a mute offering which Gray gladly accepted, brushing his own back and forth across hers. Burning with smoldering pleasures stirring to life, it was a tormentingly inadequate caress. With a small, wild cry, she twined her hands into cool black hair and stilled the teasing motion, holding his mouth against hers.

Gray softly growled, drinking deeply of the sweet peach wine of her kiss even while shifting her to lay across the hard muscles of his thighs and turning her to press full against his. Crushing her sensuous bounty tighter yet, mists of steam rose from simmering blood to cloud his eyes with passion.

Sinking into a blaze of hunger, Liz readily yielded to the devastation of his lips and melted into the pleasures of his hungry embrace. The feel of his big, hard body overwhelmed her with delicious sensations and, clinging to powerful shoulders, she helplessly shifted, brushing lush curves across muscles that, even with several layers of cloth between her flesh and his, she felt rippling in answer to her desperate movements.

Gray stroked a sweet torment down the fiery temptress's back, around her tiny waist, and up to cup lush mounds perched atop a hated corset. Moaning, she arched up and twined her arms about his neck, consumed by a longing whose source of excitement and far more thrilling end she held in her embrace. Without hesitation, she began working to free him of interfering clothing.

Thoroughly enjoying her unpracticed but tantalizing attempt to disrobe him, Gray left the chore to her while he concentrated on performing a similar service for her. By the time a determined Liz had opened and tugged the shirt from his pants to smooth burning caresses over his bare chest, he had unfastened the top of her dress. Then loosening her chemise and brushing the cloth aside, despite the still-laced corset below, he freed her bounty to his eyes, hands, and lips.

The deep sound rising from Gray's throat was muffled as he buried his face in her cleavage for a long moment. Liz cried out, shivering under the burning pleasure of his mouth again moving across her breasts, a painful joy that both satisfied an initial need and roused others. She wound her fingers more tightly into black strands, holding him to her aching flesh and trembling with a now wonderfully familiar hunger.

He lowered his head for a devastating kiss which so enveloped her, she'd no thought to spare as he shifted her to recline across the loveseat. He fought a losing battle to restrain a wildly insistent need, at least long enough to see they made it to the bed, but she fought equally hard to drive him beyond his control . . . and won. With one shaking hand, Gray lifted her skirts and petticoats while with the other he eased her underdrawers away before ridding himself of the last barrier to their joining. With hands and mouth he guided her descent into the flames of a delicious torment and shocking pleasure until she writhed beneath him, trembling wildly. Only then did he tilt her hips, lower his powerful body, and merge them in the most intimate of bonds. Gray urged her with the enticements of body, hands, and mouth into a rhythm as old as time, a rhythm pushing deeper into a conflagration's desperate abandon until it burst into a shower of searing sparks and incredible pleasure.

Exhausted, replete, they lay unstirring in each other's arms. But at last, much later than intended and shaking a dark head in self-mockery for a never before experienced impatience too overwhelming to see them disrobed and in bed before surrendering to desperate need, Gray carried his wife into her bedroom. Floating in the euphoric lassitude of complete contentment, Liz submitted to his patient aid in removing articles of clothing likely rumpled beyond saving by their play—not something she could rue. To her pleasure he then shed what remained of his own garb and joined her in bed. It was small compared to his, but far more space than the two of them needed.

Cuddling sleepily into his welcoming arms, she murmured, "They'll be waiting dinner for us."

Gray pressed lips curved with gentle amusement into a fiery tangle of curls and whispered back. "It isn't the first and, God willing, won't be the last time we substitute passion's feast for an ordinary evening meal."

Liz drifted into pleasant dreams with a satisfied smile.

A barefoot Gray haphazardly dressed in pants and unbuttoned shirt had rung for a light late supper. It was laid on a small table in Liz's boudoir by servants who discreetly withdrew as soon as they'd delivered the cold collation of meats, fruit, breads, and sweets, accompanied by a bottle of wine. During the intimate meal conversation between Gray and Liz, passion-disheveled but loosely covered by a silk wrapper, was intermittent while they appeased mundane hungers. But while lingering over a last goblet of wine, talk idly returned to serious matters. Gray found he'd a clearer view now that his bitterness had been leavened by his Lilibet's sweetness.

"Looking back, I can see that my disgust for Society was bred by both my father's hypocrisy and the blind eye its members so easily turned to all my wrongs."

Liz reached out to caress a strong hand gone tense. It instantly relaxed beneath her touch although cynicism filled the deep voice continuing to speak.

"Our, oh, so respectable Society is like carefully applied frosting on Britain's fancy cake—beautiful but hiding a rotten center."

"Though I would have wholeheartedly agreed when we first met or when I joined you here in the City, I can't now. I can't even blame Lady Charles for misinterpreting the limited information she had. She doubtless thought herself gently preparing me to meet a reality I'd surely face one day. Society is not rotten through and through, not even mostly so. It includes many good and fine people whose most serious wrong is lack of awareness and, at worst, a determination to remain so." She quietly smiled and brushed her fingers over his cheek. "Besides, there are people like you who struggle to do something about the pockets of decay in Society and fight to lessen the bitterness of the cake's bottom layers with reforms. I read your speeches and with each came to admire you more." Melting turquoise eyes moved over his solemn face like a caress. "That's why I should've trusted you, should've known you were too honorable to do what I suspected no matter the bleak hints others delighted in sharing with me."

Somehow he'd been blessed with a wife not only intelligent enough to understand the dark side of reality but brave enough to stand at his side and face it.

"The Fates must approve of my goals, for they sent me the miracle you are, one which I fear myself undeserving."

Liz was shocked to hear him speak such high praise of her, and before she could stop herself, squeaked out her amazement.

"Then I haven't been a complete disappointment, too poor a comparison with Camellia." She cringed when she heard her own plaintive plea for reassurance.

Gray rose and moved around the table to kneel at his Lilibet's side. "Camellia wasn't real, only a dream too insubstantial to survive human contact. Like her namesake, she withered at a man's touch—and in the end died. She couldn't bear to be intimate and, after our wedding night, I couldn't bear to see her bravely enduring me or listen to her quietly sobbing afterwards." Gray was shocked by his own words, words whose truth he hadn't fully admitted to himself until now. But he wouldn't unsay them even if he could.

Liz laid her hand gently against a strong cheek and, in instinctive comfort for an unsuspected anguish, tilted her head to press her lips to his.

Gray swept her into his arms, intending to carry her back to their shared bed of fiery delights.

Pleased as she was to be cradled in her lover's strong arms, Liz felt forced to remind him of a likely interruption.

"The servants will soon return to clear away the remains of our meal."

Gazing down into glowing turquoise eyes, Gray gave his head a brief shake as he laid her atop rumpled bedclothes and followed her down. "It's our home, and without our call they wouldn't dare."

Nor did they.

After a day of clear skies, no rain fell in the night, making this rendezvous even more dangerous than their first. A fact deepening the fury of the man summoned again to the back gate of Brandt House's garden.

"Lady Euphemia," he hissed the moment a woman heavily cloaked despite summer warmth was close enough to hear. "I thought you understood me when last we met here. I am not your servant, and I do not take commands kindly—yours least of all. Or have you forgotten my warning? It was not lightly spoken and, as you daily grow less useful, beware of tempting my patience."

Euphemia straightened her considerable girth into its most impressive guise. "I would never have *suggested* this meeting for any reason save one very important."

"Humph." The visitor was clearly unimpressed.

"Gray returned from Parliament early today only to discover Elizabeth absent. It put him in an unusually foul temper." Euphemia paused but when the other made no answering sound, she hurried on. "And I'm sure you've noticed, as all London has, that he accompanies her everywhere. At first I thought it merely a feeble scheme to convince Bertie and his fast friends that Elizabeth was not fair game for their hunt. But after the temper of this afternoon it's clear he has . . . feelings for her."

Unseen in the dark, the man's eyes narrowed. The disgust in Lady Euphemia's last words made it equally clear that she did not share the duke's admiration of his duchess.

"It's a fact already assumed," he softly growled. "But what has that to do with our plans? Are you begging mercy for your brother for the sake of that love?" He surmised that the sudden revelation of facts he'd suspected for some time had inspired her unwise summons. Doubtless she would suggest a twist to their ongoing plan, the same one around which he and his cohorts had already begun weaving their plans.

"No, certainly not!" Clamping down on a growing impatience and restraining her usual imperious manner, Euphemia placated herself with a hearty wish that she were able to shake sense into the dense man. "I merely suggest that Gray's foolish love for the American provides you with an infinitely more promising target. You'll never wear Gray's courage down with threats against his own safety, but were she at risk. . . ."

"Hmmm." The dark figure, half-buried and nearly invisible in the tall hedge's gloom, would never share future plans with this less than reliable conspirator. "It's a possibility, but I'm more curious to know what price you seek for your suggestion?" There was no question but that there would be a price when dealing with this woman, a master manipulator.

The night garden wrapped its cloak of thick silence more tightly about Euphemia as she mentally debated how to respond to a question so clearly couched in disdain. After a few unhurried moments, she made several firm requests and supported them with an offer to do whatever was needed to see the deeds successfully complete.

To the unmoving man her foolish demands made little sense, but the fact that in the end they wouldn't matter in the least allowed him to agree to each in clear conscience—if, and he inwardly laughed at the thought, he had ever possessed one.

CHAPTER 17

Liz lingered at the breakfast table, drifting in a warm, bright euphoria blind to the gloomy prospect of a cloudy morning beyond long windows. Gray had awakened her as he rose from her bed to join the valet waiting in his own room and prepare for the coming sober hours in Parliament. Having years of experience in dressing herself without a maid's help, Liz had rushed to don a simple chemise and front-fastening gown of bright blue in order to meet Gray for the day's first meal.

"Your Grace."

The call pierced the pleasant haze of recent memories, bringing turquoise eyes to the footman standing primly at her side extending the salver supporting a single envelope. Bronze brows furrowed. It was far too early for calling cards or invitations to be delivered.

"Thank you," she absently murmured while taking the missive in hand and turning it over to peer more closely at its ornate seal. The earl of Hayton's seal. This unwelcome fact quickly dissipated the last mists of bemused happiness.

Liz waited until the door closed behind the departing footman before breaking the seal to open the envelope and draw out a folded sheet of fine paper. She quickly read the message once and then again more slowly before folding and sliding the sheet back into its envelope.

The earl claimed to have received information from the inspector in charge of the investigation into Gray's supposedly accidental hunting injury during their visit at Hayton Lodge. Having already been so misled by Hayton's claims in regard to this subject that it had ended in the past evening's blazing row with Gray, Liz was suspicious. However, she could hardly afford to ignore his flat statement that with this news he'd uncovered details of another planned attempt upon Gray's life—one that would be put into motion within hours. He'd begged her to come and work with him to intervene and end the threat. Liz more than doubted Hayton's desire to save Gray, but this meeting surely offered her an opportunity to secure the physical evidence needed to prove the earl's involvement in wretched deeds.

Liz rose, silently reaffirming her determination to risk any danger first to protect Gray's life and then to end the continuing threats by revealing their source. While briskly quitting the room and climbing toward her suite, her mind raced over a review of the curious and surely perilous directions Hayton had given.

With irrefutable logic, the earl had stated that Gray's distaste for a public invasion of his privacy meant he'd most assuredly *not* appreciate police involvement. A reality made more certain by an Ashleigh family member's involvement in the dastardly plot. These were facts not open to dispute whether or not he was accurate in his claim of an Ashleigh connection. It was the steps the earl had urged Liz to take in coming to Hayton House secretly that stirred her uneasiness to fearful heights. Not only was she directed to tell no one of her destination but to have the ducal carriage drop her on a well-traveled street where she could summon a hansom cab without drawing unwanted attention.

"Your Grace?"

Hand on the crystal knob of the door opening into her suite, Liz paused and glanced over her shoulder to an openly curious Annie.

"Tell Ellison to have the carriage brought round before hurrying back to help me dress," Liz directed. "I've an important call to make."

"But where at this early hour?" A startled Annie asked, then bit her tongue knowing it was no business of even a lady's maid.

Liz's response was a grim smile and quick wave of her hand to rush Annie on her way. Quietly closing the door, thankful that both Lady Euphemia and her stepdaughter were still sleeping, Liz moved to sit at her escritoire and hurriedly dash off, close, and seal a brief note for Dru. One whose meaning was hopefully so enigmatic as to be lost on anyone else.

Believing herself to be no fool by anyone's standards, Liz refused to hie herself off to Hayton House in complete secret. And her hesitation was not merely born of the possible dreaded blight on a woman's reputation that would result from visiting a bachelor's home—the damage Gray had accused her of tempting. No, it was born of her certainty that the earl was the despicable leader of a ring of white slavers.

Liz stood and began unfastening the blue gown, unwilling to allow a moment's idleness to magnify the issue of personal danger. She reassured herself that the earl would no more dare assault a duchess, the Toast of the Season, than Society had blamed Gray for his youthful if wild indiscretions. Though Liz sensed a serious fault in this reasoning, one having to do with the different expectations for gentlemen and genteel ladies, she refused to allow her courage to falter by risking a closer examination.

Annie returned just as her mistress began shrugging out of the loosened dress. Anxious to be gone before the whole house was awake, Liz refused to waste precious moments in either the time-consuming lacing of a needless corset or donning of an endless number of petticoats. Soon the duchess was arrayed in her favorite gray suit with the charcoal cameo buried in a new scarlet ascot at her throat. Annie also insisted, and Liz was too rushed to argue against, that she wear the sapphire ring and earrings. Then, once abundant fiery locks had been tamed into an intricate knot beneath the rakish angle of a smart hat fitted with a red ribbon and unique black quills quite unlike the usual ostrich plumes adorning most bonnets, Liz was ready to depart.

Propping one envelope against the delicately scrolled inkstand resting atop her escritoire and pocketing another, Liz turned to her maid. "If I have not returned before teatime, see this envelope gets into Lady Drusilla's hand—only Lady Drusilla's hand."

Annie earnestly nodded to the empty doorway where the duchess had disappeared. This was an odd situation. Her Grace was in the norm open about her plans and took Annie with her most places. That she was about to depart alone and was uncertain about returning in hours was all the stranger for the fact that this was the one day of the week when afternoons were spent in Brandt House receiving callers. This was the Ashleigh ladies' at-home day.

Suffering a twinge of guilt for leaving a confused Annie behind, Liz gathered her short train up in one arm and began gracefully descending the sweeping staircase. She reached the bottom step just as Ellison opened the front door to an excited Timothy.

"Lizzy, I've found it!" He fairly shouted.

Liz waved her hands palm out, signaling a need for discretion—and less noise—to the disheveled and unshaven young man who, despite his agitated ruddiness, looked as if he hadn't slept in days.

Timothy almost leaped to Liz's side, grabbed her hands with his and pulled her into the drawing room. "I've been endlessly, fruitlessly, combing the upper house's records day and night. And finally I've found the secret hiding place of *the* 'sealed report' supporting all we've suspected!"

"What do you mean hidden and why?" Liz quietly asked the question, leaning back against the closed door while carefully tempering her own excitement. Was it possible that her journey to meet with the earl was unnecessary?

"For some reason to which I, as secretary to the House of Lords, should've been privy," Timothy jerkily began with a strong thread of indignation running through his words. "The report was concealed in the midst of voluminous pages containing the endless and boring verbatim testimony of farmers in some obscure county protesting government interference. They say these farmers are a dour lot with hardly a word to speak . . . don't you believe it. By the number of pages it took to detail each's complaint, they must go on for hours about what they view as injustices."

Anxious to get on with the point of his discourse, Liz was vexed by Timothy's unexpected ability to become completely sidetracked in the middle of an all-important announcement. Her barely restrained impatience apparently communicated itself to him though she said nothing.

Thrusting both hands roughly through tawny hair, as if to push his thoughts back into sensible order, Timothy returned to a description of his discovery. "It was a perfect hiding place: inserted into the middle of a document on a subject into which no one is likely to inquire. Even if someday found, everyone would assume it had merely been misfiled. Only I, as the one responsible for filing documents, would be blamed for putting the report where it didn't belong. But I swear I've never before seen or even heard of the sealed report." His indignation had turned to outright disgust.

Liz's impatience could no longer be restrained. She pushed herself away from the door to approach Timothy with a single, pithy question quietly asked. "What does it say?"

"Oh," Timothy flushed a bright red to equal any blush to which Liz had ever been prey. "Haven't I told you?"

Liz forced stiff lips to smile as she gave her head a brief shake that threatened to displace her smart black hat.

"It's a report written by Gray that clearly implicates Hayton in the white slave trade between Britain and Europe at the highest levels. More particularly, it ties him even more firmly with the apparently far more lucrative Middle East market for fair-skinned females."

Liz was about to ask why, if this information was known, Hayton hadn't been brought to account for his ghastly involvement? Why had the report been sealed? And why had it been so thoroughly hidden? She would never believe Gray a party to covering it up for the sake of Hayton's position in Society.

Before she could speak, Timothy added what proved to be at least a partial explanation. "Unfortunately, although Hayton was implicated repeatedly, the report states a lack of substantial evidence to prove his connection with the infamous dealer in flesh, the shadowy Badger." Dark eyes met turquoise with a knowing gleam. "Yes, the same elusive figure we've been trying to trace, but who it seems no one reliable admits to ever having seen."

Timothy was plainly elated by his discovery, but

Liz was only more discouraged. The report did indeed provide support for their theories. However, finding it provided no more a definite answer to their search than uncovering written threats had provided their author's name.

Timothy ruefully rubbed a hand over the stubble of his cheeks and chin. "I'd better hurry home and prepare myself for another day in Parliament. But perhaps you and Dru can meet me in the park between tea and dinner. I'll bring a small box of bonbons to share in celebration of this step forward."

His mention of Dru's favorite sweet in concert with the hopeful request was more than Liz had the heart to refuse. The pair had hardly seen each other during the days of his search, and it would be cruel to take all hope away. She nodded agreement despite the fact that even under the best of circumstances it would be nearly impossible to slip Dru away from Euphemia's eagle eyes during later afternoon hours . . . and the more ominous reality that she might not be around to arrange anything. This confirming report with its lack of tangible proofs merely made it all the more important for her to go to Hayton House.

Liz was anxious to be off, meet the uncertain challenge, and hopefully return, but she exercised a new talent learned in recent weeks, forcing herself to be patient. For someone with duties waiting elsewhere, Timothy's farewells were lengthy and punctuated with longing glances up the stairway to his still-sleeping love's door. It remained closed and finally, to Liz's silent but fervent gratitude, he departed.

The Ashleigh coach had been waiting beyond the front gate for quite some little time and as soon as Timothy disappeared, Liz hurried through that opening in the elegant iron barrier to settle herself inside. The journey between Brandt House and the busy thoroughfares nearer the City's center was simple, but after she'd stepped down from the ducal coach it seemed to take forever and certainly far too long to hail a hansom.

Not until she sat safely inside that anonymous public conveyance did Liz give serious thought to the possibility of an Ashleigh conspirator in Gray's danger. They couldn't possibly expect to convince her that either Dru or Lady Euphemia were involved, thus she thought the suggestion an obvious attempt to lay a false scent by moving beyond oblique implications of Timothy's involvement to outright accusations. Yes, it must be the young cousin and heir they meant to see blamed, but she knew Timothy too well. Even if she hadn't; even if he hadn't been the discoverer of the hidden report, as an aspiring M.P., Timothy was far too intelligent to form a dangerous affiliation with white slavers. It would risk scandal enough to permanently prevent him from holding office.

Of a sudden, Liz realized Lawrence and his fellow conspirators had no reason to believe that a duchess, even an American one, could possibly be aware of their "business" interests. After the way she'd accepted his comfort in the gazebo and the way she'd sought his help when the carriage broke down, Lawrence doubtless thought he could feed her charming lies and expect his claims to be believed. Well, peach-bright lips took on an impish curl, more fool he to think so little of her mental abilities.

When the hansom drew up before the now familiar facade of the earl's London home, Liz waited for the door to be opened and daintily paid the driver before turning to face the coming confrontation. Consideration of her foe's poor opinion of her had reinforced her determination, yet she'd never felt more alone in her entire life. She squared slender shoulders and resolutely approached the door despite feet that seemed weighted with iron ingots.

Though braced to meet any dangerous contingent, just as on her arrival the previous day, the same proper butler opened the door and ushered her into the same subtly decorated drawing room.

"Ah, Lizzy, you're here at last." Lawrence rose from his chair drawn near a cheery fire. "I'd begun to worry that you might arrive too late for anything to be done to divert the serious assault upon Gray that I wrote you about."

What could Liz do but gently shake her head in apparent deep regret. "I came as soon as I could get away," she quietly assured him, and as it was true, the words were spoken with the clear diction of sincerity.

"Of course." Lawrence oozed such syrupy sympathy Liz felt as if she'd been doused with the stuff and almost backed away as he come forward to take her hand in one of his and pat it with his other. "I do understand."

All Liz could think was how little he really understood.

"But please, Lizzy, sit down." Still holding her fingers he motioned toward the chair matching his across a small table. "We'll share a comforting sip of tea—a new blend I hope you'll find agreeable—while I outline the plot I intercepted before we discuss what actions must be taken to divert the scheme."

This man she knew as a villain posed as the soul of chivalry, and Liz was thoroughly disgusted by the false image. It was even more disconcerting to recognize she'd been thrust into a role in some strange play combining the civilized experience of taking tea with barbaric talk of attempted murder.

Bending a head of sleekly combed blond hair, Lawrence poured the already steeped dark liquid into the elegance of two translucent Sevres teacups.

Despite an impatience sorely tried by all the impediments earlier delaying the discussion she'd come to set into motion, Liz lifted her cup, took a small sip and politely hid a shudder of dislike for its bitter aftertaste.

"What do you mean, she's out?" Euphemia glared at the unwanted servant standing before a closed door and daring to block her will with foolish excuses.

Annie straightened her shoulders. The duchess was her mistress, not this overbearing woman who Annie knew had disliked her immensely from the first. That Annie was not Lady Euphemia's choice for new lady's maid and had been given the position without consulting her had assured the older woman's disdain . . . but somehow Annie sensed there was more.

"Merely that, Your Ladyship. The duchess—" Annie emphasized the title knowing it would grate on the older woman and taking quiet delight in that fact. "—said only that she would be out, possibly until after teatime."

Euphemia allowed an indelicate growl to escape as she easily brushed the slender Annie from her path and entered Elizabeth's suite.

As if it were a beacon, the small envelope propped up on the dainty escritoire immediately drew Euphemia's attention. She sailed toward it like a battleship at full steam. That it was addressed to her stepdaughter meant nothing to her. She rudely ripped it open, frowned over the words, and thrust it into a capacious pocket before whirling to leave.

Annie stood purposefully in the open door. Euphemia's eyes narrowed on the much less substantial figure like a threat as she moved straight forward, forcing the maid to either step aside or be pushed down and stepped on. A possibility Annie knew the other woman would enjoy for all her proud gentility.

CHAPTER 18

"The duchess departed this morning before the house was properly awake." Ellison stoically responded to his master's demand for an explanation of his wife's absence.

"This morning," Gray irritably repeated. "But when did she return?"

"She has yet to do so." The butler answered calmly, though a crack in his emotionless facade allowed a glimpse of honest concern for the American duchess to show as he added, "The carriage returned within an hour of leaving—without Her Grace."

"But, good God," Gray growled. "It's well past teatime now."

"Yes, Your Grace." Ellison nodded, striving to recover his imperturbable image.

"What evil maggot got into the coachman's brain that he dared leave her unescorted anywhere?" Ghastly images had begun forming in Gray's mind. "And where precisely did he leave her?"

Ellison met the duke's scowl without flinching. "Durst left Her Grace on Tilton Avenue, outside the millinery shop patronized by Lady Euphemia. And he would assuredly *not* have left her there alone if she hadn't ordered him to bring the carriage directly back to Brandt House."

Gray received this information with growing frustration. It would be useless to ask what reason she'd given for her reckless action. A duchess need not excuse her choices, no matter how foolhardy, to servants. But, oh, how Gray earnestly wished that his often unconventional wife had done so this time.

After dismissing Ellison, Gray found himself alone in the drawing room. Prey to growing worries, he began striding between front-facing windows and the marble fireplace opposite. Gray felt as if he'd somehow been pushed back in time to the previous afternoon. Now confident of his wife's fidelity, no jealousy gnawed at him. But that lack, rather than lightening his distress, left the field clear for his fears for her safety to double and double again.

Something had happened to his Lilibet. To Gray this was not a mere possibility but rather a harsh fact. Although she was impulsive, unpredictable, he was certain she'd never willingly have subjected him to a second day of distress and frustration. The only answer was the one he'd suspected for her absence the day before. As black-hearted as his foes assuredly were, they weren't stupid. Clearly they'd recognized a far more effective method to guard their business interests by redirecting toward his wife the threats he'd shrugged aside.

In addition to his worries for her safety, Gray suffered over the one, the only lack in their previous night's satisfying communion of body and spirit. He'd allowed fear of the vulnerability he'd steeled himself against for so long to keep him silent. But surely the opening of past wounds, confessions of old hurts, as well as the fervency of their lovemaking had shown her the love he'd been unable to put into words. It didn't matter, though able to stand strong against any physical or moral threat, he'd quailed before a brave woman's open emotion and had failed to speak the words. Awareness of that shameful cowardice deepened the dark texture of his frustration.

Again, as yesterday, it was the sound of Brandt House's front door opening that ended Gray's pacing. However, in this instance it was not the sound of swishing skirts but a man's firm tread that he next heard. That difference did nothing to slow his haste, and he reached the doorway between drawing room and entry hall just in time to hear a curious exchange.

"The duchess isn't here?" Standing motionless one step inside the opening whose door Ellison held wide, Timothy echoed the butler's statement with disbelief. It was a disbelief quickly replaced by a flare of renewed hope. "What of Lady Drusilla? Did she go out with Her Grace?" Was it possible that he'd merely missed the two of them in the park?

Gray answered before his impassive butler could. "At Euphemia's insistence, Dru is in her rooms preparing for an evening of Shakespeare to be followed by Sir Andrew and Lady Somes-Halyer's soiree."

Intent on serious concerns, Gray ignored Timothy's crestfallen expression to pursue answers to his own questions.

"Do you know where Elizabeth is?"

Timothy shook his tawny head. "Only where she isn't. This morning she promised she'd try to bring Dru and meet with me in the park after tea. I brought the promised bonbons—" He held up a small box elaborately wrapped by a famous confectioners in wisps of gauzy paper and bright ribbons. "But they didn't come."

"You talked with Elizabeth this morning?" Penetrating silver eyes narrowed on the younger man. "Where?"

"Well, here, of course." Timothy was bewildered by

both the odd question whose answer was surely obvious and his cousin's black mood.

"When you spoke, did she tell you where she meant to go?"

Timothy looked blank. "No. She said nothing about leaving Brandt House." How could he admit he hadn't given Lizzy a chance to tell him anything without also telling Gray what had so completely occupied their conversation. "But, come to think of it, she was dressed to go out."

"Yes, and she did leave Brandt House this morning, apparently shortly after you departed." Gray studied Timothy's unaccountably guilty expression. "But she hasn't returned in all the hours since then."

"How awful!" Timothy gasped, horrified by the myriad of wretched possibilities raised by their furtive investigation into equally horrible realities.

"I agree it is awful, and the fact that she promised to bring Dru and meet you in the park proves she meant to return early enough to do so." Gray pushed aside his awareness that Elizabeth had been involved in, was likely the force behind, a scheme to subvert Euphemia's decision to break the bond between the young pair.

"Oh, Timothy, I would have come if I'd known." Dru flowed into the room, throwing her tiny self into her surprised beau's welcoming arms. Then, turning about to face her stepuncle, Dru told him what she'd just been told.

"Annie came to tell me something as soon as I was alone."

Gray straightened. Did this mean Lilibet's maid knew more than she'd admitted under his questioning?

Dark curls brushed suddenly rosy cheeks as Dru shook her head to refute his unspoken accusation. "No, Annie doesn't know where her mistress is. Truly, she doesn't. But she felt it necessary to tell me about the note Lizzy left for me."

"Note?" The two men questioned in concert but it was Gray who added a second query. "Do you mean Annie gave you a note left by Elizabeth?"

"No!" Dru emphatically denied, wringing her hands in visible anxiety.

The men, simultaneously losing patience, looked like twin thunder clouds.

"Annie told me that my stepmama pushed past her to enter Lizzy's room. Once there she saw and took the note addressed to me."

"Ellison!" Gray immediately roared.

Appearing almost as immediately in the drawing room doorway, Ellison dipped his head toward a scowling duke.

"Tell Lady Euphemia that I wish to speak with her—now!"

The butler straightened his shoulders and lifted his chin to quietly answer the command. "Her Ladyship left a few moments past."

Gray's scowl deepened. He refused to continue uselessly repeating unpleasant facts like a fool. "Then please ask Annie to come and answer a few additional questions."

Ellison, relieved that he could fulfill this order, briskly turned to carry it out. And in the briefest of moments Annie uneasily curtsied to the always intimidating but now frighteningly intense duke.

"Annie," Gray began, tempering the deep frustration of his voice into a gentle burr. "Lady Drusilla tells me that my sister took a note from your mistress's suite. Is this true?"

Annie mutely nodded.

"Did your mistress leave you instructions regarding the note?"

Annie slowly nodded again while bolstering her

bravado to speak. "She said I was to give the note to Lady Drusilla if she should fail to return by teatime." Annie paused, then earnestly added, "I would have, too, if it had still been on the desk where she left it."

"But is it true that Lady Euphemia has it now?" Gray's steely eyes bored into those of pale brown, demanding honest answers. "Did you see her take it from the desk?"

The feeling that her word was being doubted lit Annie's courage. "Yes! She pushed me aside—because I didn't think she ought go into Her Grace's suite while she was gone. I saw Lady Euphemia pick up, open, and read the note. Then she put it into her pocket and nearly walked over me to leave the room, though she must've known I'd seen what she'd done and wanted the note returned."

Gray nodded, giving the girl a reassuring smile. Few servants would've dared challenge the right of any member of the gentry, least of all the overbearing Euphemia, to do as they pleased. He was impressed that Annie had gone as far as she had to impede the actions his sister shouldn't have taken.

Once a relieved Annie had slipped silently away, a deadly calm Gray spoke freezing words. "Elizabeth has been abducted. I don't know who took her, but I can guess why."

Dangerously glittering eyes narrowed. The most peculiar aspect of this action, to Gray's thinking, was that the culprits behind it—proven masters at slinking through shadows to commit loathsome deeds—had dared pluck a duchess off a well-traveled street during daylight hours. That strange behavior provided him with a faint glimmer of hope. Perhaps they were growing carelessly bold, bold enough to trip themselves up and leave a trail to follow.

"I wish I'd some indication of where best to begin my search for her." The frustration behind his words curled Gray's strong hands into fists.

He could think of half a dozen crowded public locations in the roughest areas where transactions in white slavery were suspected of having been negotiated or foul tenements where the trade's "commodities" were thought to have been stored while awaiting shipment. They were all places to whose repellent squalor Gray cringed to think of his Lilibet exposed. He closed his mind to images of her in the hands of slime who catered to humanity's depravities to prevent rage from fogging a mind he must keep clear.

Having stood motionless and quiet throughout Annie's questioning and Gray's disheartening statement, Timothy and Dru exchanged a knowing look.

"We may know something of use." Timothy paused, plucking up the courage to confess what Gray would definitely not enjoy hearing. "You must know how anxious Lizzy has been about your accidents?" Though Gray's compelling eyes went to ice and narrowed on him, Timothy determinedly continued, "Since you wouldn't discuss the danger with her, she enlisted Dru and me to join her in a what she called 'a little discreet sleuthing.' And that's what we've done."

"You have done *what?"* Although tightly restrained, the rumbled question was a small explosion. The thought of easygoing Timothy, timid Dru, and his unpredictable wife mucking about in greater danger than they could possibly understand was mind-boggling . . . and alarming.

"Uncle Gray," Dru interceded, still in Timothy's arms and feeling his heart pounding so hard she feared it would burst. Besides, Gray's disbelief was an insult to her growing sense of daring, the bravery Lizzy had encouraged her to develop. "I suppose you think us unaware of the business we're investigating? But, you see, we do know that it involves the white slave trade."

"What!?" Gray was stunned. After Timothy's

frightening announcement he'd have thought matters couldn't get worse. They had.

Timothy, too, gasped at his beloved's ill-timed revelation and sought to mitigate the damage. "Now, Gray, you know I'd never willingly allow genteel ladies to . . . to . . ." Unable to go further without doing what he was in the process of claiming he wouldn't, Timothy helplessly motioned toward Dru.

Dru took it badly and ruffled like an angry hen. "As if it were *your* choice."

"It is."

"Then how was it that not so many days ago you found yourself escorting Lizzy to the Gaiety Hall?" Dru demanded.

Now she'd done it. Timothy caught a glimpse of Gray's blazing eyes and nearly melted.

"The Gaiety Hall? What mad impulse drove you to take my wife into one of the lowest music halls in one of the worst areas of the City?" After years of investigating them, Gray knew too much about the depraved practices and perils of London's teeming slums.

Seeing Gray's rapidly darkening temper, Dru's bravado began to waver. She realized into just what unpleasant position she'd pushed Timothy, and attempted to brush away a little of the slime with which she'd smeared him. "Lizzy said either he went with her or she swore she'd go alone."

Black lashes fell as Gray clenched his eyes closed in frustrated exasperation. It sounded precisely the sort of thing "Lizzy" would say and do. Moreover, this disclosure provided concrete answers to two questions: who had preceded him to the music hall and where Elizabeth had been earlier on the night he found her in the servants' hall.

"We went, learned nothing, and then I brought Lizzy safely back home." Gazing at, and ostensibly talking to, Dru but very aware of Gray's penetrating gaze, Timothy rushed over this hideous confession and anxiously moved on to a matter surely more important and, by virtue of that fact, hopefully able to distract from the first. "I've spent days and nights searching for clues to our villain's identity—and I found something!"

"What did you find?" Gray did not move, yet his strength of will seemed to reach out and demand a quick response from his cousin.

Timothy cast a half-sheepish, half-proud glance toward Gray. "A sealed document firmly implicating Hayton as a collaborator with the Badger."

"Where did you find it?" A skeptical glimmer of silver showed between black lashes. Had his young cousin somehow found what he'd been desperately trying to locate since the middle of the previous year's parliamentary session? Or was Timothy merely expanding upon the vague rumors that had circulated about the report's existence for months?

Timothy dutifully repeated all that he'd earlier told Liz, a tale of discovery ending with the same dismal admission. "Of course, as I told Lizzy this morning and as you know because you wrote it, the report gets us no closer to the Badger's identity."

"Tch!" Dru wrinkled her nose at Timothy in fond reproof. "Even Annie provided more useful information than that." Seeing the disbelief of the two men who'd worked so hard first in preparing and then in finding the lost report, she defensively sought to justify her claim.

"Annie told Liz about backstairs gossip that has it a rough-looking man's repeatedly been seen slinking into Hayton House between midnight and dawn."

"The Badger!" Timothy's initial amazement slipped into a mild disgust curling wide lips down. "You didn't tell me."

"You weren't around to tell." Dru promptly deflected the assault with undeniable logic cushioned by a loving smile and soft sky blue gaze.

Watching the rapid-fire blasts of these two friendly foes, Gray shook his head at the ability of the lovesick to be so easily distracted from infinitely more important concerns. But rather than censure, it roused in him a deep regret for not having risked his pride to assure the woman foolishly risking too much for his sake of his love for her.

Dru saw her stepuncle's frown. It dampened emotions warmed by Timothy's nearness with the cold awareness of the menace hovering over Lizzy.

"Anyway—" Dru returned to what little further information she had to share, "—it's what Annie said that sent Lizzy, me, and Annie off to Hayton House yesterday. Lizzy was certain he'd be gone and thought we might be able to do a bit of her 'discreet sleuthing.'" Nibbling a full lower lip, she tilted her head and gazed at Gray with wide azure eyes pleading forgiveness for her earlier moment of thoughtlessness.

"You believed it was possible to simply walk into the man's home and then out with the proof which a formal House investigation failed to uncover?"

On the defensive again, Dru shrugged. "You go in the front door where your actions are expected. We thought two genteel ladies on a social visit could, sort of, come through the back and find what we sought in a place unsuspecting and unprepared."

"What you've likely done," Gray's words fell like icicles shattering on pavement, "is to bring out the villain's claws, poised to rip Elizabeth to shreds." Gray gracefully whirled toward the door, a plan of attack rapidly taking form.

"Where are you going?" Timothy released Dru and leaped forward to wrap his hand around Gray's arm.

"To find my wife and bring her home."

"Wherever that is, I'm going, too." Timothy faced his cousin with a kind of steady determination Gray had rarely seen in him. Dying firelight glowed on the silver wings in Gray's hair as he nodded acceptance of the demand.

As the Ashleigh carriage came to a halt at the gate to Hayton House, Gray gave the front gardens a scrutiny he'd never spared them before. They were adequate, but nothing out of the ordinary, certainly nothing able to inspire the duchess of Etherton's envy. If he'd paid attention to them on earlier visits, he might have recognized the flimsiness of Lilibet's excuse when she spoke it, and he might have learned the truth of her visit, and he might have been able to prevent today's disaster. He might; he might; he might . . . all useless conjectures when only action could change the outcome.

The carriage was opened by Jeremy, the senior groom serving as coachman, as Euphemia had commandeered Durst and the other carriage earlier. Gray descended first, closely followed by Timothy. When they approached Hayton House's door, a punctilious butler opened it to wave the surprised and uneasy pair inside.

"This way, Your Grace, sir—" he nodded and led them toward an open portal.

"I say, Grayson, this is an unusual time to call." With a banal smile and languid movements, Lawrence met his visitors as they entered the drawing room. "I was about to retire to my suite and change into evening wear—in time for the soiree at the Somes-Halyers', don't you know."

"We'll keep our business brief." Gray's chill response was not accompanied by a reciprocal smile.

"Business?" Lawrence idly shrugged. "Oh, surely not when the evening has begun and there are so many more amusing things to occupy one's mind. You used to be such fun, but now you've become a too staid member of Parliament. Take care or I fear you'll soon bore your lively and delightfully amusing wife."

Gray recognized the blatant taunt in the words but still it required a full measure of self-control to restrain hands itching to wipe the sneer from Hayton's face.

"Where is my wife?" The deep question rolled like thunder as Gray moved steadily forward until he towered over the shorter earl.

Hayton's answer was a burst of mocking laughter. "You've lost the charming Lizzy already? I hadn't high hopes for your ability to hold her for long, but I didn't think you'd lose her so soon!" Firelight rippled over carefully brushed blond hair as he shook his head in feigned sorrow. "What? Has she run off with the footman? Or, perhaps, one of the Prince's more amusing friends?"

Gray's icy control instantly evaporated under a burst of fiery anger. One powerful fist flew out, smashing full into the earl's too brilliant smile and laying him out flat on the floor.

Timothy, standing motionless throughout the violently abbreviated scene, was shocked. He'd known Gray his whole life and had never, ever seen him lose his temper beyond a few chilling and most effective words. When the older man turned his back on his groaning foe and strode out past the wide-eyed butler, Timothy hustled to keep up.

Though fearing to speak before they were again ensconced in a moving carriage, once Timothy sensed Gray's control reestablished he hesitantly spoke.

"Where do we go next?"

"We'll start at the music hall where neither of us found what we sought, and where I don't expect to find what we seek . . . only guidance on which will be the more likely of a few places I wish I didn't know existed." Gray glared blindly into rapidly darkening streets. "And pray to God Elizabeth still doesn't."

CHAPTER 19

Liz's nose wrinkled. A vile smell was her first conscious sensation. Then, on turning her head, she felt the relentless pounding of some nasty creature who seemed to have taken up residence there. Without risking the painful consequences of any movement more violent, her dry tongue instinctively pushed against a knot of cloth, attempting to dislodge it from her mouth while she slowly returned to reality.

Despite lashes that felt as heavy as if made of iron shavings, Liz opened her eyes—to a darkness completely without form. Lying motionless on her side, she struggled to force still-muddled wits into some semblance of order and take stock of her situation. Rough and rotting wood was imprinting its coarse texture on the flesh of one arm, hip, and . . . She was nude!

At that shocking realization Liz instantly tried to sit up. She couldn't. Her feet were bound together at the ankle while her joined wrists were fastened just as firmly behind her back.

Heart thumping out a wild rhythm painfully echoed in her head, Liz acknowledged the obvious fact that

Lawrence, the apparently charming gentleman with whom she'd shared a cup of bitter tea, had first drugged and then delivered her here. But where was here? Not the earl's posh London home. The distant sound of rowdy but vaguely familiar music gave an erstwhile sleuth her first clue. She was either in the same building with or very near the Gaiety Hall.

This fact and her state of undress left little doubt as to her intended fate. Moreover, the wily monsters responsible for this outrage were masters in their business, using a woman's natural inhibitions as a second, invisible restraint to hold her captive. Were she to somehow win free of her bonds, not even as bold a woman as Liz would run into the streets unclothed. Such an action would not be daring but just plain stupid. In this low area of the city who'd believe she was a duchess? And even if they did believe, who among the ruffians and criminals haunting this area of the city would care? They'd more likely think it a fine thing to see a noblewoman brought down to their level and subjected to their will.

For a moment waves of panic washed over Liz with chilling defeat. Her worst fears had become horribly true. If only she'd lent more credence to this possibility rather than dismissing as unlikely the notion of anyone being so audacious as to attempt abducting a duchess and selling her into white slavery. Once the initial overwhelming waves of panic passed, Liz began piecing the shreds of her usual defenses together and bolstered them with unquelled courage.

Liz's eyes gradually grew accustomed to the darkness, enabling her to get at least a sense of the tiny room in which she was confined. Wielding the sword of hope to keep panic at bay, she began praying for a miraculous discovery of something to shield her bareness while at the same time methodically searching for a means of escape. Intently scrutinizing the dim form of her surroundings, she was pleasantly surprised to see that there was a window on the wall across from where she lay. Within moments Liz was reluctantly forced to dismiss the window as a possible escape route. It was far too small for her, or anyone larger than a toddler, to wiggle through. Besides, she ruefully acknowledged, few items of clothing were likely to be conveniently waiting for her between window ledge and street below. But still the window held her attention.

Either thick clouds had gathered after she arrived at the earl's house this morning or the night was a moonless one, for there was no glimmer of it or any other form of light to relieve the darkness outside. Except, she realized after steady observation, for a faint, erratically appearing glow along the window's bottom edge. She initially found the light perplexing, then wondered if it were a result of the opening and closing of the Gaiety Hall's doors? Puzzle solved, her attention shifted.

This prison cell appeared completely empty save for herself—and a little lump of something negligently tossed into a near corner. A lump distinctly unpromising as a weapon for securing her freedom. Liz firmly closed her thoughts to the sense of impending defeat intensified by a growing chill. While she stared at the lump in disgust, the window's intermittent glow briefly gleamed on an object in its midst.

Liz instinctively began slowly, awkwardly rolling toward that momentary gleam. But each completed rotation brought such a wave of pain and giddiness that she paused after three, fearing she'd lost the right path. Another closer, brighter glimpse confirmed her direction. She clamped her teeth tightly on the gag and with sheer determination ignored the excruciating pounding in her head to continue rolling until, at last, she found her nose buried amidst the black feathers of her smart hat. Exhausted by the struggle to cover this negligible a distance, Liz was discouraged but forced herself to curl upward enough to peer inside the overturned hat—an action rewarded with the most heartening of omens.

Apparently dropped carelessly inside the neat felt oval lay the treasured cameo whose intricate silver setting had caught faint light and reflected it in what Liz chose to see as a beacon of hope.

Hands fastened behind her back, Liz couldn't be certain but sensed that her valuable sapphire ring and matching earrings had been as carefully removed and carried away as her suit and undergarments, all designed by the great couturier Worth. Apparently her captors had disdained the hat and keepsake. While the clothes and jewels might be monetarily more valuable, to Liz their loss was meaningless compared to Gray's precious gift.

The thought of Gray reignited Liz's fiery spirit and determination to find a way free . . . or at least to be prepared to help when he come for her. And come for her he would. He hadn't made a verbal declaration of love, but his actions gave her confidence in his feelings for her. She put her complete and unquestioning trust in him. The sealed report Timothy had discovered proved Gray was aware of both the earl's dirtied hands and of the Gaiety Hall's tie to the wretched trade in which she'd just become a commodity.

Liz felt certain Gray would come seeking her at the music hall below. The problem lay in the fact that he'd likely run into as blank a wall as had she and Timothy. Lacking any indisputable proof of her presence in this specific building, he might think she'd been taken elsewhere in London's dim maze of warrens and shift the focus of his search away from where all too wily foes had chosen to hide her. Therefore, despite being bound and gagged, it was plainly her role to meet the challenge of finding some way to signal him.

Like a heaven-sent omen, the window's renewed glow made a gleaming frame of the cameo's silver edging. Liz smiled beneath the gag's restraints. In that instant the keepsake, Gray's gift to her, inspired a desperate plan. The deed would require perfect timing and incredible luck, but Liz felt complete confidence in its success.

Having left the security of gaslit streets behind, an unmarked servant's coach wound deeper into the Haymarket. Inside the vehicle a fidgeting Timothy found himself glancing ever more frequently at his cousin. While his own nerves were stretched tighter with the horses every forward stride, Gray impassively gazed out the window at scenes of decay and despair without a flicker of emotion. The man had rarely spoken since they'd departed Hayton House; and, were it not for the abrasions which the earl's teeth had left on Gray's knuckles, Timothy would have begun to suspect he'd dreamed the entire scene.

From Hayton's home they'd returned to Brandt House. Gray had tersely explained the logic of exchanging the ducal carriage for the servant's coach as necessary to protect the reputation of the woman they sought to save. When they'd set off again, each carried one from Gray's grandfather's matched pair of dueling pistols, the only firearms available in the duke's City home. And they'd left a distraught Dru behind with Annie comforting her—an odd pairing.

Gray felt the younger man's eyes upon him but, mentally preparing for any of the wide variety of scenarios they might have to face, refused to permit his attention to be diverted. As he'd told Timothy earlier, Gray had no real hope that they'd find Elizabeth at their next destination. There were rooms above the music hall to accommodate patrons' brief visits with women offering their bodies to please them, but it was unlikely his wife's abductors would risk storing her, a valuable commodity, in so nearly public a site.

When the coach rumbled to a halt before the source of muffled but roisterous noise, Gray silently motioned his cousin to step out first. Descending next, he paused to glare at the first of two sets of closed doors. The pair in front of him opened to a small and poorly lit anteroom where a burly man waited to demand a fee to pass through the next pair into the hall itself or payment for use of an upper room reached via the rickety stairway ascending on one side. It was from that brutish simpleton he must wrest the truth of Elizabeth's whereabouts.

Light from the coach's lantern glittered on an odd birdlike object flittering down from above, twirling as it dove, heavy end striking the street, not more than two paces from where Gray stood. He was startled but, intent on his cause, would've ignored the strange occurrence had it not been for the sound of metal scraping over stone. It required no more than a moment's delay to step forward and lift the object.

Despite the indistinct notes of a raucous song just begun inside, Timothy heard Gray's sharply indrawn breath. He curiously moved to stand at his cousin's side and gaze at the strange item cupped in a large hand—two black feathers awkwardly tied with a scarlet satin ribbon to Lizzy's cameo. Timothy's attention lifted to a dark face gone to stone and then followed the line of an icy gaze up to where a pale fluttering appeared in a window—one, two, no, three stories above.

Before Timothy had finished counting, Gray issued a cryptic order to Jeremy, who held the coach's reins and pushed through the first set of doors. Wasting no thought on the command given a coachman, Timothy hurried in his cousin's wake. He arrived just in time to see the man assigned to collect payments robbed of his senses by a single well-placed punch and shoved aside.

"Timothy," Gray softly called as he snatched up

one of a pair of kerosene lanterns and began climbing steps two at a time, "use your pistol to keep *anyone* from coming after me."

Obeying without question, Timothy braced shoulders against the wall to protect his back and stood alone in the otherwise vacant entry with loaded pistol leveled on the bottom step as if daring anyone to try.

In the tiny, dark room above, Liz waited with breath unconsciously held. Although forced to work with hands bound behind her back, she'd managed to improvise a signal whose simulated wings were designed to both draw attention and, hopefully, limit the damage to her cameo. She'd had to roll to the window's wall, scoot herself up against it and peer around the edge until her savior arrived. Then, offering up a fervent plea for divine assistance, she'd turned her back and tossed the evidence of her presence as far out as restrained hands allowed. Instantly dropping to her knees, shielding her nude body, she'd thrust wiggling fingers through the opening, just above the window's lower edge.

Still huddling on her knees she waited. Each silent minute that passed seemed like an hour, and it felt like an eternity had gone by before she recognized Gray's step. He was moving down the corridor, throwing open every door until, at last, the one across the room from her burst open and the light from his lantern assaulted her dark-adjusted eyes.

Gray immediately set his lantern on the floor at one side of the door and began striding toward his Lilibet.

"'Alt roit ther yer 'igh and moity lordship!" At the sound of the unpleasantly guttural voice, Gray went still while Liz crossed her arms over her breasts, eyes going wide.

"The Badger," Liz gasped, instantly certain that this must be the same rough character reported to have made late-night visits to Hayton House.

"Ther Badger?" Shaggy head thrown back and chortling, the man repeated her words with contemptuous delight.

A single blast laid the burly man on his back while a plume of smoke drifted in the air between the open door where he'd stood a moment before and Gray's dueling pistol. The victor calmly shoved the lifeless body into deep shadows beside the portal. Escape path cleared, Gray moved toward the woman who, though more courageous than any he'd ever known, was so pale she looked to be in shock or nearly so. He bent down to quickly dispense with her bonds and gag. Then, stripping off his coat he wrapped the garment warmed by his heat around her chilled body. He rose to his feet, lifting and cradling her near while raining kisses on the lovely face tilted up to him like a flower seeking the sun.

"I've spent recent hours damning the Fates for giving me my perfect mate only to take her away once my stubborn heart yielded to her gentle assaults." Gray knew they should leave immediately but refused to allow another moment to pass without correcting his regretted lack by telling her how he felt. "Now I've got my love safe in my arms again." Eyes gone misty met shining turquoise. "And I do love you."

"As I love you, Gray." Fervently kissing the lips that had formed the welcome admission, Liz reveled in his confession of emotions equal to those she bore for him. Her cheeks had regained their color and she sighed, firmly wrapping about his neck an arm still cramped by hours in the same uncomfortable position. "After Hayton's earlier lies, I should've known better than to answer his summons today. Forgive me for drawing you into this danger."

"From what Timothy's admitted, I know whatever you did, you did for my sake. It would be far more unforgivable were I to blame you for an action motivated by your love for me." In emphasis of the passionate declaration, Gray fitted his mouth to peach lips and claimed an equally passionate kiss wherein their very souls seemed to meld into a single entity.

"How sweet." The unexpected voice viciously invaded the tender scene. "The frozen duke melted by a fiery-haired American."

Lowering his Lilibet carefully to her feet and thrusting her safely behind his powerful form, Gray turned with his weapon pointed toward the door. In its opening the sneering Hayton was silhouetted by a torch held high in the hand of one of the motley assortment of supporters crowding behind. He held Timothy, gagged and hands bound, like a shield while pressing the muzzle of the young man's own pistol to his head.

"In spite of the fact that I was never as good a shot as you, Grayson, at this range I cannot miss. And if you fire your weapon, though you might hit me and not him, still it'll be at the cost of your cousin's life."

Hayton could not miss, Gray silently acknowledged. Worse still, with a weapon whose single shot had already been fired, there was no possibility that he could fire at all. But, had there not been a crowd of thugs behind the earl whose immediate threat to Lilibet was too great, Gray would've gladly renewed his earlier physical assault on the man.

Lawrence forced his tawny-haired hostage to precede him into the room, opening the way for his minions to pour in and disarm the duke, leaving a shocked Liz prey to the avid scrutiny of too many. While Gray's hands were being tied behind his back, Hayton's dark eyes also glittered obscenely over the length of the duchess's shapely legs visible beneath a coat that covered only to midthigh.

"I deeply regret I was unable to be present for your unwrapping, Lizzy." His smile was no longer charming but rather a leer, and the voice that could sound like smooth cream was now nearer curdled milk. "But

I'll be the first man involved in the next step of your training."

A shudder passed through Liz at the repulsive meaning she couldn't doubt. Hearing the words and seeing her reaction, a rumble of fury rolled from a now gagged Gray.

In answer to the duke's deep growl, Lawrence turned upon him a gloating gaze. "Your emotions have muddled your wits, elsewise you surely would've known I'd not be so easily robbed of my quarry. Once you left my home, I immediately came here. Expecting your arrival, I've waited in a rather nicer room at the far end of the corridor, anxious to extract a final vengeance—for your loosening of my teeth and endangering of a most profitable business."

With both Brandt males bound, Lawrence thrust the younger into another's hands. He languidly circled the spirited duchess clutching her inadequate covering tight to her throat. Lifting a lock of bright hair, he rubbed it between his fingers as if appraising its texture. "She'll fetch a very handsome price in Istanbul . . . after I'm done with her."

Hayton dropped the red curl and turned again toward the longtime competitor he'd rarely bested but would take joy in literally beating now. "We'll leave Lizzy for the moment while I concentrate on exacting my retribution upon you."

Among the earl's supporters a minor dispute broke out featuring crude epitaphs and coarse references to the captive's attributes. They were vying for the right to stand watch over the beautiful duchess soon to drastically descend in position—figuratively and literally.

"I think not, my friends." Lawrence spoke softly and the men immediately went quiet if mulish.

These words were harder, more inflexible, than any Liz had ever heard the earl speak. She was thankful that in this matter he'd exercised control, although he killed that wisp of peculiar gratitude with his next action.

"She's no more likely to leave now than she was before—not nude." Lawrence jerked Gray's coat from her shoulders and resisting hands, then stepped back to take a long, burning look at her curvaceous body. Like a dangerous snake preparing to strike, he hissed, "Soon, very soon."

Waved into action, the earl's minions began pushing and dragging the two male hostages from the tiny room while he trailed leisurely behind, closing the door after stepping through it. Liz couldn't see what was happening to Gray and Timothy, but by the noise of their going knew they were being hauled down the corridor to some other chamber. One not so far distant that in the minutes that followed she could fail to hear either the thudding blows or the rumble of scornful taunts being delivered.

Unwilling to helplessly wait for the worst, Liz scurried to the lifeless body of the man Gray had shot. In the commotion of their arrival and the confrontation just ended, Hayton and his men had somehow forgotten their fallen compatriot. It was true that the man lay in the shadows behind the open door, but they must surely have heard the shot. Light from the lantern left behind burned over Liz's unbound hair as she shook her head in amazement while dropping to her knees beside the limp form. They'd forgotten even his weapon. Their folly was a blessing to Liz, providing her with an opportunity to alter the current course.

Liz wasted no time in freeing the body of its filthy shirt and grease-stained pants. These she immediately donned, refusing to quail at the likelihood of minute inhabitants. Employing the same rope he'd used for a belt, she cinched the clothes tight to her own narrow form, retrieved his unused pistol and moved to the door.

Cracking the door open a fraction, she peeked into an empty corridor to be certain no guard had actually been posted before stepping from her prison cell. On bare feet she moved stealthily over rough plank flooring toward the source of the continued physical and verbal abuse of the Brandt men. Upon reaching that target, she threw the room's door wide with enough force to split its decaying wood as it smashed loudly against the wall behind.

The deafening crack arrested fists midmotion and words half-spoken while instantly the attention of all within the room flew to the muzzle of a weapon leveled at Hayton's head.

"I am a *very, very* good shot." The fierce glitter in turquoise eyes emphasized Liz's slow, precisely enunciated claim. After a moment's pause for it to sink into her audience, she added, "I trust, Lawrence, that you remember how I bested all participants at the bird shoot you hosted at Hayton Lodge?"

Liz smiled with a cloying sweetness as insincere as every word the earl had ever spoken to her. "I was pleased to find that this gun holds more than a single bullet. So, if you and any of your nasty little group wish to continue living, tell your friends to pile their weapons in the corner behind Gray and Timothy while you free them. Once each person's task is done, the next is to lie face down on the floor with hands clasped at the back of the neck."

Though sweat gleamed on Lawrence's brow and upper lip, he hesitated. Liz cocked her weapon and the sound broke his never strong courage.

"Do as she says," Lawrence ordered, moving to sunder Gray's bonds with a sharp dagger. "This crazy American is unlike any female I've ever known and too likely to follow through on her threat."

"Very wise of you, my *friend.*" The last word dripped with contempt. "Because I assure you that I'd rather be shot than make the visit to Istanbul which you've so kindly arranged." With a heady sense of triumph, Liz enjoyed the clanking sound of weapons piled atop one another and the view of prone bodies stretched out in disorderly rows at her feet while Gray and Timothy shredded their foes' own clothing to provide bonds for wrists and ankles.

"Moreover," Liz offered a final declaration, "I guarantee that you'd die before I could be forced to do so."

"I don't think so, m'dear."

Liz was startled by the familiar voice of an affable family friend immediately behind. Glancing over her shoulder, she found an even more startling sight: Sir David with a gun pointed directly at her head. And, most shocking of all, Euphemia stood at his side!

"Do put the weapon down." He motioned with the muzzle of the gun in his hand while, with his usual pleasant smile and in a mild voice now outrageously inappropriate, he added, "I have no doubt that you are capable of carrying out your threat." His expression hardened. "But so am I."

In stunned disbelief, Liz did as he commanded. What was happening? What could this jovial and seemingly fatuous man, ever concerned with his own comfort, be doing in these vile environs? With, of all people, Lady Euphemia!

"Oh, yes," Sir David continued, eyes narrowing on the breasts beneath a thin shirt inadequate to cover such bounty despite its large size. "It was very foolish of you to get involved in this nasty business—though I expect to make a fine profit on you." He looked her up and down in a coldly appraising manner so utterly devoid of personal interest it was even more offensive.

"Take comfort that leastways your search has won

its goal. It's I who am the Badger." Sir David fairly puffed with pride in the infamous title.

In the announcement Gray received a more personal and hurtful blow than any delivered by the earlier physical assault. In one sorry instance he'd followed his father's example. Without a moment's suspicion he'd given the complacent Sir David years of trust, thus laying himself open for this painful betrayal.

Liz shook her head in an attempt to make sense of unsuspected revelations while one of the men she'd forced to lie prone rose up and pushed her to the floor between Timothy and Gray. Her husband immediately wrapped a protective arm about her. Fighting a growing sense of hopelessness, she welcomed the shelter of his strength, thankful that although their captors were quickly rearming themselves they hadn't yet turned their attention to physical restraints for their hostages.

Amused by the duchess's confusion, Sir David explained in a gentle tone intensifying the incongruity of it all. "I can tell all of you this now as these two will soon be dead." He again used the gun to wave, this time toward Timothy on her right and then Gray on her left. "A truly tragic end to an unfortunate struggle over the Ashleigh legacy. One which I, as a family friend, will sadly mourn." He contorted his face into a frighteningly believable sorrow.

"But you can't do that!" Euphemia interrupted, voice rising into a shriek. "You promised me Gray would not be seriously harmed."

Liz felt her husband's muscles tense and responded by stroking solace over the taut arm curled around her shoulders.

"M'dear woman," Sir David answered his overwrought companion. "That was before you made such a nuisance of yourself and before the duchess rallied the family forces to protect Grayson. It was too bad of you, of them but . . ." He dismissed annoying problems on the verge of being satisfactorily eradicated with a shrug.

"But what do you propose we do with the old dragon?" From his position a pace behind the duke and his wife, Hayton nodded toward Euphemia. He was annoyed with his partner for bringing the unstable woman here in the first place.

Sir David carelessly shrugged. "We'll return her safely to Brandt House where she's no danger to us."

"What?" Hayton was appalled by his leader's suggestion that any member of Society with knowledge of their activities would live and be a threat to his peace.

"Think, Lawrence." The disgust in Sir David's command made it clear how little he thought of the man's intelligence. "I'm sure you find it difficult, but use what good sense you can muster to consider the matter calmly."

Neither Gray nor Liz bothered to look behind, but they felt waves of frustrated resentment flowing from the earl as Sir David's quiet voice continued its emotionless litany of logical crimes.

"The bodies of Grayson and Timothy can be arranged to seem the product of self-defense and murder respectively. We can even expect Society to accept the duchess's disappearance as a result of her grief and shame. But Lady Euphemia? The same options cannot be safely applied. For our business she's too old. Hell, even when she was the harsh young woman I remember, she was never valuable enough to be worth the risk. Her death would be one too many to explain. So, why should we try?"

On one level Liz soaked in the warmth of what she feared would be her last moments in her beloved's arms. On another she watched the man she'd thought amiable, if a trifle befuddled, become a monster while her imposing sister-in-law shrank into a pallid, frightened ghost of her former overbearing, haughty self.

"Lady Euphemia has already committed herself too

deeply to risk making uncomfortable revelations." Sir David cooed with vicious satisfaction. "How can she tell what she knows without exposing how she conspired in a plot that ended her beloved brother's life or without destroying not only her reputation but Lady Drusilla's as well?"

Sir David turned a bland face toward the woman gone deadly white. "Of course, m'dear, your specific request will be granted. The duchess will be sold into some sheik's harem where her independent spirit will assuredly be broken. And I do intend to fulfill my part of our bargain. Within the week you'll have the agreed-upon amount—blood money in payment for Grayson's death."

Euphemia cried out and fell back against the cracked door hanging haphazardly from loose hinges, braced against the wall behind while Sir David shifted his attention to his noble associate. "All the loose ends are tied and a looming threat tamed." He grinned. With the action his placid mask fell completely away, and his audience saw the vile Badger truly revealed in an expression of blatant evil.

"Indeed, sir, that does tie off loose ends quite nicely."

Both Liz and Timothy quietly gasped while Gray softly murmured, "At last."

The inspector, backed by Jeremy and a large group of uniformed constables, continued. "We deeply appreciate the help you've given us with your succinct outline of past and intended crimes." Before the speaker could step aside to permit his men's entry, a growling Sir David whirled, lifting his weapon.

Gray released Liz and launched himself at the man's legs. That bullet went harmlessly wide of the mark, but other guns were fired while constables swarmed into the room, swinging truncheons to great effect. During the ensuing melee, Liz made it her mission to trip as many villains and knock them to the floor as possible. For Liz the next minutes were measured in pounding heartbeats and ignored pain while the air was filled with the sound of blows thudding into bodies, gasping breaths, fists smashed against flesh, and the sick-sweet smell of the blood spatters making the floor slippery.

After order had at last been restored and the two well-born criminals with their thugs taken into custody to be hauled away, Liz lay on the rough floor against one wall, exhausted and aching from blows inflicted by many jabbing feet and falling bodies.

"Lilibet, my brave darling, are you all right?" Anxiously kneeling at her side, Gray carefully turned her prone body over. He was relieved by the brightness of her smile despite the streak of blood, clearly not hers as no skin was broken, and the bruises beginning to discolor the flesh of her cheeks and likely elsewhere.

"In better shape than you after the ordeal you've been through tonight," Liz answered, loving concern melting turquoise eyes. She felt every one of her many bruises, but they were nothing compared to those Gray had surely sustained in the beating the villains had given him even before the just completed battle had begun.

"I've thought we'd safely won this conflict once or twice before only to discover I was wrong." Gray's rueful grimace warmed into a heart-winning smile as he carefully lifted his courageous wife from her awkward position. "This time I'm quite certain we have."

The lock of black hair fallen rakishly across Gray's forehead gave the man Liz had once thought too stuffy a justifiably roguish look. She grinned and nodded, impulsively wrapping her arms about her bold hero's neck.

Gray cradled her gently nearer, mindful of her

many bruises. "But let's waste no time in getting free of this place and its relentless parade of untrustworthy newcomers."

"Your Grace?" A quiet voice tentatively interrupted.

Both Gray and Liz glanced questioningly into a hesitant Jeremy's face.

"I wrapped Mr. Timothy's broken arm in a sling like you told me I ought."

While Jeremy nervously paused, Liz looked across the room to the conspirator she hadn't realized was injured. Even through the sling it was obvious that Timothy's forearm was bent at an odd angle. But despite a pale face, he sent Liz a smile of victory for the fine end to their adventure.

Jeremy went determinedly on with the message he'd been sent to deliver. "Now Mr. Timothy wishes to know when you intend to return to Brandt House where he wants to remind you Lady Drusilla is waiting. And, also, he wonders what should be done about Lady Euphemia." The young groom awkwardly tilted his head toward the pitiful figure still hunched against a broken door.

Liz unashamedly clung to her beloved's broad shoulders as he rose to his feet. Gray instructed Jeremy to aid Lady Euphemia to the waiting coach. Then, proudly carrying the bruised and bulky figure Lilibet was in her borrowed clothes, he led the way down to a street still filled with constables. Jeremy leading a quietly sobbing Euphemia followed, trailed by Timothy.

CHAPTER 20

Inside her Brandt House suite Liz gratefully eased a body plagued with hurts and aching muscles into the steaming water and frothy bubbles filling an elegant claw-footed bathtub. She employed a ball of rose-smelling soap and a washcloth to completely rid herself of the grit and stench of her captivity. After working up a white lather in thick red hair, she rinsed, wrung out excess liquid, and combed her fingers through its tangles. Sweeping the heavy mass up in both hands, she leaned against the porcelain tub's high back then dropped her dark-fire burden to flow over the rim and pool on the floor while she lazed in delightful comfort.

It was the habit of many genteel ladies to be pampered by their maids while bathing, but Liz's modesty had never permitted such service. A fact which made it all the more startling when she heard the door open. Liz abruptly sat up and rapidly dissipating bubbles sloshed over the tub's sides along with a fair measure of now tepid water.

Tall, dark, and stunningly handsome, Gray stood in the doorway of her small dressing room, an appreciative gleam in the silver eyes focused on full breasts saucily frosted with peek-a-boo foam.

Plainly fresh from his own bath and just as plainly bare beneath the scarlet dressing gown, Liz remained proudly erect while returning Gray's interest with equal admiration for the glimpse of wiry curls covering the broad chest revealed by his loosely tied robe.

"Don't you think it's time you came out of the water?" Gray's question was a soft rumble. "I've already bathed and dressed."

"Dressed?" Liz gently scoffed, giving a brief shake of tresses whose fire was not appreciably tamed by their dampness.

"Wearing more than I need." Gray shrugged. "And you already know it's more than I wear while I sleep." The last statement was accompanied by a teasing wink.

This uncharacteristic action won the blush she'd restrained moments past, but turquoise eyes refused to drop demurely from his unwavering gaze. Laughing in response, she accepted his hand to help steady her as she rose.

It was Gray who poured the waiting ewer's contents over her body, rinsing away the bath's residue. And it was he who took up one of several soft, clean towels neatly folded and waiting nearby to rub her hair, and then with care gently began patting her bruised body dry. He started with her shoulders and worked slowly down—lavishing too much attention on sweet, tempting breasts for his peace of mind. This wasn't his purpose in coming. Even as he sank to his knees before her, he silently scolded himself to remember that, for her sake, he must control his unruly desires. This goal was reinforced by discoveries he made while smoothing every gleaming drop from her body.

"As Worth said, your natural coloring is delightfully vivid. But I fear you'll grow far brighter over the next few days." Silver eyes gone cloudy moved ruefully over patches of creamy flesh already turning from red to purple. "You paid too great a price for your concern over my safety." He leaned forward to lightly brush his lips over a particularly nasty bruise in the curve between waist and hip.

Liz gasped. The sound was not born of pain but, so far as she could tell, Gray apparently believed it had been. Masculine cheeks darkening with what seemed a guilty flush, he instantly rose, took up another large towel and enveloped her in its folds.

"I'm sorry, my poor, brave Lilibet. You're in no condition to travel down the road to which that kind of action leads. Nor, truth be known, am I." That was a lie. He was perfectly capable and able to easily ignore his own injuries for the prize of claiming her luscious body, but he loved the woman within too much to put her through the pain it would undeniably cause her.

Liz nodded regretful acceptance of this indisputable fact. Moreover, she feared that by morning she'd be so stiff and bruised it would be difficult to move at all.

On her expressive face Gray was consoled to discover more disappointment than relief. Indeed, Lilibet seemed to suffer as much disappointment as he. But with his experience, he knew better than she how uncomfortable it would be for her were they to make love under these circumstances.

"However, we can still share a bed, comfort each other's hurts." Strong arms opened wide, inviting her into his embrace. "After almost losing you, I need to feel you near."

Gray was very much aware that this was the first time in his life he'd ever wanted to spend a night holding any woman platonically in his arms. He'd have found it a useless waste of time with anyone save his Lilibet. But even holding the woman he loved in simple comfort would mean a great deal more than ever had the meaningless physical embraces he'd shared with others.

Liz flowed forward, welcoming the prospect of closeness with this wonderful man who was, as he'd claimed her to be, a gift of the Fates.

As carefully as he had in the room above the Gaiety Hall, Gray lifted his now clean and sweet-smelling bride. Tucking her, towel and all, into the beckoning comfort of her bed, he gazed down at the exciting, unique woman he'd wed and smiled teasingly.

"Your present garb is rather more attractive than the shirt and pants you wore when we parted at your door a short time past."

Softly groaning at the memory, Liz returned his grin. "You, on the other hand, were most properly attired, despite the odd rip and smudge of dirt. But, I like you best this way, too."

The adoration in turquoise eyes nearly undid Gray's fine and noble intentions. Yet when he slipped into bed beside his wife, despite all their banter, he held her in simple comfort until, with head pillowed on his chest, she drifted into dreams. The descent of his own sleep-borne fantasies was delayed by the feel of her delicious form—from shoulder to toe and everywhere in between—pressed against the hardening contours of his body. But at length, the tensions of a very long day and physical exertions of the battle at its end allowed a deep sleep to overcome distractions.

The pale sunbeams of early morning drifted between the slightly open edges of a window's heavy drapes. They caressed Liz's cheek until heavy bronze lashes responded to their call and lifted. A smile curled peach lips as she realized upon precisely what she rested. Liz softly kissed the firm flesh and rose up on one elbow to study her sleeping husband's thick black hair with its distinguished silver wings emphasizing a broad brow. His firm cheeks and strong jaw were darkened by morning stubble while even in sleep his wide mouth was a sensual enticement. Her attention wandered lower to the breadth of his chest, muscles at rest, but plainly powerful—a strength she'd seen him exercise the night past with grave consequences for his opponents.

Yielding to an old temptation, she began softly stroking satin skin and tangling fingers in wiry curls. Next, surrendering to a wanton urge, she traced her fingers' path with her lips, allowing the weight of full, silk-soft breasts to brush teasingly across his bare form until she won what she sought.

Gray came awake, confused by the dream coming temptingly to life. His hands took up where his dreams had ended, one sweeping down an arched spine to press pliant flesh intimately nearer while the other glided up to cup a luscious globe.

The very real repetition of the tiny moan of hunger he so loved to hear convinced him that this was reality. He went still . . . until she writhed against him. Even then he forced himself to do no more than hold her lightly in his arms.

Liz had other ideas. She was sore—but not *that* sore. Pulling slightly away from the man too fearful of hurting her to hold her nearer, she resumed the sweetly tormenting caresses that had awakened him and whispered enticingly.

"You said I couldn't, but I know I can." Liz planted several more tantalizing kisses over his chest then laid her cheek across the path her lips had taken. Her hair brushed his chin as she added, "And I can see for myself that you most assuredly can."

Low laughter rumbled from beneath her ear before Gray carefully rolled Lilibet to her back and rose up to look down, silvery eyes gleaming with amusement.

"Oh, you can see that? Let's test your premise, shall we?" His mouth slowly descended to her breasts where he returned the sweet torment she'd played across his chest . . . with interest.

Only after she was so deep into passion's fires that no minor discomfort could intrude, did he move slowly above her, holding a melting turquoise gaze with one of glowing silver while his hips very gently eased down, proving her premise and possessing her completely. She gasped in welcome as his mouth covered hers, and together they moved in slow, sweet rhythm. Again they dove into a vortex of fire, deepened by tenderness, and reached new depths before crying out together with a culminating explosion fiercer and brighter for the unshielded love at its center.

"I have no dowry." The brightness of Dru's grin refuted any possibility that she regretted the lack. She was delighted by the certainty that her lack of dowry put an end to the interest of Lord Poxwell—or any other self-important suitor unwilling to make a less than impressive match. She could almost feel sorry for poor Poxwell. His only use had been the excuse he'd provided for her escape from exile in the country, for never would she have wed anyone save Timothy. "Isn't it wonderful?"

Secure in the circle of Gray's arm, Liz returned the girl's infectious grin. She gazed affectionately at the young couple sitting close together on a rose loveseat blessed with an abundance of lace doilies. It was a match, save for color, to the silvery green one she shared with Gray catercorner to the other couple's. Though every bit as stiff and sore as she'd suspected the previous day's adventures would leave her this morning, she in no way regretted the heated therapy Gray had provided brief hours past.

"Of course you have a dowry," Gray answered the claim with fond disgust.

"But I don't want one!" Dru asserted, sitting up and leaning toward her stepuncle with the earnest demand.

"Well, you'll have one." The response was firm enough to set Dru back and bring a suspicious sparkle to pale blue eyes. "At least enough to see you and Timothy nicely set up."

The threatening tears of frustrated hopes instantly turned into a physical expression of joy as an ecstatic Dru turned and flung herself against her shocked intended.

"And as wedding gift, Liz and I will provide an adequate amount to support Timothy's wish to stand for the seat in the House of Commons vacated by the discredited Sir David."

Afraid two pieces of such overwhelming good news would unman him, Timothy blinked rapidly and forced a shaking voice to momentarily distract attention—long enough to regain his composure—with an enquiry. "What has . . . what will happen to Sir David and the earl?"

Gray saw and silently applauded his cousin's efforts at control, a talent any politician must hone. "I received a report from the inspector in charge of their arrest less than an hour ago. He states that both are in gaol where, in consideration of the seriousness of their crimes, they'll stay until hauled into the dock for trial. As for what happens then?" Gray shrugged but his eyes were ice. "I doubt two born to the gentry but, by their own choice, fallen so low will find much sympathy from any jury. Hayton could insist on being tried before the House of Lords, but he'd be a fool if he did."

"Hayton. Why not Sir David?" Liz curiously asked, unfamiliar with this quirk of British law. "And why would he be a fool?"

Gray smiled down into a puzzled frown and

brushed back one fiery curl escaped from her intricate chignon to fall on her forehead. "Sir David has no landed title and is not a member of the House of Lords. Therefore, he's not entitled to that privilege."

The gentleness her nearness gave his expression faded into an old bitterness as he answered her second question. "As for why he'd be a fool . . . There's little to compare with the retribution of our class when one of our number begrimes the virtuous facade we strive so hard to maintain."

Liz heard the echo of a disdain for his own he'd revealed when speaking of Society as pretty icing on a spoiled cake, and again she sought to mitigate the wholesale contempt recent events could only have reinforced.

"The best any one of any class can do—" she softly pointed out gazing up at him, eyes gone soft with a plea for understanding "—is to try to *be* as virtuous as we strive to seem."

Slowly, under her steady attention, the frost that had molded Gray's face into a cold mask thawed.

Timothy, too, had taken note of his cousin's return to the frozen armor from which he'd thought Liz's fiery nature had freed the man. And on this day, which ought to be filled with relief and a fine sense of victory, it couldn't be permitted. Again he sought to distract—this time for Gray's sake.

"I must say, we certainly were fortunate that the constables decided to move upon the white slavery ring when they did."

"Fortunate? Nothing like that. Jeremy obeyed the order I gave him as we entered Gaiety Hall. Had you forgotten?" Black brows furrowed in a surprise not cured by Timothy's sheepish shrug.

"Jeremy tells me he had to work at convincing them to come at all." Gray continued the tale. "A lifesaving feat for which I've profusely thanked and rewarded him. A reward in addition to his new position as under coachman."

"I'll give him my appreciation, too," Timothy grinned. "It's plainly due to him that we were rescued only moments before our erstwhile friends did their worst."

"Not quite so bad as that." With a quiet laugh Gray assured both Timothy and the young woman whose sky blue eyes had widened in renewed fear of a danger past. "Jeremy tells me that the police were standing outside the door from almost the moment Sir David arrived. But they chose to wait and listen to him babble before breaking up our fine gathering."

"Breaking up, indeed," Timothy muttered *sotto voce,* restraining a mocking smile while lifting the arm a physician had splinted the evening before.

"Still and all, an understandable decision. The waiting took a toll on our nerves, but it provided proof enough to see that ring of white slavers' business at an end." Gray chose not to muddy their moment of success by mentioning the bleak certainty that where one ring ended another would begin—but hopefully without the leadership of members of Parliament.

"But how soon can we marry?" With this complete shift of subject—back to one much happier—Dru purposefully broke the tension roused by memories of a dark experience.

"At the end of the Season?" Liz welcomed Dru's action and glanced up into her husband's bruised face for confirmation of her suggestion.

But as Gray indulgently nodded, another voice intruded on the warmth of the scene.

"Will I be permitted to remain long enough to see my precious stepdaughter wed?" Euphemia stood hesitantly just inside the door.

Liz felt a pang of pity for the woman whose face was puffy and unattractively blotched, whether from tears of regret or resentment it was impossible to know. Liz suspected a combination of the two. It was certain that Euphemia's morning meeting with her brother had stripped away her former haughtiness. And lacking her usual supercilious airs, Euphemia seemed almost a stranger to Liz.

Gray, too, was momentarily stirred to pity for his sister . . . until he remembered what she'd intended for his Lilibet. After they'd arisen to meet a day destined to host an odd collage of joy, sorrow, relief, and contentment, he'd left his wife to Annie's care while he chose to have done with the most difficult chore first. He had met with Euphemia for a painful discussion of her misdeeds and their price. Her appearance here before this small group was at his command, the first on a list of conditions she must meet in exchange for his permitting her an easier punishment than that which the courts would assuredly have exacted. Nonetheless, her arrival put a blight on the sun-filled room. Indeed, it seemed to darken even the garden beyond long windows.

"A return for the wedding might be in order." Gray coolly nodded, replacing her suggested "remain" with "return." "So long as you fulfill your part of our agreement and gracefully retire *now* from this Season—for unspecified health reasons that will not improve enough for you to reappear in future years."

Euphemia grimaced, face turning purple though she meekly nodded.

"But first, as we agreed, you must confess your wrongs and their reasoning to this company. I want Dru, as well as the others here present, to understand what was done and the reason for your permanent retirement to Dell House in Cornwall."

Aware that his wife, at least, would be unfamiliar with Euphemia's destination, Gray explained. "Dell House is a lesser family holding, small but quite comfortable though far, far from anyone in the society

Euphemia has allowed to cloud, nay, completely destroy her judgment."

Gray's attention had not shifted from the sister whose jaw had moved forward into an obstinate thrust. At the end of his explanation an ominous quiet fell upon the room. No faint rustle of cloth or audible breath broke the tension while a steady silver gaze silently demanded Euphemia comply with oaths previously given.

"As I've already told you, Dru—" Euphemia looked to the stepdaughter apprehensively cringing away from her and tighter against a comforting Timothy. "Your father died nearly penniless, leaving you nothing like the amount required to see a marquess's daughter properly wed. Sir David promised to discreetly provide a marriage settlement substantial enough to seal the pact with Lord Poxwell or any suitable mate." Euphemia's voice became a whining plea for the others to accept her actions as no more than a righteous attempt to secure the best for all concerned. "All I need do in repayment of his generosity was provide a small, innocuous bit of help in frightening Gray into abandoning some unimportant political issue. And that issue one which Sir David told me could only end in tainting our family name."

"No-o-o," Dru wailed.

When her stepmama had talked of this matter an hour before she'd joined the wounded Timothy, Dru had closed her mind to its implications, focusing instead on the welcome fact removing the barriers between her and the man she loved. Now, while curled in Timothy's hold, the whole sordid plot that had nearly resulted in dreadful consequences and had caused Timothy's injury came clear. It filled her with anguish.

"To know that you did these awful things for my sake smears me in the same foul guilt!"

"Oh, no!" Hearing the condemnation of her beloved stepdaughter, Euphemia would've flown to her side but for the restraining power of Gray's deepening scowl.

"Continue and have it done." Gray demanded, anxious to have this wretched black cloud of duty behind them and future skies left infinitely clearer.

Euphemia glared in return but could not stand against her brother's dominant will. Taking a deep breath, she went on with the point she earnestly felt absolved her. *"Truly,"* she emphasized for Gray's sake as well as Dru's, "I believed Sir David's promise that no real harm would come to Gray by anything I did . . . and all I did was tell the man when my brother would be where. Surely nothing that couldn't have been learned elsewhere with only a little more effort." She nearly mewed in her desperation to be accepted.

Gray nodded. He believed Euphemia had honestly thought she could play dangerous games with traitorous men, working their end against his to win the prize she sought, but it did nothing to justify her wrongs—neither those committed against him nor worse, far, far worse, against his Lilibet.

"I acknowledge but do not accept your reasoning as excuse for actions against me. But you haven't even that minimal justification for your unforgivable actions against Elizabeth. You may have merely gone along with Sir David's plans for me, but you actually requested that my wife be sold into some sheik's harem."

"But, Gray—" A strange gleam entered slate gray eyes, one as frightening as Euphemia's twisted logic. "I was only thinking of our family name—as you ought to have done." She sounded like a nanny scolding her charge. "The Ashleigh heir's bloodlines must never be tainted with those of the merchant class."

Feeling the words like a physical assault, Liz's temper flared and she straightened away from Gray's half-embrace. In response, although Gray continued gazing at his sister, his hands rubbed comfort over her stiff shoulders.

"I suspected the American was carrying your child. I was certain that even were she rescued from foul surroundings and the slimy company of whoremongers, you'd never dare accept her babe as heir."

Silver eyes flashed with such fury that Euphemia fell back while the next instant Gray turned toward Liz. "If the villains we've defeated had instead succeeded in their vile plans for you, so long as there was life in my body, I'd have found you and welcomed home both my precious wife and *any* child you bore."

Throughout the unpleasant confrontation, Mrs. Simms had quietly waited just outside the door, but at this pause and seeming end to the scene, she moved into the room and draped a cloak about her mistress's shoulders.

"It's time, Lady Euphemia," she said with unshaken loyalty. "The carriage is waiting to take us to the station. The day's only train departure providing a connecting service to our destination leaves within the hour."

Euphemia straightened in a faint parody of her old self. "Our bags are packed and loaded?"

"Yes, ma'am." Mrs. Simms nodded, gently urging her ladyship from the room.

Once Euphemia was gone and with her the shadows she'd brought, Timothy set himself to ridding Dru of wrongful guilt and reviving her earlier high spirits. With the resilience of youth, the pair were soon involved in quiet talk of wedding plans and dreams for the future.

Forcing himself to put aside dark pain of his sister's betrayal, Gray gave his full attention to the source of such a brightness and warmth that he knew she could heal the wounds of his past with confidence for their future.

Gray rose and made a courtly bow, holding out a hand that drew a surprised Lilibet to her feet.

"Could I have a moment to speak with you privately in the library?"

The question was asked in the most proper of tones. Nonetheless, the wry smile accompanying this request made it clear Gray was purposely repeating similar requests made in their early, volatile weeks together. Liz remembered how often those first arrogant demands had been the herald of a dreaded fiery confrontation. Now she welcomed any excuse to be alone with the devastating man and enjoy fires of another sort.

"Certainly, Your Grace." Liz lifted a corner of her skirt and with one finger pressed below the point of her chin made a pert curtsy.

The focus of her mocking taunt growled, and despite lingering soreness, a laughing Liz danced into the book-lined room one step in front of him. Shutting the door as he entered, Gray instantly swept the saucy minx into his arms for a passionate kiss. She relaxed into the intimacy of the embrace and it was some little time before he returned her to unsteady feet.

Liz leaned back against a wall of books while her handsome husband made his way to the desk. He dug into the same drawer where she'd found nasty threats on scraps of coarse paper and her curiosity rose. Then as he returned to her with something clasped inside one closed hand, she knew by the gesture she remembered from an earlier time. Her face glowed with a love brighter even than her vivid mane.

Gray held out his hand and on his palm lay the keepsake, one small dent in the silver border. He'd initially given it to her with a love he hadn't admitted. Now he lifted her hand, pressed a fervent kiss into her palm, and laid the cameo atop as if to seal the caress forever, and followed the gesture with a declaration the more potent for being unembellished by flowery phrases. "I love you."

Liz's fingers curled around the treasured token and she melted against his powerful form, lifting her lips to brush loving kisses to what she could reach of his cheeks and throat while whispering over and over, "And I adore you, adore you, adore you."

EPILOGUE

Late September 1886

"Father already has a hunt organized for us at the Double H the first weekend after our arrival." Seated on a plush couch in the family parlor at Ashleigh Hall, Liz grinned up at the man just entering. Smiles now common to her husband's lips made him even more devastatingly handsome than when they'd met. "I'm afraid the pheasant hunt he took part in during his visit here left him as unimpressed as I was the first time."

"And still are," Gray murmured and bent to brush a kiss across her ever-tempting mouth before continuing. "When Samuel accepted the invitation to Scotland, I warned him what to expect. He's as stubborn as you and insisted. We can only be thankful he was at least spared the stray bullet that interrupted your first British bird shoot."

"Ah, but it didn't interrupt the British shoot but rather the American style hunt I shamed the others into attempting." She straightened, casting him a glance of mock fear. "I hope this doesn't portend a similar assault."

"I don't think it's a problem, as I doubt you've any

hidden enemies in Wyoming waiting to threaten you." A crooked smile curled Gray's lips, and while he settled on the couch beside her lightly tapped her nose with one finger. "Or are you trying to dampen my anticipation for our visit when you know how much I've enjoyed our previous journeys."

"Never," Liz solemnly stated, leaning nearer when he wrapped his arm about her and again silently acknowledged that the freedom she'd once thought could only be found in wide open spaces would, in truth, have been a prison of loneliness. She took pleasure in their visits to the ranch but had no desire for its escape. Perhaps one of their younger children would wish to live there, perhaps . . .

"Most certainly not this time when," she added, meaningfully, "I must enjoy it the more for knowing I won't be in a position to make the trip next autumn."

Gray's eyes went soft as they met turquoise before dropping to a still narrow waistline. "Shall we tell Timothy and Dru—who I've nearly forgotten to remind you will be here any moment—or leave the limelight to them?"

"We've months to share the news of our growing family while this is Timothy's great triumph. . . ."

Gray had left the parlor door open, and the pair inside were summoned by the sound of new arrivals escaping the briskness of early autumn by sweeping into the flagstone entry. Soon two couples stood in the circle of comfort cast by the roaring flames of the parlor's massive fireplace. A smiling warmth accompanied the tinkling of crystal goblets meeting in a toast celebrating Timothy's win in his first nationwide election.

Leaning closer to Gray whose strong arm was draped about her shoulders, Liz studied the other couple. Marriage had not dimmed Dru's adoration of Timothy or his for her.

"Now that it's successfully past," Timothy said in earnest relief, "I can admit how worried I was. Though they gave me the position in the by-election after Sir David's arrest, I feared the voters, given more time to consider my part in the man's downfall, might've come to view me as someone as begrimed by those ghastly deeds as he." He stopped to gaze down at his gently scowling wife. "I am most thankful it's been relegated to a forgotten past unlikely to dirty my family's future."

"The poor fool thinks—" Dru softly mocked, squeezing her husband's arm, "—that he hid his uneasiness from me . . . as if I were that insensitive."

"Insensitive?" Timothy's dark eyes widened in an exaggerated innocence backed by a purity of motive. "No! It's I who would've been insensitive to put a wife in your delicate condition through such stress."

A complacent smile warmed Dru's naturally rosy face as she patted her well-rounded belly. "The baby's fine and, judging by current liveliness, showing approval of his father's success."

"His?" Gray grinned.

It was Liz who answered, snuggling closer. "I'm told *his* father has sternly informed the babe not to disappoint the important man he intends to become."

"That's true," Dru laughed, "but there's more. Since Geoffrey was born, Timothy has insisted his firstborn will have the good sense to also be a son."

"Not so," Timothy looked hurt. "Son or daughter—doesn't matter. I'll love the child the same." After a meaningful pause he added, "But it would be awfully nice to give Geoffrey a playmate."

"Whether boy or girl, you're doing that." Liz sensibly pointed out the obvious, restraining a merry smile while teasing the politician for a less than diplomatic gaffe.

"Speaking of the scamp," Timothy wisely shifted the focus, "where is Master Geoffrey?"

As if on cue, the door opened. The boy's nanny stood in its frame, but her young charge bolted around the slender block and into the room. Black hair ruffled by his speedy flight, he threw himself into his mother's arms and, with an impish gleam in turquoise eyes, grinned up at his doting father before embarking on a lengthy, enthusiastic account of his afternoon's adventure.

Delighted by his son's antics, the warmth on Gray's face intensified as he studied his fiery-haired wife, laughing at Geoffrey's imaginative description of the wild monster he'd tracked through the woodland. His Lilibet had so thoroughly melted his icy restraint that she'd opened his heart to a previously unsuspected range of joys and satisfactions found in family . . . in life itself. His love for her grew brighter, stronger every day.

Reluctantly turning his thoughts to their guests, Gray spoke seriously to his cousin. "Since Elizabeth, Geoffrey, and I set off across the Atlantic in a week's time and the brief midwinter session begins shortly after our return, this may be the only opportunity you and I have to discuss a few of the pressing issues facing us."

Dru sent Liz a feigned grimace of despair. It was returned with a knowing grin. Each could clearly see a future in which her husband would continue the political fight for needed changes. A fact of which they were inordinately proud.

Liz glanced up at a Gray intent on the topic begun. She had the satisfaction of knowing that he would seek and listen to her thoughts on these important matters while she savored the kind of position that in New York and Wyoming she'd foolishly sought to reject. Holding her seldom still son firmly in one arm, with her free hand she lightly touched the charcoal cameo at her throat. It was her talisman of happiness.

Feeling the weight of Gray's attention, Liz glanced up into soft silver eyes now rarely layered in ice. Impervious to the other couple's amusement, he bent to claim smiling lips in a loving kiss until Geoffrey, locked between, began to giggle.

A.D. 678

Cra-a-ck!

A harshly shoved door smashed against the stone wall behind. It was the rude announcement of an unexpected visitor's arrival in a small abbey cell. The echoing sound startled the young beauty on her knees before a robed figure into settling back on her heels. She turned jewel-bright eyes toward its source—a tall, black-cloaked figure filling the open doorway and silhouetted against the brilliant rays of the setting sun, which glowed on his bright hair.

The intruder's mouth tilted into a cynical half-smile, and disgust darkened the amber gaze skimming over the woman's alluring curves. She was the loveliest creature Adam had ever beheld. But a woman condemned by the fact that as she knelt at the feet of a man of holy calling—worse still, a bishop—only a cloud of ebony hair provided a covering, of dubious usefulness, for slender shoulders and lush breasts.

"Who are you?" Bishop Wilfrid thrust himself between the newcomer and the bold woman, who with blatant appreciation eyed this man so powerfully made and wickedly handsome it too likely eased his path into sins of the flesh.

"And by what right do you enter my lodging uninvited?"

"I knocked—loudly—but no response was forthcoming. Fearing some ill had befallen you, merely did I open your *unlocked* door."

Face flushed with irritation, the bishop shifted his

meaningful glare from stranger to the door split top to bottom. Were such force an example of the man's restraint, then woe betide any who crossed him. . . .

The still-kneeling female softly purred her admiration for strength proven by the abused door. The sound earned a quick accusing glance from the bishop, who then turned back to reproach the intruder.

"Solitude and privacy bring man closer to the divine and are the gifts we here at the abbey seek, gifts we guard for ourselves and one another." The strain underlying his gentle tone made it clear that tight control was required to maintain it. "Thus, never have I had reason to fear trespassers nor to bar my door against them."

"With no reason to bar your door, my sudden appearance can hold no great alarm for you."

"You have shattered my privacy as none of the brothers here would do . . . and at a most inopportune moment." In answer to the stranger's slow, mocking smile, Wilfrid felt compelled to speak further and snapped sharply critical words. "The monks of Winbury Abbey have put aside earthly pleasures and would see this scene for what it is, while you, a man of the world, are blind to the truth."

"Truth?" Against his will, Adam's gaze fell to the woman leaning around the bishop's robes to continue her leisurely study of him. She tossed her head, rearranging the shiny mass of black curls to permit a tantalizing glimpse of tempting flesh. By that blatant enticement Adam knew she was no penitent sinner come to be saved.

Seeing the stranger's cynical expression deepen, Wilfrid followed the line of a golden gaze to the seductress wantonly returning the visitor's attention. Gritting his teeth in irritation, he leaned to the side, snatched a dark cloak from where it hung on a peg driven into the wall and swirled it around the woman before pulling her up to stand before him. With hands cupped over her shoulders, the bishop pushed the damsel a step toward the intruder.

"This is Llys, daughter of a Druid sorcerer and trained in their black ways. As our God commanded His disciples, I am striving to drive the demons out from her."

Golden gaze narrowing, Adam studied the seductive woman and saw her subtly shift into a more alluring posture.

The bishop growled his displeasure. "She excels in wielding feminine wiles able to tempt any man into sinful debauchery, but I have not succumbed. And indeed, I'd have succeeded in my mission had your untimely arrival not undone what progress had been made."

Cynicism glowed in Adam's amber eyes. Progress had indeed been made, but toward what goal? The explanation given did nothing to sway his opinion. The Druidess looked no more a willing candidate for exorcism than she'd seemed a penitent sinner. Her stunning sapphire gaze had yet to shift from him and the invitation in their smoky depths never wavered.

Adam had no trust in the bishop's excuse for this intimate scene, but the scene did offer the possible answers he'd come seeking. Disillusionment had rung clear as a church bell in his younger brother's last missive. In it, Aelfric had suggested the bishop was not what he seemed, an opinion apparently justified and one that explained his wild intention to flee from this newly formed abbey.

"I am Adam, Ealdorman of Oaklea. And, concerned by what my brother Aelfric wrote me, I have come to visit with him."

Following a momentary widening of the bishop's eyes, Adam saw shutters close the man's expression into a mask of regret.

"I fear, my son, I've unhappy news of your brother."

Thick lashes half-shielded the fire of topaz eyes while a frowning Adam waited in smoldering impatience for an explanation.

"Aelfric is dead." Even as Wilfrid spoke he fell a step back, wondering in that moment if it were not this Saxon lord who possessed otherworldly powers. His strange golden eyes flashed with fire surely hot enough to incinerate the living. Having known only the slight and devout Aelfric, the bishop had thought exaggerated the many heroic tales of Adam's physical strength and success as a warrior—but no longer.

"Did some virulent sickness abruptly strike him down?" Like twin barbed maces, guilt and regret smote Adam. For the sake of his people at Oaklea, rather than immediately setting off in answer to Aelfric's plea, he had lingered the hours required to properly delegate its management. Now it seemed that delay had prevented him from seeing his beloved brother again . . . perhaps kept him from saving Aelfric's life. The bishop's next words landed another invisible blow.

"I fear it was no ailment of the flesh but rather a weakness of the mind. . . ."

Dark gold brows furrowed more deeply still. Adam knew Aelfric better than any other living soul. Had the bishop claimed his death due to one of the inevitable waves of illness that washed over the land with depressing regularity Adam would not have questioned the words . . . but a weakness of the mind? Never!

"I, myself," Wilfrid hastily continued in an attempt to lessen the fierce warrior's obvious disbelief, "saw Aelfric drive the dagger into his own heart."

"No!" Adam felt as if that dagger had instead struck him dead to point, but the shock served to rouse him from the haze of self-guilt. He was certain the bishop spoke nothing of the truth, an opinion crystallized by the unpleasantly bright smile on the woman's berry-sweet but surely poisonous lips.

"Show me Aelfric's grave."

Adam's demand was answered by a mournful shake of the bishop's head. "I cannot, for I know not where it lies."

"Is he not in the churchyard?" Repressed fury curled

Adam's hands into fists, but knowing the answer he'd be given, he exercised stern control to hold them immobile at his sides.

Filled with a sense of self-righteousness, the bishop was empowered to meet golden eyes directly. "No man guilty of taking his own life can be laid to rest in hallowed ground."

"Then have the men who buried Aelfric lead me to the spot they chose."

"I cannot." The bishop's flat refusal was accompanied by a woman's laughter, humorless and full of cruel glee.

Neither wishing nor invited to tarry the night within Winbury Abbey, Adam and the two supporters who'd awaited him outside its walls made camp in a woodland glade a short distance into the forest. He intended on the morrow to scour the forest edge for sign of recent man-caused disturbances. It was his fervent hope to find Aelfric's grave and make certain an adequate mound of stones was piled to protect his final resting place against animal marauders and then, no matter the bishop's claim, see it marked with a cross.

Guilt for having failed his brother and thoughts of an unmourned grave kept Adam awake until the darkest hours had nearly passed. Only then did the soft breeze whispering through treetops and the faint sounds of small animals moving amongst thick foliage below lull Adam into dreams . . . for a brief time.

With the instincts of a warrior trained in defense, Adam's eyes abruptly opened to a flash of descending silver. Issuing a bloodcurdling battle cry, he rolled to the side, deflecting the descending dagger from its deadly path to his heart. Instead the blade's sharp pain struck just below the ribs on his right side.

In the next instant the sight of three mighty warriors standing firmly braced with swords drawn and waiting sent a small party of craven assailants scurrying into the shadows beyond the fire's ring of light. Two defenders would have given chase had the third's weapon not fallen from his grip while he slowly sank back against a broad oak trunk, dark liquid flowing freely over hands clasped to his side.

In part to forestall his companions' useless desire to hunt down their foes, in a voice tightened by the burning in his side, Adam spoke.

"Help me bind this wound and then leave us be off to Throckenholt with all possible haste." Through his discomfort Adam smiled at the others' disappointment. "Be it Wulfayne's pride in his wife is justified, Lady Brynna will see my paltry injury soon mended."

Although frowning with mingled skepticism for the claim and concern over a deep wound threatening to prove serious, the pair bent immediately to do as their leader bid.

Past the door opened and held wide by a young thrall, two men entered the Ealdorman of Throckenholt's hall. The amber eyes of a third, supported between them, struggled to focus on the tall man striding forward to meet them.

"Wulf. . . ." Even lacking the rough bandage heavily stained with blood about Adam's middle, the faintness of his husky voice would have been cause for concern. "Need your . . . help. . . ."

Wulfayne's dark gold brows furrowed with concern, and just as he reached out to help his friend, Adam sank into oblivion.

After carefully laying their limp burden on the mat hastily laid near the hall's central hearth, Cedric and Arnulf stepped back to watch the woman who must be Lady Brynna approach their fallen leader with a neat stack of cloths, small vial of pale brown liquid and jar of creamy unguent. To their surprise a second younger but equally beautiful woman sank to her knees across the wounded man from the other.

"Who attacked you?" Wulf abruptly interrupted the pair's absorption to demand explanation from his fellow ealdorman's supporters but added another question before the first could be answered. "Did they fall upon you on *my* lands?"

Cedric, the older and less taciturn answered. "Nay, we were resting for the night only a short distance into the forest beyond Winbury Abbey when our cowardly assailants fell upon us. Once we showed ourselves well able to return the attack, they scurried into the shadows like the vermin they are. Only our lord's injury prevented us from giving chase."

The tight disgust in these words spoke volumes, and though the answer did little to resolve the puzzle of who was responsible and why, Wulf chose not to demand additional information from men likely unable to tell more.

Wulf continued quietly speaking with the two healthy visitors as the women worked in silence to rid the wounded man of soiled bandage and tunic. Once dried blood had been washed away and torn flesh brushed with the witch hazel solution, Brynna's deft hands applied the soothing unguent and covered it with a pad, leaving the younger woman free to study the man.

Other than Wulfayne, who stood as foster father to her, the maid had never seen a man so devastatingly handsome and, despite a natural reticence, found herself unable to look away from either the masculine beauty of a face framed by thick golden hair or the wide expanse of powerful chest laid bare. She had only just begun serious training in the healing arts with Brynna and during many years in the hill-cave home had never—save for occasional glimpses of her teenage brother or the aged Glyndor—seen a man even partially unclothed. Nor had she ever expected to feel a wish to do so. Now, driven by an odd compulsion backed by curiosity, her gaze traced the magnificent planes and ridges of a chest half-shielded by the wedge of curls a shade darker than the golden hair of his head. An unfamiliar and disturbing tension halted the breath in her throat and lent a strange rhythm to her heartbeat.

Brynna glanced up and recognized the startled new

awareness in her assistant's sapphire eyes. While quickly dropping attention to the chore at hand, a wry smile curled her mouth. This was an echo of her own past. She saw again the scene wherein she'd first found Wulfayne and tended a similar wound. That initial pang of desire was unmistakable and, most fond of the girl, she was gently amused.

"If you'll finish fastening the pad and then wipe his face with cool water, I'll see to the needs of our other guests." With these words Brynna gave the maid a reassuring smile and rose to match action to words.

As Brynna had already wound the bandage around the man just above his waist, the girl had no difficulty in neatly tying its ends to secure a thrice-folded cloth square in place. She next rose and into a basin poured cold water from a ewer only recently filled at the spring in back of the house. Again sinking to her knees beside the patient, she valiantly struggled to free herself of this useless fascination. Recognizing with despair the faltering of a serenity which must be held most precious to one of her destiny, the maid took deep, steadying breaths and forced calm to trembling hands. The erratic beat of her heart she'd no hope of returning to peace and wasted no moment trying.

Wringing out a small cloth, she hesitantly brushed back a swathe of blond hair before gently wiping the man's brow, down strong cheeks to a formidable chin, then around and back up before dipping it once more into the bowl. The water was chilly enough to numb her fingers . . . and cold enough to awaken the once-unconscious man.

From beneath thick lashes, Adam peered at the source of this frigid caress.

"No-o-o . . ." In the first moment of shock he gritted out his disgust over his apparent return to the abbey. He tried to sit up and half-succeeded before a wave of dizziness overcame him. Dropping against the pillow hastily formed of his own bundled cloak, he clenched his eyes shut in hopes of clearing away this surely false image of the bold female who'd earned his disdain. He looked again only to find a seemingly sincere frown of concern on the beauty's face even as Wulf moved to stand at her back.

"Adam, it's never a fine idea to attempt too rapid a recovery." Wulf grinned down at the scowling man, apparently irritated by his unaccustomed physical weakness. "You've already won a well-deserved reputation as a mighty warrior—no need to continue the fight where no enemy threatens."

No enemy? Adam would have laughed, but the memory of a sorceress's unholy glee strangled the sound. His tawny gaze never shifted from the worry-knitted brow of the woman who, had he not known better, seemed the image of sweet innocence.

From a damp cloth tightly clenched liquid dripped between slender fingers while the focus of a fiery glare nibbled her soft lower lip. The wounded man's glare seemed to brand her with guilt . . . but for what? So far as she knew, she'd never seen him before. What blame could he place at her door?

"Adam," Wulf spoke firmly to break the strange bond. "Meet here my foster daughter, of sorts. Llys and her twin brother, Evain, reside with Glyndor in the hills of Talacharn and only rarely descend to gift us with a visit."

Llys? To Adam the name was proof that she was in truth the woman he'd met in Winbury Abbey. A certainty backed by news that she resided with the famous—hah! infamous—Druid sorcerer, Glyndor.

Wulf quietly requested that Llys allow him a private discussion with his friend. She could do naught but grant him that boon. Stifling a near overwhelming desire to demand from the glaring man an explanation for his instantaneous dislike of someone he could know nothing about, she rose with exceptional grace. She twitched her simple homespun skirt into place as if 'twere a regal gown and proudly retreated to join Brynna in serving their other visitors a tasty morning meal. Still, she cast many sidelong glances toward their devastating patient

—her unexpected antagonist. Bruised and confused by the unwarranted disapproval of one she found all too attractive, Llys made a silent vow. The reason for his wrongful condemnation of her she would find. And more, she would prove it utterly unjustified.

Unrecognizable words of ethereal loveliness held Adam spellbound. Having shaken off the bonds enforced too long by his wound, he'd escaped Wulf's home while only menial thralls were about. Now the fragrance of wildflowers surrounded him where he stood in the shadows at forest edge, every sense heightened by the tantalizing tune's pure notes. Beneath dawn's glowing hues and in the center of a triangle formed by three mighty oaks a dainty figure moved while lavender mists billowed about her feet.

Delicate face and slender arms lifted to a sky shifting from bright pastels into the pale azure of early morn she seemed an elusive fantasy come to life, one whose bewitching spell Adam fought. He shook his head in a futile attempt to see the image scatter like moonbeams. It didn't. Instead, as if in answer to a mystical summons, all manner of wild creatures joined her in the glade . . . a shy doe with her speckled fawns, long-eared rabbits, even their natural predator the wolf and the normally elusive badger. Slowly spinning at the start, Llys gracefully twirled ever faster. Masses of shiny black hair danced on the breeze and twined about a figure of unearthly beauty until her song crescendoed in wild sweetness and power.

"What is this strange power you wield over the beasts of the forest?"

It wasn't the question he'd meant to ask. Indeed, Adam hadn't meant to speak at all. But, uncomfortable in the role of spy, he boldly stepped from the shadows. He had journeyed from Oaklea on a quest to seek the truth behind his brother's odd words of condemnation for a bishop and instead had fallen into the role of secret observer of a beguiling sorceress's haunting rites.

For Llys the intruder's rude end to the spell of chanting

completely sundered an aura of peace. She whirled to face the cynical but potent smile of a far too attractive visitor who by rights should be safe abed and recuperating in the lord of Throckenholt's home. A topaz gaze locked with sapphire. Although heavy lashes half descended, Llys lost a battle she'd no experience to fight and found it impossible to look away.

Adam mistook her steady, slumbrous expression for a repeat of wanton invitations wordlessly issued in Winbury Abbey. Using the excuse of his contempt, he strode forward to accept.

Suddenly swept full against a broad, muscular frame and held there by bands of flame-forged steel, for the first time in her life Llys was wrapped in a male embrace utterly lacking the platonic nature of brother, friend or mentor. Trembling under a barrage of unruly sensations, she found herself drowning in an amber sea of fire and gasped. That response gave Adam the perfect opportunity to take what he wanted. But a kiss rough at the outset gentled into a persuasion that stole her breath. His lips brushed hers once and once again. Fiery excitement throbbed through Llys's veins and, driven by instinct, she wrapped her arms about broad shoulders, twined fingers into strands of cool gold.

Adam, too, was lost to thoughts of blame or guilt and tangled his hands into a lustrous dusky mane to crush the tender, deliciously curved maid ever nearer. Surrendering to her silent entreaty to part petal-soft lips, he claimed the deeper, devastating kiss she naively demanded. Naively?

Shocked by what he'd once have sworn was the nectar-sweet taste of innocence on her lips, Adam released her mouth and gazed down into a blue gaze gone smoky with mingled desire and confusion. Naive? Innocent? These pure words could never be applied to this treacherous female whose nature he knew, the despicable truth of which he'd seen with his own eyes and heard in her cruel laughter.

He smiled with bitter scorn for both himself and her.

Llys's training as sorceress must have honed to incredible sharpness her talent for seeming to be what she was not. Having long prided himself in accurately reading the character of others, he was vexed by his own inability to delve beyond her sweet surface to what must be a sour core. Ruthlessly he quashed lingering tendrils of guilt for having initiated an innocent into passion. To further waylay the flow of that worthless emotion, his arms fell away and he took a step back from the clearly dangerous woman.

"What manner of fool would you play me for? Do you think me so simple-witted I can be easily misled, so weak and maneuverable I might forget your cruel mirth over Aelfric's death?"

Fine dark brows met in puzzlement. "Who is Aelfric?"

Adam growled his disgust. "Next you will claim to have never visited Winbury Abbey."

"But never have I done so." With these words Llys spread her hands, vulnerable palms turned upward in wordless entreaty for clarity amidst a maze of tangled emotions and strange accusations.

Long moments passed as Adam studied the maid's apparent sincerity. Though vivid memories would ever prevent him from accepting her guileless image, plainly she would never confess to her part in that dreadful scene. That fact acknowledged, he could only deem it squandered time to further pursue her admission.

"What strange rite were you performing?" Adam's gaze went as impenetrable as cloudy amber.

Llys was startled by his abrupt shift in subject although such an action was Glyndor's favorite trick to knock an opponent off-stride. Still, she answered without hesitation. "I besought the forces of nature to grant Anya the boon of a hasty recovery." Seeing dark gold brows rise in unspoken query, she quickly added, "Busy tending her daughter with a tisane of tansy and woodbane, Brynna begged me to chant the dawn in her stead and therein seek healing for Anya."

The next moment Llys could have bitten her tongue with annoyance. In her flustered state, she'd broken the all-important rule taught first by her father and then by Glyndor: *Never* speak with an outsider of the powers unknown to men untaught. Such powers were more like to frighten strangers unwilling or incapable of understanding into violence against those able to commune with the forces embodied in all natural elements.

Determined to turn back the tide of her wrong, Llys resurrected the subject he'd abandoned. "Who is it you've mistaken me for? And what has that woman to do with the chaste men of the abbey?" Though never lacking in courage, it required every shred of Llys's bravery to stand undaunted before the man gone motionless as stone while bolts of golden lightning seemed to flash from his eyes.

What game did the mercurial sorceress play? Adam refused to ease her goal by voicing answers they both knew. Staring into her unflinching gaze, he silently wondered what purpose lay behind her questions. Did she think that by challenging his memory with bald-faced lies she might deflect his disapproval, weaken his certainty of what he'd seen?

In this new role she appeared as neither the wanton siren of Winbury Abbey nor the shy and quiet maiden of Wulfayne's abode. Was this resolute maid of unyielding sapphire gaze nearer to the true core of her being? With this fresh demonstration of her ability to switch between vastly different poses he grew more positive that he never dare trust this devious beauty. His frown deepened in disgust over thoughts suggesting such a traitorous emotion even possible.

Llys saw Adam's firm mouth twist down with derision. Clearly he meant to give no answer, yet beneath his steady golden gaze she refused to falter for so much as the briefest of instants. Rather, the willfulness of her nature lit sparks in sapphire eyes and tilted a dainty chin upward.

Thus they remained, each determined the other would give way and in so doing reveal themselves to be the one in error.

"Adam, Llys. . . ."

At the call, the pair turned in unison to meet the quizzical scrutiny of Wulfayne come to summon them home for a discussion of strange matters just uncovered.